NOTORIOUS

Katherine Sutcliffe

JOVE BOOKS, NEW YORK

This is a work of fiction. Names, characters, places, and incidents are either the product of the author's imagination or are used fictitiously, and any resemblance to actual persons, living or dead, business establishments, events, or locales is entirely coincidental.

NOTORIOUS

A Jove Book / published by arrangement with
the author

PRINTING HISTORY
Jove edition / November 2000

All rights reserved.
Copyright © 2000 by Katherine Sutcliffe.
This book, or parts thereof, may not be reproduced in
any form without permission. For information address:
The Berkley Publishing Group, a division of Penguin Putnam Inc.,
375 Hudson Street, New York, New York 10014.

The Penguin Putnam Inc. World Wide Web site address is
http://www.penguinputnam.com

ISBN: 0-515-12948-8

A JOVE BOOK®
Jove Books are published by The Berkley Publishing Group,
a division of Penguin Putnam Inc.,
375 Hudson Street, New York, New York 10014.
JOVE and the "J" design
are trademarks belonging to Penguin Putnam Inc.

PRINTED IN THE UNITED STATES OF AMERICA

10 9 8 7 6 5 4 3

Praise for *NOTORIOUS*

"With a touch of a master storyteller, Katherine Sutcliffe mesmerizes readers from the very first word by weaving an intense story of exquisite passion and deep emotions. *NOTORIOUS* is a luminous love story that shines brightly in your heart."
—Kathe Robin, *Romantic Times*

"Devoted fans of historical romance know that Katherine Sutcliffe is one of the best writers of romance in bookstores today."
—Harriet Klausner

"*NOTORIOUS* is dark and dangerous . . . and exactly what makes Katherine Sutcliffe's novels classics in the purest sense. This is absolutely one of the most compelling historical reads of the year."
—Jill Barnett, *New York Times* bestselling author of *Wicked*

"The incomparable Katherine Sutcliffe is in top form with her trademark blend of passion, pageantry and thrilling romance."
—Susan Wiggs, bestselling author of *The Charm School*

"Katherine Sutcliffe is a marvelous talent and a treasure of the genre."
—Laura Kinsale, *New York Times* bestselling author

"Katherine Sutcliffe entertains. She hits a home run every-time!"
—Kat Martin, *New York Times* bestselling author of *Perfect Sin*

"Stunning . . . this is by far the best historical romance I've ever read . . . and I can't recommend it highly enough."
—Beth Anderson, *Rendezvous Magazine*

"*NOTORIOUS* has everything I expect from a Katherine Sutcliffe novel: breathtaking action, an exquisite hero, very vivid and evocative prose . . . Edgy and intense."
Laura Novak, *The Romance Journal*

"Ms. Sutcliffe's innovative plots are written with a savvy style that makes her one of this genre's top-notch authors . . ."
—Darlene Kendall, Border's Books and Romance Communications

Dear Readers,

I would like to thank you for continuing to support me through the last many years. Many of you have become like friends to me. Your encouragement and kindness brighten my life. Your enthusiasm fills me with happiness and the hope that my stories and characters continue to entertain you still since my first book was published in 1986. I wish I could meet each of you and not merely shake your hand, but give you a big hug. Please continue to write me, and visit my Web site anytime.

Warmly,

Katherine Sutcliffe
PMB #259
2520 Ave. K, Ste. 700
Plano, Texas 75074

www.romancejournal.com/Sutcliffe/default.htm

❧ *Prologue* ❧

In the final analysis your aims and objects are quite as moral as any minister's, because morality consists in conversation of the best interests of civilization, and you are not seeking your own good, but the ultimate good of your country.

—CAPT. A. P. NIBLACK,
"Letters of a Retired Rear Admiral to His Son"

The Crimean War
Calamita Bay, 14th September 1854

Upon some broad green place, tinted by a faint morning sun, a man beheld a woman holding a whimpering child against her bosom. She looked very young, hardly more than a child herself, her face smooth and streaked with soot and tears. She knelt on her knees amid the rubble that, only twenty-four hours previous, had been her home. There was something familiar about her eyes, as if he had gazed into them before. Her lips were moving, soundlessly, and though he could not hear her words distinctly he stood frozen in the shadows, mesmerized by the image, a feeling of fear and outrage crawling up his throat.

In a voice that seemed to come thin through the smoke and morning sunlight, she began to softly wail, and he realized the babe in her arms was dead.

Vague memories came to him: a woman kneeling in a garden, snipping lavender while a baby napped in a basket—the oh so heavy silence that always ensued with the knowledge that another good-bye was imminent. There would be no pleading. No tears, not until he left. That was the agreement between them. No ties. No permanence. No happily ever after.

Forever simply wasn't in him to give, even for the sake of the child, though he would have sacrificed his life for them both.

It was *her* eyes that looked back at him from a stranger's face. As she wailed her grief, her long black hair fell over her shoulders and coiled upon the stones, moving sinuously in the stirring of air, crawling with blue ripples that looked absurdly sensual amid the awful destruction.

Then out of nowhere stepped the officer, the barrel of his gun pointed directly at the woman.

"No! Not the women and children! Put down the gun! Don't make me kill you, Lieutenant. I won't allow you to kill her, Lieutenant. Put down the gun! Not the women and children! I said—"

From the corner of his eye he saw her fall, slowly, as if time were grinding to a stop, facedown onto the dirt, her hair spreading like a Japanese fan around her head. His mouth falling open in soundless outrage, he raised the gun in his hand and turned on the officer. . . .

✦ 1 ✦

So cheer up, my son. Play the game. Take your medicine. Don't squeal. Watch your step. After all, it is a splendid profession and an honorable career.

—CAPT. A. P. NIBLACK

Victoria Military Prison
London, England, March 1857

Occasionally the sounds of silence were interrupted by screams. Maniacal. Hysterical. They would wing at Jason through the impenetrable darkness, smashing against his ears, which had long since become sensitive to the slightest sound: a rat burrowing in the straw, the whimpering of a prisoner in some distant cell, the slow drip of water on the floor when it rained. That, perhaps, was the worst: the constant, rhythmic *drip drip drip* of water that would ultimately turn his tiny cell into a fetid bog. Still, those sounds were his hold on reality, a reminder that life beyond these walls still existed.

Odd how the darkness, once his friend, now lay upon him like a behemoth. As a boy he would lie in the dark and dream of unicorns and knights in armor. As a man he'd made love to beautiful women, the darkness a blanket as soft as their sighs in his ears. He had also killed, slid silent as a viper through the blackness and struck without warning, snuffing out life after life. Perhaps he deserved this torment.

Then again, perhaps not.

Jason laughed. *Idiots.* All of them. Did they not realize with whom or with *what* they were dealing? He'd suffered far greater tortures than these. This black confinement was nothing. And the prospect of dying? If he actually gave a damn about that he would not have spent the last years of his life thumbing his nose at consequence. As his father had always preached: If something is worth fighting for, it is worth dying for.

A sound: The jangle of keys and the muttered whispers of nervous gaolers. Ah, yes, they would be nervous. They feared him *and* respected him.

The door swung open, spilling blinding light into the cell. Rats scurried through the rotting straw and the onrush of fresh air washed over him in a cool wave that made him catch his breath. A pair of gaolers stepped into the cell, clubs ready, their faces screwed into masks of trepidation.

"On yer feet, Batson," one barked, voice tight, eyes round as coins.

His eyes aching from the bright assault, Jason Batson slowly stood.

The gaolers moved aside and one pointed at the door with his cudgel. "Out with ya. And no funny business or we'll bash yer head like a bleedin' egg."

"Do you think so?" Jason replied with a patient smile, then walked between the cautious guards, out into the stone corridor. It felt cavernous compared to the ten-by-ten chamber that had been his universe for the last months.

One of the guards put down his club and took up leg irons. He went to one knee and clamped the manacles around Jason's ankles, his hands trembling in their haste to be done with the dangerous task. Then he applied the wrist irons, which were attached by a length of heavy chain to Jason's ankles, and jumped away, releasing a relieved breath as he glanced at his companion.

The group moved down the corridor, past closed cells that muted the ranting from within. They exited the building and entered another. This was softly lit and carpeted, its furnishings glowing with mellow beeswax. A sound of laughter ceased the moment the threesome moved by the office.

A short thin man with a bald head hurried toward them. "Imbeciles," he barked, then wagged his finger at them. "You were to clean him up first. Good God, he smells like a death pit and doesn't look much better. Bathe him and for heaven's sake shave him and do something with his hair. Give him some decent clothes while you're at it."

"That won't be necessary," came another more familiar voice.

Harold Dunleavy stepped from his office. "Lord Batson shan't be dallying long, I suspect." He smiled at Jason. "While he may be lethal, he isn't stupid. Quite the contrary, as a matter of fact. Come along, your lordship. Please, make yourself comfortable while Mr. Simms fetches you a drink."

Dunleavy stepped aside as Jason entered the office, his ankle chains dragging the floor and his bare feet depositing bits of rotting straw on the plush Oriental rug. He caught a glimpse of his reflection in a mirror before stopping before Dunleavy's desk.

Dunleavy moved around the desk, his step hesitant, his gaze locked on Jason. "I'll remind you, Batson, that there are guards stationed outside the door. One false move—"

"And you're dead." Jason laughed softly.

His face drained of color and his brow beginning to sweat, Dunleavy cleared his throat. He lowered his voice. "You arrogant son of a bitch, I could have you shot this very moment and no one would be the wiser. I could toss your corpse to my dogs and who would care? As far as Society is concerned, Lord Jason Batson was nothing more than a philandering ne'er-do-well who lived strictly for seducing women and cheating at faro. The populace knows absolutely nothing about your affiliation with our military *or* the fact that you are a killer for hire."

"Subsidized by the Crown, lest you forget."

Dunleavy opened a box of cigars and offered one to Jason.

Jason ignored him.

"We had such aspirations for you," Dunleavy said, putting aside the box. "Your father was very good in his day. There wasn't an enemy military commander who didn't fear him. But you . . . ah, you were even more brilliant and lethal than Randolph. You could have been Her Majesty's greatest asset. She's quite distressed about this ugly affair, you know."

"I would think she would be more distressed over one of her officers murdering women and children."

"Occasionally examples must be made. Lieutenant Grant was simply following orders. The woman was believed to have had a gun."

"I hardly think Her Majesty justifies killing the innocent, no matter the cause."

"I didn't bring you here to debate the debacle. You were wrong. You murdered an officer in cold blood."

"Then you should have stood me before a firing squad. Why haven't you?"

Dunleavy stood from his chair. "We might yet. That, of course, will depend on you."

"I'm not in the mood to negotiate. Then again, I never was. Cobra operated on *his* terms. His allegiance is to *his* men, not yours. And speaking of my men . . . how are they?"

"Alive, for the time being. That, too, could depend on you."

"Stop beating about the bush, Harold. You want something. What is it?"

"We have a . . . situation that calls for Cobra's specialized expertise."

Jason shrugged. "Not interested. The last months of not dodging bullets has given me the opportunity to carefully consider my future. The fact is, Harold, I don't need the Crown's money any longer. My tea plantation off the coast of Ceylon is extremely successful. I'm not getting any younger, either. Thirty-three next month. I want to settle down and not have to worry that some lunatic from my past is going to crawl out of the woodwork and put a bullet in my head. In short, I intend to sail away into the sunset and put memories of Cobra's bloodthirsty escapades out of my mind." He briefly closed his eyes and took a deep breath before saying more quietly, "If that's possible."

Harold's thin lips curved in spiteful amusement. "Wrong, Batson. You'll retire when *we* say you can retire."

Jason slowly turned his gray eyes on Harold. "Careful, little man. Need I remind you that I could cross this room and snap your neck so fast you wouldn't know what happened . . . should I so desire. Now pay very close attention to what I say. I'm done with Cobra. I'm going to retire to Ceylonia Plantation and bounce babies on my knee and if you come anywhere close to me again I'll remove your brains through your nose, piece by piece, while you're still alive."

Although hot color flushed Dunleavy's face, he continued in a monotone. "There is talk of mutiny throughout India—"

"Not interested, Harold."

"In a great part thanks to our distinguished marquess of Dalhousie, former Governor-General—"

"Shut up, Harold."

"The marquess was most energetic during his tenure. He instigated numerous measures that have left the Indians furious and resentful and determined to strike a blow against us. As you know, traditionally in India adopted sons were considered the equal of natural ones for the purposes of succession and inheritance. Dalhousie proclaimed that the practice would no longer be accepted, and states without proper heirs would immediately become part of the British territory. Last year we took over Oudh, and I'm afraid the resulting backlash has been ugly. The deposed royal family was not given pensions, et cetera. In short, they are destitute and fanning the fires of rebellion."

"Are you finished?" Jason asked, leaving his chair.

Dunleavy wrung his hands. "Then there is the matter of Nana Sahib. I believe you know him personally?"

Jason frowned at the mention of Nana's name. "The adopted son of the late peshwa of Poona. I know Nana Sahib. He's quite friendly with the British. My father and I attended several parties at his father's residence."

"*Was* quite friendly. Thanks to Dalhousie's succession and inheritance order, the title and pension that Sahib had anticipated inheriting from his adoptive father will now pass to the Crown. To say he isn't pleased would be putting it mildly. But I'll get back to Nana Sahib in a moment. Frankly, the Dalhousie proclamation is only the tip of the iceberg. The initial fires of discontent came about with the introduction of the new ammunition we dispensed to our regiments. They believe the damned cartridges to be greased with pig and cow fat, and therefore the sepoys—our Indian soldiers—both Muslim and Hindu alike, are offended. There have been occasional flare-ups in northern India: Jhansi, Indore, and a scattering of smaller stations. So you understand that Nana Sahib's whimpering and breast-beating is like a cinder among straw. At first we brushed him off as a man who, without the old peshwa's inheritance, was of little consequence. However, we've recently learned that he has gone looking for sympathy. Not long ago Azimullah Khan, a young sycophant of Sahib's, came to London and attempted to beg and bribe from any and all, including Her Majesty, who might help Nana Sahib get back his pension—all to no avail. Then there were journeys to Constantinople, where he gained an audience with the sultan and communicated with Russian agents. They also conferred with the caliph of Baghdad; dropped in on the Mahratta, Rajpoot, and Seik chiefs on his route from Bombay; and went on to discuss the issue with the emperor of Delhi's wife, Begum Zinat Mahal, who has been widely outspoken on restoring the Mughals to their former glory so she might place her son upon his rightful throne. The growing consensus is that should Nana

Sahib unite the sepoys who feel they have in some way been betrayed by the British, as well as the princes they deposed, the zamindars they dispossessed, the Brahmins and Maulvies they disgraced, and made a common bond with the emperor of Delhi, their combined forces could drive the foreigners from the land."

Jason left his chair and moved to a window overlooking a broad veranda paved with brick. There was a child there, attended by a nanny. The little girl had long black hair and was no more than four or five years old. Dressed in a woolen cape and tiny fleece-lined boots, she played with a doll that she pushed around in a pram. His eyes narrowing, Jason only partially listened as Dunleavy continued.

"I believe you're familiar with Compton Fontaine?"

Jason frowned, the mention of his good friend's name momentarily diverting his attention from the child. "Viceroy Fontaine," he said cautiously, his keen instinct warning him not to reveal too much about his past relationship with Fontaine. Compton Fontaine had become as close to Jason as a father through the years; they shared the belief that the Brits should stop foisting their government and religion down India's throat.

The child ran to the nanny, who swept the girl up in her arms and hugged her. His breath forming a fog on the cold windowpane, Jason did his best to force Compton Fontaine from his thoughts and studied the child's features, or what he could see of them. As her spray of black hair continued shielding her profile, a sense of frustration tightened his chest.

"*Ex*-viceroy . . . problem with discipline . . . he and his wife were always outspoken regarding the British occupation of India . . . believed we were out to dirty the waters, so to speak, when it came to forcing upon them our religion, education, morals, et cetera. When Fontaine's wife died the problem only worsened. Over the years he's become very friendly, not to mention sympathetic, to extremes of Nana Sahib's plight. The last year he's been so bold as to write letters to the London *Times* condemning our 'machinations to perpetrate evil and unlawful actions upon the helpless and naive natives of India by robbing them of their human rights and legal properties.' In short, Batson, not only has the man become a dangerous nuisance, fanning the building fires of discontent, he has become an embarrassment to the Crown."

"Who is the child?" Jason asked, placing his fingertips against the glass and nudging aside the condensation of his breath.

"Batson, we need your expertise. We must take Fontaine out quietly so it looks in no way as if our government has had any involvement whatsoever with his death. After all, once he married Lord Sheffield's oldest girl he became highly regarded. Can't have it known that we go about exterminating members of our aristocracy, can we? And while you're at it, any help you and your men can provide us by nipping the Nana Sahib problem in the bud before it becomes completely out of hand would be more than amply rewarded."

"Even if I weren't retired, I don't work for men who justify the killing of women and children," he replied as the nanny pulled the hood of the cape over the little girl's head.

"The problem is that Fontaine has taken up with Sahib at his residence in Bithur. Our attempts to lure him out of Bithur so we can . . . discuss the situation has proven futile. Which brings us to our plan. Fontaine has a daughter. Destiny Fontaine Chesterfield. I believe you knew her husband? Killed himself recently. Nasty business it was, too. Married barely three months when she found him hanging by the neck from a gable or some such."

The words jarred Jason again from the scene before him. The child blurred, and as the memories in his head poured forth he recalled the image of a dark-haired twelve-year-old with tears in her eyes as she stood at the deck rail alone, staring back at the India shores she had once frolicked on. As a twenty-two-year-old soldier, not even having experienced his first battle, Jason had been impressed by Destiny Fontaine's determination to be brave for her father, who remained on the docks, waving good-bye—possibly forever. Off and on through the next ten years Compton had regaled Jason with stories of his daughter's escapades in England, how she was developing into a strong-willed woman just like her mother, and not to forget beautiful—the sort that should appeal to a man like Jason—if Jason ever decided to settle down and become a family man—which he certainly would if he ever met Destiny face-to-face.

But Fontaine had not known the real Jason Batson: only the young aspiring soldier once eager to serve and protect his queen, then the tea planter whose fondest desire was to create the grandest tea empire in the world. Had Fontaine known that when Jason wasn't toying with tea he was assassinating potentates in their sleep, Jason suspected he would have been Compton's *last* choice to marry his daughter.

Still, Jason promised Fontaine many times that he would write to Destiny, and call on her during one of his trips back to England. But he never had—never took the time, *damn him.* Now Dunleavy stood there with his bald head sweating and informed Jason that Destiny had married, and was widowed, and in big trouble, by the sounds of it.

An absurd sentiment rolled in his chest. He shook off the unsettling feeling and focused again on the little girl.

"*Who* is the child?" he repeated more coldly, knowing the answer, experiencing a sense of anger that made breathing next to impossible.

"Lady Chesterfield must be handled carefully. She's astute and uncompromising when it comes to her loyalties and is extremely loyal to her father—thinks he can do no wrong. If she believes remotely that we're using her to get to her father and harm him in any way, she'll revolt. Did I mention she's attractive?"

"That's my daughter. Isn't it?" Jason turned from the window, understanding now why Dunleavy had ordered the manacles on his wrists and ankles. And why, even as he felt the first wave of fury turn over in his gut, three armed guards now stood just inside the door, between himself and Dunleavy.

Dunleavy swallowed. "I'm sorry to inform you, Batson, that the child's mother is dead. She's been dead a little over a year. We didn't tell you for obvious reasons. It was imperative that we keep control of the situation. Had you known about Michelle's demise you would, of course, have wreaked havoc to get to the child. I know what you're thinking. You think that we had something to do with Michelle's death. Quite the contrary. 'Twas an illness, nothing more. You should be grateful for our intervention. Since you and Michelle were never married, the child was at the mercy of the courts. God only knows where she might have ended up—a misbegotten waif and all. So we took her and provided her a home and caretaker, suspecting that there would come a time when you would desire to be with her again.

"Come, come, Batson, you needn't look so murderous. Look at her, for God's sake. Is she not healthy? Happy? The two of you can be together if you cooperate. Help us with this little matter with Fontaine and the two of you can happily spend the next years of your lives together at Ceylonia. You may wash your hands completely of Cobra once and for always . . . with my blessing."

"And if I don't?"

Dunleavy shrugged. "How do I say this tactfully? If you and your men are of no significance to us any longer you shall be shot before a firing squad and the child will be deposited on the steps of the nearest orphanage. And if that is not enough to convince you, perhaps the prospect of certain powers learning that your father was the original Cobra will be enough to assure you that you would be wise to help us. Cobra has made some very powerful and lethal enemies throughout the world. I wager your father would be dead within a fortnight. A shame, I'm sure. I understand he's enjoying his retirement."

Jason stared into Dunleavy's round eyes and replied,

"My father is a ruthless, cold-blooded son of a bitch whose greatest accomplishment, in his own mind, was training his sons to be just as ruthless. And, speaking of my brother, where is Trevor? Why wasn't he considered for this assignment?"

"Because this particular assignment requires a certain finesse. Trevor is . . . dangerous. We employ his expertise only in situations that require complete, quick annihilation of the enemy."

"Like father like son."

"With one difference. Trevor has no conscience."

"And my father has?"

Harold replied with a tight smile "Touché. You're right, of course. Your father and Trevor would never have allowed themselves to get in your situation. But here you are, nevertheless, with chains on your wrists, staring out through a cold windowpane at a daughter you hardly know."

His eyes narrowing, Jason said, "You're going to regret this, Harold."

❧ 2 ❧

Hotaru koe midzu nomasho;
Achi no midzu wa migaizo;
Kochi no midzu wa amaizo.

"Come, firefly, I will give you water to drink.
The water of that place is bitter;
The water here is sweet."

A JAPANESE CHILDREN'S SONG
—Author Unknown

Two Weeks Later

"Will our shame never cease? Our son, *her* husband,
barely dead three months and she's cavorting on horseback
and spending time with that dreadful little Japanese gardener. The gel might at least feign some semblance of
grief, if not for her husband's memory then for our benefit.
We, after all, have agreed to pay her a yearly stipend,
which, if she isn't careful, could be cut off like *that*." Lady
Clara Chesterfield snapped her bejeweled fingers and positioned herself behind her husband's chair.

Lord Chesterfield patted her hand reassuringly and regarded his hosts with a forlorn expression. "Please forgive
my wife. She leans toward the dramatic, I'm afraid. We
have no intention of cutting off your niece's allowance . . .
unless, of course, she finds it necessary to discuss the . . .

circumstances of her marriage with anyone outside the four of us."

"It's blackmail!" Lady Clara pounded the chair with her fist.

Lady Diana Sheffield Shaftesbury jumped from her chair. "*Blackmail,* you say? How dare you make such an accusation! You knowingly encouraged that union for one reason only: to allay suspicions regarding your son. You cared nothing for Destiny's happiness and future. The fact that now she's considered a pariah among her peers doesn't bother you in the least. I've a good mind to march out these doors and announce to our guests just what sort of people you are. Not only that, but what sort of . . . *man* your son was. Blackmail, you say? The pitiful amount you intend to toss her each year is barely enough for a peasant to live on, much less a young woman of her breeding. Your son's demise has destroyed her future entirely. Tell me, with everyone believing she drove her husband to hang himself, what sort of man will have her now?"

"There, there, Diana, keep your voice down." Lord James Shaftesbury adjusted the cuffs of his shirt and smoothed the sleeves of his jacket. "The matter is hardly important enough to warrant this tantrum—"

"*Tantrum?*" Diana stared at her husband. "Oh yes, you would call my defense of my niece a tantrum. You're just as much to blame for this horrible fiasco. You were in on it the entire time. You tossed her to the lions simply to be rid of her."

James rolled his eyes and shook his head, deflecting her accusation with a wave of his hand.

Lady Shaftesbury narrowed her eyes. "I wonder, my lord, just how well you made out on this sham of a marriage."

"And what if I did make out, Diana? I think it's the least I deserve, considering I've been forced to tolerate the gel's intrusion in my life for the last ten years."

Diana flashed the smirking Chesterfields a look, and took a deep, steadying breath. "Destiny Fontaine *Chester-*

field is a thousand times finer a human being than either of you. Since your son's death she has been victimized by the most horrible gossip—that she somehow *drove* her new husband to suicide. Her entire future is ruined and her reputation is besmirched, yet instead of defending herself she continues to protect his memory and reputation—such as it was."

"Well!" declared Lady Clara. "I can certainly see where Destiny gets her penchant for vulgarity."

"Careful, Clara. I just might show you to what level of vulgarity I can sink." Diana raised one eyebrow and speared Lady Clara with a look so wicked the plump woman feigned a slight swoon, causing Lord Chesterfield to jump from his chair and frantically fan his wife's face with a hanky.

James stood and gave the Chesterfields an apologetic nod of his head. "If you'll excuse us."

Taking hold of his wife's arm, he propelled her out of the room, into the adjacent parlor. He closed the door behind them as calmly as possible before glaring down into Diana's face. "How dare you behave in such a manner to the Chesterfields?"

"I refuse to continue to stand silent while you malign my niece and subject her to the whims of people like the Chesterfields. They used her in the most despicable fashion—"

"No one twisted her arm and forced her to agree to the marriage, Diana."

"She knew you wanted her out of this house—out of our lives."

"Ever since she was plunked on my doorstep, wearing little more than a *chuddah*, she's been a source of constant irritation."

"Irritation only because you could not break her spirit and mold her into your suffocating expectations."

"For God's sake, her parents allowed her to grow up behaving like a hoyden—riding astride, dressing like a farmer's brat, associating with a lot of black infidels who believe once they die they are coming back as a cow! And God help me, Diana, you find it all delightful. I'm certain when my back is turned you even encourage her outrageous behavior."

Diana righted her shoulders and stuck out her chin. "She hasn't worn a *chuddah* in years."

"The chit worships Buddha by candlelight."

"I vowed over my sister's grave that I would care for Destiny as if she were my own. I swore to her father that she would be raised in the kindest, most caring, and warmest environment our position could offer a young girl with such promise. Not only have I let Destiny down by closing my eyes to the travesty of the marriage in which she was thrust, but I've disappointed myself."

"In what way?" James demanded with a short laugh.

"By settling, my lord. For remaining married to a way of life; for giving up my own dreams of love for the position and respect your bloody money could buy me."

"Ah! Then you might have preferred your sister's fate—winding up in that insufferable India, married—"

"To a man who adored his wife; who sought to make her every wish real; who would have moved heaven and earth to protect his family at the risk of his own life and reputation. *How I envied my sister!* And still do. I would gladly trade the so-called respectability of your name for the freedom of entrusting my heart, not to mention my life, to a man who married me out of love instead of the sick necessity to spit him out an heir every nine months."

"A lot of good you've done me there," James proclaimed with a huff. "Ten years and no child? You're fortunate that I haven't tossed you aside for a younger, healthier, not to mention prettier gel. Someone who *is* capable of 'spitting me out an heir every nine months.' "

"Oh, you crass—"

"I beg your pardon," came a voice from the door.

Lady Shaftesbury snapped her mouth closed as the majordomo stepped into the room, offering them a slight bow of apology.

"I do hate to interrupt." He cleared his throat and sniffed. "Someone has arrived straight from London who says it is of the most dire importance that he speak with your niece as soon as possible. A Mr. Dunleavy, I believe, with news regarding her father."

The old garden walls, mossed below their ruined coping of tiles, enveloped Destiny Fontaine Chesterfield in fantasy, transporting her as if by magic carpet to another time and place. This place, this garden of Eden, had been Destiny's solace since coming to England. Arriving at Sheffield House, she had been angry and resentful, believing that her father, the Honorable Compton Fontaine, had abandoned her, sending her away from India though she had begged and pleaded with him to allow her to remain and care for him. Normally children were immediately shipped back to England on their seventh birthday to begin their rigorous education. Thanks to her mother's perseverance, however, Destiny had remained in India, tutored by her parents, immersed in a way of life that would forever remain in her heart and soul. India, after all, had been the only home she had ever known, up until her mother's death shortly after Destiny's eleventh birthday.

Soon after arriving at Sheffield House, Destiny had discovered this garden, much separated from the grand manor house by meandering pathways and high hedges; and she'd discovered the ancient Japanese gardener, Saito Kumataro, who, after twenty-two years, continued to manicure each blade of grass, each flower bud, frog, and Buddha statue as meticulously as she had when Destiny's mother had wandered here as a girl. Here there were no sounds but the voices of birds or the solitary splash of a diving frog. There was a charm of quaintness and serenity in the air, a faint sense of something viewless and sweet. Even in the faint spring light drifting across the gray strange shapes of stones and statues, there came to Destiny the tenderness of her mother's presence.

It was here she came to escape reality, just as her mother had done so often in her times of crisis.

Her black Arabian mare grazed nearby on a patch of grass. Destiny sighed with pleasure as the horse, Sasaki Takatsuna, turned its big black eyes toward her and nickered.

"Saito, I dreamt last night of a horse. And the night before that of flying through the dark skies, gobbling up stars."

"But that is very good, Hotaru. To dream of the horse means good luck awaits you."

"Does it not also mean that I shall be traveling a great distance?"

The old woman nodded. "It is time for you to travel, I think. Your wings are strong. To remain here would bring much heaviness to your heart. But it is the dream of the stars that intrigues me. Such a dream signifies that you will soon become the mother of a beautiful child."

"That's a lot of poppy-poop. We both know there isn't a titled man in this country who would dare ask me to dance, much less to marry him. Have you heard what the snobs are calling me now? The Black Widow. I'm so wretched a wife, not to mention so disreputable a human being, that only a man with a death wish would even consider me as a wife. I'm doomed, I tell you. I'm fated to spend the rest of my days dodging the barbs of malicious gossip. I shan't ever marry again—or have children. Not that I care to marry again, mind you. I determined on my wedding night that my parents' marriage must have been a veritable fairy tale. Too perfect to be true."

"You should not take it personally, Hotaru. They speak out of ignorance."

"They speak out of arrogance and meanness, not to mention stupidity. They condemn me for something they know absolutely nothing about. Ah, me." She sighed. "I warrant I'm not exactly an example of the perfect woman. I'm headstrong. Occasionally volatile. I ride astride, and though in the last few years I've tried desperately to conform to Society's standards, I'm still happiest when I'm wiggling my toes in the sand and turning my face into the sun. I love to wear my hair free. And petticoats make me itch. Let's not forget shoes . . . Saito, I spent most of my years in India running barefoot with the natives."

Saito laughed softly and nodded. "You are like the filly that, once given her freedom to run, stares sadly to the green hills from her box, her heart bursting with the longing to be free again."

Destiny sighed. "I have so desperately missed India, and my father. He once said I was special enough to make Buddha fall in love. Yet, here I am a widow. And there is not a solitary male peer who looks at me as something other than disaster. Am I not attractive just a little? Is my hair not a rich enough brown? My eyes not green enough? My teeth straight enough? Is my body too hard from riding Sasaki? Is my skin too dark from the sun? Are my breasts not voluptuous enough? My hips not wide enough to safely heft around children in my womb?"

Destiny glanced at her old friend. Standing no more than four feet eight inches tall, bandy-legged, her face yellow and round, her eyelids heavily drooped, Saito shuffled amid the mounds of plants and stones. Her hair, braided into a queue that reached her knees, fell across her stooped shoulder.

"Never mind," Destiny said, crossing to the low wall that was covered in thick green moss. She watched the parade of well-dressed men and women meander across the estate grounds. "Look at them, Saito. What will this soiree accomplish, other than the pairing up of blue bloods and the assurance that the upper class will be continued through marriages of convenience instead of love? I simply don't understand. I was willing to stoop to such a level; I played by their rules—married a well-titled man as much for my aunt's sake as my own. I'm well aware that Uncle James wanted to be rid of me. And my father *certainly* approved. Chesterfield was a most pleasant sort—or was, until our wedding night. And I found him . . . appealing to look at, though he wasn't the sort who normally snags my eye. A bit pudgy about the middle, you know, and his skin was a touch too pink. And I never cared for fair-haired men in the least, but the chances of me stumbling across a titled man who didn't look as if he'd spent his life in a snail shell was somewhat remote, don't you think?

"What I mean is . . . even if we didn't actually *love* one another, the . . . joining might have been satisfactory. In time we might have come to care for one another and I might at least have had a child to love, and who loved me even if his or her father didn't. I think I might make a very good mother, Saito. Don't you think so?"

"Very wonderful, Hotaro," she replied as she stooped to pluck an errant weed. "But you should not give up hope."

"So Aunt Diana has been told repeatedly by her physician. I see what being childless has cost her. Imagine having nothing to look forward to every morning but facing Uncle James. Had she not had me to occupy her these last years I'm afraid she would have been dreadfully unhappy. I've been sorely tempted to return to India and take her with me. There are a thousand men there who would happily go to their knee and cherish her for the remainder of her days, child or no child. Then again . . . Aunt Diana might be shocked by the Indians' flagrant appreciation of coital relations. The colorful and detailed images are plastered everywhere, on walls and ceilings of public buildings, men and women in the most intimate of positions, their most private body parts exposed in the delightfully grandiose fashion." She lowered her voice and smiled. "I'm ashamed to admit that I found it all quite . . . beautiful, among other things. Thanks to my own mother, who wasn't appalled at all by the art, I learned that such relations between a man and woman were to be celebrated and enjoyed, and I came to better understand their own passion for one another. Unlike most of my peers, I quite looked forward to my wedding night. I didn't consider lying with my husband a duty. Quite the contrary. . . . Does this conversation unnerve you, Saito, because if it does—"

"Not at all, Hotaru."

"It's just that you're the closest friend I have. My only friend really, especially now. Every time I attempt to discuss the situation with Aunt Diana she flees the room in tears."

"I am listening, Hotaru."

"I suppose my enthusiasm shocked Chesterfield," she said, frowning. "I should have feigned a degree of apprehension. I'm afraid my awaiting him in the marriage bed with something on my face other than fear or repulsion gave him the wrong idea of my character. On the other hand . . ."

She followed Saito Kumataro down the path paved by blue pebbles, toward the pond fringed with large flat stones, rushes, and water lilies, and watched as Saito paused to stroke the back of a frog that basked on a rock in the fading spring sunlight.

"On the other hand, Saito, if the old adage be true, if it walks like a duck and quacks like a duck then it must be a duck, then perhaps the string of expletives and accusations he hurled at me might have merit, although I cannot imagine how one can be accused of being a harlot when one had never been allowed to be alone with a man longer than it takes to discuss the weather." Raising one eyebrow, she added, "Unless one can be deemed a harlot because of her thoughts, which, I confess, have a tendency to fixate on images that are more physical than cerebral.

"In short, I horrified Lord Chesterfield to the point that he stood at the foot of the bed, with his pink face sweating, his body shaking as if with the ague, spewing reasons why he simply would not, *could* not perform his marital duty on a woman so brazenly uncouth. What could his parents have been thinking to demand he agree to such a match? He simply could not go through with it. Then he fled the room."

Destiny looked away. "After a month I gave up trying to reason with him. My attempts to appease and console him only made matters worse. He paced the floor throughout the nights; he holed up in his library and wept inconsolably. When I entered the room he stared at me as if I were a . . . a *kamakiri*. Yes! A *kamakiri*, Saito. A giant praying mantis, the eater of small children. I pleaded with him to forgive my initial conjugal enthusiasm. I would wait patiently for as long as it took for him to accept me willingly in his bed—oh, but that set him off all over again, wailing and cursing his fate: Why, oh, why had he been born the only male heir? . . . If he was doomed to live an agonizing lie his entire life he would rather be dead. . . . He meant it, obviously. What was—is—so repugnant about me, Saito, that he would rather take his own life than know me completely as his wife?"

Saito was very quiet for a long while. Finally she said, "I will tell you of my brother's life, Hotaru, a story that I have shared with no other. Once, long ago, he was married. All the years he dwelt with his wife, no unkind word was ever uttered between them. And when she died, he thought never to marry again. But after two more years had passed, our father and mother desired another daughter in the house, and they told my brother of their wish, and of a girl who was beautiful and of good family, though poor. The family were of our kindred, and the girl was their only support; she wove garments of silk and of cotton, and for this she received but little money. And because she was filial and comely and our kindred not fortunate, my parents desired that my brother should marry her and help her people; for in those days we had a small income of rice. Being accustomed to obey our parents, my brother suffered them to do what they thought best. So the *nakodo* was summoned, and the arrangements for the wedding began.

"Twice my brother was able to see the girl in the house of her parents. He thought himself fortunate the first time he looked upon her; for she was very comely and young. But the second time, he perceived she had been weeping, and that her eyes avoided his. His heart sank for he thought, she dislikes me and they are forcing her to do this thing. Then my brother resolved to question the gods, and he caused the marriage to be delayed. He went to the temple of Yhanagi-No-Inari-Sama, which is in the Street Zaimokucho.

"And when the trembling came upon him, the priest, speaking with the soul of that maid, declared to my brother: 'My heart hates you, and the sight of your face gives me sickness, because I love another and because this marriage is forced upon me. Yet though my heart hates you, I must marry you because my parents are poor and old, and I alone cannot long continue to support them, for my work is killing me. But though I may strive to be a dutiful wife, there never will be gladness in your house because of me; for my heart hates you with a great and lasting hate, and the sound of your voice makes a sickness in my breast, and only to see your face makes me wish that I were dead.'

"Thus knowing the truth, my brother told it to my parents; and he wrote a letter of kind words to the maid, praying pardon for the pain he had unknowingly caused her. He feigned long illness, that the marriage might be broken off without gossip, and we made a gift to that family. And the maid was glad, for she was enabled at a later time to marry the young man she loved. Our parents never pressed my brother again to take a wife, and when they died, soon after we met your mother's mother, who brought us to this country and offered us a peaceful life."

Laying her hand on Saito's sleeve, Destiny said, "Are you suggesting that Chesterfield loved another?"

"It is not beyond reason."

"If that were true, would his sadness not have been reflected in his demeanor when with his friends? It wasn't! When Lord Rosebury came around, which he did often, Chesterfield was joyous and lighthearted. They drank together and rode together and hunted and . . . they were inseparable. But the moment I walked into the room his mood went from buoyant to crushing despair. Once he hurled an entire decanter of fine sherry at me, barely missing my head by inches.

"I wish my mother were alive," Destiny said, touching her reflection in the water. "She was so wise and kind and understanding. There wasn't a problem she wouldn't confront and rectify if it was in her power to do so."

"You are much like your mother, Hotaru. Your spirits are free and your hearts are much full of love. It is no wonder she turned to a man like your father, who blessed her with the freedom to grow as a human being worthy of much respect. It is sad that her father never understood this."

"My grandfather was cruel and demanding and . . . I'm glad I never knew him. I shouldn't have liked him at all, I think. Imagine refusing to allow my father to court her, just because there was that hint of controversy regarding his affiliation with socialism. To this very day I believe my grandfather had everything to do with my father's being shipped off to India. Did he actually believe that my mother wouldn't follow him? She would have followed him to the ends of the earth."

"Their marriage was hardly of calm water. There was much fire and tumult within their relationship."

"There was passion, yes. Passion for India. And passion for each other. But at the end of each day they were happy and content and in love. I never saw them retire to their room angry with one another. My father respected my mother's opinions and her right to voice them. He admired her attitude toward the Indian people. Unlike the other English wives, she wasn't content with separation from the masses. She felt if they were to live among them, they should respect and understand their culture; not attempt to 'civilize' them to our ways and beliefs. After all, Buddhism and Hinduism existed long before Christianity."

"I will hardly argue the point," Saito replied, squatting beside the figure of a stone Buddha.

Destiny dropped to her knees beside her. "Saito, I have a secret that I must confess to someone. If I tell you, will you promise not to think too badly of me?"

"Have I ever thought badly of you?" she replied, gathering a large green stone in her hand.

"The last few days . . . I've been meeting someone, a man. In the forest of wild ponies." She pursed her lips and watched Saito's inscrutable face, knowing there would be not so much as a flicker of shock—not from Saito. "He happened upon me as I was feeding the ponies from my hand. I felt as if . . . in a moment as if . . . I had fallen into a fairy tale. Oh, Saito, he's so handsome. I look into his face and reality subsides. We sit for hours discussing such mundane topics as weather, cattle, horses, India. Do you know how long I've craved a companion with whom I could discuss my life in India—who isn't overcome by distaste when I reveal how I played with the native children, ate in their homes, dressed in their clothes—prayed in their temples?"

Sitting back on her heels, her gaze drifting to the sky, which was fast building with clouds, Destiny sighed. "His name is Jason. I lied and told him mine was Mary. I don't dare tell him my real name, Saito. Were he to learn my true identity, the fiasco with Lord Chesterfield would pale in comparison to the scandal of my clandestinely meeting a stranger in the woods, even if it is only to read poetry to one another and talk about India." She smiled, thinking of the first time she looked up from her book to discover him standing at the edge of the clearing watching her, a lazy smile on his face and his dark hair falling into his eyes. "I can't be certain, but I think he might be a farmer, or a groom—or even a gypsy," she added with a conspiratorial giggle. "He's far too earthy to be a man of any financial substance. His dark hair is too long. And although his boots are fine, they're too scuffed and muddy. A gentleman would never appear in public in scuffed boots, would he? And his eyes . . ." She smiled. "Gray as yonder rain clouds, and just as turbulent. This is going to sound dreadfully childish and silly, Saito, but I think I might be falling in love with him. Have I shocked you yet? Is it possible to fall in love with someone so quickly?"

"Love cannot flourish under the shadow of subterfuge, Hotaru."

"A forever relationship is impossible and I know it. I simply couldn't ride off into the sunset with a plowman or a gypsy—think what such a scandal would do to Aunt Diana. Her life with Uncle James since I came back to England has been difficult enough. And even if I wanted, I couldn't invite him into my world. Uncle James and his peers would tear him apart like hyenas on a carcass."

"If you know so little about this man, Hotaru, what do you find in him to love?"

She thought a moment, her mind acknowledging the acceleration of her heartbeat as she visualized his face. "We share a common interest in books. He enjoys my reading to him. He makes me feel smart, and beautiful. He oft compliments my hair and eyes and enjoys my laughter. Did I mention that he's very handsome? Not simply appealing, but . . . extraordinarily rakish. Were he a member of Society there wouldn't be a woman who wouldn't fight to snare him for herself or her daughter. In truth, he's too bloody handsome to be real."

"And would you enjoy this euphoria if he were not so pleasing to look at, Hotaru? Would your eyes grow misty if he did not mend your wounded dignity with his charming compliments? And if you were to snare him—would you not be fearful of other women who would try to lure him from you? Would your happiness soon become tainted by insecurity?"

Destiny frowned and averted her eyes from her friend, who regarded her with an all-knowing intensity that made reality sink like a stone in her chest. "I don't know," she finally replied.

"And if this man were to fall in love with you, and you were unable to satisfy his need to be with him forever, would this not cause him great pain?"

"I hadn't thought of it that way, Saito. I've only considered how the relationship could affect me." She shrugged. "It is impossible, isn't it? Two strangers falling in love. We might as well be from different stars. But the idea of never looking into his face again . . . of never hearing him laugh, of never watching him feed wild ponies from his hand . . . all those things made yonder reality more tolerable." She motioned to the distant manor house. "I don't want to spend the remainder of my life alone, Saito. I'm twenty-two, a widow, yet haven't had the pleasure of a solitary kiss or caress even from my husband. I don't want to be so desperate that I would be forced to marry some man old enough to be my grandfather just for the sake of security—as Diana's been forced to do. I think I would rather be dead than to be as unhappy as my poor, sweet aunt."

Drawing back her slender shoulders, Destiny set her chin and forced a strength into her voice that she did not feel in her heart. "You're right, of course. It's not my way to intentionally hurt people. My mother and father taught me better than that. I'll end it today. I'll tell him I can never see him again—for his own sake."

With her face partially hidden beneath the brim of her large hat, Saito sat on the ground near the Buddha and crossed her legs, waiting as Destiny sat down before her, crossing her long legs, in loose cotton Japanese trousers, beneath her. "I think it is time for your lesson," Saito told her.

"Once there lived in the Izumo village called Mochida-no-ura a peasant who was so poor that he was afraid to have children. And each time that his wife bore him a child he cast it into the river, and pretended that it had been born dead. Sometimes it was a son, sometimes a daughter; but always the infant was thrown into the river at night. Six were murdered thus.

"But as the years passed, the peasant found himself more prosperous. He had been able to purchase land and to lay by money. And at last his wife bore him a seventh child, a boy.

"Then the man said: 'Now we can support a child, and we shall need a son to aid us when we are old. And this boy is beautiful. So we will bring him up.'

"And the infant thrived; and each day the hard peasant

wondered more at his own heart, for each day he knew that he loved his son more.

"One summer's night he walked out into his garden, carrying his child in his arms. The little one was five months old.

"And the night was so beautiful, with its great moon, and the peasant cried out, 'Ah! Tonight is truly a wondrously beautiful night!'

"Then the infant, looking up into his face and speaking the speech of a man, said, 'Why, father! The last time you threw me away the night was just like this, and the moon looked just the same, did it not?'

"And thereafter the child remained as other children of the same age, and spoke no word.

"And the peasant became a monk."

Destiny frowned and scratched her head. "I'm not sure I understand."

"You will, Hotaru," she told her. "You will when the time is right."

❧ 3 ❧

Before you pronounce on the rashness of the pro-
ceeding, reader, look back to the point whence I
started; consider the desert that I have left.

—CHARLOTTE BRONTË, *Villette*

Despite the mounting rain clouds that sent James and
Diana's guests scurrying for shelter, Destiny rode her
mare Sasaki beyond the far-reaching boundaries of the
Sheffield estate and down the meandering road beyond
Bournemouth, where the scrubby heath gave way to the
dense pinewood forest. She took with her a grain sack of
corn and oats and a book of Shakespearean works so worn
the spine had become cracked and the pages smudged by
fingerprints and the imprints of flowers she had pressed.
Once coming to the grassy glade, she dismounted the
hard-breathing horse and sat on the downed trunk of a
tree, sack on her lap, her fingers drumming the book in anticipation as she waited and watched in silence as the
birds trilled around her and the light began to fade with
the onslaught of rain clouds that rumbled frequently with
thunder.

They never set a definite time for their rendezvous; that,
of course, would have been far too brazen and implied
much too much familiarity. For him to invite her to such a
remote area would have shown tremendous lack of respect
for her reputation. On the other hand, for her to request his

company would have painted a most shocking and unappealing portrait of her character.

There were no appointments struck. No hints provided to issue so much as a glimmer of an invitation between them. He—the stranger named Jason with storm-kissed eyes and windblown leonine hair—simply arrived, as if he somehow gleaned from the stars that she would be there, waiting, trying her best not to reveal the intense pleasure his company brought her. They would go through the ritual of pretending surprise to find one another there. Eventually, their initial nervous banter would ease into gentle conversation, dreamy introspection, arousing exchanges of veiled flirtations that made her skin flush, her heart race, and her mind whirl with what-ifs.

What if he tried to kiss her?

What if they discovered that they *could* defy the world and fall in love?

What if? What if? What if?

Sitting there today, however, with the pressure of humidity pressing down on her, she did not pray that he would walk from the woods looking like a deity of temptation. She prayed that he would not come, but leave her sitting on the rotting trunk of a tree, shivering with rain-touched wind, clutching a book of love sonnets to her breast. Because Saito was right, as always. Love could not flourish under the shadow of subterfuge. If he walked into this glade now, she would be forced to tell him good-bye, but not before she accomplished what she came here to do.

Time passed. The sky grew darker, the clouds heavier, the wind colder. Lightning danced along the distant horizon and thunder crawled through the forest, growling like dragons in the undergrowth. Eventually, the wild, shaggy ponies that roamed the wood eased into the glade, ears perked and nostrils flared, eyes watchful and hopeful as they were lured by the scent of grain. Destiny tossed them handsful, smiling as they inched closer and closer. Eventually they would eat from her hand, sniff her fingers, allow her to lightly touch their matted forelocks and perhaps scratch their withers.

It was they who first noted Jason's approach; their heads raised suddenly, their every sense focused on the darkening wood; they whirled on their haunches and as swiftly as deer dissolved into the trees and undergrowth.

He rode from the wood on a snorting, lathered, blood-bay horse, his boots and breeches muddy and his loose-fitting white shirt slightly drooping off one brown shoulder. His hair was thick and dark—not black exactly, but somewhat long, to the tops of his shoulders, a mass of loose waves that framed his face in a wild, gypsy-like manner. His cheeks were slightly gaunt, his brow hooded, his mouth . . . wide and twisted with a secret irony that made her flush with a kind of embarrassment—ashamed for sitting in the woods alone feeding ponies and waiting for him.

"Do you make a habit of going about scaring people and animals?" she called out, trying her best not to reveal, even to herself, the incredible pleasure and relief the sight of him gave her.

"Do you make a habit of trespassing on people's property?" he replied in a sharper tone than normal as he allowed his frothing animal to move toward her.

"If this prove to be your property, then I should apologize," she replied just as sharply, then bit her lower lip to keep from smiling.

"It's not."

"Then why should you care?"

"I don't."

"Then what are you doing here?" she asked.

"I might ask you the same."

"Feeding ponies, of course. I can't imagine any worthier excuse for braving this miserable weather."

"There are men about who prey on bits of fluff like you."

"I beg your pardon?" She raised her eyebrows.

"Bandits and such. They have no scruples, you know."

Destiny tried to breathe. Jason was close enough now that she could smell the heavy scent of hot horse flesh and hear the grinding of the animal's teeth on the bit. In a silky voice, she tipped her head and asked with a lift of one arched eyebrow, "Are you a bandit? Because if you are there is little here to rob except a gunny of corn and a worn-out book of sonnets and such. You're welcome to the corn, of course. Your animal looks as if it could use a few more pounds on its ribs."

He slid off the saddle and onto the ground, causing his horse to shy to one side. For a moment he appeared hesitant; he looked from her back to the trees, as if deciding whether or not he should stay.

"I don't recall inviting you to join me," she told him.

"Do I look like a man who cares?" He gave her a flat smile.

"You look like a . . . *bounder.*"

"Do I?" He laughed, the sound slightly self-deprecating. "Why so? Because I have no coat on? Because my leathers are frayed? Because . . . ?"

"Because I've never seen a gentleman who looks like you. That's why. Your skin is dark. And there's stubble on your chin. Not to mention that you're riding without gloves. No gentleman would *ever* ride without gloves. His hands would become brown and calloused. Let me see your hands. I'll tell you if you're a gentleman or not."

"Dare I come that close, bounder that I am . . . or could be?" His lids drooping a little, he moved toward her, mouth curled slightly, his hands extended, palms up for her inspection.

Destiny regarded his hands, with their long fingers and well-manicured nails. They were not massive hands, like a plowman's or blacksmith's, but they were brown and very calloused. "You ride a great deal," she said, pointing to the rough areas between his fingers. "Your clothes, or what there is of them, are obviously of superior cloth and cut, though you don't strike me as the sort who would frequent Bond Street. And your boots are of fine leather, if scuffed and overly due for a shine. You might well be a groom who's been handed down a few fineries from his generous employer, or a gypsy with a penchant for robbing the wealthy."

He sat down beside her, his elbows on his knees. There was an intensity in his eyes that slightly unbalanced her, and for an instant Destiny acknowledged that the man could well be a bounder after all. Certainly his previous carefree behavior had turned to an intentness that made his rakishness all the more mesmerizing, if not unnerving.

He said in a slow voice, "Is it not more likely to come upon a man riding in the wood than it is a woman sitting in a glade, and feeding wild ponies, no less?"

"That would depend on the woman, I suppose . . . especially if she were a lady."

His eyes regarded her up and down, and the realization occurred to her that he had sat more closely to her than normal. His nearness aroused a warmth in her that made her throat tight.

"A lady would never wear her hair down outside of her boudoir, of course," he commented, drawing her gaze to his lips, which carried a shadow of sardonicism. "Nor would she gad about in public dressed like some Japanese rice farmer. For that matter, a *lady* wouldn't be caught in that getup at all."

"Well," she replied with a smile, "I never said I was a lady . . . did I?"

"No. You didn't. But I suspect that hidden beneath that crown of windblown curls and your pitiful excuse at flirtation lurks a proper sort of young woman. My question is why she would risk her reputation to meet a total stranger in a forest glade."

Heat kissed her cheeks. "If you have something to say, sir, then say it. I came here to read and to enjoy the ponies. Need I remind you that *you* are the interloper here."

"So I am," he replied wearily, and looked away. A long

moment of silence passed before he pointed to the book on her lap. "Shall I read to you today?"

"Ah. So you *can* read." She smiled and raised her gaze from his lips to his eyes. They looked more blue now than gray.

"About as well as you can ride," he replied.

"I happen to be a very good rider."

"I know. I've watched you ride."

"Shocking, isn't it?"

"That would depend on who you are—or, rather, *what* you are."

"And if I be a lady, would you retreat to a more respectable distance? Would you flee into the woods? Would you think of me as too scandalous to know?"

There was silence between them that seemed to stretch forever. His gaze never left hers; his body did not move, yet it felt to Destiny that the world narrowed into a hot pinpoint of his existence alone. His smell, his body heat, the touch of his leg against hers swallowed her entirely. "Well?" she demanded in a weak voice. "Would you hate me if I were a lady?"

"No," his lips replied.

She struggled for a breath. "Why do you stare at me so?"

"I might ask you the same." His mouth curled sensually. His leg pressed closer to hers.

"You're very . . . rugged."

"And you're very feminine, despite this pitiful and unbecoming garb you're wearing. Despite that you ride like a man and prefer the company of wild ponies to young women your own age."

"I'm hardly prone to girlish chitchat." Lowering her lashes, she tipped her face away and, working up her courage, admitted, "I've been married, you know."

His dark eyebrows slowly raised and his face clouded.

"I'm a widow," she hurriedly explained. "Does that please you better?"

"I suppose that if I must make a choice between your being a widow and being married, I would have to say yes.

However, I think I would like it better if you had never been married at all."

The exhilaration started in her chest, along with the what-ifs and the barrage of realities that Saito had forced her to confront. Something new vibrated between them—an intensity that flustered her, a danger that magnified every sound, smell, and color surrounding them.

Clutching at the book on her lap, she shoved it at him and tried vainly to continue their banter. "If you can truly read, then read to me."

He continued to stare at her, his face and eyes hard. "I would rather talk about you."

Caution tapped at her brain. She opened the book and attempted to focus on the page.

The man plucked the book from her hands. "Did you love your husband? Did he make you happy? Did your father approve of him?"

"My father?" Flustered by his odd questions, Destiny nodded. "Yes, my father approved."

"I don't believe you."

Destiny frowned. "My father would never disapprove of something if he thought it was what I really wanted."

"Nonsense." He laughed sharply. "If your father thought for a moment that what you wanted might harm you he would give his life to stop you from making a mistake."

"How do *you* know what my father may or may not do?" she replied as sternly.

Frowning, he shrugged, and when he spoke again his voice maintained a monotone. "Fathers are not in the habit of allowing their daughters to make matrimonial mistakes. A young woman marries for either love, money, or a position in Society. I'm simply interested in why you married . . . whomever you married."

She did not respond.

A muscle bunched in his jaw and with apparent effort he looked away, into the woods where the wild ponies peered out at them from the brush and vines. A sudden wind blew his hair over his brow and under his chin, rippled the sleeves of his shirt, and wove through the tall grass like invisible serpents. Suddenly he stood and paced a few feet away before turning on his heels and glaring down at her. "This is insane," he finally growled. "I don't know what the hell I was thinking to come here like this—to get involved with you like this."

Surprised, she shook her head. "I don't know what you mean, 'involved.'"

"Don't play naive. You aren't the naive sort. If anyone was naive here, it must have been me." He ran one hand through his hair and briefly closed his eyes. "I should have run like hell the minute I saw you riding your damned horse. I don't think I've ever seen a woman handle a horse quite like you, ride like you, as if you become a part of the beast. You don't even have the good sense most of the time to use a saddle."

"I'm sorry if that offends you," she replied, unable to look away from his suddenly angry gaze. "And when have you seen me ride?"

"Who hasn't seen you ride? You fly about the countryside like a bat out of hell. Not two days ago you took a wall and you and your horse landed smack in the middle of a funeral procession."

Her face flushing, Destiny turned a shoulder to him. "What I do on my horse isn't any concern of yours."

"You're going to get yourself killed."

She peered at him from under her lashes. "And that bothers you?"

He did not reply, just turned the book over and over in his hands. Finally he sat beside her again, flung open the pages, and searched the words, riffling the gold-leafed edges with his thumb in silence until his breathing evened and the flush of anger melted from his cheeks. Oh, how she ached in that moment to reach out and touch her fingers to the fall of dark hair on his brow! She felt euphoric that he cared about her welfare. She wanted to tell him the truth about her dreadful match with Chesterfield. No, she had not loved him. She had only wanted to do what Society ex-

pected of her and, along the way, appease Uncle James and
therefore make Diana's life a little more peaceful. Never,
at any time, had she experienced the kind of emotions she
now felt thumping in her breast. Dear God, she must be insane.

"Would you like to talk about India some more?" she
asked.

"No," he snapped. "Don't bring the topic up again. I've
grown bored hearing about it *and* your father."

Destiny frowned. "You're very rude today. And angry.
Are you in some sort of trouble?"

He flashed her a dark look. "I'm well accustomed to
dealing with trouble should trouble arise. However, I
hadn't anticipated that it would come this time in the
form of a woman."

Destiny stared hard at his features. Had he somehow discovered her identity? Did he now know that she was, indeed, a pariah of Society?

He focused on the book and began to read in a voice
smooth and rich as black velvet:

> "Shall I compare thee to a sumner's day?
> Thou art more lovely and more temperate:
> Rough winds do shake the darling buds of May,
> And summer's lease hath all too short a date."

His voice fell silent, and slowly he shut the book before
reluctantly raising his head. The temptation to reach out to
him filled her. She touched his cheek, allowing her fingertips to slide over the rough stubble on his jaw and trace the
strong line of his chin; they drifted to his lips, which
slightly parted as he turned his face into her hand, breathing warmly into her moist palm.

"Do you think me pretty?" she asked, holding her
breath.

"Pretty?" He made a sound in his throat. "You have a
complexion like peach blossoms. Your eyes are as green as

an Irish glade. And your lips . . . I'm certain I've not seen lips as lovely as yours. . . ."

She could not breathe suddenly. The air felt charged and heavy. Every nerve began to tingle, and she wondered if the throbbing she heard in her ears was her heart or the thunder of the approaching storm.

She tried to speak, but failed. The place where he had breathed into her hand burned both hot and cold. The whisper of admonition for remaining in this glade, sharing space with the gypsy-like stranger, dwindled in her mind like ice on fire, replaced with a sense of rawness that made even the touch of coolness in the air painful upon her flesh.

"It's starting to rain," he whispered.

"I don't mind the rain," she heard herself reply.

For a brief moment it seemed to Destiny that he would reach out for her; a multitude of emotions swept his dark face—anger, confusion, frustration—then he backed away, just slightly, and slowly shook his head.

"Those months with nothing but thoughts, regrets made me a little crazy . . . maybe. Then I heard about this wild, beautiful creature who rides the back roads on her black Arab, who frolics in the woods with wild ponies, and I had to see her for myself."

At last he reached for her. He slid his fingers around the back of her head and, with an insistent move, drew her close. "Have you ever made love in the rain?" he breathed in her ear.

"Of course," she lied, catching her breath as he pressed his mouth against the pulse in her throat.

"Have you ever made love in a glade with a stranger?" He kissed her temple and traced the shell of her ear with his finger.

She laughed nervously. "Do I look like the sort of woman who would do such a thing?"

"Yes. You look like a woman made for love, to drive a man wild with desire to hold you, to taste and smell your flesh, and make him mindless with pleasure."

She drew away, not out of mortification, but because his

shocking murmured words filled her with a headiness that made the air reverberate with a thunderclap so sharp and startling her consciousness flickered like a flame. As he stood, he lifted her with him.

He could have been anyone: a bounder, a bandit, a groom, a farmer, a gypsy. She did not know his identity, but neither did he know hers. She was just as much a stranger to him—two strangers meeting in a forest glade who found one another incredibly appealing. She might never again have the opportunity to share such an experience with a man who so epitomized her most secret fancy. Why not share a kiss, then go on their merry way, never to meet again, to partake in nothing more than the memory of a few shared forbidden moments—

The rain began, trickling through the tree limbs and making tiny splashes like music upon the leaves. It beaded upon Jason's dark hair and on his skin, turning his white shirt transparent so she could see the shadow of dark hair on his chest. As he cradled her face between his hands and tipped back her head, the water fell softly upon her closed eyelids and parted lips. He bent his head over hers, slid his mouth onto hers . . .

So this was kissing. This heat and wetness, the easy molding of his lips with hers, the tentative teasing of his tongue, the warmth of his breath upon her face. Odd how she felt it all the way to her toes. It sluiced through her veins to her fingertips and rushed through her belly to ignite like fire then expand like sunlight above a misty eastern horizon to settle in a slow pulsating glow at the apex of her thighs.

She pressed close.

Even on her wedding night Destiny had not felt like this. The reality occurred to her in that instant that she might never feel this way again.

Trembling, reason screaming in her consciousness, she tugged her shirt over her head. Her chemise clung to her skin in a fine pink film, and with a tug of a single ribbon it fell open, exposing her breasts, which felt aching and sensitive to every minute raindrop. If he rejected her now she would die.

"Foolish woman," he whispered. "Why?"

"Because I've decided that I won't see you again—ever. Because I need you to hold me before you go. *Please.*"

He murmured, "Oh, my God." Then he stepped away and turned from her; he moved haltingly toward his grazing horse before stopping, head down, as the rain fell harder on his shoulders. Slowly, slowly, he turned again and his look became fierce. "Once is all you want from me, sweetness? Then I simply disappear? Fade into the sunset? Years from now I'll fleetingly cross your mind, perhaps when you're nestled in your husband's arms, and I'll be a naughty secret that will occasionally make you smile. What if I tell you that I want more than that?"

"It's impossible," she said softly.

"Because you think me a bounder? A gypsy? Not worthy enough for you? Well, I imagine there are a few women in my past who must have felt what I'm feeling right now. What the devil. One way or the other I'm going to hate myself tomorrow."

He reached for her so swiftly she lost her breath, dropped to one knee before her and slid his hands around her waist, drawing her close so he could open his lips upon her nipples, tug them and nuzzle them with his tongue and teeth. She gasped and whimpered. She twisted her hands at last into his thick dark hair and arched her back, giving herself up to his caresses.

His hands slid down her body, into her clothes and between her legs; they nudged away her breeches, which slipped easily off her hips and bunched around her ankles.

He untied her bootlaces, slid the boots from her feet, set them aside. With rain running in rivulets down her hair and shoulders, beading like teardrops on the tips of her erect pink nipples, she watched as he disrobed, revealing his man's hard, honed—and shockingly scarred—body.

Naked and aroused, every muscle glistening with rain, he stood, his eyes embracing her, his lips no longer sardonic, but gentle and whispering words she could no longer hear because her heartbeat was drowning out even the thunder overhead. He wrapped her up in his arms and kissed her again; his knees nudged her legs apart with an insistence that both frightened and thrilled her.

Falling, falling in his arms to the ground, rolling as he opened his mouth upon her breasts, licking and teasing with his tongue and teeth until she no longer knew her own body, or cared that it was no longer hers, but his to do with as he wished, to make her a woman, to give her the wedding night that her husband had robbed her of—if she never married again she would at least have this.

Twisting in the cold, wet grass, the rain driving harder, her hands buried in his thick hair, she kissed him back and arched her body into his, opening her legs and wrapping them around his narrow hips in blatant invitation. He made sounds in his throat, deep, guttural, and yet he held back, allowing his hands to explore her, gently, roughly, hungrily, fingers delving, stroking, gliding around and in and out until she gritted her teeth and cursed him.

Then he pinned her to the ground, arms and legs spread, as he rocked onto his knees and poised, head fallen forward. His eyes closed briefly and opened, then looking into her face and slowly lowering his body onto hers, he thrust into her with a force and pain that raised her hips off the ground and caused her to cry out.

The sound of rain filled up the glade and forest.

He stared, expressionless, buried inside her. "You're a virgin," he finally said, shock melting from his face, replaced by confusion then dark anger.

"You needn't look so despairing. I didn't lie to you. My husband wouldn't have me. Not on our wedding night nor any night of the three months we were married. He hung himself so he need not trouble himself ever." She tried to smile. Odd that she could not manage it. After all the many weeks and months that she had been forced to contain her humiliation, now it rose like a lava flow from within her chest. It burned like quicksilver in her eyes. "So you need not worry that I care who you are, bandit or bounder. You only did what another could not find in his heart to do."

❦ 4 ❧

It is too painful to think that she is a woman, with a woman's destiny before her—a woman spinning in young ignorance a light web of folly and vain hopes which may one day close round her and press upon her, a rancorous poisoned garment, changing all at once . . . into a life of deep human anguish.

—GEORGE ELIOT, *Adam Bede*

Their bodies entwined, flesh pressed against flesh and damp with sweat and rain and mud, they remained silent, unmoving. Jason, with his eyes closed, buried his face in Destiny's damp hair. As a soldier he had made few mistakes in his career; as a man and a lover he had made several. This being the worst, no doubt about it. Months in solitary confinement had obviously diminished his common sense, not to mention his self-control. Now what the blazes was he going to do?

"What difference does it make that I was a virgin?" Destiny touched his face.

"A virgin deserves better than a mud puddle for a bed and weeds as her pillow," he responded through his teeth, his mind still musing over Compton Fontaine's reaction should he learn that Jason—friend and confidant—had deflowered his precious daughter.

"A bride deserves better than a groom who flees their marriage bed in tears," Destiny countered. "Obviously we don't always get what we deserve."

Jason rolled to his back, allowing the light rain to wash the sweat from his brow and clear his mind. It wasn't as if he had been the instigator here, he thought. Not by a long shot. It was obvious the lady had had every intention of using him—a stranger—to take care of the business her husband had not, could not, accomplish on their wedding night.

Taking his shirt from the ground, Jason proceeded to gently clean the blood and semen from between her legs. He did not look in her eyes. Roughly catching her arm, he helped her to stand, then snatched up her clothes and began to dress her.

She frowned. "Why are you so angry? Would you have preferred my being the sort of woman who would lie down with just anyone?"

"That's exactly what you've done," he snapped as he reached for his breeches. "I could have been a madman. A murderer. A disease-infested—"

"I would think you would be grateful. It's not every day a man is so generously offered a woman's virginity. Then again, my husband wasn't so thrilled either, was he?"

He fastened his breeches and turned for his boots. "Perhaps before you marry again you should better learn your husband's idiosyncrasies. One would have to be blind not to know that Chesterfield enjoyed the company of his own sex. He and Rosebury were lovers—had been for years." The words tumbled out before he realized it. His boots hanging from his hands, he slowly turned his gaze back to hers.

Destiny stared at him through the rain, shock and realization glazing her eyes.

Damn, he thought.

"Oh, my God," Destiny whispered. "You're no farmer or groom. . . . You know who I am. You've known all along. *Who are you?*"

Wearily, Jason tossed his boots to the ground, drew himself up, and offered her a slight bow. "Jason Batson, Lady Chesterfield. I'm—"

Her eyes widened further as she cried, "Batson! Oh, my God. Oh! You know my father; he's written of you and—oh, my God." She covered her mouth with one hand and backed away.

He took a step toward her. "Let's not get hysterical."

"You're a friend of my father's!"

"Which is why I'm here—"

"Detestable fiend! He would shoot you if he knew—"

Jason narrowed his eyes and pointed one finger at her. "Don't get sanctimonious, sweetness. *You* seduced *me*." For an instant he thought she might faint. "It's obvious I've bungled this badly," he explained as calmly as possible. "My intention these last days was not to . . ." He waved his hand toward the crushed grass at their feet. "I had not meant to . . . enjoy your company so . . . much. Then again, before happening upon you here I had not expected you to be so alluring as to make me forget my priorities. Which is obviously what I've done."

She backed away again, shaking, a hot red flush creeping up her neck and spreading along her jaw. A breath slid through her clenched teeth and her hands fisted. "I cared for you, naive little idiot that I am. I became swept away by some silly fairy-tale fantasy that you cared for me as well. I only wanted to know a few wonderful moments of being appreciated; I wanted to know what it is to be desired by a man who—"

"Oh, I desired you all right. How could I not when you stood there naked as a wood nymph? Regardless, I came here to discuss your father. I have to know what you know about his association with Nana Sahib."

"Then you admit it." She drew herself up and lifted her chin. "This was all some ploy to weasel from me information about my father. Who sent you, dammit? Tell me now, or I shall . . ." She looked around frantically, her gaze locking on the riding whip she had tossed aside.

"I work for a man named Harold Dunleavy."

Dunleavy's name sent another spasm of fury through

her. "Dunleavy," she hissed, causing Jason to raise both eyebrows. Obviously he had hit a nerve—*another* one.

"Dunleavy," she repeated, doing her best not to fully lose control of her senses. "That deplorable little man has done his best over the years to ruin my father. So this is how he intends to do it—by using me? . . . I beg your pardon, by *your* using me? Is Dunleavy's plan now to blackmail my father? If my father doesn't desist his support of India's plight, Dunleavy will spread the word to all of England that I'm a promiscuous doxy who rolls about forest glades with strangers? Because he knows my father would do anything, even walk away from his beloved India in order to protect my reputation."

Jason allowed her a thin smile. "First, I resent the insinuation that I used you. Secondly, I came here to learn just how much you know about Compton's involvement with Nana Sahib. I decided days ago that you don't know a hell of a lot. I kept coming back because . . . I found you . . . pleasant company."

"Liar." She sprang for her riding crop, and before he could grab her she struck at him, barely missing his face. He lunged, took the crop from her, caught her struggling body against his, and pinned her arms to her sides.

"You bloodthirsty little termagant. If this is any indication of how you treat men when you become angry, I don't doubt Chesterfield hanged himself."

She struggled furiously, though it did little good. Her beating his arms and chest felt about as effective as if he'd been a stone wall. "Stop it," he shouted, shaking her. She began to kick at his shins. He thrust one knee between her thighs and dragged her up against him. "For God's sake, be still and listen to me."

Her head falling back and her eyes glazed by anger, she cried, "My father loved you. Traitor! I despise you. And when I inform my father what you've done and why, he'll despise you as well."

"I can't help your father unless I know the truth."

"You mean help Dunleavy—"

"Forget about Dunleavy!" He howled in pain and bent double as she kneed him in the groin, slid out of his arms, and ran for her horse. Stumbling, he made a grab for her. Both hit the ground hard, she beneath him.

"If you touch me I'll scream," she declared with such vehemence he almost laughed, considering her sorry circumstances. Still, the sight of her beneath him had a sobering effect. The damp, transparent chemise barely covered her nipples. His body responded with a surge of hunger that made the ache between his legs unbearable.

"Be quiet. I said, be quiet. And still. Because if you knee me again I'm going to forget that I've tried damn hard to be a gentleman these last many days. I'm going to forget again that you're Compton's little girl and I'm going to rip the clothes off of you, spread your legs, and bury myself so hard and deep in you, you won't be able to sit that bloody horse of yours for a fortnight."

She gasped and the color drained from her cheeks. Her eyes looked like two green pools in her face.

For some asinine reason there were things he wanted to tell her—his reasons for spending all these pleasurable afternoons in her company—reasons that had nothing to do with his assignment. He was fascinated by her spirit, intelligence, and enthusiasm for life. Her warmth melted the cold that had settled in his bones during those long months in prison when he had festered in the dark, imagining that somewhere there would be a woman whose very presence could wipe the memories of war and horror from his mind; who would sail away with him to a tea plantation where his heaven was a rambling white house overlooking an endless green sea.

But the soldier in him had wanted to discover if she knew anything at all about her father's involvement with Nana Sahib. Obviously, if Dunleavy was right that Compton Fontaine was in league with Sahib to overthrow the Crown's occupation in India by way of violence, then Jason would be forced to deal with the unpleasant situation one way or another.

But it had soon become obvious to Jason that Compton's daughter knew nothing about her father's most recent activities with Sahib—if, indeed, Jason was to believe Dunleavy's stories of high treason. As far as Destiny knew, Compton was simply rattling Parliament's windows by dashing off letters to the newspapers about the injustices and inequalities among the Brits and natives.

Sorrowfully, he realized that during the last few days, indeed the last few minutes, he had ruined any opportunity to know Destiny Fontaine in any capacity other than . . . as an enemy, a traitor to her father. He could not turn back the clock to the moment he first approached her in the secluded glade. He could not, in a dashing manner, kiss her hand and proclaim that her father's greatest wish was for the two of them to ride off into the sunset together. She would never again trust what he said. She would never believe that she had stirred something inside him that was foreign and unsettling and filling him with regret—a sentiment that was alien to him, until now.

Her chin began to tremble, yet she glared into his eyes with the ferocity of a tigress. He could feel her heart pound against her ribs and her every breath was a struggle.

"You're a manipulating, scheming fraud," she finally said, "and I shall hate you to the day I die."

"Be that as it may, you're going to listen to what I have to say. Your father is in trouble. Dunleavy suspects that he's helping Nana Sahib ready an uprising to expel the British from India. Should he discover this to be true, he fully intends to assassinate your father, along with Sahib, with the nod from Parliament, of course."

Destiny's face turned white. She did not blink or breathe. At last she found the strength to ask, "Who is to do it, kill my father?"

"Me," Jason replied softly.

Her face turned to stone. He lightly stroked her cold cheek, fully aware of the shock and fear she would be experiencing in that moment. "Trust me, sweetness, I don't believe for a moment that your father is guilty of treason.

Compton might be zealous about his love for India, but he would never put the lives of his fellow countrymen in peril. Destiny, I would rather turn a gun on myself than harm your father."

"I don't believe you." Her voice sounded wooden. "If you truly cared about my father, you would never have come here for Dunleavy in the first place. You would never have lied to me and allowed this sordid mistake to take place."

"I've only Dunleavy's word on what's been going on in India in the past months. I had to know for myself if Compton has gone over the edge. As I spent these days here with you, I realized that even if your father had become so involved with Sahib, he would never have implicated you in any way with his decision.

"Dunleavy is going to try to convince you to help him. Don't trust him. Your involvement would jeopardize not only Compton's life, but your own as well."

"And I should believe anything you tell me." It was not a question. Her eyes narrowed. "I think not, sir."

Her hand moved too fast for him to deflect the rock that she drove into his temple. The sudden pain against his head reverberated through his skull like a bolt of lightning, and the world turned black.

An hour later Destiny stood shaking in the butler's pantry of her aunt's manor house, covering her mud-streaked face with her hands. She dared not close her eyes because she would certainly see Batson's still face, a pool of rain-diluted blood beneath him. "I fear I've killed a man, Diana. Oh God, what am I going to do?"

Diana clutched her niece and whispered urgently, "Hush. Hush before someone hears you. Merciful heaven, Des, you're a mess—"

"Did you not hear what I just said?" Destiny stared into Diana's round eyes and stepped away, slapping Diana's hands aside. "I fear I killed him. I bashed his head with a rock. There was blood and—and—he just lay there white and still and I'm certain he wasn't breathing—"

"Quickly, we must get you upstairs before James sees you. And, God forbid, our guests."

Grabbing Diana's shoulders, doing her best to see through the little clumps of mud stuck in her eyelashes, Destiny whispered, "I should go back—"

"You're going nowhere except to your room and into a bath. James is furious. He's been searching for you for hours. If he were to see you now—"

"Diana!" came James's bark, causing Diana's eyes to roll and a slight whimper to rush through her lips. She turned on her heels, positioned herself between her husband and Destiny, and squared her small shoulders as if preparing for battle.

James, with several men following, moved out of the shadows and into the pantry. His eyes narrowed as he acknowledged Destiny, peering over her aunt's shoulder, her hair wild from wind and rain, her face and clothes filthy. His step hesitated, and his expression went from shock to murderous. "Good God," he declared. "What the blazes has the chit got herself into, Diana? She looks like a damnable bone grubber."

"She fell from her horse," Diana explained with a lift of her chin. "You can hardly fault her for that, considering you yourself tumbled last week." Directing her attention to the nervous servants, she said, "Blankets quickly. Destiny is wet and freezing. And bring cotton and salves for her injuries. Draw her a hot bath. Warm her some milk."

"To hell with hot baths and warm milk," James sneered, roughly shoving Diana aside. He glared down at Destiny, jaw locked, teeth grinding. "Daft girl, we've been frantic the last hours looking for you. Someone has arrived from London with word of your father."

"My father?" Destiny glanced to the line of unfamiliar men standing behind James, all somber faced and assessing her as if she were a swine to be purchased and slaughtered.

James caught her arm in a death grip and ushered her out of the foyer and along the back gallery, followed by the men in dark suits and emotionless expressions. Diana trailed, wringing her hands.

As they entered the library, James directed Destiny to one of several high-backed chairs. He shoved her into it, whipped a kerchief from his pocket, and rubbed at the mud and water on his hand.

"Here she is, gentlemen. You're welcome to her. Now, if you'll excuse me, I have guests." Catching Diana's arm, he forced her to the doorway, where he paused and looked back. "Once this meeting is finished, Destiny, you're to retire to your rooms immediately and remain there until I give you permission to do otherwise."

Without waiting for her reply, James exited the room, Diana struggling to be free of his hold on her arm.

One of the men walked to a row of crystal decanters lining a table near the bow window. He poured several drinks, one of which he put into Destiny's hand, forcing her stiff fingers around the glass. Another man, older and more distinguished looking, sat in the chair next to her.

"Go ahead," the older man said, pointing to the drink in her hand. "You look as if you need it."

"You're here about my father?" she heard herself say in a dry voice. Her hands trembled as memories of the last hours tapped like sharp little spikes in her brain. Caution stiffened her spine. She couldn't breathe.

"Drink," the man ordered, crossing his legs and relaxing in the chair.

Raising the snifter to her mouth, Destiny sipped the sherry, shuddered, and briefly closed her eyes. Not good. Batson's image swam into her mind, his handsome face disappearing behind rivulets of blood. Oh, dear lord. First Chesterfield, now Batson. Jason. Her father's friend. The man with whom she had become so enamored, whom she had seduced like she was some . . . brazen hussy. With the sherry warming her and sending a tendril of lethargy through her, she again focused on the stranger's face and released a shaky breath.

"What's wrong with my father? What's happened to him? Why are you here?"

"Lady Chesterfield, I'm sure you're aware that in recent months there's been a great deal of unrest spreading through India."

"My father wrote of it."

The man's eyes narrowed. "Indeed. And what, *exactly,* did he write?"

"What else? That the British were on the verge of insulting the entire nation, of course. And that Dalhousie had done more to alienate the nationals than any Brit who ever walked the face of the continent. My father was appalled by the Crown's growing arrogance and hunger to control and manipulate the populace."

A flicker of some emotion crossed the man's face.

"Who are you?" Destiny demanded, bracing herself, knowing even before he responded what the answer would be.

"Harold Dunleavy."

Destiny set her drink aside and stood up. "Dunleavy. Of course. The man who for the last few years has attempted to convince Parliament that my father is a traitor. During his brief term as viceroy you caused him immeasurable trouble. Correct me if I'm wrong, sir, but did you not instigate the investigation that ultimately removed my father from office?"

"Should Her Majesty not concern herself with a Crown official who appears to care more for the rights of a lot of heathens than he does for his own countrymen?"

Destiny turned and was brought up abruptly as a man stepped before the door, blocking her escape.

"I'm not here to dredge up old grudges, madam."

She faced him. "No? I've been told that you were passed over for the position of viceroy in favor of my father. Perhaps you begrudge him the very air he breathes."

"It was a long time ago. What does matter is that you

should be made aware that your father's safety has been greatly jeopardized by a few radicals who've grown irate over the Dalhousie rule of succession and inheritance."

"My father is greatly respected, Mr. Dunleavy. I can't imagine who would turn on my father for any reason, regardless of the mess Dalhousie made of the country."

"You're familiar with Nana Sahib?"

"Of course. He's my father's closest friend."

"We've received word from Sahib himself. He's threatened severe consequences to all of Her Majesty's subjects living in the region if steps are not taken to rescind the succession edict."

"I don't believe you. Sahib would never turn on the English in such a way."

"I'm afraid it is true." He withdrew a letter from his coat pocket and handed it to her. "Read it for yourself. He warns us of a far-reaching mutiny if we don't act in their best interest."

"Why have you come to me?" Her voice quivered as she focused on the letter. Surely there was some mistake. Nana Sahib adored her father. He'd thrown Destiny birthday parties in his own home. And when her mother died, he'd opened the doors of his own sacred chapels to lay her body in state.

Destiny looked away, the memory of Batson's warning ringing in her head: *You're going to listen to what I have to say. Your father is in trouble. Dunleavy suspects that he's helping Nana Sahib ready an uprising to expel the British from India.*

"Lady Chesterfield, I've come here in an attempt to help your father."

"Why would you help my father when you fought for years to destroy him?"

Dunleavy left his chair and walked to a window. For a moment he remained silent, his expression thoughtful. "Granted, my dear, I've been outspoken regarding your father's behavior. But only because I feared that his fanning the embers of discontent would result in the sort of situation we're now facing. Obviously, your father has tremendous influence with Nana Sahib, and could prove to be an invaluable mediator, but all attempts to communicate with your father these past several months have proven ineffective."

"What do you want from me?" she asked in a low voice.

"Your help, of course."

"I can't imagine how I could be of any help to you."

"We know how close the two of you are. He'll listen to you. You'll reason with him, convince him that, should he not cooperate by influencing Nana Sahib to forget this outrageous rebellion, his hands will be filthy with the blood of both the British and his beloved natives. On the other hand, should your father cooperate and help us with the Sahib matter, his previous transgressions will be forgiven . . . and forgotten."

"You want me to go to Cawnpore? To discuss this issue with my father in person?"

"As our emissary, so to speak."

Destiny glanced around the room at the other men, who stared back at her with hard expressions.

He fully intends to assassinate your father, along with Sahib, with the nod from Parliament, of course.

"We have a ship prepared to sail at the end of the week," Dunleavy informed her. "I've arranged for a special company of men to accompany you. If anyone can get you into Cawnpore, and into Sahib's compound, they can. They specialize in the . . . impossibly dangerous, so to speak."

Who is to do it, kill my father?

Me.

Breathing as evenly as possible, Destiny took a long moment to respond with a simple nod. "I'll consider it and let you know."

Dunleavy regarded her with sharp eyes, his smile less than believable.

❧ 5 ❧

I hold it truth, with him who sings
To one clear harp in divers tones,
That men may rise on stepping stones
Of their dead selves to higher things.

—TENNYSON, *In Memoriam*

Lying on the bed, doing his best to ignore the noise from the tavern below, Jason watched the light and shadows from the lamp dance seductively across the ceiling. He'd hoped for sleep. But obviously that was not about to happen. The injury on his head throbbed like hell, and every time he closed his eyes, the vision of Destiny Fontaine swam up before him, her lips parting and her body arching to invite him deeper inside her. Her scent permeated his nostrils and her soft groans continued to whisper in his ear.

What could James Shaftesbury have been thinking to sacrifice Destiny to a man like Chesterfield? The woman was smolder and fire. Thunder and lightning.

Touching the swelling on his temple, Jason winced.

A virgin. Christ, he had made love to a great many women, but he had never had a virgin. Would never have taken one, unless it was on their wedding night. A man simply didn't walk away from a woman whose virginity he had taken . . . even if she had cracked his head open and left him to die.

Now what?

Dunleavy was at Sheffield House that very moment, discussing her father's situation with her, explaining how her help was necessary to save not only Compton's life but the lives of thousands of others. Thanks to Jason, she knew about Dunleavy's plans, so there was no possible way she would agree to make the trip to India. That, of course, would not stop Dunleavy. He would hog-tie her and haul her on board Jason's ship if he had to. Good. Very good. As long as Jason had control of the situation and the girl was in his possession, Dunleavy and a dozen of his goons could not harm her. The trick was going to be getting her aboard his ship—and keeping her there. No doubt, the moment she realized that the captain was the same man who not only made love to her, but admitted he was supposed to assassinate her father, she was going to revolt, But he would cross that bridge when he came to it. First things first, and that was to get Destiny out of Dunleavy's hands and back into his own.

Sitting up, Jason reached for a glass and a bottle of rum. The door opened.

He glanced up and made a noise in his throat. "I must be slipping. I thought I'd locked that damn door."

"I'd be careful with that rum. Remember, it's been a long while since you've indulged. You're liable to get drunk and do something stupid."

"Since when have you ever known me to do something stupid, Harold? Ah, let me take that back. I mean other than getting involved with you."

Dunleavy walked to the little window overlooking the countryside. "You've spent time with the girl, haven't you, Batson? Don't deny it. I had you followed this afternoon, to the forest glade. I don't recall that our plans were for you to seduce the young woman. In fact there were no plans at all for you to have met the chit before she boarded your ship. You realize that your intimacy with the woman changes everything."

Jason poured himself a drink. The cut on his head began

to bleed again, or perhaps it was simply sweat beading his brow. The air felt uncomfortably hot.

Harold laughed. "I should have realized that you would think her too beautiful to resist. My mistake, I'm afraid. Tell me, what have you told her of our plans?"

Jason drank the rum, wincing as it hit his empty stomach. "She doesn't know anything, Harold. Just because I made love to her doesn't mean I spilled my guts to her. Hell, I've been locked away in solitary for months. If a woman wants to spread her legs for me, why wouldn't I climb on for the ride?"

Harold turned his sharp gaze on Jason. "I don't believe you, Batson. I think you're hiding something. Or you're up to something. Must be, or you wouldn't have been meeting her in the first place."

Jason stared directly into Harold's small eyes, his mind ticking over the details of his meeting that afternoon with Destiny. Someone had obviously followed him to the glade, but while they might have enjoyed a perverted moment from the forest shadows, overhearing his conversation with Destiny would have been impossible. The tree line had been too far away.

"I wanted to find out for myself how deeply involved her father is with Nana Sahib. I haven't stayed alive this long without first thoroughly investigating a crisis before I move in for the kill." Pointing to the cut on his temple, Jason smirked. "Besides, were we sharing secrets, I hardly think she would have rattled my brains with a rock."

"Why, exactly, did she smash you with the rock?"

"I told her she was the best fuck I'd ever had."

"My, my. Has Cobra lost his touch with the ladies? Perhaps nearly a year in solitary confinement has caused you to go a bit rusty. Tsk, tsk. You *are* going soft, old man. But then, I suspected as much when you murdered Lieutenant Grant."

"He shot a woman. I would do it again. And I will, if I have to."

"Are you threatening me, Batson?" Dunleavy moved to the side table, picked up the bottle of rum, and refilled Jason's glass. Then he laughed. "Killing for you is as natural as breathing. That's all you're good for, you know. Someone as inhuman as you really doesn't deserve to move among normal beings. Who will care when you die, I wonder? Come to think about it, there will be joyous celebration from the many wives, mothers, and children of the men you've slaughtered through the years."

"Only because worms like you don't have the guts to do it yourselves." Jason downed the rum and slammed the empty glass on the table. Then he stood, towering over Dunleavy by six inches, causing Dunleavy to back toward the door. "I don't like you, Harold. You're a little man with a nasty brain and shit for guts. Weakness arouses you. The only way you can feel good about yourself is when you crush the helpless. I'm finished with you and your bloody Covert Operations by Radical Agents."

"You can't walk away from us, Batson."

Jason clenched his fists. The rum made the room swim as he took a step toward Dunleavy. He grabbed the bedpost for support. "My father did," he slurred. "He walked away."

Harold laughed. "Do you think so?"

He tried desperately to focus on Dunleavy's mouth, to make sense of his meaning. What the hell was he implying?

". . . Shame he had to go so suddenly. . . . Believed to be a heart attack—"

"My father is dead?"

". . . Believed to have passed away quietly in his sleep. Your mother was most devastated. After all these years of living virtually alone, she was thrilled to have him home with her again. Of course she never had a clue who he was or what he was doing when he was away for weeks and months at a time. We were quite good at delivering his letters to her, government business abroad and such—same as we did while you spent the last year rotting in solitary. She believed your father was an ambassador or something as ridiculous, just as she believes you and Trevor are off gadding about America. Imagine how she'll grieve to discover that her own flesh and blood is nothing more than a mercenary—a killer for hire."

Jason flung himself against Dunleavy with a force that drove Harold off his feet and against the wall. His hands twisted into Dunleavy's collar; his knuckles dug into Harold's throat. "Did you kill him? Answer me, you son of a bitch. Did you murder my father?"

"Your father didn't give a damn about dying, any more than he gave a damn about his family and home. They were simply a pleasant sojourn from bloody wars. A place to hang his hat and warm his feet. Had he actually given a fig about you boys do you think he would have involved you in his operations? 'Two chips off the ol' block,' he called you and Trevor. And he was right about another thing: he said you would be the first to fold—said you didn't have Trevor's hunger for the kill. That your softness for women and children would eventually break you."

Gritting his teeth, Dunleavy peeled Jason's fingers from his shirt and shoved him away. "What's happened to you, Batson? Did those months in solitary give you too long to think about the men you've killed? Did their faces awaken you in the middle of the night? Did their screams haunt you?" He smoothed his collar and coat. "If it helps, just continue to tell yourself that you're a soldier dedicated to fighting for the downtrodden and weak and try not to think of the money you got for cutting their throats."

Harold reached for the doorknob. "You're finished with the Chesterfield woman. Do you understand me? We no longer need your services where she and her father are concerned."

Jason did his best to focus as Harold walked from the room, leaving the door open behind him. He stumbled to the threshold and watched Harold move down the corridor. "What the hell do you mean, I'm through with the Chesterfield woman?" he shouted. "Look at me, you son of a bitch."

Dunleavy descended the back stairs. Jason ran after him, bracing his hands against the narrow walls as he took the steps two at a time. The noise from the tavern crashed against his ears, disorienting him. He should never have drank the damn rum—stupid—stupid as allowing himself to succumb to a wood nymph feeding wild ponies. Christ, he wasn't some inexperienced kid in knickers who had never seen a woman smile so brilliantly or laugh with so clear a tone he might have mistaken it for a birdsong. He'd simply been too long without a woman—months, for God's sake. He was only human. Oh, yes, despite what Dunleavy claimed, he was human. He'd saved as many lives as he'd taken, goddamn him to hell. If he got his hands on Dunleavy again . . . he burst through the back door, skidded in the mud in the darkness as the rain and wind hit him like a cudgel.

He never saw the men who grabbed him—another mistake, he thought as he was thrown face first into the wall and held there, his cheek cut by sharp stone edges. Someone drove a fist into his kidneys and pain sluiced like a blade up his back. Another buried his hand into Jason's ribs once, twice, until he felt his knees start to buckle. Fingers twisted into his hair and drove his face into the wall again and again, until blood filled up his mouth and nose and he thought he might drown. At long last, they released him. He slid down the wall to his knees.

"You heard the man, Batson. If yer smart y'll forget Lady Chesterfield and go under awhile. Maybe then y'll grow yerself a new set of balls. Obviously somebody stole yers when y' wasn't lookin'." A burst of laughter from several men rewarded this remark, and with a final kick to his ribs that sent Jason sprawling facedown in the mud, the assailants moved off through the dark.

Rain drove into his back and though he tried to lift his face from the mud, he couldn't.

"Well now, look here," came a familiar voice.

Several pairs of hands gripped his shirt and hauled him over.

"Looks like we're a bit late, don't it?" said someone else.

A face neared Jason's, grinning widely. "Gum, but I think he's still breathin'. A right mess he is, though, ain't he? Think we should fetch a doctor or wot? Wot say, Cap'n? You gonna live or die?"

Jason spewed mud and blood from his mouth. "Seems I've lost my touch, gentlemen."

"Not fer long, Cap'n. Aye, not fer bloody long."

Paolo Tosti was blond, blue-eyed, and slightly built . . . and lethal with a garrote. With a sliver of wire he could cut a man's jugular so swiftly and cleanly the poor bastard never knew what hit him. He did not, however, care for knives—too messy—and guns made him nervous. Paolo had been blessed with extraordinary hearing. He could hear a snake slithering in the grass a hundred yards away. He was also brilliant at disguise—not his own, but Jason's. Paolo's ability to mold rubber and wax into humanlike features was uncanny.

On the other hand, Conrad LaTouche was as tall as Jason and outweighed him by a hundred pounds. Unlike Paolo, Connie prided himself on his ability to wield a knife. He could put a knife into a bull's-eye at twenty-five feet. He carried them on a belt around his waist—sometimes ten of them, just in case he found himself in a pinch. He'd collected knives from all over: Russia, China, Japan—even a Bowie knife from America. That was his favorite. It was big and curved and could split a hair as if it were warm butter. Connie took pride in his ability to cut a man's throat cleanly and painlessly. Jason had saved him from the hangman the very morning Connie was to be executed for the murder of a solicitor who, according to Connie, had attempted to collect money from Connie's mother for services never rendered. Dunleavy had not much cared for sparing Connie, as the solicitor had been Harold's second cousin.

Gabriel Hirsch stood six feet ten inches in his bare feet. He had hands as big as platters and strong enough to crush steel. He rarely spoke, due to a tendency to stutter. He'd spent four years holed up in the guts of a hulk—buried in the prison ship for pummeling a man who called him a freak. Gabriel did not care much for people, except children. Jason surmised it was because mentally Gabriel was a child himself—except when it came to killing. He was ruthless and uncompromising. He would go through walls to waste a man with his bare hands.

Franz, Fritz, and Zelie Lussan grew up in Seven Dials, a criminal district where seven streets of thieves, murderers, and prostitutes converged in the area of St. Giles. The brothers held a fascination for things that exploded. Firearms were their expertise. When not shooting someone or blowing something up, they entertained themselves with inventing weapons that would shoot straighter, faster, or take down more of the enemy with the pull of a single trigger. Franz and Fritz delighted in experimenting with ammunition. Their most recent claim to fame, according to them, was the new cartridge that was doing much at the moment to instigate trouble in India. To replace the cumbersome process of loading a gun separately with shot, powder, and then wadding to keep the first two in place, a soldier would be issued a paper cartridge containing a shot and the right amount of powder. He would simply bite the top off and load his gun, pushing the paper, which had cleverly been greased with pig or cow fat, down the muzzle. Not to be satisfied with the status quo, however, the brothers were now working feverishly on an even more simplified version of the cartridge—something that could be loaded into chambers and automatically fed into the weapon's barrel without a lot of packing and that could discharge within seconds. No doubt the brothers were geniuses. Zelie, however, had a problem with opium. It permeated his every living cell. Of course Jason had argued with him over the unpleasant habit, to no avail. Zelie was certain that anyone with any shred of creativity needed the poppy to enhance their mental capabilities, and since he was undoubtedly the brains of the brothers, his peregrinations into oblivion were absolutely necessary.

Jason was convinced that the group of individuals hovering around his bed and drinking his rum were as mentally and emotionally combustible as a keg of the Lussan brothers' gunpowder. But then, that was exactly why he had chosen them for his company. Cobra existed entirely for the purpose of marching into situations deemed too risky or secretive for Her Majesty's military. Cobra moved in when all else had failed—all hope was lost. By orders of the Crown, they slid through night shadows and assassinated potentates and military leaders who posed a threat to the Empire's security. Cobra was not a company for men who gave a damn about dying. And for that they were paid exorbitant amounts of money.

Zelie smiled at Jason and shook his head. "I haven't seen you so badly bruised since Calamita Bay. I'm quite tickled, actually. It's usually one of us who takes the beatings."

"I've obviously upset Harold." Jason winced and clutched his side. Christ, the bastards had broken a rib.

"That's putting it mildly," Fritz declared. "If you're not very careful you'll find yourself in solitary again. What's worse, we'll find all of us in solitary again. I should beat you to a pulp myself before I allow that to happen."

Bending near, Zelie purred, "Would you like a touch of my opium, old man? It will do you wonders. Won't feel a thing in a bit. You'll drift away and think yourself on some beach in Jamaica. Ahhh." His eyes drifted closed. "I can almost feel the sun on my face now. Where is my pipe? Someone fetch me my pipe."

Connie dragged a chair to the bed and sat down. He'd grown a lush beard since Jason had seen him last. It gave him the appearance of a red bush with eyes. "You want I should kill the bastard for ya, Cap'n? Ain't none of us who wouldn't like to see his carcass hanging from a scaffold."

"If anybody kills Dunleavy, Connie, it's going to be me." Jason took a deep breath, or tried to. Perhaps his rib wasn't broke, but it was damned sore, for sure. "He's removed us from this mission. I can't let that happen."

"Look, Cap'n. Maybe it's time y' packed it in. Y've made enough money over the years to buy yer own bloody country. Take yer wee daughter and buy her a pony and make up for the years y've missed with her. She'll be needin' her daddy now that Michelle is gone."

Jason noted the concern on their faces.

"What Connie is meaning," Franz said, "is that you always said if there came a time when you no longer had the heart to see out a mission properly that you would put down your gun and walk away, move into that pretty house you built on Ceylonia Plantation, raise tea and horses and babies you can bounce on your knee—enjoy all the things you didn't enjoy growing up."

Jason looked at Paolo, who stood near the window, his arms crossed over his chest. "You know something I don't?"

Paolo shrugged. "Dunleavy has reassigned this mission to another company. Under the leadership of someone who won't be swayed by his conscience when the time comes for confrontation, and the tidying up afterward. Harold intends to use the young woman to lure her father out of Sahib's compound, where he's taken refuge the last months. Compton won't think twice about surrendering . . . at which time he is to be quietly and efficiently assassinated. Destiny Fontaine Chesterfield is to be eliminated as well. Can't have any witnesses, you know."

Jason lay in the heavy silence, the pain in his body suddenly no more than a dull, throbbing ache as he stared at the ceiling. Of course Harold would eliminate Destiny. Why had he been so damned obtuse? No way Harold would allow Destiny to return to England with stories of the government assassinating their aristocracy. Gritting his teeth, Jason rolled from the bed. The room swam, as did the faces of his men. Focusing on Paolo again, he demanded, "What else have you heard? If he's taken me off the mission, then who's to deliver Destiny to her father?"

"As I said, someone Dunleavy can trust to carry out the mission. Who won't have any qualms whatsoever in taking out Sahib, Fontaine, *or* his daughter."

"Who, goddamn you?"

Paolo averted his eyes and replied, "Your brother, of course."

༂ 6 ༂

With women the heart argues, not the mind.

—MATTHEW ARNOLD, "Merope"

As the tall case clock chimed midnight, Destiny paced to the window, where she stared out over the dark, rain-drenched grounds and the road she had ridden down that afternoon to meet a man she had so *ignorantly* believed she loved.

Jason Batson. One of her father's closest friends. How very convenient. Her father would open his arms to Batson, and Batson would shoot him in the heart.

Or would he?

He *did* confess who and what he was. He *did* warn her about Dunleavy.

Dear God, what if she had made a mistake? What if he was telling her the truth, that he wanted to help her father, not harm him? Ridiculous! He used her, manipulated her heart with his casual flirtations, gentle touches, and charming compliments. He set out to make her fall in love with him, to trust him, to be willing to give her all to him—even her father, no doubt.

Had she killed him?

No. She wouldn't believe it. She'd only wanted to hurt him. She'd wanted to escape his arms and body and eyes, which could confuse and enrapture her even as she trembled from the possibility that he could harm her father.

Why would his memory not leave her alone, even now,

after all that had transpired? There was anger, yes. Immense anger. Frightening anger. But there was hurt as well.

Destiny shifted her thoughts to her father. Another time she would have thanked God that he was not here to witness her erosion of character. But she needed him tonight. Not just to hold her and assure her, but because she wanted desperately to know that he was not guilty of the dreadful accusations Dunleavy made against him. Because if it was true, if Compton Fontaine had in any way provoked the unsettled situation in India, he was in tremendous trouble. Unless she sailed immediately for Cawnpore there was absolutely nothing she could do to help him.

Her aunt Diana sat in a chair, her white hands clasped amid the multitude of folds in her blue velvet skirt. "I'm waiting, Destiny," Diana stated in a tremulous voice. "Who is the man you supposedly killed? And why were you with him?" Diana tipped her head and stared harder at Destiny's profile. "I don't care for that look on your face," she said softly. "It frightens me, Destiny. You're up to something."

"Am I so predictable, dear aunt?"

"The only thing predictable about you, Des, is your unpredictability." Diana smiled a little. "I often wonder what I would have done all these years without your unpredictability. I have so looked forward to it every morning."

"'Twould have been nice if a little of it had rubbed off on you," Destiny replied.

"Are you so certain it hasn't?"

"I think I catch a glimpse occasionally."

Her fair brows drawing together and her look becoming serious, Diana declared, "There is more to me than meets the eye, niece. As my own mother used to say, still waters run *very* deep. Now tell me all the details. I must know everything if we're to confront this sorry situation with any hope of remedying it."

"I'm dreadfully concerned about my father, Diana."

"Then you *do* believe Dunleavy?"

"Hardly. He's been nothing but trouble for my father for years. Why would Dunleavy want to help my father now?"

"Smashing!" Diana declared. "Then you won't consider leaving with him for India."

"Absolutely not. I'll go alone."

Diana blinked and her mouth fell open.

"I'll need money, of course." Destiny looked at her aunt, watching Diana's eyes grow round as saucers as Destiny's meaning sank in.

"I couldn't possibly finance such an escapade, Destiny. James would divorce me."

"By the unhappiness I see on your face day in and day out, I suspect that wouldn't be such a horrid fate."

Diana raised both eyebrows. "How very cheeky of you."

"It's the truth, isn't it? You're not in love with James. We both know who you're in love with and have been since the moment you set eyes on him—the very day my mother met him."

Her fair cheeks turning dark as plums, Diana sank back in the chair and bit her lip.

Going to one knee beside her aunt, Destiny took Diana's hand. "You're in love with my father, Diana. It's fine, really. You needn't look so aghast."

"How did you know?" she asked, turning her face away.

"'Tis there in your eyes. It trembles your lips and flushes your cheeks when I so much as mention him."

"Oh my. I had no idea. I feel so . . . ashamed. Will you ever forgive me, Destiny?"

"Forgive? For what?"

"He was my sister's husband." Her eyes brimming with tears, Diana took Destiny's face between her hands. "Do you know how often I have imagined that you were my own daughter? Every morning that I look into your eyes I see him there, smiling back at me, just as he did that stormy spring day your mother and I happened upon him on the old highway. We were driving a pair of shaggy white ponies and they spooked and ran away with us. Suddenly he was there, beside us, leaning down from his horse and grasping the harness to stop us. As I recall, your mother was most perturbed and told him so. She was quite capable of handling the situation, and he should stand off immediately. I think it was that very moment that he fell in love with her, and I, him. But your mother was older, a radiant and sophisticated eighteen, and so beautiful, full of pride and temper and rebelliousness, and I was only thirteen, hardly blossomed and as timid as a mouse. What a curse is youth occasionally!

"I'm ashamed to admit that the day she decided to follow him to India I tried desperately to talk her out of it, not because it was dangerous and unseemly and our father would disown her, but because I was jealous. Over the next many years I lived for the day when I would receive letters from your mother. Always your father included a few lines and I would fantasize that he was slipping me coded messages of his love for me. Of course, I knew in my heart that he loved only one woman, and would until his dying day."

Searching Destiny's eyes, Diana whispered, "Do you despise me now, niece? Do you think me a shameful person to have fallen so in love with a stranger and continued to love him even after he married my sister?"

"No." She shook her head, frowning as her aunt's words brought the day's catastrophe back with a rush of heat and despair. "We all fall prey to our emotions from time to time. It's what makes us human, Diana, and occasionally, perhaps too often, makes us foolish."

Destiny moved again to the window. Rain fell heavily over the dark countryside, extinguishing even the lights from Saito's residence in the near distance. "For the last several days, I've been meeting a man in the forest glade where I feed wild ponies."

Worry crept into Diana's voice as she said, "What do you mean, exactly, that you've been meeting him?"

Focusing on her reflection in the windowpanes, her dark hair a wild spray of tangles, Destiny smiled wryly to herself. "I thought him a farmer, or a groom. I even fantasized that he was a gypsy."

"Tell me his name."

"In the beginning I didn't want to know his name. If I didn't know his name he needn't know mine. But that was before we confided our dreams. Before we fed wild ponies together from our hands. Before I read him Shakespeare and saw his eyes light up when he laughed. He has the most wonderful laugh, Diana. It vibrated inside me like a harp string, all full of rich and vibrant melody."

Diana left her chair and moved up beside her; she placed her hand gently on Destiny's arm. "You became smitten with him?"

"Smitten?" Laughing, Destiny shook her head. "The word is far too inadequate to describe what I felt for him—or thought I felt for him." Turning away so Diana could not see the despair on her face, Destiny shook her head. "I don't want to think about it.

Diana grabbed her. "Tell me what happened, niece."

"I dare not, Diana. My appalling behavior would only upset you—"

"Tell me!"

"He confessed his name is Jason Batson . . . and that he's a friend of my father's. He also confessed that he works for Harold Dunleavy . . . and he is, or was, under orders to murder my father."

"Oh, my God," Diana whispered. "There's more . . . isn't there?"

Covering her face with her hands, Destiny shook her head. "Thinking back now I'm not certain if I seduced him or he seduced me. One moment we were talking and the next . . .." Her eyes drifted closed and a warmth suffused her. " 'Twas my right," she announced in a steely voice. "My husband robbed me of that right on my wedding night. Why shouldn't I turn to another? He at least held me and kissed me—"

"Oh!" Diana covered her mouth with one hand. "Destiny, you didn't . . . didn't—"

"I did," Destiny said in a flat voice and allowed her mind to wander again, seeing the rain bead upon his naked shoulders and on the ends of his dark hair and eyelashes. "And it was wonderful. Everything I always imagined it would be. He made me feel . . . beautiful and desirable. He kissed my eyes and lips and breasts and . . ." Glancing at her aunt, she discovered Diana's face white and her eyes slightly glazed. "He glibly informed me of Chesterfield's relationship with Lord Rosebury."

"What a dreadful fiend. I *wanted* to tell you, Destiny. James wouldn't allow it. You know how forceful he can be. We all hoped . . . that is, you seemed to like Chesterfield well enough, and . . . there was always the chance that he would accept his responsibility and . . . change. It's happened before, you know. Quite often, as a matter of fact. At the least, we all hoped he would father an heir, and we both know how much you long to have a child of your own."

The case clock ticked in the sudden silence that fell like a hod of stone between them. Destiny listened to her heart thump like a drum in her ears.

Diana cleared her throat. "Destiny . . . Did he . . . What I mean is . . . Could you . . . Is there any possibility of . . ."

"Of my being with child?" Destiny swallowed. "Oh . . . I hadn't thought . . . I didn't think . . . I don't know."

"You must know. You were there."

"We were . . . intimate."

"Yes, but did he . . . oh my, how do I say this? A man experiences certain . . . physical reactions when he . . . You cannot become pregnant unless he . . . What I mean is—"

"Say it, for heaven's sakes!"

"He ejaculates in you," Diana whispered and squeezed closed her eyes. She proceeded to fan her face with a hanky that she withdrew from her dress sleeve. "It's all rather untidy, you see, but most pleasurable for them, or so it seems. *I* wouldn't know, really. I suppose it would *have* to be or they wouldn't demand it so frequently. You can always tell when they successfully do the deed; they become most frantic and excitable. Then there are spasms and convulsions and growls and groans and . . ." She fanned her face harder then mopped her brow. "Then it's over quickly. *Very* quickly."

"Yes," Destiny replied in a thin voice. "He might well have put a baby in me."

Diana covered her eyes with her fingertips. "Can this night get any worse?"

"My parents were intimate quite often," Destiny said. "And there was only one child. And I hate to bring this up, but you and Uncle James have tried for years—"

Diana began to laugh, and her eyes flashed. "Sweet niece, how naive you are. There are certain artifices a woman can utilize to avoid pregnancy. I had no intention of giving James a child, another human being to control and manipulate and humiliate if he or she somehow failed to live up to James's expectations. The idea of passing on my husband's cruelty to future generations was out of the question. And as far as your mother and father . . . there were certain problems after your birth. The *accoucheur* pronounced your mother incapable of having another child without a certain risk to her life. Therefore, both I and my dear sister took precautions during intimacies. Had I not done so, I suspect these rambling and gloomy hallways would be crawling with tiny likenesses of Lord Shaftesbury. *God forbid.*"

Destiny sank onto the bed and stared at the ceiling. "When I learned of his association with Dunleavy I crowned him with a rock. I didn't mean to hit him so hard. I just wanted . . . away. I was frightened and . . . my heart felt . . . broken."

"If he's a killer, he deserved to die," Diana exclaimed, surprising Destiny with her vehemence.

"But he warned me about Dunleavy."

"And that's supposed to excuse the fact that he's a murderer?"

"What if I'm with child?"

"Let's not discuss it."

"I'll humiliate you. You'll not know a moment's peace. I can't imagine Uncle James's reaction. Dear heavens, what was I thinking to have done such a careless, idiotic thing, Diana? I should leave for India immediately, put as much distance between myself and you as possible. I'll go to Cawnpore and warn my father about Dunleavy's plans."

"What will you do about money?"

"There's my stipend from the Chesterfields."

"That won't buy your way across the Channel, much less to Cawnpore. Besides, if what Dunleavy says is true, the last place your father would want you is knocking on Sahib's door. You're a beautiful, young, widowed woman, Destiny. You simply cannot go gadding about the seas unchaperoned. Or traipsing about foreign lands that are stewing in rebellion."

They sat like pale statues, listening to the clock tick and the rain whisper harder against the windowpanes. Then there came a sound from the hallway. An envelope slid under the door. Destiny hurried to pick it up and opened the door but found no one in the shadowed corridor. Stepping back into the room, she tore open the missive and tilted it toward an oil lamp to better read the words.

There is a man in Portsmouth who can help. The address is 777 Seacove. Go alone. Tell no one. Immediacy is imperative if you wish to help your father.

The night air smelled of pungent tar and rotting fish as Destiny, holding a scented cambric kerchief to her nose, moved along the piers, staying well away from the port admiral's house—a blustering man well acquainted with James and Diana who'd spent many pleasurable afternoons riding to the hounds with James's pack of cohorts. She skirted the guardhouse and wandered, confused and mountingly desperate, along the watery avenues of storehouses, rigging houses, and sail lofts that lined the Portsmouth docks. She dared not stop any wayward sailor to ask directions to Seacove Street. He would certainly consider her an unprincipled woman . . . or worse. The fate of many missing women through the years had been attributed to the occasional white slavery ships that slipped into the harbors looking for comely booty.

There came a noise behind her and Destiny, her heart leaping into her throat, turned just as a cloaked figure dove into the deep shadows of stacked crates and barrels, causing them to wobble precariously. A voice squeaked in alarm, and Destiny gasped. Doing her best to see through the mounting fog, Destiny called:

"Diana, is that you?"

With a shuffle of feet and another bump of the barrels, Diana crept into sight, clutching her cloak as fiercely as she could around her shoulders.

Destiny shook her head and rolled her eyes. She walked to her aunt. "You promised me you wouldn't follow."

"I desperately tried, Des. Honestly! I couldn't lie in bed and think that you were wandering about this dreadful place alone. I simply couldn't live with the consequences if something happened to you."

"And how do you propose to protect me if I'm attacked? Beat the devil to death with the heel of your shoe?"

"I'm prepared. See for yourself." She snapped open her reticule to reveal one of James's derringers.

"We'll be fine as long as we're besieged by a big canary," Destiny murmured.

From the dark staggered a lone sailor with scraggly hair, singing under his breath; he stumbled against a pile of hemp.

Destiny moved toward him. Diana grabbed her.

"He's socked," Destiny whispered and peeled Diana's fingers from her arm.

She cautiously approached the drunkard, keeping her cloak and hood pulled snugly around her. Reeking of whiskey and sour sweat, he slowly turned his face toward her, revealing his heavily scarred nose and unkempt mustache, which drooped down both sides of his mouth and beyond his cleft chin.

"Seacove Street," she said, taking a quick step back as

he tried to straighten, grinned with black teeth, and belched loudly.

Narrowing his eyes and rewarding her with a lascivious grin, he pointed down the dock, toward the brick paved street in the distance. "There y' be, lass. Joost beyon' that damn light. But I'm tellin' ya, ain't no place for a lass." He crooked his finger at her suggestively. "Y'll be needin' a man in there, aye. I'm yer man fer that." He attempted to stand again, rocked on his boot heels, then slumped to the pier, landing with a grunt on his backside.

Diana dragged her away. They hurried through the fog, looking back only once to make certain the drunkard had not followed—only to discover that the sailor had disappeared as suddenly as he had appeared. They followed the meandering street as best they could through the darkness, attempting to read the address of each deteriorating building with as much skittishness as if they'd been the caves of flesh-hungry dragons. At long last they found it, a soot-covered nondescript structure with boarded windows erected at the point where Seacove Street dead-ended into the harbor. Destiny's heart sank as she and Diana huddled together, shivering as much from anxiety as from the creeping cold.

"I fear we've been led down a dark path, niece. This pitiful building looks as if it hasn't been occupied in years. Come away while we still can. If we hurry we might just make it home before sunrise. As it is I haven't the slightest idea how I'll explain my absence to James."

"I didn't come all this way just to drag myself home now like a whipped pup."

Destiny banged on the door with her fist—once, twice, again, drumming harder, her fear growing that Diana could be right, that the crumbling building might be vacant and this dangerous excursion be for nothing.

There came a noise, a shifting of a bolt. As Destiny took a cautious step back, the door creaked open, allowing a sliver of light and the heavy scent of incense to boil into the street. A broad, stooped Oriental stared down at her. He showed no surprise to discover two shivering women on his porch step, at three o'clock in the morning, no less.

Clearing her throat and righting her shivering shoulders, Destiny took a breath then slowly released it. "I was told to come here," she announced in a less than steady voice.

His black eyes seemed to penetrate her. They unnerved her with an uncanny sense of familiarity that disturbed her. Impossible, of course. Had she ever shared the remotest space with this odd and intimidating creature she would remember the occasion, easily.

"What do you want?" he asked in perfect English.

She stared, unable to unlock her eyes from his. "I was told that someone here might help me."

His dark eyes shifted to Diana. "Were you not told to come alone?" he asked.

Diana moved up behind her. "She did. Or rather, I followed her. As her guardian I wouldn't allow her to come to such a place alone."

"I shan't stand here in the cold to discuss it." Destiny shouldered the door aside, forcing the man to step away and allow them in.

The room swam with the odors of incense and brewing tea. The walls were crowded by small shrines, amulet bags, and representations of Daikoku, the god of wealth. There were lacquered screens depicting two Buddhas: one with clasped hands, the other holding a lotus. Near the base of a flight of stairs was the likeness of Ni-o, the protector against burglars, a hideous creature with protruding eyes and a face and figure distorted and corrupted into exaggerated and convulsive action.

Destiny moved to the foot of the stairs and looked up; at the top of the staircase she saw a single door. "I was told to come here. That someone here could help my father." In an angrier voice, she added, "Unless, of course, this is some sort of trick. What are you staring at?" she demanded. "I haven't got a lifetime to spare. Who sent me this note?" She thrust the crumpled paper at the Chinaman, who ignored it and moved to a table that held a pot of steaming tea.

More cautiously, Destiny said, "I suspect you're fully aware of my father's situation or you, or whomever, would not have contacted me. I was told someone here could help in the matter. You may tell him I haven't the patience for games."

"Nor does the gentleman who wishes to help you," he said, sitting on a carpet and crossing his legs.

Diana tugged on Destiny's cloak. "Come away, Destiny. I'm not certain I can contain my need to scream much longer."

Raising his dark gaze again to Destiny, he pointed to a cushion on the floor. "Please. You've come all this way, risked much to be here."

Destiny sank onto the cushion as Diana hovered. "How do you know me? And if you aren't involved with Dunleavy, how are you familiar with my father's situation?"

"A mutual . . . acquaintance." He poured her a cup of tea and placed it in her hands. His fingertips brushed hers as they pulled away, and his wide lips curled. "Our friend was right about you. You have much courage and are obviously much devoted to your father, regardless of his possible patriotic transgressions."

"Is that a tactful way of calling my father a traitor?"

"Is it not why he was deposed of his position in India?"

"My father loves and respects the Indians' culture, but not so that he would turn his back on his own country. Besides, if my father *were* to turn, what reason would Sahib have in harming him? Harold Dunleavy desires to use me as a pawn to get to my father one way or another. I'll paddle the bloody oceans myself if I must, but I intend to go to Cawnpore with or without whoever sent me this note."

The Chinaman remained silent as he breathed in the steam from his tea, yet his dark eyes never wavered from Destiny's. There was an odd softness in his expression that did more to unnerve her than the idea that she and Diana were shockingly vulnerable to his whims.

At last he spoke. "He's a soldier, so to speak. He picks and chooses his wars and his armies with much care. Of course, his services come with a price."

"He's a mercenary," Diana announced, causing Destiny to look around. Diana leaned against the door, the hood having fallen from her head. Her face appeared white, her lips colorless. A realization settled like a shroud over her features. "Destiny, we should leave here immediately. I overheard James speak of these men. They fight not out of patriotism or loyalty, but for fortunes. They're deadly and unscrupulous. For enough money they would murder Victoria herself."

Destiny turned back to the Chinaman. "True?" she asked.

"A slight exaggeration, perhaps. I happen to know this particular gentleman thinks highly of Her Majesty, and she of him. I doubt he would murder her."

Destiny shuddered as Diana hurried to her, fell onto her knees, and looked hard into her face. "I don't know who sent us here or why, niece. But we should flee immediately. This entire escapade horrifies me. This place horrifies me. Your father would never approve of your association with such a man no matter what the cause."

"I would meet him first," Destiny replied.

"Not possible at this time," the Chinaman said, setting aside his empty teacup. "His life depends on his identity remaining obscure, for obvious reasons."

Destiny turned to Diana. "But if he could help my father—"

"No! You mustn't even think it, Destiny. Come away, please. Before we become involved in something we may eventually regret."

Destiny gently set Diana aside. "You said yourself, Diana, that I cannot go to Cawnpore alone." To the Chinaman, she added, "I'm not soliciting this person to kill anyone. I simply want his help to get me to Cawnpore. Once there, I'll . . . consider my alternatives."

Diana sank to the floor and held her head in her hands.

The Chinaman studied Destiny a long, silent moment, his features revealing not an inkling of his thoughts. At last, he stood, looking monstrously tall.

Diana jumped up. "She's a desperate child who has no business becoming involved in this dreadful mess. She has little money and far too much daringness for her own good."

The man glanced at Destiny once more before mounting the narrow steps.

Breathing deeply of pungent opium smoke, Zelie Lussan lay sprawled across the pile of plush Indian carpets and pillows, smiling at some inner thought as "the Chinaman" closed the door and sank against it, crossed his arms over his broad chest, and cursed under his breath.

"Is she as lovely as you recall?" Zelie asked, inhaling smoke from his hookah.

"Smoke your opium and shut up."

"Just curious. I should think that after a year of prison, a rag and bone gal could seduce you. Some forest nymph feeding ponies from her hand might appear as alluring as a goddess."

"She looked older in the glade. More sophisticated."

"You're losing your touch, old man. A bad sign, I think. As you and your father have always declared: keep the mission in perspective; the goal is not to be compromised. *He* never compromised. Once doubt began to worm into his conscience, he passed the torch to you and Trevor. I doubt a few stolen kisses in a wild wood could compromise your objective."

A side door opened and a disguised Paolo Tosti stepped in, his sailor's uniform reeking of the whiskey he had poured over it earlier in an attempt to appear the drunkard to Destiny. "Perhaps our friend Cobra should determine exactly what his objective is."

Zelie raised his eyebrows and chuckled. "Been listening at keyholes again, Paolo?"

"It's my forte, is it not?"

"Because you have the ears of a jackal."

"*This* jackal has made up for your opium-induced inefficiency at least once every mission." He sniffed and waved a cloud of smoke from his eyes. "Let's forget all the cloak-and-dagger bother. He really doesn't care if Fontaine has crawled in bed with a lot of sepoys. And there isn't a mission, not anymore, thanks to Dunleavy. The only excuse Lord Batson has to storm into harm's way is to save his lady love's pretty throat. How very dramatic and romantic. Could prove to be delightful fun."

"Batson won't allow his head to be turned by a pretty face." Zelie wagged his finger at Paolo. "Even Michelle couldn't do it, though God knows she tried, what with the child and all. There's more to Jason's plan than meets the eye. I say he wants to know for himself if Fontaine has crawled into bed with Nana Sahib. But therein is the problem, you see. What will he do should he discover that his old friend has gone sour on the Crown?"

Paolo crossed the room and sat on a stool before a mirror and stared hard at his reflection. He proceeded to peel the black eyebrows away, revealing his own lighter ones. Next came the bulbous waxen nose and cleft chin, all of which he tossed onto the table. "Does anyone care to hear my opinion?"

"No," Zelie replied.

Paolo looked around at his companions. "You should shut up and let him think. The man is in an emotional quandary, for God's sake. He's fallen in love. What does he do if he sweeps the young woman to Cawnpore and discovers that Dunleavy is right? To close his eyes to the situation would make him as guilty of treason as Compton Fontaine. On the other hand, if he doesn't sweep her away, Dunleavy will, one way or the other. And we all know what the other is. Trevor Batson."

Paolo stood and walked to Jason. "If you take her," he said in a soft voice, "Trevor will come after you. And so will Dunleavy. While Trevor might not put a gun to your head, he has no qualms over killing Destiny. If he had,

Dunleavy would not have given him this mission. If you take her, you will eventually be forced to confront your own brother. Are you willing to take that chance for a woman you hardly know?"

"This conversation is moot," Fritz said from a distant corner. "The girl will never go on board that ship as soon as she gets a look at who her savior really is. I haven't the foggiest clue what went on between the captain and the lady in that forest glade, but I have a hunch she's not going to be ready any time soon to forgive and forget."

Paolo peeled the long mustache from his upper lip and waved it under Jason's nose. "Obviously her recognizing our captain won't be an issue. Hell, she just spent the last few minutes in his company and had no inkling of his identity. By the time I'm done with him even his own blessed mother wouldn't know him."

Women's voices sounded through the closed door, causing all to hush and listen.

"Destiny! Come down from those stairs this instant. Whatever do you think you're doing?"

"You're being hysterical, Diana."

"I won't allow it, I tell you."

"Let me go."

"I won't!"

Paolo sighed and moved to the door. He flipped open a tiny shutter and peered through the peephole.

Jason pulled the cap and wig from his head, then drew the wax and rubberized mask from his face, wincing as it stuck to the injury at his temple. Running one hand through his hair, he pressed his eye to the peephole and focused on the pair at the bottom of the stairs, their voices now subdued as they argued.

"She'll be easily duped," Zelie remarked, relighting his pipe. "She reacts too much from her heart and not enough from her head."

"What do you intend to do?" Paolo asked.

"First I must make certain that all risk to my daughter is allayed."

"Done," Zelie announced with a flourish. "Gabriel is on the task even as we speak. The nursemaid Dunleavy has engaged to care for her is as cunning and protective as a hyena. They'll be expecting some sort of move from you, you know."

Jason walked to a table and sat down, searching his thoughts. If Destiny remained in England she would be at the mercy of Dunleavy and Trevor—bait to lure her father out of Sahib's compound, after which both of them would be permanently silenced. But while Jason had every intention of sailing to India to see how he could help his friend Fontaine, for him to haul Destiny into the escalating fracas in India would not be wise either.

Paolo bent over Jason's shoulder and said softly, "I know what you're thinking, my friend. You can safe-house her and your daughter in Cape Town until we're done with the mess in Cawnpore."

Jason nodded, reached for a quill and paper, and began to write. When finished, he again moved to the door and peered down the stairway. Destiny sat on the bottom step, her dark hair reflecting the light from the lamp on the wall. She stared up the staircase as she awaited the Chinaman's return, her expression weary and worried, her eyes bright with unshed tears. Once again she was the vulnerable lady in the glade, a naive seducer who had somehow wormed her way under his skin to provoke a recklessness that was unnervingly unfamiliar to him.

❧ 7 ❧

There is a garden in her face
Where roses and white lilies grow.

—THOMAS CAMPION,
Fourth Book of Airs

Sir John Barrow once remarked that Portsmouth Dock-
yard would "always be considered as the Grand Naval Arsenal of England, and the headquarters or general
rendezvous of the British fleet." As Destiny skirted
through damp avenues of mould-lofts, saw pits, and join-
ers' shops, her eyes trained on the vast docks of ships lining the harbor—all of which looked frustratingly
similar—she thought Sir John Barrow's words under-
stated. Surely every ship ever constructed to sail the high
seas was anchored along the jetties this night. Looking for
some supposed merchant ship among the countless sailing
vessels felt overwhelmingly hopeless. The hour was near
midnight and she was running out of time.

Once again she stepped within the streetlamp's light and
focused on the paper in her hand: *The* Pretender *will sail at
midnight. Good luck, Lady Chesterfield. Godspeed.*

"Godspeed," she read aloud, her voice sounding bitter.
"What does *he* know about God? A man who kills for
money. . . ." Then she reminded herself that not so many
hours ago she had virtually signed a pact with the devil
himself to get her to Cawnpore.

Wearily, she sat down on a pile of hempen, trying not to

think about the last thirty-six hours. The afternoon she'd spent with Saito in the garden seemed a lifetime ago. How ironic that she had been chatting so blithely with her friend about travel and fantasies about her future—a concern that, in that moment, had been no more consequential than worrying whether her reputation would weather the storm of controversy surrounding her brief sham of a marriage to Chesterfield.

Poor Diana. How she had pleaded with Destiny to rethink this insane notion of hers to search out some unknown ship that would, on the word of a mercenary whom she had not as yet met, deliver her halfway around the world to her father. Destiny could still see in her mind's eye her aunt weeping, as distraught as Destiny had ever seen her, wailing as quietly as possible, "What shall I do without you, Des? What shall I do if something dreadful happens? I shall always blame myself. How can you do this, Destiny, leave me here to live alone with James. Perhaps Chesterfield had the right idea, after all. Perhaps I'll simply hang myself. I would rather face a noose than one more year of this dreadful existence in a loveless marriage and with no sweet Destiny to brighten my day!"

Destiny briefly closed her eyes before looking back through the fog, where High Street converged with several others running east to west, narrow passageways crowded by weather-worn chapels, market houses, almshouses, and seedy hotels. A flutter of uncertainty and mounting fear rolled over in her stomach as she thought of spending the next several weeks surrounded by a lot of bloodthirsty soldiers. And what if she arrived in Cawnpore to discover that Dunleavy had been truthful all along? Or worse, what if she arrived in Cawnpore to discover that her father was dead—killed by the very men who had been like family to him for the past many years?

This was not a journey for a trembling twenty-two-year-old woman whose idea of rebellion was riding about the countryside dressed like a Japanese rice farmer.

She was not, however—had never been—a coward.

With one last glance at the paper in her hand, she retrieved her valise from the ground and moved down the pier, searching with mounting frustration for the ship that may, or may not, provide her a way to India. Along the watery horizon were the silhouettes of many ships that had already set sail for their destinations. Could it be that she was already too late?

Her step slowed. There, docked between a man-of-war and a well-appointed East Indiaman, was a decrepit-looking cargo vessel whose deck appeared overcrowded with crates and cables and chains with links as long and broad as a man's leg. The ship hardly looked capable of limping out of the harbor, much less making it all the way to India. And it certainly did not even remotely resemble a vessel that would carry mercenary troops into battle.

"God help me," she whispered aloud as she recognized the name on the ship as the one scrawled on the paper in her sweating hand.

The *Pretender*.

The child's cries rattled the walls and caused Gabriel Hirsch and Connie LaTouche to cover their ears. "She has the wail of a banshee, Cap'n," Connie declared. "Are y' certain y'll not want to deliver her to a kind aunt or some such on the way? I hardly think y'll be able to focus on yer objective with that sort of caterwaulin' goin' on. It's enough to put a man off his feed."

The "captain" of the *Pretender* shushed the girl, only to have her scream louder and squirm furiously in his arms. She wailed in French, "Let me go! Let me go! I want my nana! Help! Help! He is going to eat me and I shall die!"

"I am *not* going to eat you." Jason subdued her flailing arms before she could smack him across the nose again. "Look at me, Jenette."

"You're too ugly to look at! My eyes will fall out!"

Connie snickered and elbowed Gabriel. "She got her mum's temper, I see, not to mention her old man's disposition."

Gabriel agreed with a laugh and a nod. He gently tweaked the little girl's flushed cheek with his massive fingers and patted the top of her head.

Jason struggled with the flailing child. "Quiet, poppet, before you wake up the entire British fleet. If you're good I'll give you a sugarplum."

"I don't want a sugarplum. I want my nana!"

Jason put his hand over his daughter's mouth and looked at Connie. "It's well after midnight. Any sign of Destiny? There's weather moving in. If we aren't out of this harbor by the time it hits we'll be anchored here until it passes. As soon as Dunleavy discovers his ace in the hole has flown the coop, he and every naval officer in the fleet will be scouring these docks to find us. Not to mention Trevor. Christ, I'm in no mood to confront him. Not yet."

"I've sent Fritz out to search the wharf. If she's there he'll find her. As for her"—he pointed to the teary child in Jason's arms—"we'll be lucky to get out of this harbor alive if she keeps that up. Y' might try tellin' her who y' are. Might make her shut up."

Lowering his voice to a whisper and pointing to his own disguised face, Jason said, "Would you want a father who looks like this?"

Connie smirked. "Yer disguise is pretty damn ugly, fer sure. I reckon Paolo got a bit carried away. But then, he's always had a flair for the dramatic. One positive thing, sir. The lady won't be recognizin' y', fer sure. Hell, y'll be lucky if she'll stand in the same room with y'."

Bouncing the little girl in his arms, Jason told her, "There's nothing to be afraid of, *ma petite chou chou*. I'm a friend of your father's."

"My papa would never have a friend who looks like you," she declared with a haughty little sniff and a shake of her long, dark curls. "You are much too ugly and fierce. My papa is very handsome and big and brave . . . and very kind. He would not stand for snatching little girls from their beds while they're sleeping."

"How do you know he's handsome? Do you remember him?"

She shook her head and her lower lip quivered. "But my mama told me before she died that he would come back for me someday. So you cannot take me away, monsieur. If you do I shall never, *ever* see him again."

Jason searched his daughter's big eyes, so much like her mother's. How often had Michelle looked at him in such a way, anxious and pleading, hoping to hear vows and promises that he was incapable of giving because of his accursed hunger for adventure. "And what if I tell you that I'm here to take you to see your papa? Would that please you, *ma petite*?"

"I don't believe you! Let me go. I want my nana!"

"What in heaven's name are you doing to that child?" came a feminine voice from the doorway. Destiny, jaw set stubbornly, her hair tumbling from its combs, and her eyes snapping with the same alluring green fire he remembered, marched over the threshold. Her presence and her scent washed over him, and any reluctance to carry out his plan to help her was gone in the blink of her wide eyes and the saucy tilt of her head. Christ, he had never before been so rattled by a woman. Then again, he had never known a woman with her fight and courage. In that instant he believed her capable of taking on Nana Sahib's entire sepoy army if necessary to help her father. He wanted to snatch her off her feet and make love to her . . . desperately.

She grabbed the crying child from Jason's arms and gently held the girl to her bosom, stroking her mass of curls and cooing comfortingly in her ear. "There, there, little one. Is it no wonder you're frightened? What have they done to you?"

Jason raised his eyebrows as his daughter nestled against Destiny's shoulder, her eyelids immediately growing heavy and her tears drying.

At last, Destiny focused on his face. Her eyes widened briefly as she acknowledged his scarred features; uncertainty and fear flashed over her expression, but just as quickly was gone as she swallowed and stepped away, took a deep breath, and steadied her voice. "Where is the child's mother?"

"Ain't got one," Connie declared. "Poor, wee lass, virtually an orphan 'cept for her old man. Mother up and took her away from him a few years back. It's taken all this time to catch up to her—God rest 'er soul—and fetch the kid home."

Shifting his gaze to Connie, Jason raised one eyebrow, impressed by his friend's spur-of-the-moment excuse for why a lot of mercenaries would have a five-year-old on board the *Pretender*.

Fritz appeared at the cabin door, slightly out of breath. "This'll be Lady Chesterfield, I reckon. Found her frozen stiff as a corpse with fear. Tried to help her with her bloody baggage and she 'bout took me shin off with the tip of her shoe."

"What do you expect when you come springing at me from the fog?" she replied. Her arms hugging the child, Destiny stared intensely at the *Pretender*'s captain, her smooth brow glistening with sweat. She was trying desperately to be brave. Considering she was surrounded by a lot of cutthroats, Jason surmised she was doing a damn good job of it.

As Gabriel and Connie regarded Destiny with a cautious and worried expression on their faces, and Fritz leaned against the door frame and crossed his arms over his chest, obviously waiting for Jason's reaction, Jason resigned himself to the reality of the game and gave Destiny so lascivious a smile Destiny's face flushed and her breath left her. She backed against the wall and did her best to level her chin.

Jason reached for his daughter.

Destiny spun away, cradling Jenette's head against her shoulder. "If you'll show me to my cabin, Captain, I'll see to the child's comfort myself."

The men glanced at one another, then Jason said, "Perhaps the lass will do better with a woman. Show Lady

Chesterfield to her quarters, LaTouche, and *mind your manners*. We ain't out to sea yet, ya know. A woman screamin' is liable to bring the police runnin' all the way from Queen Street!"

Jason grinned as Destiny's cheeks drained of color. Her eyes, round as pennies, looked like polished emeralds in her perfectly oval face as she stared first at him then at Gabriel, who towered over her by two feet.

At just after two in the morning the *Pretender*'s sails caught the first hint of building wind from the north and slid effortlessly from Portsmouth Harbor. As the deck shifted and creaked and the riggings snapped taut with full sails, Jason stood on the bridge, his gaze fixed on the dark pier, alert for any unusual activity that would warn him that their departure had been acknowledged by anyone other than some random sleepless sailor. So far so good.

With any luck, Dunleavy would not realize for another day or two that Destiny had slipped through his fingers, and even then he would not immediately suspect that Jason was somehow involved in her disappearance. By the time Dunleavy had turned over every rock between Bournemouth, London, and Portsmouth in an attempt to locate Destiny, the *Pretender* would have put several hundred miles behind them. The only way Trevor could catch them was if the *Pretender* were to founder.

"Aye, Cap'n, it's good to be at sea again, eh?"

Jason looked around.

With his big legs braced apart and his bearded face turned into the wind, Connie sighed. "There ain't no place as peaceful as the sea, I always said."

"We're in for rough weather," Jason remarked. "If we were smart we'd have waited until after the front."

"Aye, we'll be forced to get our sea legs about us. No doubt about it. But we've got ourselves a fine crew this trip, sir. They're fully capable of handlin' the wind and anything else that might arise."

"I'm counting on that. I needn't remind you that we have a priceless cargo below."

Connie chuckled. "I take it yer not meanin' Fritz's and Franz's munitions. Bloody hell, they've packed us with enough gunpowder and weapons to put us on the frickin' moon if we blow. One thing's fer sure. We're well prepared for trouble should trouble arise."

Jason glanced at his friend. "I won't take chances, Connie. I'll run before I stand and fight."

"Understood, sir."

"How is my daughter?"

"Settled in nicely with Destiny. The lass has given the young woman something to dwell on other than us lot of cutthroats—is how she's referred to us, I believe."

Jason nodded. "Have the men front and center in fifteen minutes."

"Aye, aye, Cap'n."

The wind continued to build and blow hot and cold, east to west and north to south. The riggings sang and the sheets and shrouds popped like firecrackers, so Jason was forced to raise his voice to be heard over the cacophony. With spray stinging his face, he walked the line of drenched sailors and soldiers, all doing their best to keep their footing as the ship bucked like an ornery horse beneath them. Connie had been right. The crew was good. Very good. He'd sailed and fought with them before and trusted them with his life.

"Welcome aboard, gentlemen," he shouted. "This mission will be little different than the others. With one exception. We have on board a young woman and a child. My daughter. While in their company you are to behave yourselves. There will be no spitting, urinating off the mizzenmast, or foul language."

The crew laughed.

Jason did not, just stared each man down until the smile slid from his face. Then Jason continued. "The man who disobeys my orders will spend a week in the hole. And I

will personally kill any man who behaves toward Lady
Chesterfield in a less than gentlemanly fashion."

"Yer a bloody fool for bringin' the woman aboard,"
came a voice from the dark.

Jason moved to the hulking figure in the shadows.
"Hugo Mallet. I might have known. I thought you were
buried under a prison somewhere in Scotland."

"I was reprieved for good behavior . . . sir."

"So how did you escape?"

Hugo smirked. "Ain't a prison been constructed that can
hold me for long . . . sir. And I repeat: a woman's got no
place on the *Pretender*. I'm all for knockin' heads with a
lot of sepoys; I ain't got much use for the sons of bitches.
But haulin' a woman's arse into the fray is gonna be trouble. She'll mess up yer priorities . . . if she ain't already."

Jason turned to Connie. "What the hell is he doing on
my ship?"

"Sorry, Cap'n. We were short of men and he was available." Lowering his voice, he added, "Frankly, I would
rather have him aboard the *Pretender* than his joinin' up
with yer brother."

"What was his latest incarceration for, *exactly?*"

Connie pursed his lips. "The robbery of the Old Lady of
Threadneedle Street."

"You robbed the Bank of England?" Jason said to Hugo.

"Why not?"

Connie cleared his throat and turned back to the line
of wet soldiers and sailors. "I'm here to remind you lot of
reprobates and bloodthirsty miscreants of the Code of
Oléron, rules hereby set forth to modulate your behavior
while aboard the *Pretender*.

"Anyone that should kill another on board ship, unless
ordered or authorized by the captain, should be tied to the
dead body and thrown into the sea.

"Anyone that should kill another on land, unless ordered
or authorized by the captain, shall be tied to the dead body
and buried with it in the earth.

"Anyone lawfully convicted of drawing a knife or other

weapon with intent to strike another, or of striking another so as to draw blood, shall lose his hand.

"Anyone lawfully convicted of theft should have his head shaved and boiling pitch poured upon it and feathers or down should then be strewn upon it for the distinguishing of the offender, and upon the first occasion he should be put ashore with neither food, water, or currency.

"Anyone found using foul language in the presence of females or children will have his tongue scraped and he shall be bound naked to the mizzen and suffer no less than a dozen lashes of my cat-o'-nine.

"Anyone found guilty of offensive or reprehensible behavior toward females or children, such as extreme insult, assault, or worse, shall be executed and his body buried without prayer or ceremony.

"If you understand these laws speak now."

"Aye, aye," the men shouted, and clicked their heels.

❧ 8 ❧

The man who is liable to fits of passion; who cannot control his temper, but is subject to ungovernable excitements of any kind, is always in danger.

—*THE ILLUSTRATED MANNERS BOOK*

The violent rocking of the ship awoke Destiny from her confused and troubled sleep. Her lower body ached with an odd sensation that made her roll her face into the pillow and squeeze her eyes closed. A mistake. The images that swam in her memory were shocking, unnerving, disturbing. The woman was not, could not be her, naked, clutching, inviting an intimacy that had made her mindless with the same ache that throbbed in her now. His groans had inebriated her senses. His gasps had incinerated every sensitive nerve in her flesh until she felt as if she might burst. For that brief moment, she had never felt so treasured. . . .

Had he cared for her a little?

Had she been too hasty in jumping to conclusions?

Had he truly meant to harm her father, why would he have confessed his association with Dunleavy?

She hadn't meant to hurt him so badly.

Was he dead?

Oh, please, God. Don't let him be dead.

As the waves grew rougher and the wind howled like hungry wolves, Destiny swallowed back a sob and lay shivering on her uncomfortable berth, which took up most of the dark cuddy in which the captain had put her and the distraught child only hours before.

So, it was done. God help her.

While she had dreamt of loving a dangerous stranger, the ship had put England's shores behind them. If the remotest reluctance to set out on this grueling journey lingered somewhere deep in her subconscious it was too late now to change her mind. She was on her way to Cawnpore with a crew that put the most blackhearted pirates to shame.

The child stirred and whimpered. Destiny stroked the little girl's cheek and she drifted back to sleep.

Destiny slid from the berth and tucked the blanket snugly about the child's frame. She staggered as the ship lurched from side to side, flinging her against the wall, then bouncing her off a commode that was stationed to the floor by heavy brackets. Having slept in her clothes, she did her best to smooth the wrinkles from her skirt while trying desperately to remain standing as the ship seemed to suddenly plummet like a stone, tremble as if it would shatter into a million shards, then cut through a turbulent swell that sent them rearing like a hound horse over a hurdle.

At last she found her way from the cabin, crawled up the companionway, after several attempts that sent her sprawling backward, and emerged on the deck, where the sails full of wind bulged and shimmered like ghosts in dawn's gray mist. Cold wind cut like teeth through her clothes as she struggled upright and searched the deck. Dark figures ran here and there, all silent as they went about their business of securing the riggings in preparation for the building squall.

"There she is," came a shout, and Destiny turned just as someone grabbed her, virtually lifting her from her feet as he propelled her toward the captain's wardroom, where light, barely discernible in the haze, glimmered through round windows. Before she had time to protest, she was ushered into a room where a solitary table was cluttered with dirty dishes and utensils. The air smelled of a sweet, nauseating smoke that clung to the ceiling like London coal smog. The captain sat at one end of the table, hunkered slightly over what looked like a bowl of cold gruel, a spoon in one hand, the other gripping a cup of coffee.

He did not look at her immediately, just pointed his spoon at an opposite chair and growled, "Sit."

Hands shoved her toward a chair. She fell into it just as the ship pitched again. Clinging to the table and refusing to look at the congealing food, Destiny did her best to swallow back her sudden sickness.

The captain turned aside, offering her his scarred profile. The skin of his face from his temple to his jaw, then down the side of his neck, had been ravaged by fire. Puckered pink flesh contorted his right eye, which looked pale and sightless.

"Rule number one," he snarled, causing Destiny's eyes to widen and her teeth to chatter. "Never, under any circumstances, are you ever again to leave your cabin unless attended by myself or Connie LaTouche. Do you understand me, Lady Chesterfield?"

She nodded and tried to swallow. Impossible. Her throat felt as if she had gulped the entire sea full of salt.

He shot her a stern glance. "These men are not a lot of blue-blood puffs. When they size up a woman it's not with the idea that they desire to share cocoa with her in a stuffy parlor attended by some spinster aunt."

She nodded again and frowned at her sudden urge to cry. Dear heavens, now was not the time to show weakness or fear. The carnivore sneering at her would not appreciate tears—not from a woman who had just engaged his crew to get her posthaste to her father halfway around the world, to a country tottering on the brink of mutiny.

"Are you fully aware of what you've gotten yourself into?" he demanded.

She opened her mouth to speak. Nothing came out.

"We're soldiers, Lady Chesterfield. Our utmost priority is to confront and defeat the enemy—at all costs. We're not married, therefore we need not worry about leaving a des-

perate widow behind. Few of us have families at all. And
even if we do . . . we've been forced to cut our ties from
them completely. Do you know why?"

She shook her head and twisted her fingers together in
her lap.

"Because there isn't a man aboard this ship who hasn't
got a price on his head, Lady Chesterfield. There are a
great many very powerful men who would happily exact
their revenge on us by way of our families."

"I'm very sorry for you," she managed in a dry voice.

"Why?" he demanded, frowning.

"Because you live a cursed existence. And when you die
no one will care. Who will remember you beyond your
murderous deeds?"

He glared at her for a long moment—the white, sightless
orb reflecting the lamplight. Odd that she could not look
away. There was something almost hypnotizing in the way
he gazed at her, and though his voice was rough and husky,
and he purposefully strove to intimidate her, there seemed
to be an undercurrent of gentleness in the tone. And his
face . . . that part of it which had not been disfigured was,
oddly, as disturbing as his scars. It stirred something in her
consciousness . . . perhaps pity. Yes, pity. Obviously the
man had once been attractive.

"What are you staring at?" he finally asked, snapping
her from her trance. "Is there something about my appearance that dismays you? Perhaps a lady such as yourself has
never found herself in the company of one so . . . disfigured. Hmm? Or is it, perhaps, my character that so offends
you? And before you respond I'll remind you that we're together in this room because you came to me."

"I'm well aware of why I'm in this room, Captain. This
ship was my only recourse to get me to India. As far as
your character, sir, while I cannot reason how anyone
could kill another for money, it's not my way to judge others. Lord only knows I've been judged unfairly myself. As
far as your . . . appearance"—she lifted her chin and forced
herself to look him squarely in the face—"you *are* some-

what . . . intimidating. But I've witnessed worse. My father once employed a servant whose face had been totally disfigured by fire. He'd lost one hand as well, but he was the most loyal and the best loved of all of our servants. I learned young, sir, that a man's facade rarely represents the reality of his character." She sighed and added, more to herself than to the captain, "Even the most handsome of men too often hide a dishonest heart."

He sipped his coffee, that unnerving colorless orb still fixed on her. "Do I detect a hint of cynicism, Lady Chesterfield? Has some handsome cad broken your heart?"

"Hardly." Her face flushed with heat and she averted her eyes.

"Because I can't imagine your allowing such a devil to take advantage of you . . . unless you were willing to be taken advantage of."

Destiny frowned and shot him a curious look. Her face grew hotter.

"You have a temper." The captain laughed low, in his throat. "I suspect that were you to discover such a deception you would retaliate in some way. Kick. Scream. *Smash* him with something."

Heart thumping, she held her breath.

"An umbrella. A shoe. Or something. . . ." He smirked.

"This conversation is ridiculous and far too personal," she declared.

For a moment his look darkened, then he shrugged. "Did you rest?"

"The rocking of the ship awoke me."

"And the child? Is she still sleeping?"

"As soundly as an angel."

He smiled thoughtfully. "She's quite the angel, isn't she? Aside from her temper. Perhaps, once she grows accustomed to this"—he pointed to his face—"she'll warm to me. What do you think, Lady Chesterfield?"

She replied softly, "Perhaps."

The captain scraped back his chair and stood, found his balance easily as the ship swayed from side to side, and moved around the table. He stopped so close she could feel his body heat through her clothes, then he put his hand on her shoulder. Her back stiffened and her breath caught.

"Foolish young woman," he whispered in that unnerving voice that sent threads of wariness shooting through her. His fingers gently kneaded her shoulder. "You haven't the slightest notion of who or what I am. Yet here you are, a rose among rubble, hungry for adventure and defying decorum. I wonder what sort of devotion would drive you to such behavior."

She glanced nervously at his hand as it moved slowly into her hair. He lifted it in his palm, allowing it to slide through his fingers. "If there truly is trouble for my father, perhaps I can help him."

"And perhaps not. Occasionally there are wars that cannot be won. Enemies who cannot be vanquished. Sometimes the most fierce wars are waged within ourselves. The battle between truth and denial is often the most defeating. Our own unwillingness to face reality is our downfall." His fingers twisted gently in her hair as he said, "What will you do if you discover that your father is a traitor, Lady Chesterfield? It could be a very dangerous situation. Should the insurrection get teeth, there won't be a Brit in the country who'll be safe, including your father regardless of his loyalties. If he continues to stand by the Crown, the mutineers will kill him. If he's turned, he'll be tried and convicted as a traitor."

"My father is not and would never become a traitor, Captain. He is the most dedicated and loyal man I've ever known."

"You're not only beautiful, you're also naive."

Gathering her courage, Destiny stood, snatching her hair from his hand and moving away, stumbling as the ship shifted violently beneath her. "If you're done with me I'd like to return to my cabin."

"And if I'm not?" The left side of his mouth curled and he approached her again, his shoes scraping on the floor as she backed away, her gaze flying to the table and finding a scattering of knives. *Think, think,* her mind reasoned. He was the only thing standing between her and his malfeasant crew. If she harmed him he might toss her to the lot of curs. If she killed him she would not live long enough to see sundown.

Her back against the door, Destiny drew in a deep breath as the captain laughed in his throat. "You're a lovely little thing, Lady Chesterfield. All full of fire and determination. Not to mention passion. I wonder. How would you react to me if I wasn't so . . . ugly? Would you still tremble with fear?"

"'Tis your air of malice that disturbs me, sir, not your appearance."

"Behind this mask of scars is a man with needs and appreciations as strong as any other's. We've long days and weeks to share company. And I do intend to share your company a great deal because it pleases me to do so. Just because the fire took my face doesn't mean it robbed me of my manhood. I assure you, I'm most capable of experiencing the pleasures associated with passing time with a beautiful woman. The sea can be a very lonely place, as you'll soon discover."

She thought of telling him that loneliness was nothing new to her; she could handle lonely very nicely, thank you; as an only child growing up in Cawnpore, surrounded by few English-speaking natives, she had been forced to occupy herself in creative ways. As a young woman who preferred the company of horses and forest creatures to Uncle James's pompous peers, she'd spent weeks and months sequestered at his country estate while he and Diana frequented London. So if this man honestly believed she could somehow be lured into any kind of sordid relationship with him just because she was overcome by monotony, he was daft.

But the acerbic retort died on her tongue. Perhaps it was the weariness of his expression. Or the ghost of some odd emotion lurking behind his good eye that was as murky green as the ocean slamming against the bow. For an instant she felt curiously and disturbingly weightless—as weightless as she had those moments in the glade when a stranger had looked into her eyes and upended her every raw need and desire.

"Why are you doing this?" she asked breathlessly. "Transporting me to India when I have no money to pay you?"

He touched her cheek, traced her jawline with the tip of his finger. "Where there's war, there's money, Lady Chesterfield. A great deal of money. Your presence on this ship is simply a luxury I've afforded myself. It's not often that a man such as myself has an opportunity to spend time in the company of one so . . . fascinating."

"Cap'n!" someone shouted and pounded on the door.

A moment passed before the captain eased Destiny aside and opened the door. A cold rush of air swept in, along with mist and morning's first gray light. A small man with wild orange hair and skin as pale as a fish belly stumbled over the threshold, dragging a sodden figure behind him.

"We've got ourselves a flipping stowaway, Cap'n. Found her clinging to the deck rail by her fingernails. One more toss of the bow and she'da gone flying like a bloody albatross over the side."

As he shoved the small figure toward the captain, Destiny gasped. *"Diana!"*

The captain caught Diana before she fell. With her long wet hair hugging her skull, her clothes clinging to every curve of her body, she stared with an expression between horror and shock at her captor.

"Diana?" Destiny cried again, reaching for her aunt. "What in heaven's name—"

"Couldn't . . . " Diana began, shaking her head and still gaping at the captain, who stared down at her with as much astonishment. "Couldn't allow you to . . . go without . . . simply couldn't tolerate . . . the idea of your enduring this journey alone . . . vulnerable and at the whim of these, this, this, this—oh, my, what have we done?"

Destiny grabbed Diana as she sank to the floor, trembling uncontrollably. Her cheeks felt like ice and were just as blue. "Get her a blanket immediately," Destiny cried at the dripping sailor. Then, to the captain, "Fetch her hot coffee and get her into a chair."

"You heard the lady, Zelie," the captain snapped at the sailor, who turned on his heels and sprinted from the room.

The captain took Diana from Destiny's arms. He hauled her limp body to a chair and proceeded to rub her face and hands and slap her cheeks, muttering under his breath, "Woman, what the devil were you thinking? Open your eyes. *Breathe,* for God's sake." He reached for his coffee cup and lifted it to her mouth, forcing her to drink. She sputtered and coughed and gasped like one drowning. Finally, her lids opened and focused on his face.

"I've a good mind to toss you overboard," he said through his teeth, causing her eyes to roll back in her head and her frame to go limp again.

Destiny shouldered him aside. "You've the manners of an ogre, Captain. Can't you see she's in shock?"

"Stowaways are normally tied to the yardarm and flogged, Lady Chesterfield. She's fortunate Zelie didn't fling her into the drink." He paced, his coarse black hair spilling over his shoulders, the thump and scrape of his feet on the floor as intimidating as his mounting anger. "Just what the hell am I supposed to do with her? It's enough to have to deal with you—"

"No one *forced* you to take me aboard," she shouted back. "Uncle James will have no idea where she—we—have gone, I'm sure. Unless, of course, she left a letter. . . ." Destiny chewed her lip and gently patted her aunt's cheek.

"A letter?" The captain moved toward Destiny, his teeth showing and his hands fisted. "Tell me she wouldn't be that stupid."

Diana's lids fluttered and she raised her head, doing her best to focus on Destiny. Destiny attempted to smile. It wasn't easy with the captain glowering at her like some feral dog.

"Ask her," the captain snarled. "Did she tell anyone

where she was going and with whom? Ask her!" he shouted, causing Destiny and Diana to jump.

Destiny took her aunt's face between her hands, forcing Diana to look at her squarely. "Dear sweet aunt, did you tell anyone about our plans?"

"I . . . had to. Just a note. An apology, really. I had to make James understand why I was leaving. How unhappy I've been for so long—"

The captain shoved Destiny aside and grabbed Diana by her shoulders, shaking her hard. "Listen to me, woman. Think. In this letter did you tell Lord Shaftesbury where you were going and on what ship—"

"Only that Destiny and I were leaving for India at midnight . . . on the *Pretender*."

His expression became murderous and, grinding his teeth, he forced himself to release her shoulders and back away.

Her heart sinking, Destiny cradled Diana protectively, her consternation mounting as the captain stared at the floor in an obvious attempt to control his anger.

The door flew open and Zelie stumbled in, a blanket clutched in his arms. The captain turned to him. "Have the men meet me in my cabin immediately. Thanks to our quelling little stowaway, I suspect that by now every man-o'-war in Portsmouth Harbor will be preparing to sail."

Zelie shrugged. "This squall will delay them."

"James would never declare my desertion to anyone," Diana cried, grabbing Destiny's hands. "He would be too humiliated. He'll announce that he's decided to divorce me and, until then, he'll simply tell everyone we've traveled abroad and—"

" 'Tis not James that concerns us," Destiny replied with as much patience as she could manage.

Her eyes wide and her body shaking with cold, Diana stared into Destiny's face, realization creeping over her features. "Oh, dear God, Des. *Dunleavy*. James will tell Dunleavy on what ship we've sailed."

"Get the two of them belowdecks and have Connie and

Fritz take their positions fore and aft. Meanwhile I'll decide what we're going to do about her." The captain pointed to Diana, and as he turned away, cursing under his breath, Zelie helped Destiny and Diana to stand, tossed the blanket around their shoulders, and ushered them from the room.

Shivering and pale, Diana stared at the child huddled in the dark corner of her bunk, a blanket pulled up to her chin, staring back at her. "What is it?" Diana asked in a quivering voice.

"What does it look like?" Destiny moved to the little girl, who reached for her eagerly. "From what I've ascertained, the child was snatched from her bed and brought to the ship. The captain tells me he was commissioned to return the little girl to her father."

"I don't believe him. Do you believe him?"

Destiny wrapped her arms around the child and hugged her close. "I don't know what to think anymore."

Diana sat next to Destiny and tugged her blanket more snugly around her shoulders. She lowered her voice to a whisper. "There are fiends about who pay handsomely for children—wealthy childless couples who spend fortunes to have children snatched and transported to other countries for adoption. And as for us—we know nothing about these men, Destiny. They may well be white slavers. We could be whipped and abused and molested, spend the remainder of our days chained to beds in some dreadful brothel, forced to endure the most horrendous and perverted acts upon our persons, and eventually die of some mind-and-body-ravaging disease."

Destiny covered the child's ears and glared at her aunt. "I've been giving this some thought. 'Tis all a bit too convenient. Dunleavy might realize that I would refuse to oblige him—so he slyly put us on to these men, knowing I would be desperate for any way to reach Cawnpore. And damn me, I fell into it perfectly. Why else would this lot of cutthroats sail me thousands of miles to be with my father?"

"Certainly not for money," Diana replied, shaking her head.

"When we reach Tenerife we'll find another way to Cawnpore. Considering we have so little money, our choices will be limited, to say the least."

"Oh, but we have money." Diana tugged up her skirt and untied her boot, removed it, and turned it upside down. A wad of notes fell on the bed. "A little something I've had tucked away."

The door suddenly opened and the red-haired Zelie walked in accompanied by Gabriel the giant, who was forced to stoop radically to pass into the room.

"We'll be taking the lass now," Zelie said, motioning for his companion to remove the child from Destiny.

The little girl squealed and flung her arms around Destiny's neck. Destiny stared at the man defiantly. "What do you want with her?"

"Captain's orders. He wants the kid with him." Zelie grinned. "He's right fond of kids, especially this one."

"She wants nothing to do with him."

"That don't bloody matter, does it?"

The child screamed harder as the big man dragged her from Destiny. Destiny ran for the door, blocked it with her body, and glared at the giant. "You'll not be taking that child anywhere without me. You may tell the captain that I said so."

The men exchanged looks, their expressions amused.

With the squirming girl hooked under his arm, the giant flung Destiny aside as easily as a gunny of feathers. As Zelie followed him from the cabin, he stopped and looked back. "Gabriel's big and strong as a dozen ox but he would never hurt a woman or child. Got several of his own children scattered here and there, as a matter of fact. And as for the captain, he's got a weak place for the little ones that's big as this bleeding ocean. You've got no reason to fear he would harm her. The two of you, on the other hand . . . He hasn't got the patience for stupidity or bad manners. So you'd be very wise to behave yourselves."

"And if I don't?" Destiny demanded, rubbing her arm.

"Let's just say he has a way of dealing with troublemakers. Because of this one"—he wagged his finger at Diana—"we find ourselves up to our damned mizzenmast in trouble."

"Perhaps my aunt is right. Perhaps this crew is a lot of pirates with a penchant for kidnapping and blackmail."

"Perhaps," Zelie replied and quit the cabin, slamming and locking the door behind him.

❧ 9 ❧

Eventually the squall passed, but not the turbulence entirely. Driven hard by the chilly northern winds, the ship continued its tumultuous journey south, cutting easily through the waves that sprayed like geysers over the rails and decks. While Diana paced, Destiny lay on the berth listening to the sounds of running feet and occasional shouts coming from overhead.

"Sit down, Diana, before I'm forced to search out a *sal volatile*. You brought this despair on yourself, you know."

"Can you honestly tell me that you don't regret this rashness of action, Destiny? Here we are aboard a ship with beasts with no true interest in helping us—not if your assumption about their reasons for helping us is correct. And why wouldn't it be? Our money is hardly enough to purchase the services of mercenaries. They wage wars on entire countries! I hardly imagine that the captain might have taken on this behemoth task just because he has a soft spot for a desperate young lady with a pretty face. Men like that haven't room in their black hearts for love. Or kindness. Or gentleness. Or compassion. Or any other positive trait that normal men might enjoy. Discounting sex, of course. Dear merciful lord only knows what they are out there contemplating along that line."

Her eyes closed, Destiny recalled the captain's hand in her hair, his fingers on her shoulder. "Try not to think about it, Diana. 'Twill only upset you more. Besides, it might console you to know that the captain appears to be very concerned about our safety. He's refused us to leave our cabin without his or Mr. LaTouche's protection."

"That means absolutely nothing, Des. I've read those shocking novels of pirate fiends and such. The captain enjoys his feminine booty first and when he tires of her, he tosses her to his crew to do with her as they may. I shan't repeat to you what they do, exactly. Suffice it to say, by the time they reach land again she's not fit to live among the respectable—that is, if they allow her to live long enough to set foot on land again. One story I read had the poor dear flinging her own self into a swarming school of sharks, just to end her torture and humiliation."

Diana sank against the wall and closed her eyes, her seasickness turning her complexion ashen and causing her brow to sweat.

Destiny sat up. "I'm dreadfully sorry to have gotten you into this, Diana."

"'Tis no one's fault but my own, Des. Worrying over your welfare wasn't my only reason for following you any more than your only excuse for fleeing England was to help your father."

Destiny frowned.

Diana attempted a weak smile as her color went from gray to green. "I am running *to* a man, Destiny . . . and you are running *from* one." She tried to laugh. "But if you think about it, both excuses are absurd. I am as much a stranger to Compton Fontaine as the man in the glade is to you."

"Hardly," Destiny replied. "You've known my father for twenty-four years. While I, on the other hand, gave up my morals, not to mention my body, to a man I had known for only a few days."

"At least you have that," Diana said softly. "To remain

silent and longing all these years while my sister loved Compton . . . was torturous to me. There were times that I so envied your mother. I'm ashamed to admit that I often fantasized of seducing him."

"Why are you telling me this?" Destiny asked.

"Because I fear I'm going to die. If the captain doesn't kill us, then this seasickness will. You should know what sort of dreadful person I really am." Diana ran to the chamber pot and wretched into it. Her entire body heaved until she was forced to her knees. Destiny rushed to her, held Diana's hair back, and stroked her brow.

At last, Diana buried her face in Destiny's skirt and clung to her fiercely. "I recall a letter your mother once wrote me, not long after she and Compton married in Cawnpore. 'He glories in beauty of every kind and is fascinated by the unusual or irrational. What a contrast he presents to that which I have always known until now—the staid, predictable, and despairing monotony of our father's tyranny and obsession to conform to aristocratic standards.' Oh, niece, but I fell in love with him all the more after that. I craved your mother's letters as much as I abhorred them. They drove the knife of my discontent more deeply, yet threw open the barriers of my extreme fantasies. Please don't despise me overmuch, niece. I loved my sister devotedly, and you as well. I have no desire to fill my sister's shoes; he loved her lavishly and grieves for her still, I'm sure, and would look upon me only as a sister. Pray, that would suffice if I could but spend a mere hour in his company."

"Hush." Destiny hugged her aunt. "I don't and shall never despise you."

"Isn't it all silly, Destiny? Love, I mean. It makes us act in the most confusing and illogical manner. Though time and distance have separated me from Compton—not to mention his tremendous love for your mother—I've continued to love him regardless. And you—"

"Oh, please, let's not discuss my idiocy," Destiny declared and mopped her aunt's clammy brow. "You can't compare my relationship and feelings for a stranger to what you've felt for my father."

"But like you, I fell in love with a stranger the very first moment I saw him. I didn't know his name. It hadn't mattered. In my mind and heart, he embodied everything I imagined a man should be."

"You were only thirteen." Destiny laughed and did her best to rid her memory of Jason Batson and the bothersome emotion the thought of him aroused. She did not still love him. How could she after his confession?

Diana sighed. "Ridiculous, isn't it, how we cling to childish fantasies about people and things, no matter how old we get?" Rousing a little, her brow creasing, Diana looked at Destiny directly. "What if we're wrong about your father, Des? What if he *has* become involved with Nana Sahib? Whatever will we do if we discover he's turned on the Crown?"

The door opened and a tall, thin man with fair hair stepped in. He marched directly to Diana and dragged her from Destiny's arms.

"Where are you taking her?" Destiny demanded.

"Cap'n wants her."

"For what reason?"

"Now, that ain't exactly any of *your* business, is it?"

Diana proceeded to heave again as she was ushered out the door. Her eyes glazed with fear, she cried, "Good-bye, niece! If I ever see you again, surely it'll be as a fallen woman. Pray this torture is over swiftly. . . ."

The ship rolled and the door slammed shut on its own. Destiny stumbled to the bunk and sank onto it, her senses straining for any clue to what the notorious captain might have in store for her pitiful and despairing aunt. Still, no warning touched her ear, only the whoosh and thump of waves against the hull and what sounded like someone singing.

Her weariness bore down on her. The last hours—days—of anxiety and lack of sleep crept through her body like lead. She should be confronting the unpleasant captain, championing her aunt, but, alas, she had no strength to do it. She longed to sleep . . . and forget. Forget the present. Forget the past. Forget that Diana was correct. She was running as much *from* a man as *to* one. No matter how she struggled to block him from her thoughts, no matter how she roused her sense of indignation over his deliberately deceiving her, she couldn't shake free of her feelings. She hurt.

Her mind drifted.

Odd how in the beginning his identity had not mattered. He was handsome and kind. She had fallen in love with his odd, fascinating eyes, his smiling mouth, his soft words that once whispered in her ear, made her body hot liquid.

Your eyes are green as an Irish glade, he had whispered.

She slept for hours and awakened with reluctance. Her dreams had been gentle and rocking, awash with indistinct images of color and sound that left her damp with sweat and twisted in her skirt and blanket. Raising her head she found the lamps burned low and the cabin empty of the child and Diana. Panic seized her.

Splashing cold water in her eyes, Destiny scrutinized her reflection in the silvered glass: dark circles under her eyes; and her eyes . . . hardly green as an Irish glade—more like a peat swamp. And her hair more resembled the matted manes of forest ponies than the tame locks of a young woman of reputable breeding. No doubt she had lost weight.

What the blazes had the captain done with Diana and the child?

Destiny donned a clean blouse and skirt, wrapped a shawl around her shoulders, and made her way up to the deck. The wind had at last dropped; all was still. The sails, which caught the remaining shafts of daylight and reflected them in swaths of red and gold, hung from their masts as if weary of their earlier battle with the winds. For a moment she stood speechless, awash by the calm and silence. Overhead the evening star appeared, then one by one the stars came out and hung like golden lights in the velvety depths of the darkening sky. A light haze on the horizon hinted that moonrise was near.

Near the bow of the ship and beneath a lantern sat a group of men, smoking and drinking, their laughter convivial as they mused over a card game. The idea occurred to her that they hardly looked the bloodthirsty sort. They might well have been her uncle's own grooms passing their free time in idle banter.

The child caught her eye. She played near the group with a small doll. Destiny frowned to see a length of rope tied on one end around a man's waist, the other end attached to a sash around the child's middle. Then, as the ship made a sudden heave, sending the little girl tumbling, Destiny realized the reason for the rope: to keep her from being flung overboard by a sudden swell.

The sensation of being watched came over her. Slowly turning and searching the shadows, she finally discovered the silhouette of a man on the bridge. She mounted the stairs and found the captain. He did not acknowledge her as he leaned upon the rail gazing down at the playing child. His look was intense and distant . . . and sad.

"Need I remind you that you aren't to leave your cabin without my or LaTouche's company?" he said.

"I grew concerned when I awoke and found neither my aunt nor the child had been returned to my cabin. Where is Diana?"

"Do you suppose I tossed her overboard, Lady Chesterfield? Or perhaps I've chained her in the hold and am starving her between bouts of torture and molestation."

"I don't find your attempts at humor amusing, Captain."

He laughed to himself. "Would you be questioning her welfare if I were standing here in a military uniform, Lady Chesterfield?"

She frowned, confused.

"To reassure you, your aunt is resting comfortably in her own cabin, for the time being—once she got over her fear that we were going to tie her to a mast and flog her with a cat-o'-nine for stowing away. She'll feel better once she gets her sea legs about her. You're welcome to join me," he added without facing her.

"You appear content with your thoughts, Captain. I hesitate to bother you."

"Since when is the company of a beautiful woman a bother? Come along. You needn't be afraid. Regardless of what you think or might have heard, I rarely bite . . . unless bitten first."

Cautiously, she approached him, keeping a safe distance from him, and looked down at the child. "I've rarely seen a child so beautiful. She's as fair as her china doll."

"Her mother was beautiful," he replied softly.

"I'm certain her father must be exceptional as well."

The captain said nothing, just continued to watch the little girl.

"Do you have children, Captain?"

"Why do you ask?"

"The way you look at the child; 'tis almost sad. I thought, perhaps, you were thinking of your own children."

"Children are for responsible men, Lady Chesterfield. Not for those of us whose lives are spent thumbing our nose at consequence."

"Her father must love her very much to go to these extremes to get her back."

"Her father was an idiot to lose her in the first place."

"Then you know him well?"

He laughed humorlessly. "Well enough."

"Her mother is dead?"

He nodded.

"Poor little thing. Her mother dead and now to be swept away to some man she hardly knows. She must be horrified."

"Children are resilient. They soon learn to cope. See how she plays, when only hours ago she was crying in fear. Soon she may even come to like me a little."

Destiny moved closer to better hear him as he continued to watch the child as she played in the light of the oil lamp.

In the shadows he seemed much less intimidating; the dark washed the scars from his profile, leaving his face looking almost normal.

"The child's mother must have been very bold, or perhaps desperate, to leave her husband in such a way."

"The bastard never married her," came his flat response.

"But he must have loved her."

"Must he?" He shook his head. "Obviously not enough. The truth is, Lady Chesterfield, he feels that love somehow diminishes his manhood. Love means commitment, the giving up of one's soul. What is a man without his soul, I ask you?"

"I always considered a man's or woman's soul unwhole until he or she loves and is loved in return."

"Perhaps he's simply incapable of loving."

"We're all capable of loving, sir. I think the trick is knowing how to recognize love when we finally find it."

"Knowing how to recognize it and knowing how to act on it are two different things. To know how to act on it doesn't come naturally. Unless one witnesses the act of giving love, even experiences it for himself, he blunders hopelessly in any attempt he might make to show it."

"Yes." Destiny nodded, frowning. "I suppose you're right." She watched the child hug her doll and kiss its cheek. "This one has obviously been loved deeply by her parent."

They remained silent as they continued to watch the little girl play. Finally, Destiny asked, "What's her name?"

"Jenette." He said the name so gently and fondly, it was more like a caress. The sound unnerved Destiny; her chest and throat tightened and an unexpected pressure came to her eyes. She turned away, suddenly aware of the cold breeze that cut easily through her thin clothes, making her shiver. She had heard only one other man so reverently speak his child's name . . . and that had been her own father.

A spencer coat was slipped over her shoulders and she looked around, up into the captain's shadowed eyes. He stood very close. She stepped back and against the ship's rail; it felt cold and hard pressing against her spine.

He reached out and grabbed her shoulders, his hands at first cruel, then gentle. Her heartbeat quickened as she instinctively stiffened and her hands came up to brace against his wide chest. "Please, no," she cried quietly, anticipating that he would try to kiss her.

Yet, he did not. He just eased her away from the rail before a spray of water rushed over the side, spilling across the deck at her feet.

As he released her and turned away, she said, "I'm sorry, Captain. I thought—"

"I know what you thought, Lady Chesterfield. You needn't worry for now. Despite my looks, I don't make a habit of ravishing women . . . or even seducing them—unless they are of a mind to be seduced." Legs braced apart and hands tucked into his breeches pockets, he gazed out over the white-tipped waves glimmering like strings of pearls in the moonlight. "What exactly would it take to seduce you, Destiny?"

She felt transfixed, shocked, and unnerved by his boldness and the use of her name.

He glanced over his shoulder at her, his hair a wild dark web around his face as a sudden gust of wind whipped over the bridge. "Come, come, you don't strike me as the sort of woman who would quell from such a straightforward question. It's not as if you haven't known a man. . . . Is it?"

"What are you inferring?" she demanded.

"You were married," he said into the wind.

"Captain, I fear you know far more about me than you should. And this conversation is much too familiar for my liking. How came you to know me so personally?" Tugging the spencer more tightly about her shoulders, she moved around the captain to face him squarely. "Shall we cease playing games, sir? You know I was married and to whom. So I'm fairly certain you also know the circumstances of my husband's death."

"All of England knows the circumstances of Lord Chesterfield's death. I believe he hung himself from a belfry."

"Wrong. He hung himself from a gable."

"You don't strike me as the sort of woman who would drive a man to suicide . . . to distraction, perhaps, but not suicide." With an edge of humor in his tone, he added, "I'm certain the poor bastard didn't know what he was missing."

"I beg your pardon?"

He laughed. "If he had, he might have questioned his . . . choices in life. You're the type of woman, Lady Chesterfield, that most men would thank God to have and to hold from this day forward."

"You obviously don't travel in the same circles as I, sir. I'm hardly the quintessence of the aristocratic woman, I'm sure you'll agree."

"Yes." He grinned and his expression softened. "I wholeheartedly agree. You have a definite earthiness about you that any *common* man would find overwhelmingly appealing."

"Is that supposed to be a compliment?"

He did not respond for a moment, just stood with his long legs slightly spread and his white billowy shirt moving gently with the breeze and the roll of the ship. There was something in the way he stood, shoulders slightly cocked, his head tipped a little to one side, that flurried some emotion in her breast: a disquietude, yes. But something else more disturbing. It made her heart thump rapidly. Moments before, she had felt chilled to the bone by the breeze but now a heat centered in her belly and sluiced like an oil fire throughout her body. Thank God there was so little light or he might surely have noticed her cheeks burning.

"I should go." She turned to leave.

"Yes," he finally replied. "I meant it as a compliment, Lady Chesterfield."

Her steps slowed then stopped.

He moved up behind her. "You spurn convention. It bores and suffocates you. Chesterfield could never have made you happy, so stop beating yourself up over his stupidity. You're a desirable woman and any man who refuses to acknowledge it isn't a man in any sense of the word."

"Your flattery is kind but unnecessary."

"*Au contraire.* 'Tis very necessary, I think. I'm not certain that I've ever met a woman so unaware of her virtues. In fact, I would wager I've never met a woman more unaware of her own womanhood. Perhaps that's what makes you so charming. Your innocence is endearing, not to mention captivating."

"I hate to disappoint you, Captain, but I'm hardly innocent."

He touched her hair, gently twisted it about his fingers as he moved closer. "All the more intriguing, my dear. Would you care to tell me about it?"

"No, I wouldn't, thank you."

"Is he the reason you've banished yourself from home?"

She pulled away, suddenly nervous and agitated at herself that she had spoken so openly to this man—a total stranger.

"Need I remind you, Captain, that my reasons for leaving England concern my father, nothing more. Any romantic notions you hold that I've left some heartbroken paramour back in England is not only wrong but ridiculous. To my knowledge I know of no man who would give my desertion a second thought."

"And that makes you angry?"

"Do I *sound* angry?"

"Furious."

With a huff she turned her back on him and walked away.

"Are you certain he's not heartbroken?" he called after her.

She stopped abruptly. Whipping the spencer from her shoulders, she flung it to the deck and flashed a look at him over her shoulder. "You're far too fresh for my liking, Captain. I'll appreciate your minding your own business from now on."

"You are my business," came his stern reply, causing Destiny to raise her chin defiantly and demand:

"Do tell. And how came you to that conclusion?"

"As long as you're on my ship, and I'm responsible for your welfare, *you're my business*. Good night, Lady Chesterfield."

"Oh!" she cried, then quit the bridge, leaving the captain alone in the dark.

10

I thought there were excellent materials in him, though for the present they hung together somewhat spoiled and tangled. I cannot deny that I grieved for his grief, whatever that was, and would have given much to assuage it.

—CHARLOTTE BRONTË, *Jane Eyre*

"Thanks to the captain, who believes my stowing away on his decrepit ship is a crime of high treason, my hands are shriveled as prunes and my feet hurt. And look at my nails, Destiny. They're eroded to the quick from scrubbing the deck on my hands and knees, mind you, and that was *before* that despicable Hugo Mallet forced me to cut onions by the tubful for his stew. My eyes are swollen out of their sockets from crying. Can you imagine my humiliation when he and his malevolent friends stood around me and snickered as I sniffled and bumped blindly about the galley thanks to those bloody onions. Remind me to never again ask a servant to cut onions. 'Tis a punishment worse than flogging."

Brushing Jenette's long black hair, Destiny shook her head and frowned. "I dare say you won't have to worry about servants, Diana. Not after James divorces you and takes Sheffield House."

"Fine. I would rather cut onions for the rest of my days than spend another year in his emotionless bondage." Diana stared at her hands. "The captain says I'm to do galley duty until we reach Tenerife. That means I'll be constantly scrutinized by that dreadful Hugo creature. He goes about the butchering of meat as if it were the enemy. Perhaps you could talk with the captain. Explain that the only kitchen task I've ever accomplished was the occasional boiling of water for tea."

"Why should *I* speak to the captain?"

"Because he obviously likes you."

Destiny looked at her aunt. "Whatever gave you that idea?"

"I heard the others talking; the captain ordered them to be on their best behavior around you and that you were to be made as comfortable as possible."

Her cheeks turned warm as she recalled their conversation on the bridge the previous night. "I shouldn't take his interest as an indication that he thinks any better of me than of you."

Lying back on the bunk, her lids growing heavy, Diana watched in silence as Destiny braided the child's hair then wrapped it around the back of her head, securing it with combs. Only then did the girl squirm around to face Destiny. Her black eyes were round and her little lips red as the heart of tiny rosebuds.

"I don't want to go see the captain, madame. He's very big and he frightens me."

"I'm certain the captain would never harm you, Jenette. I think he loves children very much."

"He stares at me all the time."

"Because you're a beautiful child, I'm sure." Destiny helped the little girl off the chair, adjusted the bright pink sash about her waist, and smoothed the wrinkles from the lace-edged apron covering her velvet skirt. She then handed Jenette her china doll.

"That's a lovely doll, Jenette. She looks very much like you."

"My papa gave her to me when I was baby. He brought her all the way from Russia."

"You must be very excited to see your papa again."

"He loves me very much. My mama told me so."

"He sounds wonderful. Now come along. It's time for your dinner with the captain. We wouldn't want to keep him waiting, would we?"

"Oh yes we would," she declared with a stubborn set of her little chin.

Leaving Diana already sleeping soundly, Destiny took Jenette's hand and they made their way to the upper deck, Destiny reminding the child that there was nothing to fear from the captain and that she should mind her manners and remember to be kind. The sign of a true lady was to show compassion for those who were much less fortunate.

The captain wore a splendid black long coat with an embroidered vest to match, and a white shirt with a wide stiff collar. His hair had been combed and tied at his nape with a black velvet ribbon. He wore a black patch over his scarred and sightless eye, no doubt for the child's benefit. Still, while his dress was impressive and as fine as any gentleman's, his appearance gave Destiny pause. She tried to think of him as he was the evening before, the darkness having washed the evidence of his tragedy from his features. Throughout the previous night and all day, she had pondered over their conversation on the bridge, and of the odd and discomfiting emotions he had aroused in her, however briefly. She could not shake the feeling that they shared some odd familiarity.

As Destiny tapped on the door, the captain dismissed his companion, Paolo, a handsome young man she had met during her morning turn around the deck with Connie. Paolo and Connie's banter that morning had made her laugh and forget, momentarily, that they were conscienceless killers for hire, just as the captain had done the night before—however briefly.

The captain assessed Destiny and Jenette before he opened his arms in welcome.

"You're right on time, ladies. Another five minutes and Hugo would have been whimpering about his food growing cold."

Destiny urged Jenette across the threshold, her hands squeezing their encouragement on the little girl's shoulders.

As the captain moved toward them, Jenette flung herself against Destiny's legs and buried her face in Destiny's skirt. "Please, please don't leave me with him," she cried.

Stooping, Destiny wrapped her arms around the little girl and hushed her. "There, there, Jenette. You must never insult your host. He only wants to share dinner with you. I promise I shan't be far. Just outside this door. Should you need me I'll be here in two shakes of a cricket's leg."

Remaining near the table, his look discomposed as the child clung to Destiny more desperately, the captain said, "Perhaps, Lady Chesterfield, you would care to join us in the repast?"

"I fear, Captain, that I'm not dressed appropriately for dinner. My hair is unbrushed and my dress . . . I spent the last hours sunning on the bridge while Connie stood guard. He's been most indulgent. I hope you don't mind. I simply cannot tolerate the stuffiness of my cabin for too awfully long. It's not in my nature to cloister myself away when the sun is shining."

He did not respond, just stared into her face with an intensity that further unnerved her.

"Most women would have worn a hat," she added with a quiver in her voice. "I fear my face has become sunburned."

"You're not most women," he pointed out. "And I find the color of your cheeks *most* becoming. It accentuates the green of your eyes. As far as your turning about deck, I've no problem with that at all, Lady Chesterfield, nor with your sunning on the bridge: with one exception. Next time you'll allow *me* to escort you." With effort, he shifted his attention to Jenette. He focused on the child and the sternness of his expression mellowed. "She'd like you to stay, I think. And so would I."

Jenette turned her big eyes up to Destiny's and tugged on her skirt. *"S'il vous plait, madame?"*

Reluctantly, and with a sigh, Destiny nodded. She kissed Jenette's cheek then escorted her to the table, to the chair next to the captain's. Delicate place settings of white china with red roses and gold trim appeared out of place amid the stark, masculine surroundings of rough wood and rolled maps tossed randomly about the tables and floor. The captain pulled out the chair for Jenette, who glanced at Destiny for assurance before climbing up to the table and settling on plush, ruby red pillows.

A door opened and a brute of a man entered, his shoulders nearly as wide as the doorway. The front of his shirt was spattered with what appeared to be blood and smudges of brown gravy. He carried a tray heaped high with sliced bread, a large chunk of butter, and a bottle of whiskey, which he plunked on the table before leering at Destiny.

"Never thought I'd see a woman eatin' at *this* table. You can mark me words, sir, there's gonna be trouble soon enough, wot with three females aboard."

As Hugo stormed from the room grumbling under his breath, Destiny allowed the captain to assist her to her chair. His hand tarried momentarily on her shoulder before he sat himself and reached for the whiskey bottle. "Forgive Hugo, Lady Chesterfield. He's apt to be superstitious on occasion, and he doesn't much care for the water. His entire family drowned during a gale when he was ten."

"Then why does he sail?" she asked, nodding as he offered to pour her a drink.

"To get from one place to the other, I suppose." He grinned and shrugged. "Occasionally we must tolerate an inconvenience to enjoy that which we most cherish."

"What, pray tell, does Hugo cherish so much that he would board a ship, considering his fear of water?"

"The hunt," he replied in a cryptic tone. He raised his glass of whiskey to her. "May your journey to Cawnpore prove successful, Lady Chesterfield."

She sipped the potent drink as Hugo reappeared with a place setting for her. He returned almost immediately with a pot of steaming stew, which he ladled into their bowls.

"Don't blame me if the onions choke ya," he declared. "That bloody woman made a right mess of me food. Now ya tell me she's to help me cook until we reach Tenerife. She don't know one end of a potato from another."

Thinking of Diana's swollen eyes and red hands, Destiny said, "She's no more pleased with *your* company than you are with hers. Perhaps the captain will do you both a favor and put her to work at something else."

Hugo grunted his displeasure and slammed the door behind him as he left the room.

"I don't like stew," Jenette declared and shoved the bowl away. "I want to go to my cabin now."

The captain replaced the bowl in front of her. "It's good for you."

"I don't want it. I don't like it. My mama *never* made me eat what I don't like."

"Judging by your behavior, your mama spoiled you rotten. Now mind your manners and eat."

Her little face screwed into a frown. "I shall tell my papa about you. He won't like your being so mean to me."

"Your papa doesn't abide brashness from little girls. Your papa will tell you to mind your manners and quit acting like a brat."

Tears welled up in Jenette's eyes and her chin quivered. She jumped from her chair, spilling the pillows to the floor, and ran from the room. Destiny stood, prepared to give chase. The captain grabbed her arm.

"Leave her."

"But she's upset."

"When she's hungry enough she'll eat. Sit, Lady Chesterfield. Your food is growing cold."

"But—"

"I said to *sit*." He tugged on her arm and pointed to her chair. "Consider it an order."

Reluctantly, Destiny sat while the captain poured himself another drink and shoved his untouched stew aside. Sitting back in his chair, his intense gaze fixed on the door through which Jenette had escaped, he drank his whiskey and brooded.

"You mustn't take her rejection to heart, Captain. She's only a child and very frightened."

He drank again. "She got her mother's temper."

"You speak of her mother like you knew her very well."

"She was a firebrand. Beautiful but manipulative. It was all or nothing with Michelle. To truly love her, a man was forced to give up his—"

"Soul?" She smiled, recalling their previous conversation.

"His passions. His soul. His visions. Her emotional demands suffocated. For a man who grew up knowing neither commitment nor romantic love, her dependency was confusing and troublesome."

"How dreadful for him," she said, breaking off a bit of bread and buttering it.

"Meaning?" He slammed his empty glass onto the table, causing Destiny to jump.

"Only that he sounds like a very unhappy man. Are you certain turning the child over to such as he is wise?"

"I think you shouldn't worry overmuch about it. It's none of your affair."

Destiny stirred her stew, discomfited by the captain's sudden dark mood. "Have you some affinity with the child's father?" she asked cautiously.

"I simply don't care for your judgmental attitude, Lady Chesterfield. For one who so obviously thumbs her nose at her own peers' expectations, you're hardly in the position of casting aspersions on someone you don't even know." He poured a third whiskey and left his chair. "You obviously were gifted with parents whose commitment to their marriage vows meant something."

"Unlike their peers, they married out of love instead of convenience, if that's to what you were referring, Captain."

He replied with a sharp laugh before moving around the table. "What a unique concept. Marrying out of love instead of money and position. Tell me, Lady Chesterfield, what was it like to have a mother and father so devoted to one another?"

"It was a pleasant experience."

"Did they spend much time together?"

"They were always together. My mother even assisted my father in his duties. He never traveled anywhere without her. In fact, until the day she died, I don't think they ever spent a night apart."

He bent over her shoulder and poured more liquor in her glass. She felt his breath on the side of her face. It smelled like whiskey. Setting the bottle aside, he reached for her glass and put it in her hand. His lips near her ear, he whispered, "I don't care for drinking alone, Lady Chesterfield. Being alone isn't a state I relish, really. Not that I haven't known solitude. I can tolerate it. I just don't like it. When one's alone he's forced to confront his thoughts, and his reasons for thinking them. We won't get into the feelings part. Feelings, more so than thoughts, are much too raw and real."

He nuzzled her ear with his nose, breathed into her hair before straightening. "We were talking about Jenette's father? Ah, yes. You can't blame him, really, for his inability to commit. His father married his mother out of duty. On occasion that the father dropped in to check on his displaced responsibilities he was greeted with little more care than a stray cat. Not that he was bothered particularly. His wife's ennui in regards to their marriage simply made it easier for him to disappear for months, even years at a time."

"How very tragic for his children."

"Not at all," he replied as he stared into his glass of whiskey. "They learned at a very young age to be emotionally self-sufficient."

"I feel very sad for them."

"I don't think Jenette's father would care for or even deserves your pity, m'lady. He's chosen his course in life and ultimately accepts the consequences of his actions."

"Yes, but if he's so callous toward love and commitment, Captain, what, if anything, can he provide his daughter?"

His face clouded. "Perhaps she can teach him these things."

"I hope for her sake, and his, that she can." Destiny sighed and pointed to his empty chair. "Please sit down, Captain, and eat. The stew is quite delicious."

At last he sat, elbows bracketing his china as he stared down into his cooling stew, his brow creased, his mouth firmly set. Finally, without looking at her, he said, "Tell me about your father."

"Loyal and loving to a fault," she replied, smiling to herself. "Dedicated. He should have been a minister, I think. He's always been a champion of the unfortunate. Often I used to see him and my mother gather food and clothing from our own home and provide for the hungry and homeless. The people of India eventually came to admire him to extremes."

"He should be canonized," he replied in a droll tone.

"He took his responsibilities to the people quite seriously."

Finally, he looked at her. There was a savageness about his expression that unsettled her. "Just what would he sacrifice, aside from food and clothes, to help the people of India? His life, perhaps? Or, perhaps, the lives of his fellow Englishmen?"

Destiny frowned and put down her spoon.

The captain again stood and paced. His sudden, unexplained anger radiated around him.

Suddenly awash with disquietude over the captain's odd behavior, Destiny left her chair. "Captain, Compton Fontaine is an Englishman first and foremost."

"Is he?" The captain's lips curled as he moved toward her. "You haven't lived with your father in what, ten years? Men can change in much less time than that. Give a man enough cause and he'll come to question his every basic instinct and motive. Everything he thought he stood for and believed in can disintegrate like *that*." He snapped his fingers. "Suddenly the fog of his former reality crystallizes into the sharp ugly actuality that is truth. For most of us the actuality isn't very pretty. In fact, it's horrifying, Lady Chesterfield, because suddenly we must question our every action and reaction, determine not to make the same mistakes that we made in the past when we were so absolutely certain we were right."

"Why are you so curious about my father?" she demanded with a tip of her chin and an edge in her voice. Her own speculations of his motives for helping her reach Cawnpore rapped unnervingly at her conscience.

He raised his black eyebrows and laughed. "I'm simply fascinated over a man who demands such loyalty out of his daughter that she would brave the likes of me and this ship to get her to India to be with him in a time of crisis."

"I'm doing nothing more than any other loyal son or daughter would do if they thought their parent in trouble."

As he moved closer, she did not back away, just set her feet and squared her shoulders.

He gently touched her sun-kissed cheeks with his fingertip and lowered his voice. "What will you do if you arrive in Cawnpore too late, Destiny? What if your father is already dead? What if Nana Sahib has killed him?"

"Then I shall confront his killer myself and exact revenge."

Throwing back his dark head, he howled in laughter. "My god, child, that's the first idiotic thing I've heard you say. And here I was beginning to think you not just beautiful but somewhat intelligent." Gripping her chin in his fingers, he tipped back her head and looked down into her eyes, his lips but a breath away from hers. "How will you kill him, *chere*? With a flutter of your long, lovely lashes? A curve of your deliciously full lips? Perhaps a sway of your soft body against his. Or mayhap you'll slay him with your naivete and innocence."

"Do you make light of me, Captain?"

His expression became harsh. Holding her face more

tightly in his hand, he murmured, "I could think of worse ways of dying."

Jason was not surprised to find his comrades waiting for him in his cabin when he returned from his dinner with Destiny. Zelie lounged upon Jason's berth, smoking his opium and appearing mellow. Paolo sat at the dressing table regarding his reflection, and Connie pondered over a map. Hugo paced, his clothes still stained with blood and gravy and his expression like a pot boiling. They all looked up expectantly as Jason stepped into the room and closed the door firmly behind him.

"Well, if it ain't bloody Romeo," Hugo declared. "I was wonderin' how long we'd have to wait. Thought you might take the gal on a moonlight stroll about deck after dinner. Maybe serenade her under the bleedin' mizzenmast."

Zelie blew smoke through his lips and rolled his gaze toward Jason. "She's quite charming, old man. I think we all agree on that. And I'm certain when you're with her your moments of splendor in her arms come rushing back in all their glory. Shooting stars and such muckity-muck. You're besieged by confusion because you've always been a man of extreme emotional control."

"Like a rock," Connie declared with a shake of his fist. "Ain't none of us who could face an adversary with as much courage and grit."

"Of course, we mustn't forget your quandary over Michelle," Paolo said. "You're despondent that she died while you were holed up in Dunleavy's prison cell. You feel that your unwillingness to marry her and provide the child a proper father in some way contributed to her death. Perhaps had you been there with her to hold her hand through her dreadful disease she might have survived. You look in your daughter's face now and regret the years you missed with her; you imagine raising her on Ceylonia where you lavish upon her everything your fortunes can buy. Regrets, regrets, regrets. They all boil up in your conscience and make you question your past and ultimately your future.

"Now there is the nasty little matter of Compton Fontaine. He's your friend, true. You've shared pleasant dinners and long conversations with him through the years. He even fancied you as a son-in-law. Now you find yourself, thanks to a twist of fate, romantically involved with his daughter, and no doubt wishing you had listened to her father long ago, judging by the whipped puppy expression you get on your face every time you look at her. I think I speak for all of us when I say I never thought to see one of the most dangerous men alive turn to mush in the presence of a woman. Now you save her from Dunleavy by whisking her away just in the nick of time, convincing yourself that you'll heroically rescue her father from Nana's influence . . . and perhaps by doing so regain her trust and, possibly, rekindle the fire that made her enamored of you in the first place.

"On the other hand, fond as you may be of Lady Destiny, and her father, you're a dedicated soldier of the Empire. If it means saving your own countrymen, you'll kill Fontaine if necessary and deal with the romantic but tragic circumstances later.

"All this romance and danger is most exhilarating and satisfying, but only on the condition that you keep your focus. Which brings us to the crux of this conversation."

Connie joined in. "Do you think it wise to nurture your relationship with Lady Destiny when the possibility exists that you may have to blow out her father's brains should we discover that he's joined Nana Sahib in his little mutiny?"

Jason moved to the dressing table and motioned Paolo from the chair. Sitting, he stared at his scarred reflection in the mirror. "Christ, Paolo, did you have to make me so damned ugly? My own daughter is too terrified to remain in the same room with me."

Paolo grinned. "You can always remove it now that we're at sea. There isn't a hell of a lot Destiny can do about finding herself aboard ship with the man who was daft enough to admit to her that he was intended to murder her father."

The men laughed. Jason, however, did not.

"Of course he won't remove it," Paolo added. "And we all know why. While Destiny might tolerate and eventually warm to the *captain's* company, she would no doubt attempt to fling herself overboard in order to thwart Batson's reaching her father. Surely, there would be no more sharing Mallet's stew together or moonlight conversations on deck. She would despise you even more for, once again, tricking her, this time to board the *Pretender*."

"Oh what a tangled web we weave," Zelie cried and clutched at his heart.

"Stuff it," Jason said.

Hugo bent over Jason's shoulder and glared into his reflected face. "You've changed, Batson. The edge is gone. Yer sojourn in the slammer softened you. We all see it. It's that look yer father got just before he retired from the life. You ain't hungry for the kill anymore."

"I was never *hungry* for the kill, Mallet. Not like you. I simply followed orders like any soldier."

"Only you was paid for it." Hugo grinned. "Handsomely, I might add. Is that it? You so damn set now ya want to settle down and play papa with the kid?"

"I would advise you to keep my daughter out of this," Jason said through his teeth.

"Have I hit a nerve?" Hugo turned to the others. "I fear Cobra has woke up to his responsibilities, gentlemen. He's ready to retire and bounce babies on his knee. It weren't so long ago that Jason vowed he'd never allow a woman to get in the way of his sole mission. At least that's what he vowed when Michelle tried to snare him. Wasn't no woman worth settlin' down for, he said. Now here he sits, broodin' over a kid and strollin' in the moonlight with a possible enemy's daughter. Hell, the Cobra I used to know wouldn't have allowed a female within a yardarm of this ship.

"So where does that leave us? Do we trust our comrade to keep his instincts about him long enough to cover our asses under fire? Maybe while he's daydreamin' about home and hearth in the damn trenches we're gettin' our throats cut from ear to ear by a lot of sepoys. Mean sons of bitches, those sepoys. I'd rather go up against the whole Crimean army than a handful of sepoy soldiers." Hugo grunted and spat on the floor. "Hell, if that ain't enough we got Dunleavy and Trevor Batson somewhere behind us. He's gonna consider your grabbin' the girl and haulin' sail out of Portsmouth an act of treason. He's gonna bury our asses so far under that prison this time, we'll never see daylight again—that is, if he don't stand us before a firin' squad first. That is, if Trevor don't get to us first. Shit, I'd rather fight a pit full of black mambas. We'd stand as much chance of walkin' out alive as facin' Trevor Batson and his crew."

Sitting back in the chair, his gaze fixed on his reflection, Jason said dryly, "Maybe you're getting soft yourself, Mallet. Not only are you concerned about going up against Dunleavy and my brother, but you're afraid of two women and a child. Maybe you've lost *your* edge. Maybe all you're good for now is filling my belly with your shitty stew."

Hugo's face turned darker and his hands clenched. He stood rooted to the floor like a tree, his fleshy jowls quivering with anger, his gaze burning into Jason.

Jason slowly turned, and with his elbows on his knees, smirked at Hugo. "Something wrong, Mallet?"

"I've a good mind to rip out yer throat."

"So what's keeping you from it? I doubt that any of these men will stop you. But you won't do that, will you, Hugo? Because if you were to hit and miss, you're screwed. When Cobra strikes, he *doesn't* miss. You'd be dead before your pitiful little brain splattered on the floor."

Hugo glanced around the cabin and, finding no support, turned on his heels and made a quick exit. The others followed, Zelie pausing at the threshold to say, "Would you like me to take care of him? It would be my pleasure, you know. Never liked him much and he's dreadfully sloppy. He goes about the cutting of a man's throat as if he were butchering a boar."

Jason removed his wig and flung it on the dressing table. "Keep an eye on him. He's losing it, I think. He'll be dangerous to have around."

"Oh, jolly good," Zelie replied before leaving Jason to sink in his chair again and close his eyes.

Maybe Hugo was right. Maybe Cobra had at long last outlived his effectiveness. A year spent in solitary confinement had obviously made his reasoning rusty.

That was putting it mildly. A man in control of his logic would not have allowed himself to give in to his base urges and make love to a woman from whom he had only intended to get information. Nor would he have defied direct orders from the Crown to drop this mission to deliver her to India's shores in hopes that she could somehow help to thwart any attempt Fontaine and Sahib may make to instigate a rebellion.

But he was more than familiar with Dunleavy's methods of eliminating any evidence that the Covert Operations by Radical Agents—Cobra—had in any way been involved in the ugly business of assassination. After all, Cobra was nothing more than the shadowy underbelly of a government that would never admit it employed cold-blooded mercenaries. While there were the occasional whispers that such an organization existed, no one outside of Dunleavy and the Queen had the remotest clue of their identity. Harold Dunleavy would make certain that never changed, even if it meant murdering Destiny Fontaine Chesterfield in her sleep.

As long as she was in Jason's care, Dunleavy, Trevor, and the entire British army would have to go through him to get her. And he sure as hell had no intention of making it easy for them.

11

No one who looks at my slow (calm) face can guess
the vortex sometimes whirling in my heart, and en-
gulfing thought, and wrecking prudence.

— CHARLOTTE BRONTË, *Shirley*

Trouble was afoot. Jason could sense it as easily as he
could smell the perfume Destiny dabbed behind her ear
every morning. Like sex-starved tomcats, the *Pretender*'s
crew watched her and Diana's every move, their expressions growing more bothersome by the hour. Jason surmised that Hugo Mallet's prediction might prove to be
right. Bringing a woman aboard a ship full of cutthroats—
although normally he trusted his cutthroats with his life—
was asking for disaster. The fact that Destiny and Diana
were becoming somewhat friendly with his cutthroats didn't
help matters. Paolo spent an hour with Destiny every afternoon instructing her in art lessons—using paints and
canvases from his own treasured store of supplies—while
Diana and Connie played cards on a barrelhead. Connie
bounced Jenette on his knees, speaking to Jason's daughter in a singsong voice that belonged to a comedic thespian
instead of a bloodthirsty mercenary—his eyes, of course,
locked on Diana who, over the course of the last many
days, had blossomed into something other than the timid
troublemaker who may have put her niece's life in jeopardy by writing on a note to her husband the name of the
ship on which they had escaped England's shores.

Connie and Paolo aside, every man on the *Pretender* focused his attention on the women the moment Destiny and Diana stepped foot on deck. Someone's discipline was going to snap. Sadly, and frustratingly, Jason reckoned it was going to be his own.

The hot, thick air pressing down on him, Jason stood outside Destiny's door, listening hard for any sound that would indicate she had awakened from her afternoon nap. He had avoided her the last many days, setting an example for his men: don't look, don't smell, don't allow fantasies to scramble better judgment, and they would all live long enough to exercise their base hungers on Tenerife whores.

Yet, here he stood, lurking in the shadows, face sweating under his disguise, wondering when she would again make her appearance on deck . . . an appearance that would ultimately send him to his cabin to brood . . . among other things. But since he had informed Destiny and Diana that they would be arriving in Tenerife soon, Jason and Connie had sensed that something was up with the women. Too often they had been seen with their pretty heads together, whispering, occasionally arguing, looking over their shoulders as if anticipating their being caught in a crime.

As Diana's door began to open, Jason stepped into the shadows behind the companionway. Diana hurried to Destiny's door and tapped lightly. Destiny responded immediately, allowing Diana into her cabin. Again, Jason moved to Destiny's door and listened.

"Where is Jenette?" Destiny asked.

"Playing with her doll. I suspect she'll be asleep soon."

"Have you heard anything more regarding our reaching Tenerife?"

"Two days. Three at the most."

"We haven't much time, then."

"Not to worry, niece. I've located the guns."

Jason frowned.

"Dear heavens, Des, there are enough weapons on this

ship to supply an army. Rifles and handguns and knives—
the most lethal-looking swords and bayonets."

"Did you secure us a weapon?"

"I didn't have time. I'll go again tonight."

"Do you think this wise, Diana? Were the captain to get
wind of our plans—"

"Des, if the captain is in some way involved with Dunleavy, and if our being on this ship was devised to get us to
India so that Dunleavy can go through with his plans to assassinate your father, then we must do everything humanly
possible to thwart those plans. Once we dock in Tenerife
we'll simply . . . disappear."

"Diana, if our suspicions are true, do you really think that
these men will allow us to 'disappear'? I think not. They'll
leave no stone unturned to find us, and when they do—"

"We'll at least have weapons to protect ourselves."

"What if we're wrong, Diana?"

"Wrong? They've admitted that their reasons for traveling to India are strictly for the love of war and money. It
stands to reason that you would fit perfectly into their
plans. What if"—Diana lowered her voice, forcing Jason
to press his ear closer to the door—"the captain has decided to ransom us to your father? Compton would sacrifice his last penny to save you, Des. Therefore, we must be
brave and extricate ourselves from these men at the first
opportunity."

"Diana, would the captain have been so upset about your
leaving Uncle James a letter, giving the name of the ship
on which we're sailing, if he and Dunleavy were working
together?"

"Have you gone soft on the captain?" Diana demanded.

Jason grinned and waited for the response. It was a moment in coming.

"Hardly. I'm only attempting to understand this odd
situation. Granted, there's something very strange and
discomfiting about the captain's behavior. One minute
he's a gentleman, the next he's . . . intimidating, to say
the least. He stares at me with such an intensity I find my-

self trembling and speechless and dashing for my cabin for safety. But even here I can find no peace of mind. The solitude invites memories, and the memories drive me back on deck, desperate for anything to alleviate the images of myself opening my arms to a man who intended to murder my father."

"Don't think about it, Des. What's done is done and cannot be undone."

"I only think . . . what if I hadn't acted so rashly. What if he was telling the truth—that his reasons for meeting me in the glade were to discover for himself if my father had become involved in mutiny with Nana Sahib? That he had no intention of murdering my father. That he had actually become fond of me. . . ."

"He lied to you. He used you. Surely you can't forgive him for that."

"No. Never. But—"

"No buts, Des."

"What if—"

"No what-ifs. Were he to walk in this door this minute I would shoot him myself for taking advantage of your vulnerability. All along he knew who you were. He also knew about the circumstances of your marriage—he was aware of Chesterfield's inclinations. But even more important, he was your father's friend. According to you, Compton would have trusted your life with Jason Batson, and what does the scoundrel do? Plucks your virginity like a sweet fruit and then proclaims his so-called fondness stemmed from subterfuge. You may be certain that as soon as we see your father I shall inform him what sort of blackguard Batson turned out to be."

"I'd rather you didn't. My father would be heartbroken, Diana. And I would be . . . humiliated should my father know I'm the sort of woman who would participate in such a scandalous affair. Besides, my father may never have an opportunity to see or speak to Batson again. Don't forget I may have killed him."

Jason quietly returned to his cabin.

*   *   *

Destiny sat in a chair on the quarterdeck dabbing water-colors on a canvas. Though she stared intently at the white-tipped waves, it was neither the ocean, nor the clouds, nor even some imagined coastline that emerged on the canvas, but a watery image of a forest glade, and a blood bay horse, saddled but riderless, grazing in tall brown grass.

The image disturbed her and made her face flush with heat. Why could she not bury those moments in the glade? There were other far more important events manipulating her life: her father's welfare, for one, not to mention the fact that she was surrounded by men who may or may not be associated with Dunleavy—a possibility that she felt less strongly about every day that she spent in the company of these odd men. She dared not admit to Diana that she had grown fond of the *Pretender*'s crew, or most of them. Paolo made her laugh and Zelie enthralled her with his life theories and debates on heaven and hell. Connie fascinated her by his ability to entertain Jenette one minute and the next to command the ship with a ferocity that would make the bravest men tremble in their boots.

Then, of course, there was the captain. Disturbing, intimidating . . . absorbing. While he had kept his distance from her the last many days, she could always sense when he was near. His intensity electrified the air. When he caught her gaze he would not let it go. She felt . . . hypnotized and helpless, and shaken to extremes. Odd that she had grown exasperated by his aloofness. She had come to desire his presence as much as she feared it.

She put down her paintbrush and announced, "Finished at last. What do you think, Paolo?"

Paolo smiled. "Excellent! A masterpiece! You have talent and a very vivid imagination, *chere*. Perhaps tomorrow we'll begin a portrait of someone breathtakingly handsome, dangerous, suave—I'll pose for you, of course. Who else on this ship has the thoroughly classical features of a god, hmmm?" He gave her his profile, tilting his jaw at her a little, making her laugh so hard she spilled her paint-brushes to the deck.

Paolo dropped to one knee to collect them, stopping short as the captain came from nowhere and planted one foot on the brushes, snapping a pair in two and crushing Paolo's fingers to the deck, pinning them beneath the sole of his boot.

With a short cry of surprise, Destiny sprang from her chair while Paolo slowly looked up, up, up to the captain's face, teeth clenched to hold back his curse. "Lunatic, you've broken my brushes," Paolo finally said.

"Is that all?" the captain replied, crushing Paolo's fingers harder to the deck and fixing Destiny with a look that made her back toward the rail.

Paolo's face turned white.

Gathering her courage, Destiny cried, "Stop that! You're hurting him. He did nothing more than—"

"Occupy your every afternoon for the past weeks. Charm you with his monotonous suppositions, and act the buffoon in order to hear you laugh." Glancing down at Paolo, he added, "I'm well aware of Paolo's ability to seduce young women."

Wincing and attempting to tug his fingers from under the captain's boot, Paolo shook his head and attempted a thin smile. "I assure you . . . sir. Seducing *this* particular young woman never entered my mind. Do I look daft to you? To anyone on this ship?" he yelled, looking around at his comrades who watched the confrontation.

A dozen emotions bombarded Destiny as she stared at the captain. Again he wore a patch over his bad eye. She was learning to focus on the more normal side of his face. It wasn't so frightening. Simply . . . bothersome, as if something there nagged at her subconscious.

"Take your foot off his hand," she heard herself say. "Now."

"I beg your pardon?" he asked in so mocking a tone her cheeks turned hot. She swallowed and took a deep breath. "I said to stand back and leave him alone. You've no ex-

cuse to bully him so, when he was only giving me paint
lessons."

One side of his mouth curled. "Paolo, you seem to have
a champion. Very well." He removed his foot without taking his focus from Destiny. "We'll compromise, Lady
Chesterfield. I won't feed Paolo to the sharks if you don't
bolt for your cabin."

Paolo swept up his brushes and grabbed for his brush
box and paints before facing the captain squarely. "Your
possessiveness is understandable. It is not, however, reasonable that we should not enjoy a casual conversation
with the young lady should the opportunity arise. I suggest
that you rein in your jealousy and dampen your temper or
you are liable to wind up with a mutiny on your hands. Unless, of course, you prefer that we abandon ship in Tenerife and allow you to sail this heap by yourself to India.
Good you may be with a gun, sir, but I doubt you would
last long on your own surrounded by a hundred sepoys."

With a toss of his head, Paolo stormed away, supplies
tucked under his arms, the watchful crew smiling and nodding their approval over his remarks to the captain. They
all scrambled then as the captain shot them each a warning
glance before turning his attention again to Destiny.

"Happy now?" he asked in so cryptic a tone Destiny
considered making a run for her cabin, then decided
against it.

"I don't know what you mean," she replied. "Happy
about what?"

"You've got the lot of them panting like dogs after you.
They can't eat or sleep. They mope about in a pout when
you don't acknowledge them with a smile. They're soldiers, Lady Chesterfield, and you have them scrambling to
partake in tea parties."

"Nonsense." She lifted her chin. "Besides, do you expect
me to spend my every hour in my cabin? Perhaps if you
didn't hole up like a monk I wouldn't find the need to
search out your crew's company."

"I was under the impression that you found my company discomposing."

"Occasionally, yes. When you're in a snit, like now. A lady would hardly prefer the company of an ogre to that of a man like Paolo, who strives to make me laugh instead of cringe."

"Ah, so you do find pleasure in Paolo's company."

"I do. Yes." She nodded, still unable to remove her gaze from his good eye, which seemed to penetrate her like a pick. There was something there as curiously enthralling as there was frightening. "He's taught me how to paint," she said, indicating the easel and canvas, hoping to alleviate the tension charging the air between them.

A moment passed before he shifted his attention to the painting. He did not speak as he studied the canvas. Little by little the anger on his features melted into something softer. Finally, he said, "Looks very serene and lonely. A riderless horse usually means death. Or a loss. Have you lost something . . . or someone, m'lady?"

"To have lost something . . . or someone . . . I would have had to have had it in the first place." She shook her head. "I cannot claim that which I only perceived having."

Destiny leaned against the rail and turned her face into the sun. The wind lifted her hair and sea spray covered her lashes. Her cheeks flushed with sunlight and heat. Her skin shimmered with moisture. "Tell me, Captain. Is this enough for you, this ship, these men, the anticipation of the next battle?"

"Would it surprise you if I said no?"

Her eyebrows raised.

"Regardless of what you think of me, madam, I'm a man, not an animal. I have normal needs. I occasionally require companionship to satisfy those needs. I suspect, judging by your painting, that you're no different than I. Occasionally we meet someone who fulfills our fantasies. Alas, such infatuation rarely lasts and we're left . . . hollow and a bit calloused. Next time we won't so easily trust, or love."

"Yes," she replied softly, nodding in agreement. "I fear you're right."

"Would you care to talk about it?" he asked, and when she turned her eyes up to his, he pointed to the canvas. "The painting. The glade. The horse. Where is his rider?"

"Gone," she replied with a shrug. "He was simply a figment of my imagination. A fantasy too good to be true. I loved him briefly, or I thought I did until I realized what sort of man he really was. I needed something from him. I took it. He needed something from me. He took it. It all feels very cold now that I think about it. But we learn from our mistakes, don't we, Captain?"

"He must have had *some* redeeming quality."

"There is nothing redeeming about a liar, sir. He was a fraud. An imposter who pretended to be something or someone he wasn't. He took his pleasure at the cost of my heart, not to mention my dignity." She added stonily, "I abhor deceit. Once faith and trust are smashed by the lie it is never quite the same, is it? It leaves an indelible scar upon our soul, not to mention our heart."

The captain looked away. He gripped the deck rail and released a long breath. "And if he went on his knees and begged you? If he professed that his feelings were true, that he had never meant to hurt you, and if he could take back the lie, would you, could you not forgive him?"

Destiny did not respond to his question because she could not; she had asked herself the same thing a hundred times since she rode away from the glade, his blood staining her clothes, her body between her legs aching with a sort of pain that continued to awaken her in the middle of the night. What good did it do her to think of him now?

She gazed out at the distant dark clouds brewing on the horizon. There were spears of lightning that danced along the crest of the water. "Will it hit us?" she asked. "The storm, I mean. It looks dreadfully wicked."

"Aye, it's a bad one. But if we hold true to our course, we'll skirt the worst of it. And you didn't answer my question. Would you forgive him his deceit—"

"I can't think of anything he could do or say, sir, that would encourage any forgiveness on my part."

"Poor bastard. I'm certain he regrets his behavior and if he could relive those moments in the glade he would choose his words and actions more carefully."

Frowning, Destiny turned her gaze up to his, her heart skipping rapidly in her chest. "How do you know that we met in a glade, sir?"

He pointed to the canvas, and his eyebrows raised. "The painting, of course."

The surge of angst that robbed Destiny of breath subsided as suddenly as it had flooded her every nerve. Of course the *Pretender*'s captain would know nothing of her rendezvous with Batson in the glade. How could he? It was simply that lingering sense of hurt and guilt that continued to gnaw at her. Dabbing the images onto canvas to stare at and contemplate was not going to help her put her outrageous behavior with Batson from her mind.

She grabbed the canvas with both hands and flung it as hard as she could over the deck rail. It floated momentarily upward, caught in a wind draft, then settled lightly as a feather on the water. Destiny watched as a wave broke over the painting and dragged it partially under. Colors ran and images blurred before the water-logged canvas slid below the surface and disappeared.

Hands gripping the cool brass deck rail, Destiny watched lightning dance again on the horizon and did her best to will back the sting of tears in her eyes. The captain moved up behind her, reached around her, pried her fingers from around the rail, and forcibly turned her to face him. Catching her chin in his fingers, he tipped back her head and watched a tear creep down her cheek.

"Go on," he encouraged softly. "Cry. Get it out of your system. Take it from one who knows, the longer you hold in your emotions the more deeply they'll hurt you. If you aren't careful you'll end up like me—a heartless, unfeeling son of a bitch who couldn't possibly know what it's like to care for someone and lose them."

"I did care for him," she declared with a catch in her voice, then, despite her resolve, she sank against him, her face pressed into his hard shoulder, which smelled slightly of smoke and sweat. "I was such a fool, sir. And desperate. I had married for convenience—my uncle's convenience, actually, and too late I discovered my husband was . . . uninterested in me as a wife. Then I met a man who responded to me in ways that my husband didn't."

"And you fell in love with him." He stroked her hair.

"Yes. No! . . . Yes." She nodded and sniffed, then closed her eyes and allowed the heat of his body to somehow soothe her. His hand in her hair made her drowsy; the scent of his skin and the feel of his shirt against her cheek made her heart feel liquid. "Yes," she repeated more softly, her eyelids still closed. "Foolish, wasn't I, to love a stranger? To think he could actually love me? Uncle James is right about me. I'm a disappointment to my gender and a humiliation to polite Society. I belong back in India where I can 'move among heathens without attracting too much attention.'" She sniffed again and nestled more deeply against his shoulder. "Perhaps if I had returned to India sooner, my dear father would not be in the mess he's in now. I pray that I'll arrive in time to help him, or save him. . . ."

Destiny backed away suddenly, or tried to, her gaze flying up to the captain's face as his hands closed around her arms, anchoring her close to his body, which had felt so comforting while she had allowed herself to forget who he was, or might be. "I assure you, Captain, whatever trouble my father might be in is nothing to do with his turning a traitor to England. I would wager my life on it."

"Very high stakes for one so naive as to fall in love with a stranger." He knuckled a tear from her cheek. "So tell me, sweetheart, are you so certain that your stranger wasn't just a little in love with you?"

"He only wanted information about my father. He worked for Dunleavy."

"What has that got to do with his loving you? Trust me,

Lady Chesterfield, nothing can undo a man more than being torn between the love of his country and the love of a woman."

"Are you defending him, Captain?" she asked angrily.

"Only imagining what sort of hell he must have felt, looking into your eyes, holding your body against his, and realizing that in a blink of an eye, or a kiss of your mouth, he would turn his back on his queen in order to keep you from harm."

Again she felt hypnotized, like one focused on the eyes of a cobra, held mesmerized and terrorized by its fearsome facade. His words unraveled something in her, a weakness that angered her, a neediness that flushed her face with the realization that even this man could make her body crave an intimate touch or whisper.

She turned away, or tried to. He caught her shoulders and pulled her around, gripping her arms fiercely as she struggled. "Be still, dammit. Is this your way with men, Destiny? Crying on their shoulder one minute, the next spitting and clawing like a cat?"

"Don't touch me. Please, if you do I'll—"

"You'll what?" He shook her, snapping her head back so she was forced to look up into his face. "You'll what, Destiny? Slap me? Kiss me? For God's sake, make up your mind. Your eyes flash at me with fury but your lips quiver with passion. For the love of God, you're enough to drive a man out of his mind with confusion. Were I less of a gentleman I'd haul your pretty little ass to my cabin and spend the remainder of the afternoon between your legs. And don't think for a minute that you wouldn't enjoy it."

She gasped and blinked.

He dragged her closer, against his body, his fingers digging so hard into her pale skin her arms burned with numbness. Yet she could not move or speak. She could not take her eyes from his features, which seemed not so much fearsome as burning with a desire that made her legs turn to water.

His voice dropping, growing husky, his lips curling as he

lifted her to her tiptoes and tilted his mouth over hers, he murmured, "You'd enjoy my lovemaking, Lady Destiny, because, regardless of your ladylike manners and the veil of naivete you wear for the world, we both know that beneath that veneer is a woman who needs a man to fulfill her emotionally and physically. You're the sort of woman who, having once had a man, is going to wake up nights sweating and aching for him again. Don't deny it. Don't look at me with indignation. As a child you were raised in a country with a people who embrace their sexuality and believe their bodies are temples of pleasure. I see it every time you look at me or one of my men. Those eyes peering out from under lazy lashes. The way you part your lips . . . like now. If I kissed you, you'd slap my face. If I dragged you to my cabin, you'd fight me all the way. But the instant I was inside you, sweetheart, you'd turn into a siren."

"Monster" was all she could utter, her throat dry. "I would rather throw myself to sharks than fornicate with you."

He looked as if he might strike her.

"Cap'n!" Fritz yelled from his perch on the main spar. "We've company, sir. A ship on our stern, full rigged and coming fast."

The captain briefly closed his eyes. Still, he did not release her as he shouted, "What is she?"

"Looks like a clipper, sir."

After what felt like an eternity, he dropped Destiny to her feet and glared at her another moment before heading for the main spar. Collecting her strength, she called after him, "Is it Dunleavy, Captain?"

Stopping abruptly, he partially turned and gave her a flat, cold smile. "Perhaps. It seems now comes the true test, Lady Destiny. If, as you and Diana continue to despair, I truly am a Dunleavy disciple, now is the time I would furl sails and happily hand you over to the bastard— get you gone off my ship before you provoke my crew to mutiny."

Turning on his heels, pulling off his coat, and tossing it

to the deck, he crawled up the mast like a cat up a tree, joining Fritz on the long spar, where he easily balanced, grabbed the glass, and focused on the speck on the horizon.

"I'd wager me willie on that being Trevor's clipper," Fritz shouted. "Aside from you, Cap, there ain't another bastard on the high seas wot can manage a clipper like that. Jesus, look at her come. He's seen us, all right."

The captain slammed the glass against the mast and cursed. He looked down at Destiny, who stood shielding the sun from her eyes with her hand and watching him. He shimmied down the pole, hit the deck running, and yelled, "Hard aport, Connie, and into the storm."

"Aye, Cap'n," Connie yelled.

"Get the lady below!" He grabbed Destiny's arm and forced her toward the companionway, where Paolo waited, his expression disturbed.

"Are you daft?" Paolo shouted. "Sail into *that* storm? We'll be lucky to get out of that bugger with our keel in one piece."

"Trevor might jump feetfirst into hell, but he won't follow me into that." He pointed to the black, boiling horizon. "I happen to know he never cared for lightning."

"And I don't bloody well care for drowning," Paolo declared, following Destiny into the dark below.

❧ 12 ❧

The worth of a sentiment lies in the sacrifices men
will make for its sake. All ideals are built on the
ground of solid achievement, which in a given profession creates in the course of time a certain tradi-
tion, or in other words, a standard of conduct.

—JOSEPH CONRAD

The calm before the storm settled into every seam of the
ship as the *Pretender* hauled aport and drove as fast as possible toward the tempest. The distant clipper drew closer,
and Jason knew it was only a matter of time before the
sleek ship caught up to them. The *Pretender*'s only chance
was for him to bury her in yonder storm and pray the wind
and waves didn't send them under.

Jason oversaw his scrambling crew from the quarterdeck, Connie at his side. "The ladies are secured?" he
asked.

"Aye, Cap'n. Yer daughter is in safe hands. The women
are cluckin' over her like mother hens." Connie watched
the play of lightning on the horizon growing closer by the
minute. "She's a bad one for sure. But we both know
there's no better crew than this one to get us through it. Besides, our chances of weathering that bloody tempest are
better than Destiny's chances at Dunleavy's hands."

"And if I'm wrong, Connie? If her father *has* turned on
the Crown, if he *has* instigated mutiny with Sahib? . . ."

"You'll handle it, sir. Y' always have."

"Aye, Connie, but I've never been personally involved in the matter, have I?"

"No, sir. It's all a real mess, sir. No doubt about it. But we've all come to understand yer feelin's the last weeks. There ain't a one of us, aside from Mallet, who ain't fallen a little in love with her . . . and Diana. No way are we gonna let Dunleavy get his hands on her."

Jason took a weary breath and said, more to himself than to Connie, "She'll never excuse me—not for any of it—so what does it matter?"

"If you believed that, sir, you wouldn't be sailin' into that witch's brew. As yer father often said, if it's worth fightin' for it's worth dyin' for."

Jason frowned. "Knowing my father, I doubt he was talking about a woman."

Murky clouds crawled across the sun and daylight turned as green as bottle glass. The sails fell limp and the silence grew heavy. The crew faced the coming storm, their eyes fixed on the boil of clouds and water rising up like a leviathan to turn the sea and sky into a green frothing wall.

The roar began.

"Jesus," Jason whispered. Grabbing the quarterdeck rail, he raised his voice to be heard over the escalating noise. "Get below and secure the women. Strap Jenette to the berth. You know the routine, Connie."

"Aye, aye, sir."

As Connie sprang for the companionway, Jason shouted to the crew, "Drop the jibs and be quick about it. Lower the fore and main royals and address the top gallants. Down the shrouds and sprit sails and furl the mizzens. *Now!*"

The sudden wind took the square sails aback, slamming them against their masts and heaving the bow into the air. Jason grabbed for the wheel as the deck disappeared beneath him and the wind careened through the masts and spars, snapping taut the riggings and ropes, making the furling of the sails next to impossible. The men's shouts became lost in the growl and howl of the winds and the slash of rain that drove like knives into their skin.

The timbers groaned from the impact. The ship shuddered and heaved in the intense green darkness that was interrupted only by the lightning that danced dangerously close to the mastheads.

Jason clawed across the quarterdeck and tried to find his men among the melee. He glimpsed Fritz and Gabriel fighting with the mizzen topsail. Beyond them Connie struggled to keep his footing as a wave surged over the poop deck and drove like a battering ram into his chest.

"Man overboard!" came a shout.

Jason climbed to his feet and was driven hard against the foremast. He grabbed for a rope and tied it about his waist. He ran to the rail in time to see Paolo disappear beneath the waves.

"He's gone!" Zelie shouted.

Jason tied one end of the rope to the rail.

"Captain!" cried a female voice, and Jason looked around to see Destiny, her arms outstretched to him as she struggled with Franz, who tried to force her back down the companionway. "Don't do it!" she shouted.

Fritz grabbed him and Jason shoved him away, climbed over the rail, and dove into the water.

Hour after hour the storm, raged. It battered the ship as if it were flotsam.

Diana crouched in a corner of the cabin, hugging herself, shaking, covering her ears each time the force of water slammed into the hull and the pitch in the seams sprinkled like fairy dust over her shoulders.

Destiny huddled on the berth, her arms wrapped around Jenette. The child lay surprisingly quiet with her head on Destiny's shoulder and her china doll clutched to her little breast. She whimpered occasionally, when the ship pitched and felt as if it were a horse rearing. They held their breath, eyes squeezed closed and bodies braced for the impact, certain each time that the ship would keel up and they would plummet like a stone to the bottom of the ocean.

She tried not to think of what was taking place on deck—of the men fighting desperately to save the ship and themselves. Still, the image of the captain preparing to go overboard to rescue one of his crew kept rising up to terrify her as greatly as it had when she stumbled up the companionway to find him tying a rope around his waist.

What if he died?

Please, God, don't let him die.

The door sprang open and a churning deluge of water rushed into the cabin, carrying with it parcels and articles, boots and clothes that had been stacked about the room. Diana screamed and clamored atop the chest of drawers, crouching and shivering. "Oh God, we're going to—"

"Enough, Diana!" Destiny shouted, drawing the child closer and covering the little girl's ears with her hands.

The ship rolled.

"I refuse to drown in this detestable little hole!" Diana cried as she waded through the shin-deep water for the door.

Destiny ran after her, stumbling and slipping, caught her aunt, and flung her back.

Diana sprawled backward in the water and came up gasping, her eyes wild with fear and fury and her hair covered in seaweed. "For all we know the entire crew might have been washed overboard!" she screamed.

Her aunt was right, of course. Hours had passed since they had last heard a human voice amid the shrieking wind and battering waves. "Stay with the child!" she shouted at Diana, then turned for the door.

After struggling for what felt like an eternity, Destiny clawed her way up the companionway amid rushes of water that threatened to drown her. At last, shielding her face against the driving rain, she searched the dark deck for any sign of the crew, her panic rising. Then as lightning splintered the blackness she saw the shapes of men scrambling for a foothold amid the rain and wind. With a sinking sense of despair she wondered about the captain's whereabouts before returning to her cabin.

Destiny awoke to the sound of utter silence, darkness, and stillness. Exhausted, she rolled from the berth and stumbled and swayed in the complete blackness until she could retain her equilibrium enough to stand. Her body hurt. Her throat felt raw from the seawater she had swallowed. She clawed her way along the wall until she reached the door. A hundred images bombarded her mind—foolish images, like discovering that she, Diana, and Jenette were the only survivors. Her hands and feet slipped in the muck as she struggled to stand, then she made her way along the companion, her fears alleviated by the solitary lamp burning from a hook on the wall. Obviously someone was alive. But who? She stepped over seaweed and dead fish, her bare feet sinking inches into the sand that had settled like a carpet on the floor.

The night was windless, the sky shockingly clear and studded with endless stars. The sea, reflecting the night light, looked as eerily calm as a mill pond. Here and there a lantern burned, illuminating the decks cluttered with broken spars and shredded sails and lines that were tangled like old fish net. The *Pretender*'s crew lay sleeping among the litter, their clothes as tattered as the sails and as filthy as the decks. Were it not for an occasional moan, Destiny might have believed them all to be dead.

"This is all the women's fault," came a voice vibrating in anger. "You've sacrificed this ship, not to mention the lives of our men, all because you've let yerself go soft on the silly bitch."

"Stand down, Mr. Mallet. In case you haven't noticed, I'm not in the mood to listen to your opinion on my actions as captain of this vessel. Nor are my personal feelings any business of yours. I'll be happy to supply you with a gig should you desire to leave."

Hearing the captain's voice, Destiny nearly sank to the floor in relief.

"In case you ain't looked, sir, there ain't a bloody gig or a long boat to be found on this pitiful ship. They're gone, Cap'n, right out there with Paolo and Gabriel. And I'm here to tell you . . . *sir,* that if ya think this little stunt will put off Dunleavy for long y've gone daft as a loon."

Destiny hid until Mallet walked away, her emotions swinging like a pendulum, distressed to hear of Paolo's and Gabriel's deaths then elated that the captain had survived.

The captain sat on the transom, elbows on his knees and gaze fixed on the horizon. She moved up behind him. The need to reach out to him, to comfort him, felt disquietingly powerful.

"Captain?"

He stiffened and stood, his back to her. He walked away.

"I feel horribly responsible for all of this," she called out.

"Don't," he replied.

"Paolo and Gabriel were very kind to me. I had come to like them very much."

"They were good men. And good friends." He gripped the deck rail with a spasm of emotion, then drew back his shoulders and steadied his voice. "Were they afraid of risk they wouldn't have been aboard this ship in the first place."

"I suppose in your line of work, you grow accustomed to confronting death."

He laughed sharply and shook his head. Still, he did not face her. "You *must* think me a monster that I would have grown so calloused to losing a friend that I wouldn't grieve for him. Well, you're wrong. Aside from Connie, Paolo was my closest friend. I tried to help him. I tried. . . . One instant he was there, his hand in mine, and the next he was gone. It wasn't how he would have preferred to go."

Destiny noted his hand, heavily bound with bloody bandages. "Will you let me help you?" she asked softly, her eyes filling with tears.

"I want you to stay the hell away from me. Far away from me."

His words cut her severely, as did his tone. Weeks ago she would have declared good riddance to him and flounced away, relieved for any excuse not to share his company. Now, however, she could but stare at his broad back and wonder what odd bond had developed between them. To turn on him now felt as sore as her sorrow over Paolo and Gabriel.

"Why have you done this, Captain—taken on this mission to help my father and me? What are either of us to you other than strangers?" She moved toward him. He moved away, his back still to her. "I once thought that perhaps you were actually working for Dunleavy and this was all a trick. That you intended to use me to get at my father. Now . . . when I see how you've sacrificed so much, I only want to understand why."

His response sounded sardonic and cold as he turned to face her at last. "Perhaps Mr. Mallet is right. Perhaps I'm simply going soft. Then again, men like me don't go soft, do they?"

He moved toward her, slowly, stalking, his presence growing more menacing the closer he came. The desire to flee rushed through her, but she set her heels, instinctively knowing that if she were to run from him now the thin thread of patience holding his temper in check would snap. Yet, her traitorous body trembled as he circled her, not quite touching her, but so near the heat of him brushed her damp, chilled skin, igniting an unnerving burst of feelings in the pit of her stomach. Her breath left her, and for an instant she experienced again the disturbing sensations that had intoxicated her that very afternoon as she buried her head against his shoulder and drank in his presence—surprisingly familiar sensations that belonged to an infatuated virgin in a forest glade.

Bending near her ear, he whispered, "Men like me couldn't possibly look into a woman's eyes and fall in love, could we, Lady Chesterfield? Because a soldier capable of cutting a man's throat in his sleep couldn't possibly be capable of tenderness." He slid his cool fingers around her throat, pressed them into her skin, molding her like soft clay as he lowered his mouth closer to hers. "Such a man couldn't possibly have a conscience or give a damn if his friend dies. He couldn't possibly be moved by a child's laughter or tears. He couldn't possibly ache to feel that child's arms around his neck or desire with every fiber of his being to sing her to sleep at night. A soldier couldn't possibly grow weary of the war and want nothing more than to lay down his gun and spend the rest of his life basking in the warmth and security of a woman's arms."

"You're going to kiss me," she groaned, unable to look away from the predatory passion that burned in his shadow-washed face.

"Damned right I'm going to kiss you. I think you owe me that much."

One hand twisted into her hair, drawing her head back, ruthlessly bending her into his body as his arm slid around her waist, drawing her so close she could feel the hammering of his heart against hers. Fleetingly, she thought of resisting, but as his mouth came down on hers with a fierceness that robbed her of reason she could do nothing but swoon into his embrace, hopelessly lost to the pressure of his wet mouth prying her lips open, of his tongue sliding into her mouth, stroking, thrusting into and out of her until she heard herself whimper, felt her lips kiss him back, her arms slide around his shoulders and twist into his sea-wet shirt.

"That's my girl," he breathed into her ear; tender words, warm words, turning her world into a haze of memories that spiraled into a heat that settled between her legs. He pressed her back against the mast, pinned her there with his body, which had grown shamelessly hard and aching and shaking, and with both hands drew her blouse up, exposing her breasts to the starlight. "That's my girl," he repeated, bending to take her nipple into his mouth while his hand slid under her skirt and found the pulsating center of her being.

No protest. Like one impaled upon the mast she could but hang there, her body supported by his, her universe centered on his hand between her legs and his tongue on her breasts, her mind saying over and over, *You owe him. You owe him. You . . . want him because . . .* because oh, God, she could almost imagine she was back in the glade allowing a stranger to make her heady with pleasure—he felt the same and smelled the same and—

A sound escaped him. His hands twisted in her clothes. His teeth bared. He grabbed her hand and slid it down over the rigid rise in his breeches. "See what you do to me? Feel what you do to me. If you know what's good for you you'll get the hell back to your cabin now. Because if you don't I'm going to lay you on this deck and show you what it means to be made love to by a man with no scruples."

Shoving her aside, he turned his back and walked away, leaving Destiny to stare after him, her body throbbing like a raw nerve.

A good north wind drove them toward Tenerife, and so far there had been no further signs of Dunleavy's ship. Destiny rarely saw the captain after their heated confrontation on the quarterdeck. She supposed she should be thankful, but she wasn't. Although he had treated her little better than some wharfside doxy, she had been forced to acknowledge to herself that she had responded to him in a shameful manner. Obviously he was correct about her character. No doubt her being raised with a people who thought their bodies "temples of pleasure" had had a greater impact on her than she had been willing to admit, even to herself.

During the days he turned the helm over to Connie and only surfaced at night, long after she, Diana, and Jenette turned in to their berths. Occasionally she thought she heard him pacing. His voice drifted to her from the shadows like some ghost from the past, rousing a growing disquietude in her that made her toss and turn and avoid sleep because each time she slept she would awaken with the image of his intense face nagging at her consciousness, and the memory of his hands on her body making her ache. And not to forget his kiss. Thinking about it would make her pace her cabin, fighting the insane desire to search him out for no other reason than to satisfy her mounting need to share his company, to understand his motives and emotions, to discover why the moment he pressed his lips upon hers she had been electrified by a familiarity that had driven her to behave beyond good reason.

She dreamt repeatedly of awakening to discover herself alone on a deserted island, screaming for the captain at the top of her voice, only to have him rise from the sea and taunt her with his sardonic smile that both intrigued and intimidated. As he stood in the distance and grinned, his facade began to melt like warm wax and run in sparkling rivulets into the water. The man who stood before her was not the captain at all, but Jason Batson, the lover she had so shamelessly seduced in the glade.

Oh, to see land again. To feel it under her feet. Perhaps then she could think more clearly—focus again on the reasons why she was attempting this arduous journey: to find her father, and save him if necessary, if not from Dunleavy, then from himself. No doubt the days upon days of living on the tipping, rolling ship was beginning to take its toll on her. Her bones ached and Mallet and Diana's food was becoming less and less appealing. She simply could not smell it any longer without becoming ill.

❧ 13 ❧

He is like a lover or an outlaw who wraps up his message in a serenade, which is nonsense to the sentinel, but salvation to the ear for which it is meant.

—RALPH WALDO EMERSON, "Past and Present"

The **Pretender** *docked on a* bright, clear morning in Santa Cruz de Tenerife. While most of the crew stayed aboard, seeing to the stocking of supplies and the repairs from the storm, Franz, Fritz, Zelie, and the elusive captain, a rifle slung from his shoulder by a wide strap and a gun on his hip, escorted Destiny and Diana, with Jenette pulled along by one hand, into the capital's rambling bazaar. Stalls were heaped high with everything from clothing, flowers, and fruit to imported goods from as far away as China. The men kept enough distance to allow the women privacy, but never so far as to let them out of their sight. The captain swigged liquor from a bottle and watched them with a less than tolerant expression. Obviously he and his men weren't pleased that their shore leave was being wasted on chaperoning women with a desperate hunger to shop.

As Diana discouraged Jenette's interest in a crate of mangy, yowling puppies, she addressed Destiny quietly. "The captain rarely takes his eyes off of you these days, Des. But I suspect that you've noticed already. Has something transpired between you that I should know about?"

Destiny smiled at the girl who waved a brightly colored blouse at her. She ran her hands over the light material and sighed, doing her best to ignore the captain's presence. "The captain and I have formed a sort of truce, I suppose."

"Truce? Is that what you call the look he's giving you right now?"

"Don't be silly. The man hasn't spoken to me since the night of the storm." Recalling their intimate encounter, she flashed a look at the captain, who appeared to be lost in conversation with a pretty black-haired girl. Frowning slightly, she added, "One would think I had the plague the way he avoids me."

"Speaking of plague . . ." Diana touched Destiny's forehead, her eyes concerned. "You haven't looked well, Des. Your color isn't healthy. I think while we're in Tenerife we should have a doctor see you. Just to be on the safe side."

Destiny shook her head, forcing her gaze away from the captain, who was apparently more interested in flirting with the native beauties than in safeguarding two women and a child. She tried to focus on the young woman extending an armful of clothes to her. Not easy, she discovered. Her attention returned to the captain and the image he made, so casually moving among the people, standing nearly a head taller than those around him, his weapons enhancing the severity of his appearance. There was something so very odd about him. Disturbing. Confusing. Like now, she thought, as he turned his back to her momentarily to speak to Zelie: broad shoulders made all the broader by the fine linen shirt he wore tucked into his snug, fawn-colored breeches. Well-worn knee boots. *Riding boots*. She could almost imagine—

"Destiny!" As Diana grabbed her, Destiny blinked and looked into her aunt's disturbed face. "Are you all right, dear? You went pale as a sheet."

"I'm fine," she replied. "I simply haven't found my land legs yet. I'll be all right in another few hours."

"You've lost weight."

"From eating the food you and Hugo prepare, no doubt." She forced herself to smile. "Not to mention sweating in this unbearable heat." She regarded the island clothes enviously. They would suit her far better in this climate than the heavy dress she was wearing—the only dress she had packed in her haste to get away from Sheffield House. Alas, there was no money for clothes.

"Relax and enjoy yourself, Diana, and stop worrying about me. This place is like paradise. I daresay the next weeks will hardly be as serene and beautiful."

"Are you certain we shouldn't at least attempt to carry out our plans, Des? Find another way to India?" Diana spatted Jenette's hand as she grabbed a fruit from a basket. Too late. Jenette bit into the succulent fruit, laughing as pink juice dribbled through her rosy little lips and down her chin.

Again, Destiny looked toward the captain. The girl had placed a flower behind one of his ears. Zelie had joined in their animated conversation. "Positive," she heard herself reply. "We agreed that had the captain been involved with Dunleavy he certainly wouldn't have risked his ship and crew by sailing into that nightmarish storm."

"We also agreed not to trust them completely." Diana smiled her apology at the aggravated vendor and dropped a coin in his outstretched hand.

"You appear to be fairly trusting in Mr. LaTouche lately." Destiny laughed as Diana's face flushed and her chin squared. Holding a yellow blouse up to Diana's shoulders, Destiny teased, "This should win him over . . . as if it would take a blouse to do it. The man is positively smitten with you. I declare that if you smelled of something other than onions you would be hard-pressed to keep him away."

As Diana gasped, Destiny laughed again and tossed the blouse back to the smiling clerk. At the same moment a ragtag group of men began to beat on drums and dance down the crowded street. Some waved bright-colored streamers from their wrists, inciting many of the vendors to shout their approval and join in the dancing, their bodies moving sensuously with the rhythm.

Her foot tapping and her hips slightly swaying with the beat, Destiny picked up a broad-brim straw hat with a pale blue ribbon. She put it on, tying the ribbon in a bow under her chin. She then strolled to a table stacked high with folded skirts in every imaginable color. Pink caught her eye. Holding the skirt up to her waist, she spun around, laughing as the weightless fabric billowed lightly in the breeze. Memories of her childhood came rushing back: moments of freedom, wildness, dancing, laughing, running barefoot as hard as she could through sun-warmed sand, spinning and spinning until she became so dizzy she could hardly stand up. Like now.

The world tipped and swayed, flushing her with heat and breathlessness. She stumbled and did her best to focus on the faces surrounding her—all laughing, singing, moving like puppets up and down and from side to side, some encouraging her to join them.

"Come, come dance with us, pretty lady!"

Suddenly she was swept up in their motions, twirled from one to another, the hat flying from her head to the ground. Her hair fell from their combs and over her shoulders, spilling into her eyes while she tried to stop the momentum and explain to the revelers that she could no longer find her legs and feet—

"Diana!" she cried as she clutched the shoulders of a droopy old man with long gray hair and a beard to his belly. Her eyes searched frantically for her aunt and Jenette, then for the captain. Where was the captain and why was he allowing her to be swept away in this frantic tide? She saw him then, shoving his way through the crowd, his eyes focused like a hawk's on hers and snapping with their usual anger; Fritz and Zelie were behind him—

She could not stop her fall. Down, down she floated, the sudden dizziness and weakness turning her knees to water. She hit the ground hard, her head resting on the cobbles while the drums continued to beat deep, deep inside her.

Reaching out her hand, she cried, "Captain, help—"

He bent over her, pushing his rifle aside, and gently

touched her face. He shouted something to Zelie, who whistled to the others.

"I fear I'm fainting," she declared, clutching his shirt-front, unable to take her eyes from his features, as if they were some sort of lifeline that would keep her from dissolving into blackness. How very queer that his once frightening facade would, in that moment, bring her assurance.

As the night shadows grew long, the silent crew, scattered around the ship's deck, watched Jason pace. For the last hour Tenerife's only English-speaking doctor had been below with Destiny and Diana. Twice Jason had banged on Destiny's cabin door, demanding to know what the blazes was going on with her. Why had she fainted? If she was ill he had every right to know . . . as captain of the *Pretender*. There would be critical decisions to make. To remain in Tenerife through the night would be disastrous. While the storm had bought the ship and crew enough time to restock supplies before shoving off for Cape Town, were they forced to remain docked due to Destiny's illness there would be no hope of escaping Dunleavy's plans.

"The lass will be fine," Connie said. "I'm certain the doctor will be up momentarily to declare that her only problem is the heat and a touch of exhaustion. That damned storm 'bout took the wind out of all our sails."

"Aye," the others agreed, nodding their heads. All but Hugo, who glared at Jason and sneered, "I tol' the lot of ya that there would be trouble with them women aboard. I come on this mission to fight, not play nursemaid to a buncha women and a brat." He spat on the deck. "Best thing could happen now is for the bitch to kick it. Dump the aunt and kid here in Tenerife and let us get on about our business."

Jason stared through the shadows at Hugo, wanting to kill him.

Connie stepped between them and slapped both hands down on Jason's shoulders. He stood eye to eye with

Jason, his anger at Hugo obvious as he spoke through thinned lips. "He's an ass. We all know it. But with Paolo and Gabriel gone we need him." Lowering his voice so only Jason could hear him, he added, "I'll happily kill him for y', Cap, when the time comes. But now ain't the time. If y' want to help Fontaine and his daughter we're gonna need every hand we've got." More quietly still, he added, "I know what yer feelin', Jay. About the girl and all. We're all worried."

At last the physician appeared, followed by Diana, whose face looked drawn and ashen. She wrung her hands and bit her lip. Her eyes appeared glassy, and her chin trembled.

Shoving Connie aside, Jason joined them. He glared down at Diana, waiting for an explanation of Destiny's illness. She, however, avoided looking at him directly, so he turned on the physician. He took hold of the old man's coat front with both fists and raised him to his toes. "What's wrong with her?" he said through his teeth.

"Who the devil are you, sir?" the physician replied in a stunned, shaky voice.

"I'm the captain of this ship and I want to know what's wrong with the young lady."

Again, Connie stepped up and pried Jason's hands from the physician's coat. "He gets a bit testy when it comes to the welfare of his passengers."

"Apparently." The physician stepped away and smoothed his coat. Replacing the monocle on his right eye, he turned to Diana. "As the young woman's aunt, you should be aware of what a journey like this could mean to your niece, healthwise, that is. I advise that she remain in Tenerife at least a fortnight, if not longer, to give her enough time to consider the consequences should she decide to continue to Cawnpore. Obviously, she's been through a great deal, what with being widowed and all. Very tragic. Very sad, their being married so briefly. Perhaps this event will rally her somewhat."

"What event?" Jason demanded, first to Diana, then

again to the doctor, who stared at him as if he were addled. "Dammit, answer me, one of you. What event?"

"She's with child," Diana replied softly, reluctantly lifting her gaze to Jason's as she attempted a brave face. "My dear niece is going to have a baby."

Connie cleared his throat and walked away.

Jason remained speechless, rooted to the deck as Diana walked the doctor to the gangplank. His brain felt numb. But for the hot spot of emotion burning in his chest his entire body might have turned to wood.

A baby.

His baby.

Her baby.

Their baby.

A stranger in a glade's baby.

Jason Batson's baby.

The baby belonging to a man whose existence Destiny cursed.

A liar's baby. A fraud's baby.

A cold-blooded killer's baby.

He took a deep breath and closed his eyes. In the distance Connie shouted for the crew to make ready to shove off, followed by the scrambling of feet and the singing of spar riggings. At last, he made his feet move, slowly, down the companionway and into the dimly lit corridor, to her room where the door was closed, muffling the sound of her crying. For a long while he stood in the shadows, his body sweating, his face stinging from the grotesque mask scratching at his skin. Not for the first time he wondered what would happen if he ripped the damn thing off and presented himself to Destiny—not now, of course, but sometime. Eventually. *Maybe.* When the time was right, and that was not now.

The door wasn't locked. It swung open easily, revealing Destiny curled up on her bunk, lamplight spilling over her shoulders as she wept into her pillow.

Her dark hair a tumble of wild waves around her white face, she lifted her head. Her big eyes regarded him a long moment without blinking. "What do you want?" she asked, her voice breaking as she tried desperately to sound brave.

You, he thought.

Stepping into the cabin, he closed the door behind him. Female scents washed over him: toilet water and soap. Skin. Hair. Sex. *Her* sex. Christ, he couldn't breathe.

"Well?" she cried, her hands clenching around the pillow as she dragged it into her lap. "Surely you've seen an expectant woman before, Captain. Why do you stare at me so?"

Because you're beautiful, he thought, *and the baby inside of you is mine. And I'm too bloody confused and afraid to tell you.* Christ, he had never been afraid of anything in his life, yet this breath of a woman eviscerated him with a tilt of her chin and a flash of her eyes.

"Have you come here to gloat?" Her voice rose to a dangerously hysterical pitch.

"No," he said gently, shaking his head.

"Then why are you here?"

He shrugged. "To . . . help."

"Help?" Tears streamed down her cheeks, and she began to laugh, a dry sound that made her voice husky. "How do you propose to help me, Captain? Toss me overboard? That, of course, would help me a great deal."

"You don't mean that. I've seen you with Jenette. You'll make a wonderful mother."

"I'm penniless. Homeless. On my way to a country that could be caught up in rebellion by the time we get there. My father, the only human being aside from Diana who would give a damn about me and this child, might be dead already."

Jason moved a chair to Destiny's bedside and sat in it, elbows on his knees as he stared at his hands. Sweat beaded under his clothes. Any moment he might explode with frustration . . . and then what?

"I suppose it's nothing more than I deserve," she said with less emotion. Sinking back against the wall and hugging the pillow against her breasts, she fixed her gaze on the lamp, whose flame reflected like small fires in her damp green eyes. "Uncle James always warned me that eventually my recklessness would catch up to me. That I would be forced to contend with the consequences of my actions. I'm just sorry that a child will be forced to suffer over my stupidity."

"I doubt a child would ever suffer with you as its mother."

The cabin became quiet, but for the creak and groan of the wood surrounding them. The ship rocked side to side as the breeze caught the sails and moved the vessel out to sea.

With a little groan, Destiny pressed one hand upon her lips. "I'm going to be ill again."

Jason grabbed the chamber pot. As Destiny rolled onto her knees, he wrapped one arm around her and held the bowl under her face. She wretched and wretched, her body becoming sweaty from the exertion, and weak. She sagged against him when it was over and began to cry again. He pulled a kerchief from his breeches pocket and blotted her cheeks with it. The hair at her temples had grown damp. Her eyes were glassy. She stared up at him with a weary expression.

"I've become a royal pain in the derriere, haven't I, Captain? No doubt you're regretting your decision to help me."

He grinned and shrugged and with one finger nudged a tendril of hair from her forehead.

"I have something to confess," she said. "I may have killed the child's father. You see, when I found him out I was so angry I bashed his head with a rock and left him bleeding in the glade. I didn't mean to kill him, of course. But what am I to tell the child someday? How will I ever look at him without thinking I may have killed his father?"

"I think you needn't worry about it. I'm certain the bastard is fine. I'm equally certain that he deserved the bashing. Perhaps it knocked some sense into him."

"You must think me a dreadful person, sir."

"No. How could I think that?"

"Why shouldn't you, especially after the other night. Our meeting after the storm. I acted like a . . . a doxy. My only excuse is that I felt sorry for you, for your loss."

"You're quite the little martyr, aren't you?" He tossed his kerchief into her lap. "Sorry, sweetheart, but I don't believe it. A man knows when a woman enjoys his lovemaking. And you enjoyed it. A lot."

Anger flashed across her features, then as quickly was gone. She nodded sadly. "Yes, I did. Obviously I can't control my base urges or I wouldn't be in this predicament now. But for a moment you reminded me of . . . the way you touched me, caressed me. At least you've been honest with me. You desire me for no other reason than I'm a woman and you're a man too long without a woman. I can understand now why men and women find such pleasure in momentary trysts. Their urges can be assuaged while their hearts are left intact. Tell me, Captain, have you ever been in love?"

The lamp swayed along with the ship, back and forth, side to side, scattering streaks of light over the floor and on the walls. He recalled her urges; *their* urges that night under the stars. He'd been full of fury over his decision to sail into the storm. Sorrow over Paolo's and Gabriel's deaths had raked at his bruised insides. He'd gone at her like an animal, wanting to punish her for turning him into the sort of man who could so easily weaken. Ah, yes, that's exactly what she had done to him since the first moment he'd seen her. She had weakened him. Obliterated his reason. But love? Just what the devil was love anyway?

"I . . . don't know," he finally answered.

"You would know, of course, if you were in love. Love makes one do irrational things. It robs one of good judgment. Love . . . hurts. I don't recommend it."

Diana entered the cabin, startled to find the captain sitting on the bed with Destiny, one arm around her, her head resting lightly on his shoulder. "Sir, I think you should

leave. My niece and I have a great deal to discuss. There
are plans to be made, of course, and—"

"He can stay, Diana," Destiny stated in a surprisingly
firm tone. "He's well aware that Lord Chesterfield isn't the
child's father."

Diana dropped into the chair near the bed. Her countenance appeared as colorless as Destiny's as she looked
from the captain back to her niece. "Then I was right.
There *is* something between the two of you."

"There's nothing between us, Diana." Destiny pulled
away from him, sinking again into her bed.

"True, Captain?" Diana stabbed him with a look that
didn't falter. "Or is my niece being far too naive again?
Forgive me if I seem intense. But she obviously has a history of being swept off her feet by men who show her the
slightest bit of attention."

"Diana!" Destiny cried. "What an awful thing to say."

Diana jumped up and began to pace. "I'm sorry. Dreadfully sorry, Des. But I won't see you used and hurt again.
I'm simply so angry I can't think straight. That unthinking,
irresponsible bastard who did this to you. I fully intend to
hunt him down when we return to England and shoot him
myself. I'll have him arrested. . . . I have it! What think
you of this, Des? Since we shan't return to England for
some time, say, two or three years or longer, we'll simply
declare the child Chesterfield's—"

Jason stood suddenly, causing Diana to jump in alarm
and snap her mouth shut. Something in his look made her
cautiously back away. "Chesterfield's," he repeated in so
caustic a voice Diana shrank into a corner. "Over my dead
body. I'll marry Destiny myself before I allow that to happen."

Diana frowned.

"I beg your pardon?" Destiny again shifted to her knees,
still clutching the pillow, her lips parted, her cheeks
slightly blooming with color.

Diana panicked. "Destiny! You wouldn't dare—"

"Captain?" Destiny tipped her head to one side, her big

eyes fixed and wide as she watched his response. "Have you just proposed marriage to me?"

Had he? Jason took a deep breath and slowly released it. "So it would seem."

Stepping between them, Diana shook her head at Jason. "She's hysterical. She's desperate and frightened. Let's not forget ill. I understand this sort of sickness makes women incapable of sound reason. Obviously, or she wouldn't entertain such an offer from . . ."

"A man such as me?" He gave her a flat smile that made Diana flinch.

"What sort of existence would she have married to a man whose life is spent fighting in foreign wars? Whose home is a creaky ship with a hold full of weapons?"

"Correct me if I'm wrong, but as I recall, marriage to Chesterfield came with several estates and, once the old man dies, a king's fortune in inheritance. Position and wealth hardly bought Destiny happiness and security. And let's not forget your marriage to Shaftesbury. You're hardly in a position to throw stones, madam. If power and money were all it took to assure stability, you'd hardly be taking up space on *my* ship, now, would you?"

Diana gasped, then slapped his face.

Destiny leapt out of bed and shouldered her way between them. "Stop it, please! 'Tis my life and my mistakes, and . . ."

Her knees gave, and as she sank toward the floor in a faint, Jason grabbed her, swept her up, and returned her to the bed. Diana damped a cloth and placed it on Destiny's brow. Only then did she turn on Jason again, declaring in a quieter voice, "I don't doubt that you have a fondness for my niece, sir. But if you're truly capable of genuine affection, then you'll want what's best for Destiny. That's not marriage to a man whose accomplishments amount to little more than killing for money."

"You're a bitch," he said.

"Perhaps. But I only want what's best for my niece, Captain."

"Is that why you encouraged her marriage to Chester-field? Hmm?"

"You're despicably cruel, sir."

"At least you and I have *that* in common, Diana."

He left the room before he allowed his boiling anger to get the better of him. Diana was simply attempting to protect her niece; that did not mean, however, that her verbal barbs would not entice him to retaliate in a manner that he would ultimately regret.

The night wind felt hot against his sweating flesh as Jason walked the deck. He removed his shirt, peeled the disguise piece by piece from his face, then dragged off the coarse wig. Throwing it all into his shirt and bundling it up, he thought of hurling the parcel into the sea.

"I wouldn't if I's you." Connie moved out of the shadows, a bottle of rum in one big hand. "I'm thinkin' now ain't the time for too much honesty. Least, not while the lass is feelin' poorly. No tellin' how the truth would affect her."

Jason snatched the bottle from Connie and proceeded to drink.

"Want to talk about it, Cap?"

"Diana suggested that she pass the child off as Chester-field's."

Connie made an amused noise in his throat. "I'm fairly certain you didn't approve."

"I declared myself."

Removing the bottle from Jason's hand, Connie drank, then handed it back. "Meanin'?"

"I told her I would marry her myself before I allowed her to pass the child off as Chesterfield's."

"Did she accept?"

"Not exactly. I don't think so. At least not before Diana began her barrage of insults, pointing out that a killer like myself isn't exactly husband material." Jason drank again, deeply, and cocked a look at Connie. "If there are thoughts of romance with Diana rattling about your brain, I would forget it. Aside from being an asp, the woman continues to regard us as the devil's disciples."

"She ain't so bad once you get to know her."

"I'll take your word for it."

"So what are y' gonna do now?"

"Get drunk. Throw myself overboard."

"That won't help her or the baby." Connie watched soberly as Jason turned up the bottle and drank the dark rum as if it were water. "Once she gets over the shock of yer bein' Batson, she'll realize that it's best to forgive and forget when there's a child to think about. That's what matters most. Right?"

"Right. Damn if I'll commit the same mistakes I made with Michelle and Jenette."

"Different women. Different circumstances. Michelle used the kid to try and trap you. Destiny, on the other hand—"

"Wants no part of me."

The words hung in the humid air and scratched at his insides, along with the rum that was coiling like a hot snake in his gut. He leaned over the rail, closing his eyes as sea spray covered his face in a thin cool veil. He wished to blazes they were in India already. He felt the need for a good fight.

Destiny lay with her eyes closed, pretending sleep until Diana turned down the lantern and tiptoed from the cabin. Woozy, her stomach feeling as if she had just completed a succession of tumbles, she sat up, swallowed, and focused on the far wall until the undulations of dizziness settled in her head. Heavens, she was hungry. And thirsty. Her body shook. The cabin felt as small and stuffy as a coffin.

A tickling of fear curled in her breast as her mind raced through images of the upcoming months and years. Her father would protect her, of course, *if* he was alive. Compton Fontaine had never bowed to gossip or given a flipping fig about Society standards, which is why her mother had fallen in love with him. When he believed in something, or

someone, no one aside from God could change his mind.
Oh yes, her father would support her and the child . . . *if* he
was alive.

And if he wasn't . . . ?

How often had she daydreamed of holding a baby in her
arms? Now she would.

She groaned. The temptation to crawl back under the
sheets overwhelmed her. But she refused. Not yet. Too
much to think about and plan for. By the time she reached
India she would be . . . she calculated in her head . . . at
least three or four months along, depending of course on
what sort of winds they encountered. The captain was obviously more than adept at handling his ship. Therefore
there would be precious little time wasted in reaching
India.

The captain. She reluctantly smiled. A man whose name
she didn't even know had proposed marriage to her. He
was certainly a dichotomy. Like his face. Part of him was
feral, frightening, and ugly, scarred from the sins of his
past. The other was gentle, sad, and lonely. Perhaps regret-
ful of the actions of his past.

They had both made mistakes.

They were both alone.

She might come to care for him, eventually, should she
get to know him better. But how did one accomplish that?
He was wearisomely aloof, much to her exasperation, refusing to reveal the most minuscule information about
himself.

Still, if she allowed herself to be totally honest with herself she would have to admit that during those moments in
the last weeks when she *could* coerce conversation from
him, she found his company fulfilling and pleasant, which
had only served to pique her curiosity about him even
more and whet her imagination.

She listened closely to the footsteps moving up and
down the companion and overhead. Occasionally voices
came to her and she discovered herself closing her eyes, attempting to hear the captain among them.

Ridiculous. Obviously Diana had planted a seed of confusion in her mind. There was absolutely nothing between them. She did not become breathless when he looked at her. His nearness did not provoke desire.

Those moments in his arms had sprung from memories, pure and simple. His touch, his whispers had swept her back to a drizzly, grassy glade when she had succumbed to her naive fantasies and opened her arms to a stranger.

No stranger now, of course. His name was Jason Batson. He had put his child inside her. Even if she once believed she would someday be able to forget him and the well of feelings he had inspired in her that rainy day, that would now be impossible. He would be a part of her life forever.

. . . this heart, I know,
To be long lov'd was never fram'd;
But something in its depths doth glow
Too strange, too restless, too untamed.

—MATTHEW ARNOLD, "A Farewell"

She slept for days, rousing only long enough to eat. It didn't matter what, as long as it replenished her enough so she could lie down and sleep again without the terrible sickness churning up her throat. Occasionally she managed to open her drowsy eyes to see Diana sitting in a chair, her expression pensive and worried. Once, late, she awakened to discover the captain sitting there, his legs stretched out and crossed at the ankles, his long fingers laced over his stomach, his intense, unblinking gaze fixed on her. She watched him secretly, through the veil of her lowered lashes. It seemed he didn't move so much as a muscle. Then suddenly, and with a sigh, he leaned forward and, propping his elbows on his knees, buried his head in his hands. His broad shoulders rounded, as if burdened by the weight of the world. Somehow the image comforted her, and she fell back to sleep.

Perhaps it was the stillness that awoke her. While aboard the *Pretender* she had not felt such motionlessness since just before the onslaught of the deadly storm. The air felt suffocatingly hot. The usual creak and groan of the old wood surrounding her was absent.

The door burst open and Diana danced in. She had pinned her blond hair to the top of her head. The back of her skirt had been drawn up between her legs and tucked into a rope tied around her waist. This exposed her legs to above her knees. The usually white-as-lilies skin appeared seriously colored by the sun.

"Destiny!" she cried, throwing open her arms and rushing to the bed, where she grabbed Destiny in a bear hug. "You're awake finally. And look at you. There's color in your face. Are you feeling better?"

Destiny nodded and wondered what imposter had taken over her aunt's body. Surely this was not *her* Diana. The prim and proper Diana. The Diana who would normally swoon if so much as a flash of ankle were exposed.

"Are you hungry, dear? I hope so. I've spent hours fussing over chicken stuffed with some mushy pink fruit we picked up in Tenerife. I haven't a clue how it'll taste but it smells delicious. Of course Hugo is furious. He says real men don't eat such froufrou dishes. Men need boiled meat and potatoes. What a lot of poppycock, I told him. Men will eat anything you put in front of them as long as they're hungry enough."

"By the looks of your face, arms, and legs"—Destiny wagged her finger at Diana's exposed limbs—"I suspect you haven't spent the entire day fussing with chickens."

"I never knew how good the sun can feel on your body, Des. I positively tingle. Connie says with a touch of bronze on my cheeks my eyes appear bluer. Do they?" She batted her eyelashes and smiled.

"Connie?"

"Mr. LaTouche, of course. Des, I've had the grandest time of my life the last few days."

"While I've been lying here dying?"

"Yes." She nodded and smiled again. "But you weren't dying, dear. Your body is simply adjusting to the wee one.

It's quite normal, you see. Do you know that Connie has taught me how to fish. And how to play cards—"

"Cards?"

Diana giggled, and the shocking realization struck Destiny that her aunt was tipsy.

"You're popped," Destiny declared, sinking back onto the bed, not certain whether she should be struck with severe consternation or whether she should regard her aunt's behavior in amusement. "Positively popped." She smiled.

"Perhaps. Just a touch. The rum is smashingly potent. But smooth. Very smooth." She sniffed and twirled about on her tiptoes, dropped into the chair near the bed, and sighed. "I have a nip or two when we play cards."

"Do you play often with these men?"

"Three or four times a day."

"Oh, my." Destiny chewed her lower lip and tried not to laugh.

"You see, the winds have left us. Dead in the water, we are. Haven't had so much as a breath on us for three days. There's little to do but talk, and eat, and drink, and play cards, and drink . . . and drink some more."

"I take it your impression of the crew has changed somewhat?"

"They're as human as you or I, not including Hugo Mallet, of course." She shuddered. "Do you know that Connie has twelve brothers and sisters? Six in America. Three in Ireland. Two in Japan, and one in Brazil. His parents are still living. His father is a blacksmith. Connie sends his parents money twice a year. Isn't that sweet, Des?"

"How long have I been sleeping?"

"Days. I was growing numb with boredom, you see. I had to talk to *someone.* And once the wind died . . . well, everyone's been at loose ends, nothing to do. They invited me to join in their games and conversations—all except the captain, of course. He continues to glare at me as if I'm inhuman."

"No doubt."

"He has little to say to anyone aside from Jenette. Oh,

yes." Diana's brow knitted as she nodded. "The child has obviously gotten over her fear of him. She hangs on his leg like a monkey on a branch."

"How does he treat the child?"

Diana shrugged. "Fondly. Sweetly, actually. Jenette makes him laugh."

"Interesting," Destiny said thoughtfully; the mental image of the captain with Jenette did odd things to her heart.

"Will you join us for dinner, Des? I've baked my first bread. That despicable Hugo predicts it'll fail miserably. I should like your support, I think."

"You mean eat it even if it's dreadful?"

Diana made a pitiful face.

Destiny sighed. "Very well. As hungry as I'm feeling, I suppose that won't be so unreasonable a request."

Diana started for the door, stopped, and turned again, her expression a mixture of exasperation and capitulation. "There are some things for you in my cabin. They were delivered to the ship just before we sailed from Tenerife. Were the circumstances different I wouldn't have allowed it, of course. 'Twould not have been proper. But considering your condition I doubt that you'll want to be wearing that awful heavy dress for much longer. Gifts, niece. From the captain."

Zelie and Franz sat at a table under a lamp on deck, their attention focused on their chess game. When Jason joined them, they jumped up and walked away, leaving him staring after them, the half empty rum bottle in his hand. He dropped into Zelie's chair and stared down at the pieces that swam before his eyes.

"Good evening, Captain."

He looked up.

Destiny stood at the edge of the lamp glow, wearing the blue blouse and pink skirt he had purchased during her sojourn to the bazaar. The flimsy cloth fell so softly over her body her every curve was accentuated. She was barefoot. Her dark hair spilled like a soft cloud over her shoulders.

"Am I disturbing you?" she asked.

Jason stood, knocking the table and upsetting the pieces. "No." He shook his head and swallowed, the mind-numbing desire that had caused him to act so stupidly in the glade washing over him as he looked her up and down, noting that the light from the lamp turned her skirt diaphanous. He could easily see the shape of her legs all the way to her—

"Do you like the clothes, Captain?"

"What?"

"The clothes." She spun and the skirt lifted like a filmy cloud to her knees.

"Very pretty," he said in a tight voice.

"I'm astounded by your generosity. Had I known that you would indulge my every fancy I would have taken greater care not to show such enthusiasm while at the bazaar." In a sterner voice, she added, "Accepting such gifts, as you know, is hardly proper of me."

"Decorum rarely has its place at sea, madam. Especially under the circumstances. Where you're going that bleak little dress you've been wearing will hardly serve you comfortably."

"Do you mind if I join you?" she asked.

Frowning, he glanced at his rum bottle, then extended it to her.

Destiny laughed and took the bottle. "I meant the game, sir, but I don't mind a nip as well. I understand from Diana that it's very . . . 'smooth.' " She drank straight from the bottle and shuddered as she handed it to him and sat in the chair Franz had previously occupied. She began righting the chess pieces as Jason watched her, the lamplight overhead reflecting off her hair.

"I often played chess with my father," she explained. "I was once very good. The afternoons were so very hot in Cawnpore, the less physical activity, the better."

Jason dropped heavily into his chair, and they made a series of opening moves.

Her eyes were bright with lamplight as she focused on the chess game, contemplating it in silence. Finally, she made her move, sighed in satisfaction, and sat back in the chair. "Your move, Captain."

Jason briefly closed his eyes, then did his best to focus on the game pieces. Impossible. He could smell the same arousing feminine scents that drugged him, that drove him to lunacy, before.

Christ, was she so totally ignorant of men's desires? Had she no concept that as she sat there pondering over chess pieces, nibbling her lower lip, her slender fingers carefully stroking the little pawn, he wanted to toss her to the deck and work her body into a frenzy of passion, as he had before? Did she not realize that her very presence was eroding his willpower and unsettling his good intentions.

He had lusted after hundreds of women, occasionally toying with the possibility that if he sat still long enough he might fall in love with one of them, but those ideas had evaporated as soon as forever wormed into his thoughts. But since the day Destiny had ridden away from the glade, the concept of watching her grow old had occupied him.

"Is something wrong?" she asked.

He shook his head and drank again, still unable to look away from her face.

Her lips parted and she raised her gaze to his. As always, the simple caress of her eyes impacted him like a bullet to his chest. He could not have looked away had his life depended on it.

Funny, he thought, in a sense his life *did* depend on it.

"Sir . . . I shall ask you this bluntly because there is no other way of it. You proposed marriage to me. Did you mean it?"

With a single nod, he raised the bottle to his lips again.

"Why?"

"What would you like me to say, m'lady? Because I'm a hero, a knight in shining armor intent on saving a damsel's reputation? Nice, romantic idea, I suppose. But then, we've already established that I'm no hero. Certainly not a man with *my* reputation. Perhaps you want to assure yourself that my generosity doesn't stem from my thinking that were we to be married that would in some way secure plans to use you to get to your father. But that dog won't hunt, right? Not when I've sacrificed my ship and crew to keep you out of Dunleavy's hands.

"So . . . that brings us to the more normal and reasonable justifications for marriage. I . . . like you. I find you . . . desirable. I've been thinking of settling down of late. . . . I want a family. And you're . . . convenient."

"Ah, convenience." Her lips curled and her shoulders squared. "Where would marriage be without convenience?"

"Convenience bothers you?" He laughed softly and drank again. The rum throbbed behind his eyes and heated his blood. "Of course convenience bothers you. What was I thinking? The fiasco with Chesterfield was convenient for you both. This time you want love. Commitment. *Passion.* You want a fairy tale . . . with someone." He flashed her a smile. "Perhaps if I offer you love, commitment, and passion you wouldn't feel so badly about marrying me for *your* convenience, hmm, Lady Destiny?"

Reaching across the table, he stroked her pale cheek. "I could think of worse things than sacrificing my dignity for your convenience. But I have to know . . . were you truly in love with the man in the forest glade?"

"Briefly."

"One doesn't love briefly, sweetheart. You had an affair de coeur. The scoundrel broke your heart. Now you have his baby inside you. It happens more frequently than you know."

"Perhaps in your circle of friends, Captain. Not mine."

"Spoken like a true blue-blood. Perhaps you're more like Lord Shaftesbury and his peers than you care to admit."

She turned her face away. "Why should what I feel—or felt—for the child's father matter so much to you?"

"It shouldn't. But it does. I have to know if what happened that day in the glade will continue to haunt us."

"Captain, if I could strike him from my memory I would. But I shall never, ever again be able to do that." She placed one hand on her stomach. "You asked me once if I could ever forgive him. I've thought on that for a while and . . . No. Could I but undo what happened in that glade I would happily do so. Alas, I fear I shall pay the price forever." She sighed and focused on the dark beyond the ship. "I've wanted children desperately," she murmured. "Now there's one growing inside me and I feel nothing but fear. What do I tell him about his father?"

"You have a choice," Jason said. "You may tell him his father is a ne'er-do-well you loved briefly, or you may tell him that I am his father—should you decide to marry me, of course. Neither would be a lie."

Jason watched Destiny's face. "Or there's another alternative," he added. "We can marry in Cape Town. After a respectable period of time you can divorce me. The child will have a name and so will you. Your reputation will remain intact."

She shook her head. "I'm sorry if I appear bemused. You simply don't strike me as the sentimental sort. I can't see you bouncing babies on your knee or spending drowsy afternoons curled up with a wife."

"Neither could I until recently."

"You're meaning Jenette." She nodded and her consternation melted into a fond smile. "She's an angel. If I have a little girl I hope she's as lovely as Jenette."

"And if it's a boy?"

"Then I hope he's as handsome as . . ." Her voice dropped off.

"His father?" Jason finished.

"I'll teach him to better respect a woman's feelings." She studied his face, her own thoughtful and with a smile curving her lips. "Saito, our gardener, once told me a story of a man who threw many children into a river because he thought them ugly. When finally he was given a beautiful child, he discovered it had the same soul as the unfortunate babes who came before. I didn't understand the lesson then. I do now. One mustn't judge a man's character by his looks. Despite your scars, there is something kind in your heart. Despite your reputation, there is gentleness in your soul. Whatever decision I make, sir, I want to thank you for your compassion."

Her words, her smile unnerved him. He reminded himself that he was not a youth wrestling with a vague love-dream; he was a man fully capable of ending this madness. He would steel his heart from her as he had done hundreds of times in the past, with other women; remind himself that his calling was not spending quiet nights in front of cheery fires wrapped up in feminine sighs. Yet, as he studied Destiny's profile, all that he had put from him the last years— the ties of husband and father—burned him now with a regret that was keen and sore.

Hair damp with sweat and steam, as were her armpits and the hollow beneath her breasts, Diana bent over the tub of scalding water and scrubbed furiously at the greasy pewter dishes. Then she handed them to Destiny, who rinsed them in a tub of clear, cold water that would ultimately be used to brush down the galley floor.

"You shouldn't be here, doing this, I mean." Diana handed Destiny a plate and wrist-wiped a wet hair from her forehead. "You should rest. Sleep. At least prop up your feet. I understand that women's feet swell when they're with child."

Both paused in their chore to stare down at Destiny's bare feet.

Destiny wiggled her toes and shook her head. "I don't think so."

"Your breasts become larger, too." Diana sniffed up a bead of sweat that clung to her nose. "Are yours . . . ?"

"No." Again with the shake that caused a tendril of hair

to drop over her right eye. "Nothing aside from the sickness, and sleepiness. I don't feel sick now, however." She glanced down at the dirty dishwater and swallowed. The queasiness was there, teasing her from the bottom of her stomach, but she was not about to return to her cabin yet. There were matters to discuss with her aunt. Important matters. Matters better suited to a meeting in James's austere library than to one in a steamy, onion-smelling ship's galley with a relative who was taking out her frustration over failed bread on metal dishes.

"I'm going to marry the captain," Destiny declared.

Diana looked up, slowly. "I would ask you to repeat it but I suspect and fear that my ears haven't deceived me. What do you mean, exactly, that you intend to marry the captain?"

"You needn't try to talk me out of it."

"Are you *insane,* niece?"

"I'm a grown woman. I'm a widow, for God's sake. I'm with child. I'm perfectly capable of making such a decision."

"You're desperate."

"Which doesn't necessarily make me brainless."

"*I'll* take care of you, Destiny."

"You can't take care of yourself, Diana, much less me and a baby as well. Besides, I'm doing this for the child. I won't have him ridiculed because of his birth."

Diana took her hand. "Forgive my concern. I only want you to be happy, Des. Have you grown fond of this man?"

She thought of his kiss, and how her body had responded. No, not just her body. Something familiar had stirred in her. "I . . . he . . . doesn't frighten me any longer."

"Answer me, niece. Do you care for him even a little?"

"Yes."

"Do you trust him implicitly, not just with our lives but with your father's?"

She stared into Diana's eyes, her heart throbbing in her throat along with her sickness and the overwhelming fear of making yet another mistake. "Yes," she finally replied in a dry voice. "I trust him."

"And you're willing to settle for this?" Diana looked around her, floor to ceiling, where the steam had begun to drip like rain from the rough beams. "Des, if you're frightened of what your father will think—"

"I won't disappoint him."

Her shoulders sinking, Diana leaned one hip against the tub and sighed wearily. "Seems we've been down that road before. You married Chesterfield because you thought it was what I wanted. You thought by leaving Sheffield House that my relationship with James would flourish. Sweet niece, you were never the cause of my unsuccessful marriage to James. He simply used you as an excuse to explain away our problems because he wouldn't acknowledge his own responsibilities for our unhappiness. I should never have allowed your union with Chesterfield. But I was a spineless coward. I hoped that at least his wealth and position in society would buy you some form of happiness and freedom. Instead, here you are desperate enough to marry a man whose name you don't even know because you were so needy for reassurance and love you turned to a stranger. Des, two wrongs won't make a right. You need a man who can give you stability. Financial security."

"He's fond of me, Diana. That's more than I can say of Chesterfield. At least the child will have a name."

Her eyes narrowed and she leaned close to Destiny. "Think about it, Des. The Chesterfields would like nothing better than to present the child as proof that their son was a man. They have no other living heirs, Des. Even if they knew in their heart that the child was not his, they would pay a king's fortune to save their son's reputation. You would never want for anything the rest of your life. And think about the child, Des, the money and titles that would come with its birthright."

Destiny turned away.

Diana grabbed her, wet fingers clutching at Destiny's

arms. "If you insist on settling for something less than love, then make bloody certain it's going to be worth the effort."

With Diana's words stinging her ears, Destiny fled the galley. The hour had grown late. Zelie and Franz remained on deck, each bent over the chessboard in deep concentration. Somewhere in the shadows Fritz conversed with LaTouche. Both sounded slightly inebriated.

Where was the captain?

She returned to her cabin, but found it suffocating and hot. After having slept away the past few days, the idea of crawling into her bunk again made her head ache. Besides, there wasn't much point. Soon the nausea would return and she would be forced back to the galley to rummage for food. Diana's flat bread would suffice, she supposed. Anything to keep the horrible sickness at bay. But passing the long hours until dawn meant staring at the walls while memories and voices tumbled through her head, all reminding her of past mistakes and probable future ones.

She moved to the door and stopped.

Now would not be a wise time to search out the captain. Her meeting with him that evening had had an odd effect on her. Her resistance toward him had melted the instant he'd jumped from his chair to greet her, knocking his chess pieces asunder. Their conversation had been without its usual tug and pull—had she actually agreed to marry him?—no, no, not actually, not yet. She had only wanted to understand his reasons for making such an offer. Yet, she had walked away with no clearer understanding of his generosity than she'd had before their conversation. He liked her. He found her desirable. At least there was that.

He'd offered her divorce. Imagine that. In one breath he declared he would like nothing more than to settle down with her and bounce babies on his knee. The next he declared she could divorce him and he would not stand in her way. He was simply doing her a good turn in order for the child to have a name and a father. He would sacrifice in favor of her reputation.

Odd, she thought. Very odd.

Jason was drunk. Too damn drunk to deal with Destiny's distraught aunt, but it seemed he had little choice. Upon entering his cabin without so much as a knock, Diana stood before him, pink hands on her hips and pale hair hanging in limp strands on either side of her flushed cheeks.

"You'll make this quick, won't you, Lady Shaftesbury? I'm expecting Zelie with another bottle of rum. I intend to divest myself of clothes, drown myself in more liquor, and pass out in a disgustingly drunken sleep. I'll warn you that I'm not a polite drunk. Nor am I funny. Actually, I'm a mean son of a bitch with a low tolerance for pissy stow-aways."

"I should think you would try harder to be nice to me, considering you're attempting to marry my niece."

"You want to kiss and make up?" He gave her a humor-less smile, making her frown.

"You're up to something, sir. Otherwise, why would you offer marriage to my niece? You hardly know her."

"You're far too suspicious for your own good, Lady Shaftesbury. Besides, it's a little late now to be fretting over Destiny's life mate, isn't it, considering how you vir-tually shoved her into that sham of a marriage with Chesterfield. Is that it? Trying to make up for past mis-takes?"

Her expression turned hard and her blue eyes snapped with anger. "She's in love with the baby's father still. I don't care what she says. And while once I would have condemned the brute savagely for his unconscionable be-havior, I would rather she marry *him* than a monster who kills for money."

He slowly stood. "Daft woman, just who the *hell* do you think is going to keep Fontaine alive, if, indeed, he *is* still alive? I suspect you'll be thankful for this 'monster' should we arrive at Cawnpore and discover Sahib is in the midst of a revolution and Fontaine is involved. I expect you'll be on your knees about then, *begging* me to cut a few sepoy throats."

They stood nose to nose, breathing hard from their anger. Diana was not about to back down; he knew that. There was the same obstinacy glittering in her eyes as in Destiny's. He took a deep breath to steady his temper. He asked in a deceptively calm voice:

"So what you're telling me is, if the father of Destiny's baby walked through the door right now you would encourage him to marry her, even if the reason was to keep me from marrying her?"

"Yes," she replied with a nod and a tilt of her chin.

Somewhere in his inebriated brain Jason suspected that in another minute or so he was going to severely regret his impulsivity. But even before Diana made her unexpected entrance he had been staring into the mirror and loathing the mask that had become his prison during this voyage. He had hidden behind the grotesque barrier because he had hoped that time would have soothed Destiny's anger toward him and his outrageous behavior that day in the glade. But that hadn't been the case.

First he removed the glass from his eyes: the tiny colored disk that changed his gray iris to green, then the white opaque piece that covered the other iris.

Diana took a slow step back, her eyes widening and her jaw dropping.

He tossed the glass lenses onto the bed. Slowly, he tugged the disguise off piece by piece: the eyebrows, Paolo's creation of rubber and wax that had transformed Jason's complexion into a distortion of scars, and finally the cap of coarse black hair. His own dark hair spilled in rich waves over his brow as he watched the color drain from Diana's face.

Withdrawing a kerchief from his pocket, Jason proceeded to wipe away the remaining makeup from his skin. "Voilà, Lady Shaftesbury. Allow me to introduce myself properly. The name is Jason Batson. *Lord* Batson for those who, outside of my work, know me intimately. My father was Earl Falkland, deceased now, as I understand it. And at the risk of sending you into a state of complete apoplexy, I confess to being the father of the child that Destiny is carrying."

She sank toward the floor.

He caught her and carried her to a chair, where he fanned her face until she roused enough to stare up at him again.

"Oh, my God," was all she managed.

Jason dunked the kerchief in a ewer of water, then pressed the damp cloth to her cheeks. "I began meeting Destiny in the glade, hoping to gather information from her. I hoped to discover just how involved Fontaine was with Sahib. It soon became obvious to me that Destiny knew little to nothing about her father's dealings with Sahib. By that time I had grown fond of her. I tried to convince myself that my feelings were little more than base urges that had not been satisfied in nearly a year of solitary confinement in prison."

Jason tucked the kerchief into Diana's trembling hand. He walked away, swaying, the rum making his legs unsteady. "I take full responsibility for what happened between the two of us. I'm old enough to rein in my . . . appetites, while she . . ." He closed his eyes briefly, and released a weary breath. "She's a child," he finally said, softly. "A naive innocent, whether she realizes it or not. I suspect she was emotionally damaged more than she'll ever admit over her marriage. We were both too damn needy. . . ."

Jason looked back at Diana, who continued to stare at him as if he were a specter. "I attempted to explain myself—she wouldn't listen. I could hardly blame her, considering. Then Dunleavy informed me of his plans to use Destiny to lure out her father. By then Harold suspected that I had crossed the line regarding my feelings for her and would, therefore, be of no further use to him in his plans. At that point I was forced to take the matter *out* of his hands, for Destiny's sake. Dunleavy would have few qualms about killing her, if necessary."

Diana shook her head. "But why this dreadful ruse—this disguise?"

"I had to get her away from Dunleavy any way I could. I knew she wouldn't trust me, not after what transpired between us. The disguise was going to be temporary, or so I thought, until I realized the depth of her hatred for me. She was far more likely to spend time with the captain than with the man whom she believed abused her sensitivities, not to mention her body." He laughed and passed one hand over his eyes. "Christ, I must be drunker than I thought or I wouldn't be standing here spilling my guts to a woman who would like nothing better than to shoot me."

They heard a noise at the door. Jason turned, expecting to find Zelie with his bottle of rum.

Destiny stood in the threshold, her eyes big and her face white as milk. Her red lips moved, silently, forming the words *Oh my God oh my God;* her eyes swept the cabin, then found the discarded mask—"Oh, my God, it was you all along, you lying bastard."

"Des—" he began.

She screamed and fled. He followed, cursing the rum in his blood that made him stagger and trip over his feet. "Destiny!" he yelled, stumbling against the wall before clutching at the companionway and dragging himself up.

The deck was dark and hot and so still Jason fought to find a breath. Sweat beaded on his temples and ran down his jaw. He shouted Destiny's name, his fear overridden by his mounting anger and frustration. He saw her then, at the front of the ship, against the rail, gazing down into the dark as if contemplating jumping.

"Destiny!" he shouted and slowly approached her.

She looked around, backed against the rail, hands clutched at her breasts and her face twisted in despair and disbelief.

"Come away from there," he ordered her.

"Liar!" she cried. "Despicable fraud! Don't come any closer or I'll jump!"

"You don't want to do that, Des. Think of the baby."

She screamed again in anger and stomped her foot. "Just when I had become fond of the captain—of you—again—oh, *damn* you—"

"I can explain."

"No. You can't! Because anything out of your mouth will be a lie, won't it?"

"No more lies, Destiny."

"Liar!"

"I said to come away from there!"

"Captain?" came Diana's voice behind him. He turned unsteadily and saw her standing in the dark. "Or should I say Lord Batson? I vowed that if I ever met the man who took advantage of my niece that I would shoot him."

He stared at her hard, barely able to discern Diana from the shadows. What the devil was she saying—?

Her arm raised and she pointed the gun straight at him. She pulled the trigger.

The impact of the bullet knocked him backward. He didn't fall at first, though the night exploded with a roar that came from all around him—a roar of screams and shouts of alarm, running feet, blood pounding in his ears. He weaved from side to side as he attempted to turn back to Destiny—

Then the pain.

He looked down at his chest—dark where his shirt should have been white. Behind him Connie's voice could be heard over the melee of confusion: "Get her below and keep her there—Christ, the damned woman has shot the captain!"

Connie ran to his side. Jason did his best to fix his gaze on his friend's. But his eyes wouldn't work. Couldn't shift them. Too much pain all of a sudden.

Jason dropped to one knee, clutching at his chest; it felt hot, sticky, and sodden. Connie fell beside him, muttering curses and shouting orders to the crew, who were scrambling to be of assistance. The sounds buzzed into an indistinguishable hum that made little sense to him. The void was there, the blackness; he'd experienced it too many times before not to recognize it now. With his last thread of strength he raised his head and found Destiny, a wraith against the darkness, her white face partially covered with her white hands as she stared back at him in horror.

"I'm sorry," was all he managed before he succumbed to the nothingness.

❧ 15 ❧

And ah for a man to arise in me,
That the man I am may cease to be!

—TENNYSON, *Maud*

"Y've always been the luckiest son of a bitch I ever knew, Jason. If y' was a cat y'd have nine lives. Or had. Y've used up at least eight by now. I reckon I ain't ever seen no man who could cheat death like you."

Jason winced and tried to sit up. Not easy, considering his shoulder felt as if someone had ripped his arm from the socket. *Idiot, idiot.* He should have taken greater precautions the moment he overheard Diana and Destiny discussing filching guns from the arsenal, but he had thought them harmless enough. Besides, although he trusted his men with his own life, he wasn't necessarily apt to trust them entirely on a sea voyage with women. If their packing pistols about in their petticoats made the ladies feel safer, then so be it. *Idiot.*

"Down." Connie gently pushed Jason back against the pillows. "I said y' was lucky, not miraculously healed. There's a hole in yer shoulder I could stick my finger through. Y've lost blood and yer weak, so if y've a mind to murder Diana I would suggest y' wait until yer stronger. The woman can fight like a cornered fox. She took Zelie down with the damnedest kick to his—"

"Where is Destiny?"

"Barricaded in her cabin. We ain't heard nothin' from her in hours."

Gritting his teeth, Jason rolled from the berth. Connie had done a respectable job of bandaging his shoulder but that didn't stop the sudden throb of hot, warm blood from oozing from the wound. The room swam. He caught the edge of his berth and tried to regain his equilibrium.

Connie hovered. Aggravation seamed his weathered features.

Blinking sweat from his eyes, Jason tried to breathe evenly. He'd learned long ago that the human mind could outsmart the body when it came to pain. Focus on other things. *Pleasant* things. *Important* things. Breathe deliberately. Such equanimity could frustrate the most dedicated sadist.

The door opened and Zelie stepped in. "Bloody hell, Cap'n, I've seen dog turds look healthier than you. I'll fetch you a touch of my opium. You'll be feeling top of the world in no time."

"What have you done with Diana?" he asked, bothered by the hoarseness of his voice. Obviously he wasn't concentrating intensely enough. His shoulder hurt like the devil.

"She's locked in the hold, sir. Quiet as a mouse, she is, no doubt fretting over what's to become of her." Zelie looked at Connie, who stared at Jason with a cautious and worried expression.

"What's to become of her." Jason tried to straighten, slowly, breathing, forcing the dizziness back into the recesses of his brain. "What do we normally do to someone who attempts to murder the captain of a ship?"

His attention still fixed on Connie, Zelie said, "Strapping and keelhauling feels a bit extreme for a woman, sir."

"I could think of tortures for Diana that would make keelhauling seem like a picnic in Hyde Park." Jason took a short step toward the door. He swayed and felt his body break out in a sweat.

"If it's any consolation," Connie offered, "she says she didn't mean to hit y'."

"Oh, then by all means let's forgive her." Jason cocked a look at Connie that made the man's face flush, then he curled his fingers around Connie's nape and pulled him close. "As captain of this ship, who is suffering at this moment with a bullet hole in his shoulder, I have the final judgment on what punishment is to be inflicted on the lady."

Connie nodded. "Aye, sir, y' do."

"If there's going to be a problem between us, LaTouche, let me know it now."

"Yer the captain . . . sir." Connie cleared his throat and added, "I'll remind y' that whatever decision y' make regardin' Diana will ultimately influence yer relationship with Destiny."

"I hardly need to be reminded of that, do I?"

Connie averted his eyes and slowly shook his head.

Jason turned and unsteadily made his way out of the cabin and up the companionway. A slight breeze stirred the prepared sails, just a breath of air, but enough to make his hot skin prickle with a chill that made his teeth clench. The gathered crew stopped what they were doing and watched him, each man prepared to jump to his aid if necessary. All except Hugo, who tossed down his coil of rope and came toward Jason like a frothing mad dog.

"We're doomed, I tell ya. Them damned women are gonna be the death of us. Look at ya, for God's sake, standin' there with a hole in yer shoulder and lookin' weak as a cat-mauled mouse. The bitch deserves a bullet between 'er teeth and I'm just the bastard willin' to do it."

"Stand down, Mallet," Connie shouted, stepping up beside Jason. "The captain will do what the captain has to do."

"Right." Hugo snorted. "Big talk from a man who sniffs after Diana like she's a bitch in heat. That puts the rest of us in a fine pickle, don't it? The captain is so bloody lovesick after Destiny he can't think past his achin' dick, and his second in command is itchin' for Diana. We should be talkin' war and the two of ya are wankin' off and thinkin' this." He made an obscene gesture with his tongue. "Yer a pair of fuckin' pussies. Dunleavy should've shot y' fer treason back when y' killed that lieutenant."

Silence.

Jason glanced toward the rigidly cautious crew, their faces' expressionlessness itself telling him their thoughts. They were in agreement with Hugo about the women, though they would never admit as much, at least not to Jason's face.

He squared his shoulders as much as possible, considering the pain, and stepped around Hugo. Fritz jumped to open the hatch that led down into the bowels of the ship— the supply storage, the weapons room, and the prison hold. Connie followed, lifting a lantern as they descended the stairs. Unlike the warmer, cleaner living quarters of the old ship, these vast caverns of darkness smelled of mildew and aged oak. Dampness crept under Jason's bandages and gnawed at his wound. Heat swallowed him. He was forced to grab the banister and swallow back his sudden need to vomit.

Connie moved by him, fumbled with the ring of keys attached to his breeches, located the cell key, and drove it into the lock. The door swung open. Connie stepped aside, keeping the lantern high so the tiny hold was flooded with light.

Diana crouched in a corner of the cubicle. She flung up her hand to shield the light from her eyes as she tried to focus on Jason's face. A look of surprise and relief swept her features, then defiance. Slowly she stood, back pressed against the wall, her face gaunt with the fear she had no doubt undergone the last hours. Jason knew from experience what such captivity could do to a person.

"Surprise," he said without smiling.

An instant passed as she appeared to collect her fractured nerves. "You're alive. At least I won't be punished for murder."

"Don't be so certain, Lady Shaftesbury. I have every right to inflict any punishment I so desire. Keelhauling has been suggested. You do know what that is, don't you? We tie your arms and legs and pass you under the keel of the ship. If you don't drown, and if there's any flesh at all left on your body after being raked across the barnacles on the hull, you get to spend an indeterminate amount of time in here."

She opened and closed her mouth, saying nothing.

"You're a pain in the ass, Diana. I would think that the near fiasco you caused by leaving your husband the name of the ship on which you and Destiny took flight would have been enough to encourage a thread of common sense in your brain."

"Apparently not," she replied softly.

"Killing me isn't exactly doing Destiny any favors."

"I'd give my life to protect her *and* her father."

"And you continue to think I'm a danger to them."

"You've lied about everything else, Captain: your reasons for befriending Destiny in the first place, your identity the last weeks. Why should we believe your reasons for wanting to marry her? I suspect you fully intend to use her to get to Compton Fontaine."

He stared into her eyes, unblinking, checking his desire to wrap his hands around her throat and choke her and make her understand his reasons for it all. "Compton Fontaine is my friend as well, and has been for years."

"That's why you took advantage of his daughter, I suppose, because he's your friend. He'll be thrilled by your loyalty, Captain." The barb stung him. She must have sensed it; her lips thinned and curled in something short of amusement. "And speaking of loyalty, what *will* you do if you learn that Destiny's father *has* joined Nana Sahib in the rebellion?"

"We'll simply have to wait to find out, won't we, Lady Shaftesbury?" He turned away.

"Wait!" she cried. "What do you intend to do with me now?"

"Consider your punishment, of course."

She turned her frightened eyes toward Connie, who regarded her with a sympathetic expression. Raising her chin and jutting it toward Jason, she said, "If you harm me, sir, you'll completely destroy any chance of reclaiming Destiny's trust, not to mention her affection."

"That blade can cut two ways; if she doesn't cooperate I'll toss you in the drink. So there you have it. You've given me the perfect weapon to use against your niece. I suspect she'll do anything to keep me from harming you." Lips curling as he noted the flash of fear in her eyes, he raised one eyebrow. "Enjoy your stay, Lady Shaftesbury."

He slammed the door hard and waited for Connie to lock it. Key clutched in his big hand, Connie stood rooted to the floor, jaw set, eyes fixed in disbelief on Jason's face. "Lock it," Jason directed.

"You ain't really goin' to leave her down here, are y'?"

"Yes." He nodded and winced and concentrated a little harder—the pain was obviously getting the better of him. Refusing to acknowledge Connie's discomposure over abandoning Diana to the dark, he pointed at the lock and repeated, "Lock it."

"She ain't cut out for this kind of punishment."

"She's cut out for shooting people, isn't she?" Jason turned for the steps. "*Lock it.* If you don't I'll toss you in there with her for insubordination. Then again, I'd probably be doing you a favor. Alone at last with the lady asp. I thought you had better taste in women."

The ship shifted beneath him and, above, voices shouted excitedly in the night. The wind was back. Good. The crew could concentrate on something other than women and mutiny.

Behind him Connie cursed under his breath and locked the door. Jason forced himself to ascend the steps despite the lead weight of his legs and his escalating light-headedness.

The sails snapped and billowed as the north wind sifted around and through the riggings. Each shiver of the ship gouged through his shoulder like a pick. Connie moved up beside him and slid one arm around Jason's waist, offering support. Jason shoved him away and turned on him.

"When I give you an order, LaTouche, you damn well better follow it."

Connie stepped back. He stared.

"Do you understand me, LaTouche?"

"Aye, aye, Captain. I understand."

"This is *my* goddamn ship. *My* crew. *My* prerogative to lock up some petticoated assassin in the hole. So stop looking at me like I've just boiled a puppy. Mallet's right. I've allowed Lady Chesterfield to skew my judgment the last weeks. I've become some flipping besotted youth who can't think beyond the feel of a woman's body beneath me. What the *hell* are you staring at?"

"Just thinkin that if y' lose much more blood y' won't have a lot of say about this ship anymore."

He glanced down at his shoulder. The once white bandage looked black in the darkness. Beads of blood ran down his side, tickling his rib cage. "Stop mothering me."

"All right then. Die."

Connie moved around him and made for the bridge. He shouted orders to the crew, who scurried to their posts, whooping their pleasure over the gusts that had begun to drive the *Pretender* hard into the water spray.

Jason maneuvered the companionway steps carefully, almost sagging to the floor when he reached it; he caught himself, grimaced, shoved away from the stairs, and wobbled to Destiny's door, leaving a trail of blood behind him. He banged on the door with his fist.

No response.

He banged again, teeth clenched, eyes squeezed shut as he tried to focus on anything other than the spear of lightning that had centered in his shoulder and chest. "Open the bloody door, Destiny."

"Go to the devil, Batson."

"As far as you're concerned I am the devil, Lady

Chesterfield. If you don't open this door now there is going to be hell to pay."

"I said—"

"If you don't open this door now I'm going to have Diana shot."

A noise. A whimper? He grinned, feeling malicious and delighting in it. He had not felt malicious since Calamita Bay. If anyone had a right to feel malicious at that moment, surely it was he, what with his life's blood forming dark splotches on the tips of his boots.

Oh yes, Lady Shaftesbury's stupidity was going to make his life a whole lot easier where Destiny Fontaine Chesterfield was concerned.

The lock shifted; the door creaked open. He shoved it with his good shoulder and it flew back against the wall with a crash that hurt his ears.

Destiny backed against the wall, shoulders square, chin level. The need to scream almost choked her. It wasn't her anger at him, however, that rose up to suffocate the emotion in her throat. It was fear. Cold, strangling, unbridled terror like she had never before experienced. Then again, she reminded herself, never before had she come face-to-face with Lucifer himself. Before her was no tempting and tantalizing glade god of seduction. No grotesquely scarred and soft-spoken sea captain who seduced her with subtle flirtations, whose marriage proposal she'd actually considered.

Shirtless. Sweating profusely. Bleeding. Breeches stained by blood. Long damp hair falling into his narrowed eyes and framing his face. His teeth showed. His chest labored. He spread his legs slightly to counter the dip and sway of the ship but his eyes, gray as steel, never left her. They were sharp and cold as a sword blade.

"Rule number one," he snarled. "Never lock that door against me again.

"Rule number two. You're to avail yourself to me anytime I so desire. Morning or night. No more mister polite captain who gives a damn about your sensitivities. As you've so often reminded me, I'm a cold-blooded killer for money and as such I have no scruples. *None.* I don't know what got into me in the first place. Never had much use for guilt. It gets in the way of business."

"I . . . " She swallowed and took a deep breath, hoping it would infuse some of her old courage into her. "I want to see Diana."

"No." He shook his head and came toward her.

Her knees weakened. The blood-soaked bandage on his shoulder made her stomach turn.

Towering over her, face sweating, the outer edge of his stormy eyes pinched in apparent pain, he twisted one hand in her hair hard enough to make her catch her breath. "So tell me, Lady Chesterfield, are you pleased to see me again? Relieved? Just a little? *Humor* me. I'm in the mood to be humored. No? Then tell me again what a scoundrel I am. A liar. A fraud. Or perhaps we'll discuss the intelligence and morals of a woman who would seduce a total stranger in a forest glade then attempt to bash out his brains with a rock."

The blood drained from her face. If not for the hand gripping her hair so fiercely, she might have sunk to the floor, not out of fear, but from humiliation. But that would give him too much satisfaction. It was more than apparent that he wanted nothing more than to scare her into submission.

Her brain fumbled for some slick retort, but all she could focus on were his eyes: they were hot as ash and glazed as glass. They reminded her of another time, when desire instead of anger had turned his eyes into a dark tempest.

"Let . . . her . . . go!"

The child's voice jolted them.

Barefoot and clad in a nightgown, her black hair a riot of curls around her cherubic face, Jenette propelled herself against Destiny, burying herself in her skirt as she peered with one tear-filled eye back at Jason.

Destiny dropped to one knee and drew the child against her. Jason backed away, his previous anger evaporating at the sight of Jenette curling her little arms protectively around Destiny's neck.

"Who is he?" Jenette asked as she looked up and into Jason's dumbstruck features.

The question hung in the air.

Destiny frowned. The truth, that Jason Batson was, or had been, the scarred captain that had once terrified Jenette seemed way too complicated for a child—especially one who trembled as if she were on the verge of shattering. How did one explain such chicanery to a five-year-old?

"This is the new captain," she explained cautiously and smoothed Jenette's hair. The child's bravery in the face of her fear made Destiny's heart ache. The thought that in the not so distant future she would be consoling her own child made her dizzy—dizzier as she looked up into the babe's father's dark, angry eyes, which still regarded her murderously.

Her fine brows knitted and her rosy lips puckered as Jenette considered the revelation that the man standing before her was the new captain. "Where is the old one?" she asked.

"Gone."

"Where?"

Silly that she should look to Batson for help, when he appeared to be not only lost for words but on the verge of total collapse. Her heart quickened at the image he made, oddly spellbound by the child, his face bloodless, his mouth curled under slightly, no doubt due to the pain in his seeping shoulder. He looked the mercenary for certain, battle weary and bloody. But there was something else as well, an unexpected vulnerability and helplessness as he focused on Jenette. The image made her momentarily forget her anger and experience again the breath-robbing emotion that had turned a needy, naive young virgin into the sort of woman who would parlay her virtue for a chance at love.

Unsteadily, Jason eased down on one knee, causing Jenette to duck further into Destiny's skirt. Destiny could see he was struggling to hold on to consciousness. His hands had begun to shake. His eyes looked sleepy and threatened to roll back in his head.

"Ma petite," he said softly.

His expression became intense, as if some cruel realization had clamped onto his thoughts. He looked at his bloodied hands, down at his shoulder, then to Destiny, back to the child. "I wasn't hurting her, Jenette." Voice dry as dust, he added, "You must realize I would never hurt her *or* you. Don't look at me that way, dammit." A steely edge to his tone, he said to Destiny, "Tell her I wasn't hurting you."

A look passed between them. "Of course he wasn't hurting me, Jenette. We were simply . . . sharing a difference of opinion."

"He's bad. I liked the other captain better, 'cept he was ugly, but he was nice." She sniffed and turned her big eyes up to Destiny's. "Where's Diana? I want Diana. I can't hardly sleep unless she's wif me."

Batson made a noise, and, with a poisonous glance at Destiny, he managed to stand. "Lady Shaftesbury is detained at the moment and she's likely to be for some time." With what little strength he maintained, he started for the door. Without looking back, Jason stalked from the cabin.

Mind tricks. His father had taught him plenty of them, how to divert memories, guilt, pain down golden roads of pleasure.

The first lesson had come on his tenth birthday. Father, or "God," as he and Trevor had christened their parent, had bought Jason a stud horse named Beelzebub, a big, blowing, striking black with eyes and nostrils like fire. As the groom struggled to quiet the beast, Jason had stood straight and tall at a distance, mouth dry, knees knocking, thinking he was going to piss his pants the moment his father looked down his straight nose and ordered him to mount. Trevor stood at his side, hard eyes fixed on the horse, mouth set, shoulders squared—already wise to his father's lessons. Don't speak without permission. Don't shake, because fear was for cowards and cowards were not worth the excrement that filled their pants. And whatever you do, don't cry. Or beg. Or Father would give you something to cry about that you would remember for a long, long time.

"Jason! You're up!" The booming voice of God.

He stared at the devil horse, unable to move.

"You're up," Trevor whispered, staring straight ahead. "Jesus, Jay, move your butt or—"

"I won't," Jason hissed through his teeth. "He can't make me."

Trevor shifted slightly and looked at him from the corners of his intense eyes. "You daft? Do it or—"

"Jason!" God tapped his riding crop hard against his boot. "We're waiting"—waiting, waiting—"Do you need my help?"

Trevor made a sound in his throat, then poked Jason in the small of his back. Of course Jason was familiar with Father's sort of help—it was a lash across the backs of his legs with the crop, another lash if he so much as whimpered with pain.

Woodenly, he moved toward the horse, heels slightly dragging, watching that tapping crop peripherally while Beelzebub slashed at the ground with one forefoot then danced in place.

The groom stepped forward, eyes concerned yet attempting to convey encouragement as he cupped his hands and said softly, "Do the best ye can, lad. I won't be far."

With a leg up, Jason dropped into the saddle and reached for the reins, drawing them into his sweating hands while the animal shifted beneath him like sand propelled by a storm tide. The sudden explosion forward unbalanced him; he rolled off the rear of the horse—heard rather than felt the snap of bone as he hit the ground so hard blackness sprinted momentarily before his eyes. Then the pain, fiery and streaking up his arm, igniting a howl in his chest that stuck in his throat as Father planted his foot

*in the middle of Jason's stomach and pinned him to the
ground.*

*Father stared down at him, mouth curled in smug satis-
faction, hooded eyes challenging. "Rule number one.
Never cry."*

*Jason looked down his arm, where the bone between his
wrist and elbow bulged. Tears stung his eyes and pain
made him nauseous. "But it's broken—"*

*"Rule number two. Never acknowledge the pain. Think
of something pleasant and soon the pain will go away. To
acknowledge pain will make you weak. You'll be a sissy. I
won't have a sissy for a son. Do you understand me?"*

*He nodded and tried not to blink. If he blinked then the
tears would spill and that would make him a sissy.*

"Close your eyes and think of something pleasant."

*He groaned. The foot on his stomach made it hard to
breathe and he wanted to cradle his broken arm but he
couldn't reach it with God's foot in the way. To move it
made it hurt anyway so he just let it lay there in the dirt
and throb so badly he wanted to shout something foul, but
that would not do either because he'd been strapped
enough times with the crop to know that those lashes could
hurt almost as badly as the broken arm—*

"I said to close your eyes, Jason."

He swallowed and closed his eyes.

"What do you see?"

Red pain. Swirling pain. Throbbing pain.

"You like marzipan, don't you?"

"Yes, sir."

"Then think of marzipan."

*How did one think of marzipan? One ate marzipan. One
did not think about it.*

*"Almonds. Sugar. Butter. Creamy. Imagine it on your
tongue. The roof of your mouth. Sticking to your teeth.
Don't swallow it. Savor it. Feel the fine granules of sugar
on your tongue. Now count them. Each tiny individual
grain. Then imagine yourself sitting under your favorite
tree on a warm summer day, and indulging yourself in all*

*the marzipan you want. Take a deep, steady breath and
hold it. Release it, slowly, slowly, holding that wonderful
sweet in your mouth, more treasured than gold. . . . There.
Very good. Now tell me how you feel."*

He opened his eyes and stared up at his father's emotionless face, his arm hurting like hell. *"Fine, sir."*

*"Good boy. I'll make a man of you yet, just wait and
see."*

Thoughts of marzipan had sufficed for a few years, then
there were women, with their intoxicating bodies and
husky laughter and intimacies that could hold his mind
spellbound through pain and torture. Oh yes, he'd eventually become very, very good at divorcing himself from
pain, like the pain that ate up his body now, clawing at his
subconscious, screaming to be acknowledged.

Odd that he could not force *this* pain away. Obviously
there was too much guilt squirming around in his thoughts.
Guilt could get in the way of his concentration.

He did not want to think that at long last when he could
finally present himself to Jenette as her father, her first introduction to him was of his splintered temper, bloodied
hands, and foul disposition.

He did not want to think that he had become the sort of
man who would lock a woman away in a ship's prison hold
for attempting to defend her niece's honor.

He did not want to think that he had become the kind of
man who would lie in the dark and worry about such triv-
ial worries. Hugo was right.

Jason Batson, Cobra's most notorious soldier, was going
soft. Instead of visualizing marzipan and whores to keep
away the pain he saw only Destiny Fontaine Chesterfield
sitting on a fallen tree trunk feeding ponies from her hand,
her stomach swollen with his unborn child, his dark-haired
angelic Jenette sitting at her side cradling a china-faced
doll in her arms. Except there was no rain-dreary forest
glade in his dream. Instead they sat in the garden of Ceylonia Plantation, sunlight spilling over their shoulders,
smiling, eyes brimming with serenity.

Still, the pain gnawed like an animal at his shoulder and he tried to reason why.

Squeezing his eyes closed, breathing through his clenched teeth, he struggled to hold on to the sun-dappled image of his fairy-tale family, only to have it liquify and fall like raindrops into a pulsating hole of hurt.

With no warning, realization twisted like a knife blade in his chest. *Reality* was the key. To grasp something with the mind, to hold it there with no fear of it vanishing, the vision had to be of something real, something once experienced and cherished, burned into the soul and scarred upon his memory so no amount of pain and torture could erode it. His fairy-tale family was nothing more than that. A fairy tale. A figment of his imagination.

Rule, number one:

Never cry.

❦ 16 ❧

There are two tragedies in life. One is to lose your
heart's desire. The other is to gain it.

—GEORGE BERNARD SHAW, *Man and Superman*

His fingers closed around Diana's wrist, Jason hauled her
closer to the table on which he lay near the open fire of the
galley cookstove. The room sweltered and the flames
painted their sweating faces yellow and orange. He wanted
to see Diana clearly—or as clearly as possible considering
the sweat blurring his vision. But more importantly, he
wanted her to see what her idiocy had done to him. He
wanted it scored into her brain so every time she closed her
eyes she would visualize his face.

"I'm dying, Diana. Are you happy now?"

Eyes ringed by dark bruises of exhaustion, Diana stared
down at Jason, her parched lips parted in horror, her hair a
rat's nest of tangles that fell over her shoulders and pooled
on Jason's sweating chest.

"Y' ain't dyin' yet," Connie declared with a snort of irritation. "But we're gonna have to cauterize the damned
wound or y'll sure as hell bleed to death." Connie shoved
a knife blade into the flames then reached for his rum bottle. He drank, belched, then gently raised Jason's head and
pressed the bottle opening to his lips. As Jason drank, Connie grinned. "Y've had lots worse done to y'. Remember
the time y' got that bayonet stuck through yer leg? Went in
one side and out the other, spitted y' like a damn hog

against a tree. Y' hanged there for five hours before we found y'. Y' didn't whine so much then as y' are now. Maybe Hugo's right. Maybe y' turned into a pussy when I wasn't lookin'."

A shiver passed through Diana as she tried vainly to twist her wrist out of Jason's fingers. She looked on the verge of fainting.

"Diana?"

Jason looked around.

Destiny stood in the doorway, her wide green eyes fixed on her aunt, obviously uncertain of what to make of the goings-on. While Jason had suffered the last two days, slipping in and out of consciousness, Destiny had pled with Connie to release her aunt from the hold. However, like a faithful second in command, Connie had ignored her in deference to Jason's orders, though he was not happy about it. Jason suspected that LaTouche had spent as many hours keeping Lady Shaftesbury company in the hold as he had in ministering Jason's shoulder.

Diana struggled again, her lips pressed against her teeth as he gripped her more tightly, refusing to allow her her freedom. Dammit, if he was going to suffer, so was she.

Yet, as Destiny turned her accusatory stare at him, he opened his fingers and allowed Diana to slip away. She ran to Destiny; they grabbed one another, rocked from side to side, and cried in relief.

The rum made him woozy. But not woozy enough. Jason suspected that he could down the whole damn bottle and it would not be enough to black out the agony he was facing. But it made him dizzy enough to take the edge off his dread and allowed him the pleasure of watching Destiny smile. He had not seen her smile in a while and had forgotten what the sight did to him. He suddenly felt drunk and stupid and helpless.

"What the hell are you waiting for?" he snarled at Connie, who had leaned back against the wash sink, watching the two women share their relief over Diana's freedom.

"Blade ain't white yet," Connie replied and tipped up his

bottle again. "Won't cook good if it ain't white. Y' don't want me to have to do this twice, do y'?"

Finally, Destiny focused on him. Her face appeared ashen and pinched. Cautiously, she approached him.

"I'm dying," he announced, waiting for her reaction.

"No, he ain't," Connie countered. "Don't believe him."

"Fine then. I'm suffering. Will that appease you? If I bleed enough will you stop looking at me as if you want me castrated and hanged from a gibbet?"

Her mouth thinned and she raised one eyebrow. "I'm not in the habit of relishing the misfortune of others, Captain Batson." The words were soft and tremulous.

"Unlike Diana—and my name is Jason."

"I'm fully aware of your name . . . *Captain*."

Zelie entered the galley and Jason, gritting his teeth through a spasm of pain, pointed at Diana. "Grab her."

Diana made a dash for the door. Zelie grabbed her, ignoring her flailing arms and thrashing feet as he carried her across the room and plunked her down next to Jason. Like before, Jason seized her wrist, blinked the sweat from his eyes, and focused on her horrified features. They were beginning to swim unsteadily in his eyes. Another time he might have welcomed the black senselessness, especially in light of what was soon to follow, but not yet. He was going to make good and damn certain that Diana Shaftesbury learned a lesson from her stupidity with a gun.

Releasing her wrist, he twisted his fingers into her lacy blouse front and drew her down over him, so her face was near his and he could stare into her blue eyes for full effect. Feathers of darkness fluttered on the fringes of his vision; what little strength he had seeped out his pores with his blood and sweat. The image of Diana's face contorted, melted, and transformed as if she had donned one of Paolo's masks. He did his best to force aside the weakness; alas, although he clutched her close and focused on her eyes the chasm of blackness yawned before him and around him—he had too damn much to say—could not let go yet—

"Pay close attention, Diana. This sort of suffering happens when you're sloppy in your attempts to kill a man. Rule number—"

Three. Make the kill quick and clean. If there is enough life left in the enemy he will attempt to destroy you with his last breath.

The soldier, no older than Jason's twenty-two years, thrashed in pain and clutched at his stomach, making Jason think of the fox that had been cornered by hounds and partially mauled—delirious with pain and fear, it was going to die but with its last ounce it fought to live. His rifle in one hand, Jason stared down at the pale-faced young man, only vaguely hearing the distant gunfire of war and his father's shouting, his brow sweating and his stomach turning and his knees shaking—Christ, he had not expected this gut-churning horror of guilt that would come from killing the enemy.

"Incompetent young fool!" his father yelled. "I thought I taught you better than this. Finish him off, Jason. Put the gun to his head and pull the trigger!"

The soldier turned his eyes toward Jason and his lips moved like a gasping fish out of water. What was he saying? Help me? Don't do it? Do it and end my suffering?

"What are you, a coward? I won't stand for a coward—"

"I'm not a goddamn coward!" Jason shouted back, but no matter how hard he tried he could not raise the rifle again or pull the trigger again, not with those helpless eyes staring up at him—

Then the soldier's bloody mouth began laughing, and he rolled, raising the gun from nowhere and pointing it at Jason. The bullet buzzed like an angry hornet by his ear even before the sound of the gun firing jolted through him. Dropping his rifle, he stumbled back as Trevor threw himself on the soldier and thrust his knife into his throat.

"That's my boy," his father declared, slapping Trevor on the back, his face beaming with pride. "You're a chip off the old block, Trevor. A son a father can be proud of."

The words rolled over and over in his head.

Nightfall. A torrent of rain drove the enemy back and into their tents to wait out the storm. Jason crawled on his belly through the grass and mud, knife gripped in one hand, body shivering with cold—at least, that was what he told himself. It was cold and not fear that made his teeth chatter as he neared the soldier's tent. He'd learned a valuable lesson that afternoon: Make the kill quick and clean. If there is enough life left in the enemy he will attempt to destroy you with his last breath.

Inside the tent, the enemy sat at a table, his back to Jason as he bent near the lamp and wrote on paper. The pen made scratching sounds in the silence.

Jason slid his arm around the soldier's neck and drove his knuckles up into the fleshy place under his chin, locking his jaw shut so he could not scream. He made a deep, fast slice with his knife across the man's throat.

Quick and clean. No sound. No flailing other than the momentary exhalation of air from dead lungs and a convulsive tightening of his fingers on the pen in his hand. Jason stared down at the letter. It began, My Darling Wife.

His father had been proud that night.

But Jason had tossed and turned in his cot, sleepless, not satisfied that he and Trevor had pleased their father, nor troubled by the soldiers' deaths. He'd been haunted by those words scrawled in black ink upon pale linen paper: My Darling Wife.

Rule number four—his own rule.

A soldier should never marry.

Destiny felt starved for oxygen in the miserably hot galley. But it was the bothersome racing of her heart that unnerved her. She was afraid. From the moment Diana had pointed her gun at Jason and pulled the trigger, from the instant he'd dropped to the deck with his shirt covered with blood, she had agonized. No matter how insistently her head reasoned that she should distrust, even dislike Jason Batson, her heart argued for understanding and forgiveness. But more than that, all the old, familiar stirrings of fondness had rushed through her, no different from on those rainy days she waited for him at the glade. The anticipation hummed in her veins. The excitement vibrated her soul. For the last two nights she had dropped to her knees and prayed harder than she had ever imagined possible for God to save him.

His hands twisted in Diana's blouse, Jason spoke softly in her aunt's ear—so softly Destiny could hear nothing more than Diana's occasional whimper. When she attempted to escape he pulled her back down, teeth clenched as he continued to speak for her ears only. Diana grew still. She nodded. Sniffed. Her body relaxed, and when she finally moved away her face appeared white and emotionless. She glanced briefly toward Destiny before backing toward the door, then she fled the galley.

Weak, sweating, and breathing hard, Jason turned his head toward Destiny. His eyes narrowed as if he were attempting to focus. She moved closer. His mouth curved, just a lopsided tip of his lips that made her knees go soft. Closer.

"You're still here," he said.

She nodded and tried her best to appear righteous and indignant. She was not about to let him think she would forgive him so easily for what he had put her through, even if he did look as if he were tottering on death's door.

"Jenette." He winced and frowned and his eyes rolled back a little before he outwardly struggled to rouse himself and focus on her again. "Is she—"

"She's fine," Destiny replied softly.

A shadow of anger crossed his face and, more to himself than to her, he said, "I didn't want her to see me like this. Not this side of me. It's too damn ugly and frightening. She'll think me a monster."

Connie gently raised Jason's head and tipped the rum bottle to his lips. "Drink deep, friend, and for the good Lord's sake, just take the dive, would y'? This'll be a hell of a lot easier on all of us if y'd just go ahead and pass out like yer body is tellin' y' to. Quit fightin' it, Jay. Y' ain't got to prove to any of us what a man y' are."

Jason laughed dryly, his gaze still fixed on Destiny. "Hugo disagrees."

His hand opened and slightly extended toward her. Destiny stared at it as Connie turned toward the fire, flipped the knife blade over, and began to hum to himself. Jason raised one eyebrow and gave Destiny a lazy wink. "He always hums when he gets nervous."

She touched her fingertips to his. Closer. Her fingers slid over his, which were hot and damp with sweat and slightly shaking. Threading his fingers between hers, he closed his hand around hers and drew her near, lifted her hand to his mouth, and pressed his dry lips against it. Those gray eyes watched her with an intensity that made the breath rush from her lungs.

"Forgive me?" he asked, the tone surprisingly desperate. His hand gripped her possessively. "Careful how you answer, love, because I'll hold you to it."

"I . . . don't know," she replied, curling her fingers around his and feeling emotion swell in her throat.

"How's our baby?" Again with the grin that made his face look all the more gaunt and haggard.

Frowning, Destiny did her best to look away, before he could see the rise of tears in her eyes. Too late, they trickled down her cheeks. "Unfair," she declared with a little stomp of her foot.

"Know how it makes me feel to look at you and know you're carrying my baby?"

"Stop." She smiled and sniffed, on the verge of surrender.

"Helpless," he whispered, eyes closing, his hold on her hand becoming weak, as if he were fading away before her eyes.

Spurred by a sense of panic, Destiny gripped his hand in both of hers—she squeezed hard and leaned close, her dark hair forming a soft curtain on both sides of his face. "Sir, we each have much to forgive. Much to understand. When you're better—"

Connie put a hand on her shoulder and gently squeezed. "It's time, lass. Y'd best go."

Zelie moved around the table and began to strap Jason's ankles down, then moved up beside Destiny, nudged her with his elbow, and grinned. "He'll be good as new in no time." He separated Destiny's hand from Jason's and buckled his wrist to the table. " 'Course, I'm not so certain he'll ever be fit for soldiering again, not as soft as he's gone over you."

"Enough." Connie flashed Zelie a warning look. "Y've been listenin' to Hugo again. Get this through yer opium-occluded brain: ain't nobody livin' or dead as trustworthy and capable of takin' care of business as Batson. I'll be the first to slice out the tongue of anyone who says otherwise." Remembering Destiny, Connie looked back over his shoulder at her, shrugged, and said, "Sorry." Then he added, "Go. Y' don't want to be here for this and I'm thinkin' he don't want y' here either."

"You're wrong," she said, working up a courage that both surprised and pleased her. Connie paused and looked at her. "I think he does want me here. I won't leave him. It's my fault this has happened, and . . . it's the least I can do."

She bent near Jason again and took his face between her hands. "I'm here . . . Jason."

His eyelids fluttered. His lips parted. He attempted to raise his hand, but the strap on his wrist stopped him.

Connie turned from the fire, the knife in his hand. The deep distress in his features caused Destiny's heart to squeeze painfully. He did not want to inflict the hurt any more than Batson wanted to experience it.

It all happened fast—so fast, the sudden searing of flesh, the instant reaction of a body in the throes of shock and agony, constricting, bowing, bone, tendon, muscle straining out of skin, wrists and ankles wrenching at their bonds—and the groan, deep inside him, boiling to erupt, but not doing so—no cry, no gasp—just that first instinctive reaction to escape the suffering—then nothing but his fixed, glazed eyes staring up at her, face void of emotion—as if his mind had miraculously withdrawn from the body.

The unbearable heat pressed down on her. Dear God, she needed air.

The room swam.

Zelie swept her up and hurried her from the room, out onto the deck, into the wind and spray that briefly robbed her of breath. He carried her to the rail and sat her down on her feet. "I'll get you a drink," he offered and hurried away.

Desperately hanging onto the rail, certain if she let go she would completely collapse, Destiny did her best to focus on the undulating horizon and the scattering of pink clouds across the setting sun. She had never witnessed such suffering. The extent of it horrified her. And yet he had endured it with a silence and stoicism that did not seem human. How, she wondered, did a man endure such torture without it destroying him in some manner?

A noise. She turned, anticipating Zelie had returned with her drink.

Hugo grinned down at her. "What's wrong, Lady Chesterfield? Somethin' insult yer sensitivities? Come up for a little fresh air, did y'? Couldn't stand the stink of fried flesh and the whimperin' of a wounded man?" He moved closer. She backed against the rail, legs braced apart to keep her balance as the ship pitched and shuddered with a sudden gust of wind. "Are ya happy now?" he goaded. "Y've done exactly what I said y'd do—brought bad luck to this ship and crew. The way I see it, if y' ain't gone from this ship soon there'll be more bad luck. Worse than this. Ain't no woman worth the ruination of a ship and its crew."

"If you're not careful," came Zelie's voice, "the only one to be gone from this ship soon is going to be you." Destiny sank back against the rail, relief turning her knees to water. A cup in one hand, the other resting on a gun tucked in his breeches, Zelie gave Hugo a thin smile and motioned with his head toward the galley. "Captain's awake. I'm certain he wouldn't think too generously of your attempts to safeguard his ship and crew, especially if it meant sacrificing his lady love."

"When are y' gonna realize that the captain ain't worth a rat's fart anymore when it comes to soldierin'? Hasn't been since he got a whiff of *her*. Then again, maybe he ain't been worth much since Calamita Bay, when he murdered one of us over a damn woman and kid. I don't know about you, man, but I sure as shit wouldn't want him watchin' my back when I'm surrounded by sepoys."

Zelie handed Destiny the cup of water, which she took with both trembling hands. "Go below," he told her. "And stay there . . . *please*."

She nodded, but as she stepped toward the companionway, Hugo planted one foot in her way. "It ain't as if I don't like women. I like 'em just fine. Just not on this ship, not with these men, and not muckin' the captain's priorities around. Truth is, I wouldn't mind a little sniff and taste of what's under them petticoats myself. Must be real nice, to have twisted up the captain like it did. But be that as it may, don't for a minute misunderstand what Batson really wants—and that's yer father. Batson is gonna take that son of a bitch traitor down with a bullet between his eyes just as soon as he sees him. And if he don't . . . I will. Count on it."

Destiny backed away, her gaze shifting from Hugo to Zelie, who would not meet her eyes. As she moved toward the companionway, a sense of panic growing in her chest, Zelie joined her, caught her arm, and would not let go until she faced him. He was forced to raise his voice to be heard over the whipping of sails and the hiss of sea spray.

"Take no notice of him, lass. He's mean and crude and a pain in the ass, good for nothing but—"

"Killing people." Destiny shoved the water cup back into Zelie's hand. "That's why you're all here, isn't it? Because you anticipate killing someone. And that someone is my father."

"We're soldiers." He shrugged. "It's what we do, love; we destroy the enemy."

As Jenette slept soundly on her little cot in Diana's cabin, Diana lay on her own berth, one arm slung over her eyes. Destiny sat near her in a chair, hands clasped in her lap as she waited for her aunt to control her emotions enough to continue. At last, Diana sighed and, rolling her head to one side, stared at Destiny through the shadows.

"I fear I made a grave mistake, niece. About so many things, actually. Spending days locked in a pitch-black hold gives one time to assimilate their life, I suppose, and to understand one's motives for doing what they do. How is the captain?"

"He's been moved to his cabin. Fritz assures me that he'll be as good as new in no time."

"You were very brave to stay with him. I wish I were so brave. Do you still care for him a little?"

"I don't know." That, of course, was a lie, and had Diana not been wrapped up in her emotional quandary she would have taken one look at Destiny's expression and recognized the truth.

"I have something to tell you. Something he told me, secretly, in my ear. Perhaps he really thought he was dying. Or perhaps he simply wanted me to feel even guiltier about shooting him. He's . . . Jenette's father."

Destiny sank back into her chair and slowly turned her gaze across the cabin toward the sleeping child. "Of course," she said softly, a lump swelling in her throat. She pressed one hand to her stomach. "I can see the resemblance now. All those comments he made about her father were nothing more than self-deprecation over his not marrying Michelle."

"He made me promise that if something happens to him, I'm to make certain you and Jenette are taken care of. And the baby, of course. He intends to marry you when we reach Cape Town, whether you like it or not. Just so there's no question as to . . . inheritance. Des, he claims to be very wealthy. He owns an island off the coast of Ceylon. An entire island. He grows tea there." She covered her face with her hands. "Oh, God, what have I done?"

"Y' haven't killed him, if that's what yer worried about," came a voice from the doorway. Connie stepped into the cabin and closed the door gently behind him.

Diana sat up, her face brightening. "Is he conscious?"

"Sleepin'. He'll do a lot of that over the next few days." He nodded at Destiny. "I'm glad yer both here because I got somethin' to say to y'. Zelie told me about yer conversation with Hugo earlier. 'Bout what he said about the captain and his plans for yer father. I'm thinkin' it's about time y' know exactly who or what yer dealin' with, ladies. Our actions have left a lot of room for speculation and I'm feelin' we need to clear the air a bit before somethin' else happens like what happened with the captain. But before we start sharin' secrets, I've brung y' a little somethin' to help y' better understand Jason."

He cleared his throat and addressed Destiny. "Fact is, the captain has had a great many opportunities to marry. Maybe he should have done it long before now. And maybe he's just tryin' to make up for his past mistakes. And maybe not. Come to think on it, he ain't never been the kind of man to do nothin' he didn't want to do regardless of the consequences. I guess what I'm sayin' is, I know he's come to care for y' a great deal. And I think if y' could let yerself look beyond his reputation as a soldier for hire y'd find a man worthy of yer admiration."

"I realize you admire him, Connie—"

"Admire him? Aye, lady, I admire him. He's saved my arse more times than I care to count. He's taught me about discipline and honor, not to mention courage in the face of adversity. Hell, if it wasn't for him I'd be stuck on some damn hulk thinkin' I was good only for thievin' and wastin' my life and ambitions on ale and gamblin' and immoral women. Least, that's the way it used to be, before I was introduced to Cobra.

"We make a sworn vow when joinin' the force that we never speak to a civilian about Cobra. You can count on one hand the number of men, aside from the soldiers themselves, who know of our existence. Cobra is a militia of highly trained agents who are paid to confront and destroy any hostile group or individual who is deemed a threat to the Crown.

"The captain would probably get real angry at me for showin' y' this. He don't hold much stock in medals and such—says they don't accomplish nothin' but unearthin' the memories that go along with 'em."

He took Destiny's hand and placed something in it. "What yer holdin' there, my lady, is the Crimean War Medal, awarded for distinguished valor in the line of duty, above and beyond. It's a sterlin' silver disc bearin' the diademed head of Queen Victoria on one side, and on the other is a Roman legionary carryin' a gladius and circular shield bein' crowned with a laurel wreath; to the left here is the legend 'Crimea.' The suspension there is an ornate floriated swiveling suspender unique only to the Crimea Medal; the clasps here are also unique, bein' in the form of an oak leaf with an acorn at each end. Lady, each one of these clasps represents action in Alma, Balaklava, Inkermann, and Sebastopol, awarded in a private ceremony by Her Majesty herself. Y' see, Cobra don't get no parades. He ain't stood up before the Queen and scores of fawnin' admirers and applauded for his heroism. He don't exist, not in the newspapers or in the archives, or in Society's drawin' rooms. He's called on to take on the tasks that would sicken them scrubbed-face infantrymen still wet behind the ears. Cobra goes toe-to-toe with the devil so them boys don't have to."

Destiny closed her fingers around the medal.

"Knowin' the captain he'll want you to have it. Just keep it. And when you start thinkin' that y'd be better off married to some puffster who can't even dress himself in the mornin' without the help of servants, take this and look at it hard and thank yer lucky stars that yer married to a real man of honor."

Destiny pressed the medal to her heart. Certainly she had heard of the brave men who had fought the terrible Crimea battles. James and Diana had sent out numerous condolences to the parents and wives of those men who had died in the war. She had even read in the London *Times* of the ceremony in which Albert had awarded medals to the soldiers. There had been parades and banquets and lavish parties thrown in their honor and women had wept when hearing of their brave escapades. "There be true heroes," James's peers had declared with a lift of their sherry glasses.

As Diana sank back on the bed, burying her face in her pillow, and Connie sat down on the berth beside her, rubbing her back, soothing her with gentle words and assurances that the captain was not about to expire from his bullet wound, Destiny left the cabin. She paused in the dark with the medal still pressed against her rapidly beating heart, then proceeded to Jason's cabin, where she discovered Franz dozing in a chair near Jason's bed. Drowsily, Franz smiled up at her, stood, then tiptoed out of the cabin.

Jason slept.

Destiny sat in the chair, hands gripped together as she studied his face. Dear God, how normal he looked in that moment—no evil mercenary, no hero, just a man exhausted by pain and injury. But, regardless of the medal biting into her hand, of the child growing inside her, of the swell of feelings for him surrounding her heart, he was still a threat to her father—even more so, now; Cobra would strike at and destroy anything or anyone perceived as a threat to the Crown.

A man of Jason Batson's honor could do no less.

❦ 17 ❦

I hold it truth, with him who sings
To one clear harp in divers tones,
That men may rise on stepping-stones
Of their dead selves to higher things.

—TENNYSON, *In Memoriam*

Destiny smiled at Jenette and squeezed her little hand in encouragement. In truth she needed a little emotional fortification herself. She had avoided seeing Jason over the last few days—she needed time to think, and trying to come to some logical conclusions about her feelings for the man would have been hopeless in the circumstances. Seeing him helpless and in pain made her reasoning disintegrate.

"Jenette, I'm certain you're going to like the new captain. He's not nearly so fearsome as the other. And much more handsome, don't you think?"

Jenette studied the closed cabin door as if anticipating being thrown to a dragon. Finally, she turned her big eyes up to Destiny's and asked in a pitifully tremulous voice, "Is he going to grab my hair and shake me like he done you?"

The door opened suddenly and Fritz stepped out, glanced from Destiny to Jenette, and said, "The captain is ready to see you now."

Her voice low, Destiny said, "If he's not yet up to this—"

"He's as ready as he's ever going to be. Best to get it over with."

She caught his arm as he attempted to step around her. "Is something wrong, Fritz?"

He shrugged and frowned, then attempted a less than believable smile. "Don't know what you mean, lass."

"You appear concerned."

He again glanced at Jenette, his expression tense. He lowered his voice. "Just that we're all a bit worried over how this father thing is going to affect him. Let's face it, he ain't exactly been himself for a while now, for obvious reasons. His priorities are mucked and so are his instincts."

"And you blame me for that."

"It happens eventually to us all. Just not when we're sailing into a potentially ignitable situation. These men look to Batson for leadership and guidance. He can't do either effectively when his brain is scrambled by familial responsibilities."

Destiny watched Fritz ascend the companionway. Time and again, the last week, she had happened upon the men in deep discussion, their looks toward her and Diana growing more concerned by the day. At first she had believed them worried over Jason's condition, but, according to Connie, Jason's condition had rapidly improved.

She knocked on the door.

"Come in," came the deep response.

"Do we got to?" Jenette pleaded and gripped Destiny's skirt.

"The captain has a wonderful surprise for you," Destiny whispered.

"A new doll?"

"Something much better than a doll."

With a deep breath, Destiny opened the door and ushered Jenette into the cabin.

Jason closed the logbook and set aside his pen. Somewhat stiffly, he left his chair and turned to face her.

For an instant Destiny was lost for words. She could only stare, her breath caught in her lungs.

Batson wore a fitted gray uniform with gold buttons and epaulets. There was a dark red sash slung around his hips.

His hair had been trimmed and brushed into place. He had lost weight the last week. It gave him a lean, raw-boned, dangerous look that heightened his image of a mercenary. His shoulders appeared broader, his hips slimmer, his legs longer. His eyes were like smoke.

She knew in an instant his reasons for the uniform, to assure Jenette that he was no pirate intent on harming her; Destiny's heart squeezed so painfully she thought she might faint again. Her legs turned soft as aspic. He must have noticed. His mouth curled in amusement. Or perhaps it was simply arrogance. She was certain she had never seen anyone as handsome as he in that moment.

Finally, he cleared his throat. "Ladies." He looked down at Jenette, who ducked behind Destiny's leg and regarded him suspiciously. "There's tea and biscuits." He motioned toward the china pot and cups on a table.

Destiny bit her lip to keep from smiling. Jason was obviously nervous. He was hardly the kind of man accustomed to tea parties, especially with a child to whom he was about to confess that he was her father. She nudged Jenette toward the table, forcing herself to breathe evenly as he moved up beside her, brushed her arm with his, then pressed his hand gently against her back.

As Jenette struggled to climb onto the chair, he caught her about her waist and righted her on the pillow, stroked her dark ringlets, then backed away. His brow and temples began to sweat, causing him to tug a kerchief from a pocket and blot his forehead with it.

Destiny placed a biscuit on Jenette's saucer and reached for the teapot. "I assume, Captain, that the tea is yours?"

He frowned.

"You grew it on your island?" As he nodded, Destiny smiled at Jenette. "The captain grows tea, Jenette. On a very big island near Ceylon."

Jenette nibbled the biscuit, sprinkling crumbs over her lap.

"I assume he has a grand house—"

"Thirty rooms," he inserted. "On a hill overlooking the

harbor. There are stables as well. And horses. *Ponies. . . .*"
he added, his eyes shifting briefly to Destiny. It was all she
could do to look away and force her hands to stop trembling as she poured Jenette's tea.

"You got puppies?" Jenette asked as she reached for a
second biscuit.

"Yes, as a matter of fact. One. Named . . . Dog."

"And kittens?"

"I think there are probably several cats—at the stables.
Do you like cats?" He pressed the kerchief to his upper lip
and watched Jenette intently.

She nodded, causing her ringlets to bounce. "I had a kitten once. But it died. My mama said she would get me another, but she didn't cuz she died, too."

Silence settled like a pall over the room. Jason's face
paled; his eyes turned dark and intense. Something in his
expression made Destiny's chest ache.

She looked away, focused on his daughter. "Jenette, the
captain has something he wants to tell you," Destiny said
in a dry voice.

Jason looked into Destiny's eyes. *I'm not ready,* his confessed.

It's going to be fine, hers assured him.

Jenette turned her big eyes on Jason, waiting.

He took a deep breath and slowly released it. "Jeni . . .
I . . ."

Nothing.

Muttering a curse, Jason turned away, ran one hand
through his hair, rubbed his shoulder, paced the floor.

Destiny put her tea aside, took Jenette off her pillows,
and, holding the child's hand, walked her to Jason. She
sank down on one knee, smiled, brushed crumbs from
Jenette's white lace collar, and cupped her rosy cheeks in
her palms. "What the captain is trying to tell you, Jenette,
is that he is your father."

Silence.

Jenette stared up at Jason, unblinking, unmoving, and as
each second ticked by his face turned to stone. He might

have been wearing a mask again, Destiny thought. His emotionless countenance was nothing more than a facade to hide his embarrassment and disappointment over the child's lack of enthusiasm.

"Jenette, your father's come a long way to see you, and—"

"He's not my papa!" she blurted, suddenly furious and red faced. "My mama said Papa was very nice and this man is *not* nice, 'cuz I seen him hurt you."

Jason clenched his fists.

"He didn't hurt me, darling. See? Do I look hurt to you? Would I allow him to touch you if I thought he might hurt you? Look!" Destiny stood and reached for Jason's hand, pressed it against her own cheek, and kissed it, lingeringly, her eyes drifting closed and her voice dropping to a husky whisper. "He'll be gentle, I'm sure, because he loves children. You must give him a chance to show you how much he loves you. Come now, and give him a little hug. Please? For me?"

Jenette's little mouth screwed to one side as she contemplated first Destiny's request, then the tall dark stranger standing in front of her, a man who appeared to be on the verge of fracturing the instant she refused.

She did not refuse, however. Raising her short arms in the air, she waited as Jason knelt to one knee, then slid up against him, locking her arms around his neck. "Are you really my papa?" she asked in his ear.

He shut his eyes and held her close. "Yes, Jeni."

"Will you give me a pony? And a puppy? And a kitten?"

"I'll give you whatever in this world makes you happy."

"Even a monkey? I like monkeys, too!"

Jason laughed and hugged her, emotions suddenly raw on his face. "I'll buy you a dozen monkeys. I promise."

Destiny stepped from the room, closing the door as gently as possible behind her. She had to escape before she allowed her own feelings to get the better of her. Seeing Jason holding the child had shaken her to her very soul and filled her with unreasonable expectations. Perhaps, if he came to love her, and the child inside her, enough, he would forget his soldierly obligations when it came time to confront her father.

She hurried toward her cabin.

Behind her, the door opened. "Des?"

Her steps faltered. Reluctantly, she looked back.

Standing partially over the threshold, Jason smiled. "I'd like to see you later."

"I don't—"

"There are arrangements to discuss."

"You're—"

"Much better." He smiled again, though not so brightly. "I thought that day in the galley, perhaps you had forgiven me. I thought that we might start again. Fresh." The smile slid from his lips. "Des—"

"I'll let you know." Her voice broke, and she hurried into her cabin, sank back against the closed door, and covered her face with her hands.

Although he had sent a note to Destiny requesting that she join him for dinner, she did not show. Now Jason moved to the deck rail; the wind drove from the northeast, cooler now as they neared Cape Town. With any luck they would arrive in another two, maybe three weeks. Along the way they would encounter rough weather as the hotter northern winds collided with the cooler southern ones. Turning his face into the wind he could almost smell the storms brewing. The air felt electrified and stung his nostrils like burnt gunpowder, like those moments just before he charged into battle. His instincts vibrated. His blood hummed. He felt a little mad, as if his sanity had been pulled taut as a piano wire.

"He's no good to us anymore. There ain't one of us standing here tonight who would trust him to guard our backs."

The voice drifted to him from the quarterdeck, followed by others.

"He's not been the same since Calamita Bay. Spent

nearly a year in solitary, and for what? The woman the lieutenant shot was hiding a gun under her baby's body. She could have killed any one of us with it."

"Now this mess with Dunleavy. We'll be lucky to come out of this without our necks getting stretched. All because of a woman again."

"A woman whose father is up to his ears in trouble, according to Dunleavy. Bastard he may be, but he ain't usually wrong about situations such as this. If he suspects Fontaine is involved with Sahib, he probably is."

"Which puts us between a rock and a hard place." Connie's voice. Jason rocked back against the rail and squeezed his eyes shut. *Son of a—* "Jason is gonna have to make a choice sooner or later. He's either gonna have to turn his back on Fontaine's crimes, if Fontaine is involved in treason, and walk off into the sunset with Destiny, or he's gonna have to face up to his responsibilities. There are a few thousand British citizens whose lives depend on his gettin' his head straight. He's a soldier, dammit. A trained fighter. A killer. There ain't a one of us who, at one time, wouldn't have shook in our boots at the thought of confrontin' him."

"So what are we gonna do about it?" Hugo demanded.

"I'll think about it," Connie replied.

"We take the goddamn ship," Hugo declared. "That's what we do about it."

"Hold yer tongue, man. Yer talkin' mutiny."

"Aye, mutiny. We take the bloody ship off him, La-Touche, before it's too late. Forget about Batson's need to play hero where the woman is concerned. We wait in Cape Town for Dunleavy and Trevor. We hand over the woman to him and we get on with Dunleavy's original plan."

Jason bent at the waist, eyes closed, rum churning deep in his stomach. He tried to breathe past the anger—anger at his crew, the men with whom he had fought through a hundred bloody battles, and anger at himself. They were right, and he knew it. A battle had never been waged and

won by a solitary soldier. They moved as a unit. If one link
in that chain was weak, they all suffered.

Christ, just when had he become the weak link?
Calamita Bay? The instant at the forest glade when he
pressed his body into Destiny's and realized he'd been seduced by a virgin? Or, once spent of his lust, when he'd
looked into her eyes and realized that in some perverse
way he had dishonored a friend; not only had he questioned Fontaine's loyalty to the Crown, but he had defiled
Compton's tremendous trust and respect for Jason Batson.
How often had Compton turned to Jason as they drank together on Fontaine's veranda and offhandedly hinted that
Jason would be good for his daughter?

The ship shifted beneath him and the voices in the distance were dashed away by the deep drone of wind in the
riggings. An unnerving chill crawled up his back that had
nothing to do with the northeast wind driving the *Pretender* toward Cape Town. The realization struck him that
he and he alone stood between his crew and Destiny,
Diana, and his daughter—a crew that no longer respected
their captain because of his weakness for a woman.

Destiny's body was changing, little by little. The frail
chemise she wore beneath her blouses now felt more snug
across her breasts. Her waist felt thicker. Certainly no one
else could tell a difference, but she could. Everything
about her existence had shifted slightly out of kilter. There
was a raw edge to her emotions that left her jittery and
mentally unbalanced—far too unbalanced to sit in a room
with Jason Batson and politely discuss their future over
roasted fowl and fruit in brandy sauce.

Dear God, she was hot. That, too, had become a problem. Hot one minute, shivering the next; one instant hysterically happy, the next close to tossing herself into the
sea so she would not have to dwell any longer over her circumstances.

Stripped down to her chemise and drawers, Destiny bent
over the china washbowl. The Crimean War Medal that

Connie had given her swung back and forth from a ribbon around her neck; she tucked it into the chemise. She splashed water on her face, allowing it to run down between her breasts. She felt desperately hungry. And daft for having so stubbornly buried herself in her room in an attempt to avoid the inevitable meeting with Jason. She had never been the sort of woman to run from any situation. Yet, she continued to do just that—avoid—where Batson was concerned. Since the moment she'd stepped into his cabin and discovered him maskless, she had thrashed like one drowning in her confusion.

She loved him.

She hated him.

She feared him.

She craved him . . . with every fiber of her being.

The sight of him that afternoon, dressed in his military finery, had struck like a flint at her insides. His very presence had consumed her. The feel of his hand on her back continued to burn like a brand into her skin. The very air that had shifted around him had smelled of . . . what? Talc. Bay rum. Soap. Sweat. Then there were the images of him holding his daughter. . . .

The sudden pounding on the door made her jump.

"Open the door," came Jason's annoyed voice.

Heat spread like a rush of fire through her body. Of course he would be angry. Very angry. She was surprised that his storming the threshold had taken this long.

"I said to open the goddamn door, Destiny."

"Go away," she replied, sinking deeply into the berth.

"I'll count to three then I'm kicking the door in. One."

She set her chin.

"Two."

Squared her shoulders. Surely he wouldn't be so brutish as to—

"Three!"

Screaming, she leapt off the bed as the door crashed against the wall. She backed away as Jason stumbled into the cabin. No aristocratic officer this, with his hair windblown and his shirttail hanging loose, nearly to his knees. He held a mostly empty rum bottle in one hand.

Destiny opened and closed her mouth, mentally reminding herself that this was hardly an appropriate moment for antagonizing him further with a rebuke. The fire snapping in his quicksilver eyes was warning enough that his tolerance was at its end. She could hardly breathe in that moment, much less speak, or even make a grab for the clothes she had earlier tossed over the back of a chair.

Slowly, without taking his eyes away from her, he reached back for the door and shut it. Locking it, however, was out of the question. The latch dangled, splintered, from the door. It made rusty squeaking sounds as it swung back and forth in the silence.

"What the devil do you want, Batson?" she managed breathlessly as she backed toward the washstand.

"What do you think I want?" He tipped his head and curled his mouth. His eyes looked slumberous and deep as gray water as they leisurely appraised her.

"To chastise me, no doubt, for refusing your invitation to dinner. I . . . apologize. I wasn't feeling well. I'm not feeling well now, so if you'll excuse—"

"Shut up." He pushed away from the door and tossed the empty bottle aside. It rolled one way and then another as the ship moved from side to side. "I don't want to hear how you feel, Lady Chesterfield. I really am tired of giving a damn. There are more important matters I should be concerned about. Like how you've emasculated me in front of my men. Turned me into an ineffectual fop unfit to captain my own ship. You've skewed my thinking. Rattled my reasoning. My crew is contemplating mutiny all because I can no longer think beyond our future together."

"I'm sorry."

"No, I don't think you are. You now have me exactly where you need me. You're with child. My child. And you know damn well I have no intention of walking away like I did with Michelle. All I have to do to assure our happily ever after is vow to you that I won't hunt down your father and destroy him, regardless of his alliances with Sahib. How the hell do you expect me to do that if he's plotting to destroy his own countrymen?"

"He's not," she declared. "I know my father. You know my father. How can you think for a moment that he would do such a thing? He's been passionate in his love of India, and its people, but never so that he would consider treason."

His gray eyes narrowed and his lips thinned. His voice took on a sharp edge of bitterness that cut Destiny to her heart. "I know what passion can do to a man, sweetheart. The kind of passion that makes a man sick inside, that warps his logic and fractures everything he once believed in and stood for. The kind that leaves him worn out and weak and crazy with confusion. Passion is a man's worst enemy. It's the one greatest factor in his life that he cannot control."

His head tipped forward slightly, and he gazed at her through the fringe of his fallen hair. Destiny backed away as he approached her; her knees trembled, not out of fear but from the animal image he made, like a stalking predator and she with no hope of escape, even if she wanted to.

She sidled away as he reached for her. She needed time to think—

He lunged, twisted his hand into her chemise to stop her dash for the door. It ripped, easily, one half coming off in his hand, the other sliding off her shoulder and breast. For a frozen instant she stared at the tattered cloth in his fist, then into his eyes, which at once looked stunned as he noted the medal hanging from her neck, then ruthless.

"Bastard," she breathed and crossed her arms over her breasts, knowing the effort was futile and ridiculous. It wasn't as if he had not seen her before, but that had been her choice, not his.

The material slipped from his fingers and floated to the floor. His lips curved. His eyes narrowed. "Very pretty," he whispered just as he grabbed for her again.

Dancing aside, she darted for the door. He caught her

midstride, locked his arm around her waist, and propelled her against the wall, hard. He pinned her arms above her head with one hand as he might have done an enemy and planted both knees between hers. With her hair spilling over her breasts, breathing hard, she met his challenging gaze with one of her own.

"If you're done now with asserting your dominance, you can release me."

"No." He shook his head. His gaze raked her. His breathing quickened.

"Then perhaps this is simply a ploy to humiliate me. If so, I hate to disappoint you. It'll take a great deal more than this to humble me."

"Is that what you think I intend to do to you, sweetheart?" He laughed and toyed with the medal between her breasts, his knuckles faintly skimming her flesh, then he slid his hand across her stomach and tugged the string on her drawers. They instantly swagged over her hips and slid to her knees.

"You're drunk."

"Yes. I agree. I'm very drunk."

His hand eased between her legs, cupped her, parted her, slid inside her. She gasped and quivered and tried futilely to escape, only to have him grip her wrists more tightly and press his big body against hers, holding her in place as he probed more deeply into her, drawing a groan from her chest. She couldn't control the fire that his fingers were igniting inside her. She felt like hot liquid. Her control shattered little by little as he explored her gently, then roughly, dove deeply, then withdrew to circle, dart, slide until her body squirmed, not out of its need to escape, but to open to him as much as possible.

He tried to kiss her. She turned her head and whispered, "I hate you for doing this to me."

"For doing what? Reminding you that all it takes to climb between your beautiful legs is to be in the same vicinity as you for five minutes?"

The insult snapped something inside her. She bucked

wildly, forcing him to shift his shoulder against her chest. She jerked hard, knocking his shoulder, too late realizing it was his sore one; he caught his breath and his face turned white. For an instant he sagged away. She held her breath. Her mind scrambled with confused thoughts: guilt, spite, concern, all the while her body ached and throbbed and burned with the treasonous fires he had kindled inside her. She almost apologized, then he blinked and refocused, drew himself up, and with a guttural curse swung her away from the wall and flung her onto her berth.

Backing into the corner, drawing her legs up beneath her, Destiny grabbed a pillow and flung it at him.

He rolled his eyes a bit drunkenly and laughed as he knocked the pillow aside. He pulled his shirt up over his bandaged shoulders and head as he moved toward her and tossed the shirt to the floor. His hands moved down to his breeches and began to finger the buttons on his fly, releasing them one by one.

"You must admit," he said, "that I've treated you much nicer than I should have, considering. Have I not been tolerant of your tantrums? Answer me, damnit."

Her brows knitting together, Destiny nodded, her gaze drawn to the vee of skin and dark hair he was revealing as his breeches peeled back from his fingers. The rising ridge beneath the cloth brought heat to her cheeks and a quickening of her heartbeat.

"I put my ship and crew in jeopardy in my attempts to help you out of a very dangerous situation with Dunleavy. I lost two good friends in that bloody storm, all because I allowed my head to get muddled by a lot of nonsense: responsibility, guilt, desire, friendship. My crew believes me addled enough to commit treason should your father turn out to be a Judas to his fellow Brits. And the sorry truth is, they may be right. I can't reason any longer without wondering how my actions will affect you. I keep remembering the pleasant evenings I spent in your father's company, listening to his stories about you and thinking that a father's adoration for his daughter must certainly prejudice his perspectives. Then I saw you in the glade, feeding ponies from your hand. I watched you ride your horse like a bat out of hell and held my breath when you flew over stone walls as if with wings. I hid in the shadows of stone Buddhas and listened to you wax on about love and desire and running barefoot over Indian sands. And I thought that the compliments your father had paid you had not done you justice. Not even come close."

Sinking down into the sheets, her breath catching as his breeches parted and slipped low on his hips, Destiny wondered how she could feel so moved, aroused, yet outraged at the same time. She shook her head as he propped one knee on the berth and allowed his breeches to slide down his thighs, freeing him. A sound escaped her. She tried to roll away. He caught her, wrestled her onto her back again, and slid between her legs.

"Do you intend to rape me?" she demanded hotly, hating her own body that felt so taut and raw with desire.

"If that's what it takes," he replied in a husky whisper, then caught her fists as she tried to push him away, pinned them to the bed above her head, and with his free hand explored her breasts, gently squeezing her nipples, then down again, slowly, between her legs and to the apex of such delicious pain she cried out and attempted to twist away. They struggled. He hissed as she elbowed him. She cried out but he muffled the sound with his mouth, kissing her hard; she bit his lip. He cursed her. She thrashed her legs and bucked like a wild horse, rolled onto her stomach, and attempted to rock to her knees. Burying one hand in her hair, he twisted his fingers through it and held her face to the mattress, cupped his knees under her thighs, and hoisted her buttocks into the air.

"Gotcha," he declared, breathing hard and running his free hand caressingly over her butt, then under, spreading her, dipping into her so she quivered and made helpless noises in her throat. "We can do this one of two ways, or both if you prefer. I can fuck you. Or I can make love to you."

"I would rather—"

"Throw yourself to sharks rather than fornicate with me, as I recall."

She struggled again. He pinned her harder. "Funny how you'll seduce a stranger, submit to a grotesquely scarred and randy sea captain whose name you don't even know, but God forbid you would acquiesce to me—"

"I despise you."

"I don't think so." He slid his sex between her legs and pumped his hips. She gasped and went still. Held her breath. Her heart pounded in her throat while a shocking spear of anticipation streaked through her. A moment passed before she realized that he had released his hold on her hair. His hands splayed along the curves of her buttocks, molded and massaged them, then he leaned over her back, and, nudging aside the hair from her ear, whispered in a voice craggy with his desire, "What the hell do you want from me, Des? What will it take for you to stop fighting me? A promise? Is that it? If I vow to close my eyes to your father's crimes, will you stop this madness?"

He made a sound in his chest, and turned her over. His dark eyes burned into hers. "I love you," he confessed softly. "Isn't that enough?"

Her heart seemed to stop in that instant. She wondered if the out-of-control rocking of her world was due from surprise or if the ship moved by a sudden swell of waves.

Lowering his head, he kissed her mouth, gently, lingering, his potent, rum-flavored lips brushing hers and his tongue tasting her. Sweet seduction. Now it was he who seduced, titillating and teasing, making her body crave in a way she had never experienced—not even that rainy afternoon in the glade. His hands seemed to be everywhere at once, fondling, tantalizing, turning her body hot and liquid so she writhed beneath him, not out of pain but out of mind-blinding pleasure and need. Then his mouth, on her breasts, lightly nipping, licking, then her stomach, kissing, breathing softly and whispering words to his child, pressing his ear to her flesh as if he expected some response, then down, lower, nuzzling, embarrassing her and shocking her and making her feel brazen and abandoned. This was wicked! Dear God, she had never imagined! Oh, oh, but what glorious rapture, this intrusion of his mouth and tongue. Tunneling her hands through his leonine hair she pressed his face harder into her and bowed her back, control lost, her body swept away by its frenzied hunger for a kind of surcease she could not yet comprehend. It magnified with every dip of his tongue and tug of his lips and growl of desire that escaped him. Yet, just as it seemed she was ready to implode he shifted, mounted her, drove his body into hers with a swiftness and completeness that momentarily robbed her of breath.

His fingers dug into her buttocks as he lifted her higher, thrust deeper, his narrow hips pumping as he clenched his teeth and watched her face, sweat forming drops on his temples and above his lip.

A sound escaped her and she heard herself pleading, chanting over and over, "Please, please, please." Her hands reached for him, dug into his flesh, nails scarring with blood and causing him to moan and lower his body onto hers.

"Witch," he hissed and slid his tongue into her ear. "You want it rough, Des? Sweetheart, I can give you all the rough you can handle."

He rode her hard then. The sweat and blood from the scratches made their bodies slippery; their flesh came together again and again until the pressure began to build again and the scream in her throat clawed like razors for release. "Come on, come on, come on," he pleaded in a desperate voice, his own body hot and wet and straining with each thrust, each bunching of his muscles and tightening of his buttocks making his body like granite.

It burst on her suddenly, like a lightning explosion, static, convulsive, shockingly hot and uncontrollable. She fought the sublimity, not understanding—their first encounter had not ended this way, with this beautiful pain and helplessness—it was frightening, the submission, the letting go, the spiraling into an oblivion that made her cry out, twist her hands in the sheets, and grow still, poised on the precipice as he worked his body into and out of hers, at last driving her over the edge.

Forever, it seemed, the spasms shuddered through her, lifting her up then dropping her. He buried his face in the soft hollow of her neck as she clutched at his shoulders, holding him, needing to absorb him, unable to grip him tightly enough, wanting desperately to never let go.

And still he rocked her, his own climax building, his desperation mounting. His body sweated. His breath came in short bursts. She found the rhythm again, took his face between her hands and pulled his head down to hers, opened her mouth over his and slid her tongue inside him. A sound rolled in his chest and he tore away, cords standing out in his neck as he threw back his head and shut his eyes. She felt his coming, it burst inside her like hot fire, pulsed like a heartbeat; his body shuddered, emptied. He collapsed on her with a low moan and a soft curse.

∽ 18 ∽

Weary of myself, and sick of asking
What I am, and what I ought to be
At the vessel's prow I stand, which bears me
Forwards, forwards, o'er the starlit sea.

—MATTHEW ARNOLD, "Self-Dependence"

The ship shivered. It lifted and dropped, rocked and shimmied as Jason groggily opened his eyes, uncertain for a moment where he was. He shook his head of the sleep that nagged at his brain and carefully shifted from under Destiny's weight. She made a sound and curled around his pillow. He slid the sheet up over her naked shoulders and, bending, pressed a light kiss to her cheek.

He dressed quickly and left the room. The ship heaved; he staggered his way to his cabin, retrieved his loaded pistol and tucked it into his trousers, then made his way to Connie's cabin. The door was unlocked. Connie lay sprawled on his berth, snoring. Moving as quietly as possible, Jason retrieved the ring of keys from a peg on the wall, then made for the companionway.

Wind and the first slash of rain drove through the sheets and shrouds with a force that robbed Jason of breath. The sheets had been lowered to quarter mast and the lines secured as firmly as possible. He took a fast inventory of the crew, or what he could see of them in the dark. Everyone appeared to be at his post, alert and intent on their responsibilities. Should the storm gain momentum the bell alarm would be rung for the others.

He headed for the cargo hold, stopping only long enough for a lamp. He battled with the locks a moment, cursing under his breath as the rusty lock refused to give. Finally, the lock clicked and the hatch swung open.

Raising the lamp, he searched the crates of weapons. So far so good. Everything in its place. No rifles missing. Christ, he was becoming paranoid. He grabbed a pair of handguns from a crate and shoved them into his waistband next to his own.

"What the hell are y' doin', man?"

Drawing his gun, Jason spun on his heels and leveled the pistol between Connie's stunned eyes.

Connie blinked and stepped back. "Shit," he muttered, never taking his eyes from Jason. "Yer losin' yer touch, Jay. Next time y' sneak into a man's room to steal his keys try tiptoein' a bit more softly." He shrugged and added, "Wanna put down that damn gun before it goes off . . . by accident?"

"I don't think so," Jason replied.

Connie nodded. "You heard."

"I heard."

"It was just talk, Jason."

"Sorry, but I take mutiny seriously, old friend."

"Ain't nobody about to mutiny, Batson. We're concerned. That's all. For now, y' just might not be the right man to follow into battle. Not this battle. If there is a battle. It's all conjecture now, ain't it? We're thinkin' that it might be smarter for y' to take the women and kid back to Ceylonia. Kick back and enjoy the family life awhile. Grow tea and babies."

"You want to turn *Destiny* over to Dunleavy."

"Hell, that was just Hugo spoutin' off."

"He'll kill her to silence her. You know that. It's why I took her. It's why we're—"

"Runnin'." Connie averted his eyes and shook his head. "That's a mighty big bone that's stuck in the men's craw,

Jay. Cobra ain't known for turnin' tail and runnin', from nobody. Then there's the consequences of takin' the lady. If it turns out that Dunleavy was right about her father, we're gonna spend the rest of our lives in prison and yer gonna have to face the fact that y' might well have caused the deaths of a lot of innocent people, should Fontaine instigate the rebellion." He shrugged. "Y' know Fontaine better than we do. Y' got to deal with your own conscience about that."

"You knew what you were letting yourselves in for when you agreed to crew this ship."

Connie laughed and scratched his head. "Right. Guess we misjudged yer feelin's for the girl. Can't blame us, can y'? It ain't as if y've ever committed yerself to a woman for very long."

"Fontaine is a friend. I have to give him the benefit of the doubt until I know otherwise."

"And if y' find out he's with Sahib? Are y' gonna follow through with Dunleavy's plan and put him down before he can fan the fires?" His eyes narrowing, Connie asked, "Is she worth yer life, Jason? Is she worth the lives of the British families livin' in India?"

Destiny awoke, gasping for breath as she sat upright, the pillow clasped to her naked breasts. Had she dreamed it, the passion she and Jason had made together? No. Her body felt sore and bruised. His scent filled her nostrils and tingled her senses. Her gaze swept the floor, acknowledging the shreds of her chemise and the discarded drawers.

Destiny sank against the wall and closed her eyes, curled her fingers around the medal hanging from her neck, and felt flushed, suddenly, with heat. Had he really confessed his love for her, or had he simply been so inebriated and swept up by his desire that he would have admitted anything— even love?

Her stomach churned with hunger.

She needed air. And food. And water. Desperately.

Trying her best to ignore the rise of nausea in her throat, Destiny pulled on her nightgown then stumbled barefoot from the cabin, sagged against the wall as the ship rolled, then she made for the upper deck.

Shivering, her bare feet sliding on the damp deck, she ran for the galley, grabbed a tin cup, and plunged it into the scuttlebutt of fresh water. She splashed her face and neck, closed her eyes, and did her best to focus on something other than the pitch and sway of the floor and the undulating light from the whale oil lamp on the wall. Where was Diana's miserably bad bread when she needed it? Destiny thought.

"Well now, wot have we got here?"

Destiny looked around. Hugo stood between her and the door. Shirtless, his broad chest a canvas of snake tatoos that coiled down his arms to end in cobra heads just above his wrists, he looked like some terrible leering gargoyle— half human, half reptile; the lamplight painted his face in gyrating shadows.

"I'm ill," she said, doing her best to draw back her shoulders and appear as if his presence didn't terrify her.

"You don't look so ill to me," he slurred. "Fact is, you look bloody good. I can see why the cap'n's gone all spooney on us. Got his priorities screwed wrong, he has. He's already cost us lives—all because of you." He stumbled toward her and she backed away, against the wall beneath the oil lamp. Laughing, Hugo shook his head and narrowed his eyes. " 'Course, if you was to somehow go away the cap'n might get his senses back. I'd be doin' the whole crew a favor by tossin' ya overboard. Like I've said all along, a woman's got no place aboard the *Pretender.*"

He lunged at Destiny, clumsily stumbling over his feet as he grabbed at her nightgown, his fingers ripping the cloth and tearing at her skin as she scrambled to escape. He spun her around, drew back his fist, and drove it into her cheek. The terrible pain radiated through her face bones and exploded in her brain. She sobbed and attempted to cover her face as he slapped her again then buried his fist into her stomach so hard her feet left the floor. Clutching her middle, unable to breathe, to move, to make a sound, the only thought to flash through her mind was, *Oh, God, don't hurt my baby!*

Her attempt to scream was futile. He wrapped his meaty fingers around her throat and squeezed, choking off her voice and breath, making her head feel as if it would explode at any moment. She kicked out, landing a blow to his groin. The hands fell away as he doubled over, but only briefly. As she tried to stumble around him he caught her arm and flung her against the wall so hard the oil lamp popped loose of its mooring and shattered in an explosion of glass and fire that traveled like some demon spirit along the floor, which ignited like dry tinder.

Stunned by the blow, her head reeling, she did her best to blink away the flashes of light popping before her eyes. Pain clawed at her legs, and as if through a fog she stared down at the flames climbing up her body, eating up the hem of her gown, climbing faster. Terrified, she clawed at the gown, ripping at its seams, trying her best to smother the flames—the pain set in, awful and searing Destiny's eyes. The agony swept all else from her consciousness in that instant—Hugo and the fire and smoke that suddenly raged around her, choking the air from her lungs.

"Fire! On deck, ya bastards, we're burning like a bloody torch!"

As the alarm bell rang frantically, Jason shoved Connie aside and dashed for the deck, Connie hot on his heels. Whipped by the wind, the flames lapped at the galley walls and danced along the trestletrees of the masthead. As black smoke boiled from the doors and portholes the crew scrambled with water buckets and slapped at the flames with canvas and blankets. Skidding over the damp deck, Jason grabbed a bucket in each hand and ran for the rain barrels where Zelie and Fritz were already dragging out pails full of rainwater and passing them to Franz.

"Captain!"

Jason looked around. Diana, her nightgown plastered to her body by the wind, shouted at him and screamed something.

"Get below with Jenette and Destiny," he yelled. "And stay there until I tell you otherwise!"

"Destiny . . ." The words were lost, but the horrified expression on Diana's face was not. Jason dropped the buckets and stumbled toward her, coughing as the wind-driven smoke rolled over him, clouding his vision. ". . . is not in her cabin!" Diana cried, grabbing Jason's shirt and staring into his face. "I've looked everywhere below. She's isn't there!"

"She has to be. I left her in her cabin not twenty minutes ago!"

"She isn't there, I tell you!"

He turned away, his gaze rushing to the burning galley as panic erupted in his brain. He swept up a water bucket and ran through the smoke and flames that ate at his boots and growled like some ravenous dragon as it gnawed with fiery teeth at the walls and ceiling. He shouted her name and tried to shield his eyes with his forearm to better see through the roiling clouds of smoke. Making his way into the galley, he searched the flamed walls, the radiating floor, flung the water in the bucket over the skittering flames so steam and smoke hissed and popped and spewed in a suffocating density into his face. With his flesh feeling as if it were melting, Jason backed toward the door.

He saw it then, the blackened garment discarded in a heap near the wash bin. He dove for it, snatched it up in his hand, and staggered out of the room, out onto the deck, where he wretched and gasped for air and squeezed his eyes closed to stop the horrible burning. The crew moved with precision around him, shouting orders, hefting the water buckets, and drowning the flames.

The garment, still hot and smoldering, seared Jason's hand as he clasped it.

"It's Destiny's," came Diana's choked voice. "Her nightgown. Oh, my God—"

He shook his head. "She wasn't there. I looked for her. She wasn't there."

"Oh, God—"

"Shut up!" He rounded on her, one soot-covered fist raised as he stared frantically down into Diana's terrified eyes. "She wasn't there, Diana!"

"Then where is she?" she yelled back as furiously.

The smoke cleared in that moment, briefly. There was a movement on the prow. He blinked and looked again. Desperation seized him. He knocked Diana aside with a sweep of his arm and moved woodenly, at first, then faster. He plowed into Connie, who followed his focus to the pair in the dark distance.

"Don't!" Jason shouted and shook his head. "Don't do it, Mallet. Put her down, you son of a bitch!"

Hugo looked around, showing his teeth in a malicious smile. Naked and unconscious, Destiny hung from his arms, limp as a rag doll, her dark hair whipped by the wind.

"Don't do it," Jason shouted again as he moved closer, cautiously, one hand slowly lifting as if the action would somehow impede Hugo's intention to toss Destiny into the white-capped sea.

"I was right, wasn't I?" Hugo grinned and nodded. "I told you these women was gonna bring us trouble. Now she's about burned up the whole damn ship."

"Put her down, Mallet."

"She's dead already." He wagged her from side to side. "Just thought I'd save you the effort of throwing her overboard."

"Down. Put her down." *Please, God, please. . . .*

"Look at ya, Batson. Standin' there like a whipped dog. It ain't right what y've done to this ship and crew, turnin' us all into a lot of cowards. We're runnin', by God. All because of her." He shook her again and made a move toward the rail.

"If she's dead let me bury her myself!" Jason shouted, voice tight with panic as he carefully closed on Hugo, his eyes fixed on Destiny's limp form.

With a grunt, Hugo hefted Destiny against the rail. Her body slumped over it and she hung there precariously as the ship lifted and dove and rolled from side to side.

If Hugo gave her the slightest nudge—

Zelie slid out of the shadows and rammed a crowbar into the base of Hugo's skull. He dropped like an anchor to the deck. Jason ran, leapt over Mallet's prone body, and grabbed for Destiny just as she began to slide toward the water. He stumbled back with her weight and fell to the deck next to Hugo. Clutching Destiny's cold, still body against his, he looked down into her face and howled in fury.

"Get a grip on yerself, man. The lass is alive, Jason, and yer not gonna be of any use to her unless y' calm down and get yer head straight." Connie slammed Jason against the wall outside Destiny's cabin hard enough to antagonize the wound in his shoulder. Pain obliterated his anger for an instant. He gritted his teeth and groaned. "Diana and Zelie are with her. They'll do everythin' they can to help her. I ain't lettin' y' back in her cabin until yer rational."

Closing his burning eyes, Jason tried to breathe evenly. Calm. Calm. He needed calm. Think. Destiny was alive. That was all that mattered. He focused on the racing heartbeat throbbing in his ears. Gradually, it slowed. His body cooled. His shaking diminished.

Cautiously, Connie backed away. "Good man."

Jason rubbed his shoulder and relaxed against the wall. "The fire—"

"Out. I'm afraid Diana won't have such a pretty galley to cook in no more, but it'll suffice until we reach Cape Town."

"Hugo—"

"Is locked away until we determine what's to be done about him."

Jason looked away, frowned, then took an unsteady breath and released it. Christ, his chest hurt. He'd been nearly beat to death once by a tribe of irate Bedouins when he'd attempted to steal a horse, and it hadn't hurt nearly so much as this emotional misery. "Zelie saved her life, Connie."

Connie nodded and grinned. "Aye, sir, he did at that."

"He could've let her go. Your problem would have been solved."

"Don't nobody here want that, Jay. Not except Hugo, of course." A kindness that Jason had rarely seen settled into Connie's blue eyes. "I ain't certain any of us realized how much we'd come to care about her, until now. I think I speak for the men when I say we'll support y' in whatever decision y' make concernin' Fontaine. Yer right. We knew what we was gettin' ourselves into when we come on this little jaunt. There ain't a one of us who didn't wanna thumb our nose at Dunleavy just on spite. There's been too damn many long days at sea and too much rum to drink. Too much time to think and distort our reasonin'. But we've always moved as a unit, and always will. There ain't a man on this ship, sir, who wouldn't follow y' into hell if necessary. Y've saved our scruffy necks too many times for us to walk away now . . . jest cause y've gone all soft and sappy for a woman."

Connie grinned and winked.

Jason grinned back.

The amusement slid from Connie's features, replaced by an intensity that made his blue eyes burn like fire. He took Jason's face between his big hands. "Yer like a frickin' brother to me, Jay. And I'm determined to get you through this damn fracas one way or another. Yer gonna settle down on Ceylonia with yer wife and kids and put these nightmares behind y'. Now let's go see yer Destiny." Connie shoved open the door and stepped aside.

Diana sat in a chair, elbows on her knees, her head cradled in her hands. Her shoulders sagged. She did not look up.

Zelie sat on the berth, blocking Jason's view of Destiny. The steamy air smelled pungent, due to the scattering of open salves strewn over the floor at Zelie's feet.

Zelie looked around. His face appeared pinched as he glanced from Jason to Connie. As Jason moved toward the berth, Zelie stood, blocked his path, and planted his hands on Jason's shoulders. "I've done what I can for her, sir. I've cleaned her up. The salves should help the burns somewhat. They aren't nearly so deep as we thought. She'll be tender for sure. There will be some peeling, but for the most part they're superficial. Looks like Mallet hammered on her pretty good. I checked for broken bones. I won't know for certain until the swelling goes down. I . . . think there could be a problem with her eyes."

"Her eyes." His voice sounded dry.

"The fire." Zelie shook his head. "There's damage. I've bandaged them. I don't know what else to do. Only time will tell, I guess."

Jason nodded in understanding.

"There are bruises. Severe ones. Her throat—he must have attempted to choke her, her breasts, her ribs, her stomach . . . her thighs."

"What are you saying?" His pulse slammed and his chest constricted. "Did he rape her? Is that what you're saying?"

Zelie looked away. "I don't know."

Palming his eyes, he tried to dismiss the image in his head of Mallet on Destiny. "The baby. What about the baby?"

"Nothing yet."

"That's good, right?"

Zelie smiled and nodded. "Aye, that's good."

"There must be pain," Jason said.

"No. She roused enough earlier so I was able to give her

something. I fed her enough opium to embalm her. She'll sleep for a week. I would suggest you do the same, sir." His voice dropping, Zelie placed a compassionate hand on Jason's shoulder. "I'm sorry, Cap'n."

Zelie, followed by Connie, left the room.

Diana had not moved. Her head in her hands, her pale hair streaming toward the floor, she looked like a haggard statue.

Destiny lay amid her tangle of dark hair, the sheet tucked snugly under her shoulders. Her face was unrecognizable, her skin slick and damp from the coatings of salves Zelie had painted over her burns. The left side of her face appeared grotesquely swollen and black, no doubt from Hugo's beating. Bandages covered her eyes.

Had it only been a few hours ago that he had lain in that bed with her, marveled on her beauty, kissed her delicious mouth, and melted at her smile? Christ, he had come so close to losing her. Had he not seen Hugo when he did . . .

"I came to her cabin earlier," came Diana's unsteady voice. "I thought she should eat. I . . . saw the two of you together."

He closed his eyes. "You're angry."

"No. I've given up the anger. As I said earlier, I only want her to be happy."

"Well, I've done a smash-up job of accomplishing that, haven't I?"

"You can't blame yourself for this, Jason. Hugo Mallet is an animal."

"But he's right. If I'd kept my mind on my business, on this ship and crew, he'd have had no reason to strike out at her."

Diana stood and moved against him, laid her head on his shoulder, wrapped her arms around his waist. The action stunned him momentarily, until he felt her body shake. The realization occurred to him suddenly that through the last horrible hours she had shown no signs of her normal hysterics and irrationality. Her soft, quiet sobs against his chest were her only show of distress.

Wrapping his arms around her, he held her close and rocked her, with his eyes closed and his cheek resting on her head.

"What shall we do if she's blind?" Diana wept softly. "You have to know Destiny to understand the import of this dreadful accident. I've never known anyone who so enjoys life and the beauty of the world. The sky is not simply blue to Destiny. A red bird isn't simply red. She drinks in her reality with every breath and glories in its splendidness. And dependency simply isn't a word in her vocabulary."

Diana moved away. "She thinks I don't realize why she remained with me when she could, at any time, have returned to India to be with her father. Her presence in my life has been a godsend. Losing her would have meant life as I had once known it, before she joined me at Sheffield House—sunless, laughless, empty. Though she would never admit it to me, I know why she agreed to marry Lord Chesterfield: to give me a refuge of escape from my marriage. She thought to take care of me for a change. It's her way, you know—to care for others—and she does it very well."

Sinking onto the chair, Diana whispered, "I have never in my life been without someone to take care of me. Nannies, servants, my husband, and Destiny. Looking back now, I see that even when she was a very young woman, Destiny has always been there to bolster me. I wouldn't know the first thing about taking care of myself or of her."

"You needn't worry," he said, as he reached out and stroked her hair, a smile curling one side of his mouth as she turned her big, blue eyes up to his. "I'll take care of you both."

Jason packed the gun's chambers with powder and bullets, then tucked the weapon into his breeches.

Dawn light burned through gray clouds as he returned to the deck, where the wind whipped around the scorched mast and flapped the remnants of the charred sails that hung in ribbons from the spars. The crew stood at the stern of the ship, their heads turning as he approached.

Franz and Zelie stepped aside, revealing Hugo, his abraded, bloody wrists bound by ropes, manacles locked about his ankles. There were scratches across his cheek, and his neck appeared seared by fire.

"You have a choice," Jason declared, drawing the pistol from his belt. "You may jump into the sea or I can shoot you. It's up to you. You'll last perhaps an hour in the water before the sharks find you. A bullet in the head will at least get the ordeal over swiftly."

"Yer bloody daft," Hugo responded with a short laugh as he glanced around at the others, finding only cold indifference to his plight. His brow began to sweat. "What did I tell the lot of you? His reasonin' is gone. You can't trust no bloody commander who lets a woman screw up his priorities."

Looking at Franz, Jason asked, "Where is my daughter?"

"Asleep below, sir."

Jason raised the pistol to Hugo's head and pulled the trigger.

Hugo's body dropped like a stone to the deck.

Zelie raised his eyebrows and sighed. "This calls for a smoke, I think. Will anyone join me?"

Connie and Franz hefted Hugo up and tossed him into the sea.

"Have someone mop up this mess before my daughter sees it," Jason ordered, then walked down the companionway to Destiny's closed door. He entered without knocking.

Her face drained of color, Diana stared at him with her mouth partially open. Only then did he realize that he was covered in Hugo's blood. "Should Destiny wake up, you may assure her that she won't be harmed by Mallet again."

Turning on his heels, he went to his cabin, closed the

door, and locked it before dropping heavily into a chair. He set his gun aside and regarded his blood-splattered features in the mirror.

His reflection stared back at him: a handsome face with lifeless gray eyes and a man's brains staining the front of his shirt.

He released a weary breath.

19

'Twas thine own genius gave the final blow,
And helped to plant the wound that laid thee low:
So the struck eagle, stretched upon the plain,
No more through rolling clouds to soar again,
Viewed his own feather on the fatal dart,
And winged the shaft that quivered in his heart.

—GEORGE NOEL GORDON,
Lord Byron
English Bards and Scotch Reviewers

"Destiny? Dear niece, try not to move. I'll be as gentle as possible, I promise. Can you hear me, dear? It's Diana. I'm going to remove the cloth from your eyes now. The bandages must be changed."

Diana's voice seemed to come to Destiny from far away. Swallowed by incredible blackness, she turned her head toward the sound. Pain sluiced through her face and brought her whimpering back to full consciousness. The welling of tears in her eyes felt like daggers. As she lifted her hand to touch her face, to wipe away the tears, Diana caught her wrist and forced it down to her side. Odd how cold Diana's fingers felt upon her flesh—like tiny bits of velvet ice.

Where was she? What had happened?

"Why are there no lights?" she demanded with a catch in her voice. "Why does my face hurt so horribly?"

"The fire," came the quavering reply. Then more closely

to her ear, "The lamps are lit, Destiny. Do you not recall? There was an accident in the galley. An explosion and fire. . . ."

She shook her head as the memories surfaced, dispersing almost as quickly as they came. Still she did not understand. She could not grasp Diana's meaning and searched with mounting despair and fear for a light.

"Hugo. He hit me and flung me against the wall. He was going to toss me overboard, I think. The lamp fell to the floor and . . ."

There came a sound and she realized suddenly that she and Diana were not alone in the cabin. In that same moment the impact of Diana's words hit her: the lamps were burning yet her world was black. She grabbed for her aunt and tried to sit up.

"I cannot see," she said, shocked at the desperation she heard in her hoarse voice. "Diana, am I blind?"

"Who's here? Someone's here—*there*. I hear breathing."

She tried to rise from the berth. Suddenly there were stronger hands about her, pressing her gently down onto the bed, pinning her arms beside her until she quieted and ceased her thrashing. Only then did she detect Diana's weeping from somewhere across the cabin.

"Be still," came Jason's stern voice, commanding yet gentle and as powerful as the ocean roiling against the walls. Those moments she had spent in his arms came rushing back to her—his vow of love, the incredible security she had experienced knowing that he cared. "Listen to me very closely, Destiny. There's been injury to your eyes caused by the fire. You must try to remain as still as possible and keep your eyes shut." Placing his fingers upon her swollen lids, he tenderly closed them and held them closed until she calmed down. He stroked her brow, and when hot tears leaked from the corners of her eyes he swept them aside with his thumb and whispered, "I'm here, love."

"It's been over a week, Captain. My niece's sight hasn't returned. She doesn't eat. She refuses to leave her cabin. She refuses even to spend time with Jenette and you know how she *adores* your daughter. She won't even discuss what happened with me. I don't know what else to do." Diana paced and mopped the sweat from her temples and throat. She fanned her face with a damp hanky, then the back of her neck. She had tied her hair to the top of her head with a length of muslin ribbon. Pale tendrils drooped around her ears. Her cheeks blazed as red as apples. If she experienced any discomfiture over conversing with him alone in his cabin while he sat before her dressed in nothing more than a pair of trousers, she didn't show it.

"Give her time," he replied. "She's alive. We have that much to be thankful for."

"She has, in her more lucid moments, asked about you."

Jason continued to make notes in the ship's log.

"Captain, I can't understand how you can remain so composed over this tragic turn of events. You, of all people, should realize what such a loss means to her."

Not for the first time, Jason experienced a spear of guilt. He blamed himself for what had happened to Destiny. Mallet had been making threats toward the women since the night they had shoved off from Portsmouth. Had Jason had his wits about him he would have dumped Hugo in Tenerife and been done with him. But it wasn't only Destiny's injuries that had him unbalanced. The damage the fire had caused was enough to slow their journey to Cape Town down to a snail's pace. Most of the mainmast, its sheets, and shrouds had burned before the crew had managed to put out the flames. If Trevor's ship topped the horizon now, Jason's crew wouldn't stand an iceberg's chance in hell of outrunning him.

"I have a ship and crew to oversee, Diana. This last fiasco has damaged us severely. If Dunleavy were to find us now the few men we lost during the storm will hardly compare to what will happen if we're swamped with boarders. Nor will Destiny's ordeal hold a candle to what Dunleavy will subject her to. This ship is crippled, Diana. Every day we limp along without our mainmast and shrouds, Dunleavy grows closer. Besides"—Jason threw the pen down and slammed the log book closed—"I've attempted to see Destiny several times. She wants none of it."

Diana frowned. "When has that ever stopped you?"

"She's upset. I don't see why I should exacerbate her problems by subjecting her to my company if she doesn't want it."

With a shake of her head, Diana stared at him in disbelief. "She's horrified that you think her ugly."

"Ugly." He might have laughed if the comment had not been so idiotic.

"What is she supposed to think? One day you're sniffing like a hound at her skirt hem, the next, after the fire, after she's injured, you bury yourself away and pretend she doesn't exist." Her eyes darkening and her brows drawing together, she added, "Or perhaps there's more to it. Perhaps the idea of Hugo—"

"Don't." He stood, suddenly, causing Diana to back away. The madness that had been eating at him over the last week was there, tapping at his brain. The memory of his and Destiny's lovemaking was ruined, replaced by filthy images of Hugo Mallet, his big, beefy fingers clawing at her, spreading her—

"That's it, isn't it?" came Diana's voice. "It's eating you up inside. You believe he raped her, don't you?"

He kicked his chair. It crashed against the wall. "Son of a bitch!" he shouted, then kicked the chair again, harder. "I want to kill him all over again every time I think of her . . ." He turned and drove his fist into the wall. Pain exploded through his hand and shot into his shoulder. Closing his eyes and gritting his teeth, Jason laid his forehead against the wall and swallowed back the groan in his throat.

Diana laid one hand on his back. "You must ask her, Jason."

"For God's sake, Diana, I've done nothing but hurt her. If I hadn't tricked her onto this ship, this entire crucifying experience would never have happened."

"No matter what quirks of fate brought her to this moment, the bottom line is, she needs you desperately. She needs to know you still care, regardless of the fire or of what might have happened with Hugo."

"Of course I care," he said softly. "Of course I care."

The sky was cloudless and the sea relatively calm, adding to the heat of the day. Zelie was just exiting the companionway, a tray of food in his hands, as Jason, pulling on his shirt and buttoning it, stepped on deck. Jason regarded the uneaten porridge and bread, then Zelie's expression.

"She isn't well," Zelie informed him. " 'Course this bloody heat don't help. It's like Calcutta in June in her cabin."

"Where's Jenette?"

"With Connie. He's teaching her how to tie sailor's knots. I wager she'll be able to sail this crate herself by the time we reach Cape Town."

Jason grinned. "Set me a table on the quarterdeck. I want that porridge warmed. And bread with butter."

Zelie nodded.

Jason discussed the ship's course with Fritz, who stood at the helm. He then went below and, without bothering to knock, entered Destiny's cabin. There was so little light in the cabin Jason was forced to squint to see that Diana was brushing Destiny's hair. "Good God, it's dark as perdition in here," he declared and moved toward the lamp on the wall.

"No!" Destiny cried, her voice trembling with panic. "And go away, Batson. *Leave*. I don't want to see you again. Ever."

"That might be difficult, considering I plan to marry you once we reach Cape Town."

"Never. I won't marry you."

"Of course you will."

"I won't."

"You're being irrational."

"I won't abide your pity."

"You don't need mine—you've got enough for the both of us."

Her shoulders snapped back and her hands clasped the chair arms in a death grip.

"Go away. I don't think I like you any longer, and besides, you're much more frightening when I cannot see you. You sound so much bigger."

"I swear to you I haven't grown an inch since you last saw me."

Jason and Diana exchanged looks. She put down the hairbrush and, with a last pleading glance at Jason, left the cabin. He walked to Destiny's side. She wore the blue blouse and pink skirt he had purchased for her in Tenerife. As usual, she was barefoot. "I've come to take you up," he declared. "It's a fine day. Perhaps a little sun will restore your energy and appetite."

"No," she replied and turned her face away, shielding it with one upraised hand.

"You've buried yourself away in this stuffy, dark little hole long enough. You're going up."

She shook her head and turned her back to him.

His frustration mounting, Jason bent to one knee beside her, gently caught her little chin in his fingers, and forced her face around. The skin around her eyes was still red and puffy. The fire had burned away her eyelashes and singed her eyebrows. But Zelie had been right. The burns were superficial. While he was certain they hurt her like hell for the moment, eventually the skin would heal and there would be little if any trace of the accident. Her eyes, however, were another matter. Zelie had suggested they remained bandaged until they reached Cape Town and she could be seen by a physician.

"Don't look at me," she said.

"Don't be daft. You're beautiful."

"Liar."

"You're starting to annoy me."

"I must look like that horrid mask you wore."

His eyebrows went up, and he laughed. "Good God, I

think not." He reached for the tin of salve Diana had set on the washstand. He dipped one finger into it and began to tenderly smear the foul-smelling concoction over her cheeks. She winced and pulled away. He slid it over her chin, across her nose, along her brow line.

"It stinks." She wrinkled her nose. "What is it?"

"Knowing Zelie, I'm certain if you ingested it you would float, delirious, off the ship."

A smile twitched her mouth. Her hand came up and touched his face. Her fingertips traced his lips. He kissed them. They wandered over his cheeks, hesitated along his jaw.

"You haven't shaved in a few days." She tipped her head and her lips curled slightly. "I like it when you don't shave. You look like a pirate."

"Yo ho ho." He smiled and closed his eyes as she inched her fingers along his brow, down the bridge of his nose, again to his lips, which parted and closed gently around her fingertips.

Her eyelids grew heavy and her breathing deepened. "I think I'll go mad if I never see you again, Jason."

He bowed his head and she ran her hands into his hair. The touch aroused him. His breathing quickened and his skin warmed. His need for her frightened him like no enemy's weapon ever had. He was lost.

Searching her face, he asked with all the gentleness he could muster, "I have to know if he raped you."

Destiny became very still. The hands in his hair remained there, heavy, caressing. He heard her swallow. "No," she replied in a whisper.

"No." He wanted to believe it. He caught the hem of her dress with one finger and slowly lifted it. There were red streaks on her calves. He avoided them, sliding his hand along the inside of her thigh while she stared at him blindly, her parched lips parting with a slight exhalation of air. "I keep thinking of our last time together, before the fire. I worry that I wasn't gentle enough. I can be gentle, Des. I simply wanted you too badly, and I was confused, drunk with self-pity, I guess, and too much rum. I thought you didn't want me any longer. Thought you didn't love me any longer. Do you still love me?"

She caught his wrist and pushed his hand away, then sank back in the chair. "Leave me alone, please. I just want to be alone."

After a moment, he stood, swallowing his frustration. "No. I won't leave you alone. I don't intend to stand here and argue the issue. This is my goddamn ship and if I order you up, you will up." He plucked her out of the chair and held her in his arms, anticipating a struggle. He didn't get one. Lifelessly, she sagged against him.

By the time he reached the quarterdeck Zelie had placed the table and food. He sat Destiny in a chair, then glared a warning at his men, who hovered close. Dragging his chair next to Destiny's he sat down and put a spoon in her hand.

"Eat. That's an order. If you don't eat, I'll feed you myself."

Her brows knitted and she dropped the spoon in his lap. "I don't want to eat."

He picked it up and wrapped her fingers around it.

She dropped it again and turned her face away.

Jason scooped a spoonful of porridge and, catching her chin, put the spoon to her lips. "Eat. *Please.* Think of our baby, Des."

A moment passed; her lips parted. She ate the porridge, her expression a portrait of intense displeasure.

Jason sat back in his chair. In daylight he could see that the skin was healing nicely, although Destiny's complexion appeared as pale as the porridge, all but the bruises, which had gone from black to green and yellow.

At last, she turned her face toward the sun. "Describe the sky to me," she said.

"Blue."

"Simply blue? No hint of green or pink or gold?"

He shook his head. "Light blue. Cloudless."

"And the water?"

"Tranquil."

"I can *feel* tranquil. Describe the water to me."

Jason searched the water. "Reflecting the sky. You can hardly determine where the sea meets the sky on the horizon. The waves are moderate. A touch of froth now and again."

He offered her another spoon of porridge. She took it and licked her lips. "It's all so very . . . odd, how the senses expand. The sun feels warmer on my face. The sea is almost overwhelmingly pungent to smell. I can feel the texture of sugar on my tongue. And the sounds. Every thump and bump of the riggings, every creak and groan of the timbers are as clashing as cymbals in my ears. And voices—so distinct. One never truly listens to sound, I think. We hear the individual words, but not the tone in which they're uttered. For instance, in the last week I've learned the sound of Zelie's voice. He rolls his *r*'s and whines his *n*'s. And Connie . . ." She managed a smile. "The words rise up from his chest like air from a whale's spout."

Jason laughed. "If that's a nice way of saying he's a blowhard, then I wholeheartedly agree."

"Tell me about Ceylonia," she said.

He smiled as the images of his home rose up in vibrant detail before his mind's eye. Talking about the island plantation off the coast of Ceylon was a favorite pastime, and anyone who showed the slightest interest would be occupied for hours were they inclined to listen. "I raise tea; *Camellia sansis.* I bought the island seven years ago for a pittance when a coffee grower lost his crops and subsequently his fortune when disease wiped out his plants. I replaced them with tea."

"It must be very beautiful there."

"Paradise. There are mountains, plateaus, and valleys. There are flowing rivers and cascading waterfalls and tropical forests with jackfruit trees that produce fruit so large if they fall on your head they'll kill you."

"No!" she gasped.

"Yes. My overseer was once knocked silly by one. He

was unconscious for three days. And there are amazing animals. Elephants, of course, which we use for labor, clearing forests and plowing fields up the mountainsides, where it would be too difficult for horses. There are birds of every imaginable color, and tiny monkeys that would fit in the palm of my hand."

"Jenette should like that very much." Destiny laughed.

"One day I saw a lizard as large as a man, and another time I saw several hundred bats with wingspans greater than my outstretched arms.

"The mountaintops are always covered with haze. Occasionally the island is completely hidden by mist so thick a ship could collide with another and even then you would not be able to see what you'd hit. Then, with no warning, the mist parts and there before you is this emerald jewel rising up out of the sea. My home occupies an entire bluff that overlooks the harbor. There's a big brass bell on the docks to announce the return of my ships."

"Ships?"

"I own my own shipping company. Two rings of the bell announces my cargo ships. Three rings announces to my staff that I've come home. That's always a fine excuse for a celebration."

"It's been a long time since you were last home?"

"Two years."

Lifting her head, she turned her face in his direction. "Why, when you have such a wonderful home, would you choose to leave it for war?"

"Because it was lonely. I might work my fingers to the bone during the day, but nights were damn long and empty. And there was always that nagging thought that perhaps I could make a difference in a fight. Rescue the innocent. Deliver the downtrodden. Vanquish evil. But somewhere along the way I began to question my ideas of evil. For the enemy, I was the evil, and the lines between the righteous and the unrighteous began to blur. I began to think back on all the men I had killed, and questioned if I was right to do it." He looked away, out to sea. "I don't doubt there is distinct evil. I've confronted it. I've looked it in the eye and learned to recognize it. You can smell it. Feel it. Taste it. It creeps into the flesh and turns blood to ice. Evil cares nothing for innocence, Des. Or humanity. It destroys indiscriminately."

"Hugo was evil," she said.

"Yes."

"And you killed him."

". . . Yes. I would kill him a thousand times again for harming you."

Her body relaxed. She lay her head on his shoulder again, and said softly, "Your home sounds so wonderful. And beautiful. It saddens me to think I might never see it."

He curled his hand around hers. "I'll be your eyes, Des."

"Jason?"

"What, sweetheart?"

"My father isn't evil. You believe that, don't you?"

"Yes." He closed his eyes. "I do."

They sat in silence. He felt her hair against his flesh, wild, soft, fragrant, tying him up in their coils and robbing him of reason. He turned his eyes from the brilliant sky and focused on Destiny, her soft, thoughtful, and sad expression. He shut his ears to the sounds of his crew talking, laughing, the wind popping the sheets and the waves whooshing against the hull.

I love you, he thought.

Fontaine was not a topic he wanted to address. But Jason's future with Destiny was, and, alas, he suspected he wouldn't be able to broach one without dealing with the other.

"As soon as we arrive in Cape Town, we'll be married. I'll buy you a pretty dress for the occasion. And a hat. One of those flimsy things with netting on it and beads and such. Of course, there's business to attend to: the supplying of the ship, the hiring of new crew members; we should be able to learn quite a lot about the state of the situation in Cawnpore. I have contacts there.

"We'll spend our wedding night at the Cape Hotel.

You'll like it. It overlooks the harbor. The beds are clean and comfortable. The food is excellent. . . . The next day we'll leave for Ceylonia."

Her head raised, and she frowned. "You mean to drop off Jenette. Right?"

"Yes."

Her features relaxed.

"And you, of course."

Hot color stained her cheeks. She was trying desperately to contain her anger and disappointment, and failing miserably. He knew her thoughts: what good would a blind woman do her father? Now she would be forced to trust Jason. Her father's life was in his hands.

I love you, he thought again. *Trust me.*

20

After a youth and manhood passed half in unutter-
able misery and half in dreary solitude, I have had
for the first time found what I can truly love—I have
found you.

—CHARLOTTE BRONTË, *Jane Eyre*

Cape Town, South Africa

"You've contacted the company?" Jason carefully ran the
sharp razor edge across his lathered jaw and mentally
ticked off his list of things to do, which included meeting
Diana at Henry Mason's Fine Jewelry down on Bond
Road. He wanted her help in picking out a ring for Destiny—then he, Diana, and Jenette would drop into the
Carousel, a shop that specialized in dolls from around the
world.

He studied his reflection. There were shadows of fatigue
under his eyes; normally the very thought of marching into
a brewing war would have put a flame of fire in his cheeks.
Instead, all he could think about was how it was all going
to affect Destiny.

Connie laughed and nodded. "Aye, as always they're
chompin' to get to it."

They would be, Jason thought. He had fought with these
particular men before, at Calamita Bay, Balaklava, Inkermann, and Sebastopol. They were lethal. They were also
loyal to Jason. They would stand against Dunleavy if so

ordered. They didn't care for Dunleavy any more than he did.

"They were expectin' to hear from one of us, what with the stirrin's of problems in Punjab. Word is, there was recent situations with the Thirty-fourth Native Infantry. There's talk that Canning intends to disband them. Major-General Hearsy concurs such a move would help the morale of the Brits, if nothin' else."

"What have they heard about Fontaine and Sahib?"

"Not much. Only that he was seen two months ago at a soiree put on by Nana Sahib. Said he looked ill, racked by coughin', and was forced to excuse himself from the party."

Jason tossed the razor into the bowl of frothy water and toweled off his face and neck and the front of his damp chest.

From his window Jason could see the *Pretender* perfectly, the blackened mast, the charred remnants of the mainsail. There was no way in hell the ship could be repaired within a week. And while the tempest had put time and miles between the *Pretender* and Trevor's clipper, if Jason's calculations were right, and Trevor had the wind with him, his brother could easily arrive in Cape Town in no more than two or three days, if not sooner. If he was going to outrun Trevor, he was going to need a better ship.

He scanned the water, his attention fixing on the sleek clipper anchored near the mouth of the harbor.

Connie joined him at the window. "Nice ship, that one. I know what yer thinkin'. If we had that ship we'd stand a chance at outrunnin' yer brother and Dunleavy. I've already inquired about her. She's constructed of teak. Length two hundred twenty-five feet, beam forty feet eight inches, depth twenty-one feet six inches. Built at Aberdeen by the celebrated Messrs. Hall; entirely copper-fastened and resheathed with yellow metal; has a full poop and top-gallant forecastle, with good heights between decks, and is very efficiently secured with iron knees and riders. The captain was blowin' that he's made the run from Shanghai to London in ninety-eight days. With that baby we'll see Calcutta in three weeks tops. And to answer yer question before ya ask it, she ain't for sale."

"Everything is for sale." Jason reached for his shirt.

"We know that, but her captain is gonna be tough to convince."

"Simply tell him to name his price. And if that doesn't work, explain to him how his health, and the health of his crew, will suffer sorrily if I don't get my way. You might include a vivid description of my fits of temper."

Connie chuckled. "Y' mean like how y' poked out a man's eyeballs and cut off his tongue because he wouldn't part with his pocket watch?"

Jason winced.

"Too exaggerated?"

"A bit."

"How about the one that yer Bluebeard's grandson, and yer favorite pastime is hangin' men by their scrotum till they—"

"We'll sail in three days."

"She'll be ready and so will we."

Jason moved the desk and picked up a stack of papers. He handed them to Connie. "Explicit directions regarding the dispersal of my personal belongings should something happen to me. Everything is to be left to my wife and children, including Ceylonia Plantation and the shipping business. Send it immediately to my solicitor in London."

"So when do y' plan on exchangin' yer vows?"

"Tomorrow afternoon. I've a meeting at the registrar's office in an hour to formalize the arrangements. Afterward I plan on paying a call to a physician I know. I'd like him to have a look at Destiny's eyes."

There came a knock at the door. Connie opened it as Jason reached for his coat.

The stunning blond smiled up at Connie. "Hello, La-Touche."

Connie shook his head and laughed. "Julia Howard, y' get prettier every time I see y'."

"And you were always an outrageous flirt." She patted Connie's cheek before stepping around him, her smile widening at Jason. Her cheeks flushed and her blue eyes glistened with tears. "Jason! I came just as soon as I received your note."

"Hello, beautiful." He opened his arms. She flung herself into them and held him as tightly as she could as Connie left the room, closing the door gently behind him. Jason spun her around before setting her back on her feet. Still she clung, smiling up into his eyes, her hands fiercely gripping his shoulders.

"It's been so long, Jason. I worried, we all worried that something dreadful had happened at Calamita Bay."

"I rubbed Dunleavy the wrong way, I'm afraid, and spent a few months in solitary."

"You might have written. We've all been frantic."

"Sorry." He cupped her fair face between his hands and smiled. "You look well, Julia."

"I wish I could say the same about you. You look dreadfully tired."

"It was a rough ride. I lost a couple of men on the way. Paolo and Gabriel."

Her face clouded and she covered his hands with hers. "I'm sorry. I know Paolo was especially dear to you." More softly, she said, "Thank God, you're all right. I have an idea. You'll come to the house tonight for a decent meal. I'll have the help prepare one of the extra rooms. You can stay over and we'll catch up. We'll get smashed on fine brandy and reminisce. Say yes, Jason."

He pulled away and buttoned his coat. He had suspected for a number of years that Julia Howard had fallen in love with him. She had never outwardly conveyed it—she wouldn't, of course, she was too much of a lady, and besides, she would worry that he would reject her and then their friendship would have become strained. Not that he would have rejected her without a great deal of consideration first. Undoubtedly she was a beautiful woman. Vibrant, intelligent, a few years older than he, gentle and soft-spoken. A relationship with Julia would have been very . . . comfortable. But she was the widow of a man who had fought at his side for a number of years, who had saved Jason's life a time or two before catching a bullet himself during their campaign in Persia.

"How are the children?" he asked.

The smile still on her face, but slightly more strained, she shrugged. "Wonderful. Claudia is ten now. Michael is four. They'll both want to see you, of course. Perhaps tonight. At dinner?"

Jason slid his hands into his coat pockets and forced himself to meet her hopeful, watchful eyes. "You still have the shop? Sell ladies' ready-mades and such?"

She nodded. Her fine blond brows drew together. "The best ready-mades in Cape Town, thanks to you."

"Fine. . . . I need a favor." He took a deep breath and watched a shadow of dread move over Julia's blue eyes. "I'm getting married."

"Married?" Drawing back her shoulders, Julia cleared her throat and moved away, putting distance between them. "My God. I never thought I'd see the day. You've always been so dead set against marriage while you were associated with Cobra."

"Because it isn't fair on the wives."

"Well." She laughed and turned away. "You're certainly right about that. So, the young woman must be special to have made you change your mind."

"I haven't changed my mind. I'm getting out of the business."

"Oh? Then she *is* remarkable. And lucky. *Very* lucky that her husband will love her enough to walk away from his passion for fighting." Reluctantly, she looked back over her shoulder at Jason. Her cheeks appeared pale and her eyes slightly red. "When do I get to meet her?"

"I have an appointment at the registrar's. If you'll walk downstairs with me, I'll tell you about her."

He offered his arm to her. After a moment's hesitation, she smiled and took it.

Cautiously, Destiny removed the bandage from her eyes and allowed it to fall to the floor. Both Diana and Jason had given her implicit orders that she was not to discard the bandages without the doctor's approval, but she had to know. She was desperate to know. Time was running out. If her sight was permanently gone, then she would, without further protest, retire to Ceylonia and remain there with Diana and Jenette while Jason went to look for her father. But if Zelie's prediction was right, that her eyes had healed, then she would demand to go to India with Jason, just as she had always planned.

Carefully, she opened her eyes, little by little.

She thought at first that she was dreaming, as she so often did; a dream of awakening to a vibrant, colorful world with recognizable faces. But she was not dreaming presently. She focused hard on the room's interior, making out the drab shapes of furniture. They were as indistinct as ghosts in heavy fog, but they were there, nevertheless, distinguishable from the blackness that had suffocated her the last weeks.

Rolling from the bed, her hands before her, she moved clumsily across the floor, her equilibrium still pitching from the many weeks of living aboard ship. Light poured in through the double French doors. She opened them.

Oh, the pain—

She turned away swiftly, her hands over her throbbing eyes. Gradually she opened them again, cautiously, allowing her eyes to focus slowly.

The light and colors blurred, faded in and out, sending spears of sharp pain through her eyes. She moved to the balcony balustrade. The images in the distance were vague, like washes of running watercolors on canvas, blending into indistinctness. There were vast and endless waves of blue with patches of green and brown and splashes of white. And there was movement. Movement!

She could actually see the carts and horses and buggies and people traveling along the brown strips that were roads; and there were men moving like scurrying ants amid the stacks of cargo waiting to be transported onto the dozens of ships situated along the wharves. If she focused very hard she might even see the *Pretender* and her crew . . . *and her captain.* . . .

No. Trying too hard, too soon might prove harmful. . . .

Oh, how her heart raced with the idea of sharing her good news with Diana and Jason—the man who would be her husband by this time tomorrow. Her husband. . . .

Destiny laughed aloud. She hugged herself and pirouetted on her tiptoes, then laughed all the harder as she realized what a sight she must be for those who might look up and catch a glimpse of her jigging madly about in her dressing gown.

As minutes passed, her sight sharpened, as did the dreadful ache in her eyes. Still, she visually feasted upon the most minute detail: the scrolled-leaf design of the iron balustrade around the balcony, the wood grain of the floor, the smudged fingerprints around the doorknob that once might have made her wrinkle her nose and complain about the untidiness of the room. The crystal prisms dangling from the lamp globe were as brilliant as diamonds in sunlight. The lace counterpane on her bed looked as finely intricate as spiderweb, and the flowers—oh, the flowers that had arrived that morning from Jason, dozens of them with petals like colorful velvet and that turned the stale air of her hotel room into glorious sweet scents. After long, piercingly painful moments she finally made the words out on the card, signed simply:

With love, Jason.

With a bouquet of flowers pressed to her nose, she danced again onto the balcony and focused on the carriages below.

There was a man with his arms around a woman, and her arms around him. He pressed a quick kiss onto her lips before climbing into the carriage.

Jason?

The woman smiled brilliantly and kissed his cheek. She backed away and waved, watched as the cab disappeared down the street, then she turned back to the hotel.

Heart racing and her eyes burning, Destiny returned to the room and closed the French doors hard, blocking out the sunlight. Her knees felt like water, and she tried to tell herself that it was because of her excitement over her eyes and not because of fear that her fiancé was being unfaithful. She sat in a chair and chastised herself for focusing more on some sense of confused jealousy than on the fact that her eyesight had returned.

Someone knocked on the door.

"Who is it?" she called, sounding snappish when she hadn't meant to.

"My name is Julia Howard," came the voice. "I'm a friend of Jason's."

She glanced at the bandages on the floor. "What do you want?"

"To speak with you." The door opened and the pretty blond woman stepped in. Her face appeared cautious and worried. "Please, don't get up, Destiny. Jason told me about your accident." She closed the door and smiled. "He was going to introduce us, but he was pressed for time." Julia walked to Destiny and reached for her hand, shook it, patted it reassuringly. "Well, he said you were very pretty, and you are."

"Did he?" Destiny lifted one eyebrow and withdrew her hand. She thought of informing the woman that her eyesight had returned, then decided against it, prompted by a tickling of devilishness.

Julia dragged up another chair and sat on it. "I have a ready-made shop not far from here, Destiny. Jason asked that I meet with you, get an idea about your sizing, and perhaps bring you something pretty in which to be married tomorrow."

"How do you know Jason?" she asked, looking directly into the woman's blue eyes.

Julia sat back and returned the look with an intensity that might have made a sighted woman shrink. But Destiny wasn't supposed to be sighted and therefore was not allowed to flinch. "I've known Jason for nearly ten years. He and my husband . . . worked together."

"You mean with Cobra."

"Yes." Julia nodded and clasped her hands together in her lap. Tilting her head slightly, she studied Destiny sharply.

"Then you're married?"

"Not any longer. I'm a widow."

Heat rushed into Destiny's face. She averted her eyes, turned them toward the French doors, then quickly away when the sunlight through the sheer curtains made her eyes throb. "I'm sorry."

"Perhaps you and I will become friends, eventually. We all do. We must. Without the support of one another I fear we would all go mad with worry. Then again, Jason tells me he plans to retire once he has this India thing behind him."

"What did he tell you about India?"

"Only that he and his men were going there to assess the situation with Nana Sahib. I'll pray that it all turns out to be a tempest in a teapot and that he can return to Ceylonia as soon as possible. Otherwise you may be rattling around the house for months, waiting for some word from him. Should you grow weary of the isolation, you could come back to Cape Town. You'll be welcome to stay with me. I'll introduce you to the others."

"Others?"

"The wives, of course. We have Jason to thank for bringing us together. Mostly, we're widows, you see, and might have been left destitute upon our husbands' deaths had Jason not begun a financial aid plan for the families. He set up an account to finance businesses for the widows or children of the men killed during action. I now have a very successful ready-made shop for ladies. Mary Anderson runs a boardinghouse. Maggie Theisen owns a bakery and Carla Justice produces the ready-mades I sell in my shop."

Julia's mouth curved in a smile as she sat forward and propped her elbows on her knees. "Is something wrong, Destiny? You're suddenly looking very pale."

"So many widows," she replied with a sinking heart and a rising sense of panic.

"A great many, I'm afraid. But . . . we knew going in what the odds were of happily ever after. I'm not quite sure why we do it. Perhaps it's simply the kind of men they are. The sort that fairy tales are made of: chivalrous, dangerous, courageous. Forbidden. Unattainable. Unpredictable. Still . . . it doesn't make it any easier when the inevitable happens. Yet, were I given the opportunity . . . I would do it again . . . for the right man."

Julia caught Destiny's hand and helped her to stand. She walked around Destiny, running her hands over her waist, along her back, down her arms, humming quietly and whispering mental notes to herself. Destiny stared at the wall, fear growing as a pressure at the base of her throat and squeezing fiercely at her heart. The idea of Jason dying terrified her.

Finally Julia stepped away, although she continued to regard Destiny with an intensity that grooved her brow with deep lines of worry and sadness. "You're expecting a child," she said.

Destiny nodded and, once again, looked into Julia's eyes.

"And you can see." Julia smiled.

Chagrin crept over Destiny's features. "I'm sorry. He doesn't know yet. It's only been since this morning. . . . I'm sorry, Julia. I wanted to determine what your feelings were for Jason."

"And did you determine them?" she asked.

"You're in love with him."

"Yes." She sighed. "I am."

Destiny paced the room throughout the afternoon as she waited for Jason's return. She was tempted to dress and hunt for him, then convinced herself that to do so would be irrational if not outright idiotic. She would never find him, and even if she did, what would she say? That suddenly she was terrified of his storming into India to find her father? For heaven's sake, she had just dragged him halfway around the world to do just that. And if she did convince him not to traipse into Cawnpore, what would that mean for her father?

As the afternoon shadows lengthened and dusk crawled over the town, Julia returned with an entourage of smiling women who each introduced herself with a friendliness that brought tears to Destiny's eyes. She recognized their names immediately: Maggie, Carla, Mary. The merry widows, Destiny thought with a fresh spear of pain and fear.

With Julia came boxes of clothes. As excited as a child, Destiny flung them open to find a trousseau of gowns and shoes and lacy shawls. But it was the wedding dress that gave her pause. Her hands trembled as she held it up to her body, allowed her fingertips to caress it.

The dress was of terry velvet, ornamented with passementerie and lace. The body was high, and very close, prolonged down to the hips. It was trimmed in front with buttons and guipure, and ears of satin passementerie laid in chevrons. A narrow engrelure bordered the bottom of the body, which terminated in a slightly tucked lace. The skirt fell in beautiful lace flounces, and a gathered lace collar fell over the body. A frill of tulle illusion ruche rounded the neck and the sleeves were a pagoda form trimmed in three rows of lace.

Destiny wasted little time in undressing, tossing aside the tired dress that she had worn the last many weeks aboard the *Pretender*. Carefully she donned the splendid gown, holding her breath in fear that it would not fit her thickening waist. But it did, barely.

She did her best to study her reflection in the mirror, turning one way then the other as she regarded her silhouette. Her image sharpened then waned, blurring over in fragments of haze that threatened to discourage her until she repeatedly reminded herself not to expect too much too soon.

Her hair would be a problem. How was she to dress it? For her first marriage Diana and several servants had arranged Destiny's hair with a narrow bandeau of white lilac. But there were no servants here and she would be forced to make do. Perhaps she would leave it down and pin within it a flurry of orange-flowers that would cascade over her shoulders.

The door opened and Diana walked in, leading Jenette by one hand. The child carried a new doll and proceeded to hop up and down in excitement as she saw Destiny in her dress.

"This must be Jason's little girl," Julia declared, and the group of exuberant women all began to babble enthusiastically at once and swarm around the child like bees around honey.

Laughing, Diana stepped away, toward Destiny, leaving Jenette the center of the clucking women's attention. "Thank God," she whispered toward Destiny. "While I adore the child, don't get me wrong, Des, having spent the entire day doing my best to entertain her, I fear my feet won't ever recover. Perhaps it's good that James and I never had children. I'm not certain I would have had the patience or the stamina for raising them. I'm positively exhausted."

Destiny nodded. "Yes, I suppose she would be active, especially after spending all that time on a ship." Narrowing her eyes to better focus, Destiny watched Diana's brows draw together as her aunt finally shifted her attention to Destiny, noted the dress she was wearing, then up, to her eyes. Seconds passed as Diana studied her, then said softly, uncertainly, "You've removed the bandages, Des. Zelie told you not to . . . That is, until the doctor . . . Oh, my God. You can see me, can't you?"

Destiny nodded and laughed.

"Oh! That's wonderful!" Diana flung her arms around Destiny and hugged her.

"It comes and goes, but not completely, of course, but still and all, I can actually see again and—I have to tell Jason. Won't it be a wonderful wedding gift, Diana?"

Her eyes brimming with tears, Diana stepped back and regarded Destiny's face, her own a bit colorless and her smile slightly strained.

It was in that very instant that it happened, the tiny flutter in her belly, like butterfly wings batting the air. Destiny gasped. Again, tickling and floating; Destiny began to laugh; she looked around, into the women's curious faces. "The baby moved," she cried. "It's dancing in me like a little hummingbird!"

With an eruption of excitement the women surrounded her, hugging, offering their best wishes: Julia had the perfect baptismal gown in her shop, and if not Carla would be happy to provide one when the time came.

Jenette joined in the celebration, tugging on Destiny's skirt and squealing, "You're going to be my new mama soon! *Oui?*"

Destiny dropped down and smiled into the child's bright eyes. "Will that please you, Jenette?"

"Oh, yes. Then everything will be right again. I'll have a mama and a papa who will give me all the kittens and puppies and monkeys I want. My papa told me so!"

Laughing, Destiny swept Jenette into her arms and held her fiercely; she kissed the top of her head. Then Destiny looked at Diana, standing alone, her arms folded, her expression remote and worried. Destiny's own smile faded as a shiver of apprehension rushed through her.

"Something's wrong," she said quietly.

Gradually the din of excitement faded. The women focused their attention on Diana, neither speaking nor moving.

"There's trouble," Diana finally replied. "A ship arrived this afternoon from Calcutta with the news. It seems that a war is imminent. An urgent request for troops has been sent out. Jason has spent the last few hours preparing for their departure tomorrow afternoon. There won't be time to go first to Ceylonia. He intends for us to remain here until he returns."

Destiny slowly stood. She looked at Julia, whose expression had become one of sad resignation, then the others, who turned away, silent, their faces reflecting the memory of their losses.

Slouched in a chair, his legs outstretched and crossed at his booted ankles, Jason rolled the slender gold wedding band between his fingers as Connie paced. He was having a hard time keeping his thoughts focused on business, as discomposing as it was. They kept drifting to Destiny and Jenette. He recalled the child's pleasure that afternoon as she chose her doll. He thought that in exactly fifteen hours he would stand before the registrar and marry Destiny Fontaine Chesterfield. He thought about the surprise on Compton Fontaine's face when Jason broke the news to him that he had finally gotten smart and married Compton's cherished daughter . . . and that they were expecting a child. . . .

"Seems all hell has broken out, Cap'n. On Friday, April twenty-fourth, Colonel Charmichael-Smyth of the Third Native Cavalry attempted to alleviate his most elite sowars' fears that our government was out to dirty their souls by feedin' them animal fat on their ammunition. He declared that the rumors of such were false and those who believed as much were stupid. He permitted them to rip the cartridges with their fingers to avoid defilin' their caste, if they so desired. When he distributed the cartridges, all but five sowars refused to take them. . . . Are y' listenin' to a word I've been sayin', Jason?"

"Yes." He nodded. "I'm listening."

Franz joined in. "General William Hewitt ordered those who refused the cartridges imprisoned to await court-martial. There's been movement and dissension ever since among the natives."

"In February," Fritz added, "chupatties began to circulate among the Indian constables and village watchmen of the Doab. It was believed that these cakes were concocted out of flour and lotus seeds by Dassa Bawa, Nana Sahib's associate. Dassa Bawa distributed the chupatties among the watchmen of Bithur, who spread them throughout the North-Western Provinces, declaring that Nana's suzerainty would one day extend as far as the chupatties reached."

Franz shook his head. "Such an act has been known in the past to prepare the peasants for some imminent up-heaval. Those who ate the chupatties dedicated themselves to obey whatever orders their chief might declare."

Connie spoke up again, albeit reluctantly and wearily. "There's little doubt that Compton Fontaine is somehow involved with Sahib. He's livin' at Sahib's compound, Saturday House, at Bithur, and has been for the last year."

Closing his fingers around the tiny ring, Jason shut his eyes and whispered, "Damn."

The door flew open and Destiny ran in.

Jason jumped to his feet as she flung herself against him, arms around his neck, fingers clutching his shirt. He was forced to peel her arms away in order to look at her, the vision she made, dressed in the gown she would be married in tomorrow. Obviously Julia had not let him down. Destiny looked like some spirited angel, all in white with her hair a riot of dark curls that cupped her porcelainlike face. Her eyes were two big green jewels that reflected the lamplight.

Her eyes . . . "Christ," he whispered, cradling her face between his hands and staring hard into her eyes. "You can see."

She nodded and tears spilled. "Isn't it wonderful? And something else that's wonderful. Our baby moved. It's real now, Jason. I felt it. It fluttered inside me like a butterfly. And, oh, God, I can't let you go. You mustn't! I won't have it. Please, please promise me that you won't go. I love you, Jason. I can't bear the thought of losing you."

Had she strolled into the room and gut punched him he would not have been so winded as he was by her plea. He wasn't certain if he was moved more by the return of her eyesight and the announcement that their baby was apparently flourishing, or because, for the first time since their long, arduous journey together had begun, she had, at long last, come to care more for him than how he might help, or harm, her father.

"We'll all go to Ceylonia. Together. You. Me. Diana. Jenette. You'll let Connie and Zelie and the others deal with Nana Sahib . . . and my father, if necessary."

"Sounds like a plan to me," Connie said, not so teasingly.

"Aye. Me, too," Franz said.

"And me," Fritz joined in. "Consider it a wedding present."

"Please," she said again and sank against him. "I'm sorry I've been so selfish and self-centered these last weeks, thinking only of my father's welfare and never of how this war could affect you. Don't make me one of them—a widow. I simply couldn't live with it, Jason. I want to spend the rest of my life with you. I want you to raise our children and teach them how to grow tea and promise me, damn you, that you won't go." Her fingers twisted into his shirtfront, and she shook him. "Promise me!"

Jason felt his heart swell as he looked down into Destiny's desperate eyes. She was crying now, not because of her fear for her father, but because of her intense love for him. Suddenly those fairy-tale images of home and hearth and forever glowed vibrant and hot. There wouldn't be a solitary soul who would look upon his decision to retire to Ceylonia as anything but wise, considering the circumstances.

Drawing her close, he smiled and whispered, "Des, I would love—"

A sudden explosion shook the building, shattered the glass from the windows, and rocked the globe lamps on the tables so fiercely they nearly toppled. From the hallway came the sounds of women screaming. Destiny stumbled and would have fallen if Jason had not grabbed her and set her on her feet. He, Connie, and Fritz ran onto the balcony as shrieks of alarm rioted through the streets and adjoining rooms.

From the harbor bloomed a ball of fire and streaks of light that shot like skyrockets over the black water. Bells began to ring and the shouts of "Fire!" ricocheted from the docks. Narrowing his eyes against the glare, Jason focused on the burning vessel, knowing even as he did so what he would discover.

Within minutes the flames crawled up the *Pretender*'s masts and along her shattered decks. They devoured the sails and dripped down the companionway to incinerate the low cabins, or what was left of them. There was little to be done; the inferno, fed by the arsenal of gunpowder and rifles in the bowels of the ship, reached a hundred feet into the night sky. The crews of nearby ships scurried to douse the sparks that shot onto their sails and decks. Others hurled bucket after bucket of water onto the *Pretender*'s hull and riggings, only to see the flames grow to greater heights and fill the air with boiling black smoke.

Shirtless, his body streaming with sweat and soot, Jason shouted directives to his crew as they fought the hot, hungry beast, and when it became apparent there was no saving the ship, they turned their energies to saving the others moored close by. Bodies aching and flesh seared raw by the heat, the men fought the flames until the *Pretender*'s blackened skeleton groaned like a dying animal and crumbled into the sea.

Spent, his hands blistered, Jason dropped onto the hot wharf and stared at the remains of the lopsided blackened mizzenmast sticking up out of the debris-filled water. Connie and Zelie fell down beside him, their throats too dry and parched at first to speak.

At last Zelie shook his head. "There was no warning. Nothing. No spark. No smoke. She simply lifted out of the water right before my damned eyes as if raised by God's hand. Then she disintegrated like *that*." He snapped his fingers. "Blew me back fifty feet. Thought I'd been hit by a bloody train."

Jason lay back on the dock and did his best to breathe. He tried to collect his thoughts enough to rationalize, to make sense of what had happened and why.

Fires aboard ships were not uncommon, but usually it happened at sea due to idiotic mistakes like Hugo's, spilling lamp oil, or some sailor grown lazy and careless by smoking. Jason prided himself in running a tight ship and such disasters as this were minimal under his command. One would have had to intentionally set such a fire amid the storehouse of gunpowder to have caused such an explosion.

He sat up and scanned the dispersing crowds and the line of ships anchored in the harbor. A fear of realization shimmied up his back. It clamped on his heart so tight he lost his breath and couldn't speak. Connie looked at him, his eyes indicating the same alarm.

"Destiny," they said in unison.

Jason jumped to his feet and began running. Connie followed, shouting to the others. They pushed and shoved their way through the crowds that had formed to watch the *Pretender* burn, all the while their gazes searching the many faces who stared back at them in curiosity.

It seemed an eternity before he reached the hotel, which was no more than a minute's walk from the docks. The proprietor cried out his disapproval as Jason and his men plowed through the lobby, their boots leaving muddy stains on the rugs and their sooty hands smearing over the walls and banisters as they took the stairs two at a time to the third floor. Destiny's room was at the end of the long corridor.

The door was slightly ajar. He shouted, "Connie, check my room!" He toed the door open cautiously, eased his way over the threshold. A single lamp burned on a small table near the bed, casting just enough light so he could scan the clothes- and tissue-littered floor before calling softly, "Destiny?"

Silence. Emptiness. So much emptiness.

Then he heard crying.

Zelie emerged from another room, Diana tucked under his arm, her face flushed and wet from crying. The other women followed—Julia, with Jenette in her arms, trailed by Carla, Maggie, and Mary, their faces chalk white and dazed. Diana wailed hysterically as Jason took her by her shoulders and demanded, "Where the hell is Destiny?"

"Gone," she choked. "They took her."

Jason ran down the corridor toward his room, his heart climbing his throat and panic seizing him senseless. There was no way in hell Trevor and Dunleavy could have crept into town without his knowing—but of course they had, or his ship would not be lying in a thousand shreds on the bottom of the sea. He kicked the door back against the wall. Connie stood rooted to the floor, his eyes fixed on the bed.

The coiled cobra lifted its hooded head and hissed.

❧ 21 ❧

Let those love now who never loved before;
Let those who always loved, now love the more.

—THOMAS PARNELL

Calcutta, India, June 1857

Memories of her childhood flooded back, reviving Destiny's lethargic senses to a pinpoint of nostalgic pleasures despite her sorry predicament. As the ship crawled its way along the treacherous Hooghly River toward Calcutta, Destiny looked out on the lush green countryside, allowing her eyes to feast on the luxuriant dates, coconuts, and bananas and the vast rice paddies that resembled corn in the distance. The air burst with smells that made her dizzy: garlic, cooking oil, pungent tobaccos, added with hot dust and the tang of spices—chilies, turmeric, ginger, cloves, and the fragrant scent of jasmine and sandalwood that had often scented their home in Cawnpore. Amid the lushness of the vegetation, bamboo coastal huts gave way to dingy, flat-roofed houses with narrow casement windows, and along the lip of the muddy river buffaloes sank up to their bellies to avoid the constant irritation of flies and gnats.

Although Destiny searched hard for any clue that there was something amiss among the people, she could not see it. The only thing appearing slightly out of place were Cobra's armed guards stationed along the deck rails, their eyes constantly searching the river for signs of trouble.

Trevor Batson looked much like his brother, but for one difference. There was a lifelessness in Trevor's eyes that made Destiny's blood run cold. True, she had felt anger and distrust at Jason, but never had she experienced the dread that swallowed her when in Trevor's presence. She had no doubt that he would kill her if she crossed him. The disturbing idea continued to haunt her that he might kill her regardless—if told to do so by Harold Dunleavy.

For the last two and half weeks, since Trevor Batson had kicked in her door at the hotel in Cape Town, she had resisted their attempts to make her talk about her father, choosing instead to remain as much as possible in the comfortable cabin, at least until the heat of the day forced her on deck. There she would remain until the sun set and the air cooled. Unlike the *Pretender*'s stark, dark cuddy, her little cell aboard the *Mirage* was furnished with a sofa, a mattress, a washstand, a hanging lamp, a chest of drawers in two pieces, and a bucket and rope to draw salt water, with which to bathe, up through the porthole.

This day there was a difference, however. The somber, steel-eyed crew were intent on cleaning their Lee-Enfield rifles, adjusting their sights, polishing the barrels. They were obviously preparing for war.

"We should be arriving in Calcutta soon," Trevor said as he moved up beside her.

She turned away, refusing to acknowledge him.

He grinned. "If Dunleavy was smart he would employ you. Your tenacity would be an asset to Cobra. Come, come, sweetheart, we only want what's best for the Crown. Dunleavy will go much easier on you if you co-operate."

Destiny flashed him a look. Tall, his right cheek carved by an old knife wound, his dark hair reflecting the sunset, he regarded her thoughtfully. Finally, she said, "I don't understand his hunger to destroy my father."

"Despite his probable good intentions, your father's

turned on the Crown. Your father is a traitor. Your father has roused a multitude of problems for the men, women, and children residing in this godforsaken country."

"Indeed." Dunleavy joined them and offered Trevor a cigar that he took from his pocket. Then he mopped the sweat from his brow. "We attempted to reason with your father long ago, asking only that he cease his zealous enthusiasm over the natives' fear that we were somehow encroaching on their freedom and spiritual beliefs. He only dug in his heels more deeply, thus forcing us to remove him from office. We tried to deport him. That's when he moved in with Nana Sahib. You see, your father has set a sorry example, hasn't he? It's rather difficult to deny such monstrous accusations as those the heathens are making against us, when there are respectable Brits supporting them—pounding their chests and harping about perceived injustices, firing off irate letters to Her Majesty, not to mention ranting to the *Times* that our whole intent is to pillage the country and its natives not unlike immigrants have done to the American savages. In short course, my dear, your father's become an embarrassment, not to mention a danger, which we can no longer abide."

"Nana Sahib and those like him have every reason to question that which would rob them of their inherent rights."

"Spoken like a true Fontaine." Dunleavy snorted and grinned at Batson.

Destiny stood toe-to-toe with Dunleavy. "I think there's more to your concern over my father's behavior than meets the eye, sir. You act like a man afraid of losing something."

"Indeed I am, young woman. With the Daulhousie ruling, the Crown has every opportunity to expand its empire."

"And perhaps you see yourself as overseer of that empire."

"Someone has to do it, and it won't be some bleeding-heart nonconformist who sees himself a savior of a lot of savages."

As Dunleavy walked away, Trevor flashed Destiny a

smile. "He's a little man with big aspirations. He's also an ass. He would cut his own mother's throat if he thought it would win him esteem."

"And you wouldn't?" she replied with a lift of one brow.

He shrugged. "I don't know. I've never been faced with that dilemma."

"You will be. Soon, I suspect."

"Ah. You mean my brother." He regarded her closely. "Could prove interesting. He's lethal, no doubt about it. Aside from myself and our father, I suspect Jason is one of the Crown's finest soldiers. Or was. But he's gone soft. Grew tired. He aspired to retire to his plantation and raise tea and babies. Doesn't surprise me, actually. He always had a weak spot for children."

As if by instinct Destiny laid one hand protectively on her stomach.

Trevor sighed and ran one hand through his dark hair. "Now that you're of a mind to communicate, you might elaborate on your relationship with my brother."

"What difference would it make to you?" she responded, refusing to look at him.

"That rag you're wearing, or what's left of it: it looks like a wedding dress."

"And if it is?"

"Then I have to assume that you and I were very close to being related."

She opened and closed her mouth, took a deep breath, and shook her head. "I loved him from the first moment I saw him—fell in love with his handsomeness and his pretty way with words. I loved that he was the antithesis of a high-stocking—a man unafraid of his manhood." Turning her eyes up to Trevor's, she said, "How does it feel to face the probability that you may have to kill me, thus murdering your own flesh and blood?"

His dark eyes narrowed as he lit his cigar with a match. His gaze raked her, leisurely, then he tossed the match into the water and waited for her to explain.

"I'm with child," she told him pointedly and noted the

faintest flicker of some emotion in his eyes as his gaze dropped to her stomach, then came back to her face. "I'm carrying your niece or nephew, sir. Jason's son or daughter."

Trevor looked away.

"Unlike you, sir, who may have to confront your brother if you continue to be so hell-bent in supporting Dunleavy, and in that moment decide whether or not you can kill Jason, if Dunleavy so orders, I tell you here and now that regardless of what stand my father has taken, he is my father and I will not harm him. If you're forced to kill me for that, then so be it."

Although life teemed about the streets of Calcutta, there was an air of disquietude hovering as heavily as the dust and heat among the people. Word of uprisings farther north was spreading. There were rumors that British families were being routed in Meerut like cattle, robbed, abused, and worse. One weeping woman declared that she had heard of a baby being speared and flaunted before its terrified mother before being summarily tossed like an old gunny into the river swarming with long-nosed alligators. Another spoke of a pregnant infantryman's wife being eviscerated by a Muslim butcher.

While Trevor made arrangements for their journey to Cawnpore, Dunleavy's mood nosedived as more English families began to arrive in Calcutta with horrifying stories of murdered women and children, of entire troops massacred by Meerut rebels. Most curious, however, was the rumor that Nana Sahib remained neutral and friendly, going so far as to take in the wives and children of the English officers, providing them sanctuary from the upheaval.

One night, Destiny did her best to sleep, despite the heat and the constant drone of conversation between Dunleavy, Trevor, and several government officials who refused to acknowledge that the situation north was fast becoming dire. Lying in the dark, she stared at the ceiling and did her best to focus her thoughts on something other than the harsh reality that her father might have helped instigate the terrible upheaval that was costing entire families and infantries their lives.

Finally, she left her bunk and walked to the window overlooking the Ganges. The moon reflected brightly from the water, stirring up memories of her many weeks aboard the *Pretender*.

She thought of Jason.

Where was he? As during those long weeks without her sight, she could almost sense his presence. It vibrated the night air as sharply as the insects and the jackals yapping in the distance.

"Can't sleep?" came Trevor's voice behind her.

"No," she replied.

He joined her at the window. "Good news. Dunleavy is considering leaving you here. You'll be no use to him now that the mutiny has caught fire."

"I suppose I should feel relief."

He grinned. "I should think so, since the likelihood of my having to kill you is alleviated."

"Would you have done it?" she asked. "Kill me?"

He looked out into the dark. "Yes. If you were a threat to the Crown, I would have no choice."

She smiled. "I understand now why your brother risked life and limb, not to mention his crew, in that tempest."

Trevor laughed softly. "Crazy bastard. It might have worked, too, had the damn storm not blown you so far off course that we were able to reach Cape Town before you."

Destiny looked at him squarely and steeled her voice. "I intend to go to Cawnpore and find my father. I'll go with or without you, of course. I haven't come this far and risked this much to quit here."

"Stupid," he said simply.

"I'm not convinced of my father's duplicity. I'll find out for myself."

He remained quiet for a time, thinking. Still gazing out the window, he said, "These many weeks I've wondered

exactly what kind of woman you were to have so ensnared
my brother and bogged up his priorities. Now I know."

Their Arab horses lathered and breathing hard, Jason
halted his troop's progression near a sandbar on the shallow Ganges. Since arriving in Calcutta four days ago and
learning he had missed catching up with Trevor by a mere
two days, he had driven himself and his men hard into the
sweltering heat. Much to his frustration, their progress had
been hampered by dust storms and a scattering of British
refugees who wailed about the unspeakable atrocities happening along the way. But even their numbers had dwindled.

Diana, her hair soaked by sweat and stringing down
around her sunburned face, slid from her horse and ran toward the river. Jason ran after her and caught her as she fell
to her knees in the slimy ooze, desperate to find surcease
from the heat by plunging her face into the water. He
caught a handful of her hair and hauled her back. She
screamed and kicked and clawed at his hand like a wildcat,
spitting obscenities and threatening to kill him when she
got half a chance.

"Quiet!" He shook her. "I'll tie you to a tree and leave
you for the rebels if you don't behave." He dragged her to
her knees and forced her to look at the river, and at the
refuse that had collected along the bushy shoal. There was
brush and weeds and dead fish and . . .

She made a sound in her throat, as dry as the dust she
had been breathing the last few days.

Amid the tangle of garbage, blackened by rot and feeding flies, the corpses of a European lady and gentleman
stared up at her.

With a strangled groan, Diana sank to the ground and
covered her eyes with her raw and bleeding hands. "Oh,
God, I know she's dead. Dead, I tell you. And Compton,
too."

Jason sat down beside her, wearily took her in his arms,
and stroked her head. A thousand times over the last cou-

ple of weeks he had kicked himself for allowing Diana to accompany him and his men to this apparent nightmare. He should have forced her to remain in Cape Town, with Julia and Jenette, but she had begged, and when that hadn't worked, had threatened to do herself bodily harm. Try as he might he could not muster the energy to allay her fears. If there was guilt to be laid at anyone's feet then it should be at his, not hers. He should never have agreed to transport Destiny to India, even if his intentions had been only to help her. Then again, who would have believed that such hell could have befallen the land in such a short space of time. He had fought in a great many wars and witnessed unspeakable bloodbaths, but not at the price of innocent civilians: merchants, bankers, priests . . . children. This was not a war. It was a massacre of the most fiendishly wicked kind.

Around the nearest bend came a horse and rider, a European cavalryman slumped over his saddle, his broken brow slinging blood over his horse's withers. Connie and Franz rode for him, and as he briefly managed to lift his head and focus on the advancing riders a look of horror crossed his bludgeoned features; he slid off the animal's back and crawled on his belly toward the rise of tall grass near the river, screaming at the top of his lungs when Connie caught up to him at last.

Connie wrestled the young man, pinning him down into the grass as he thrashed. "Quiet, lad. Quiet, there's naught here to harm y'."

At last the terror evaporated from his eyes and a look of realization settled into his drawn features.

"Have y' come from Cawnpore?" Connie asked.

Franz ran up with a canteen of water. He held it to the man's cracked, bleeding lips and allowed him to drink. Finally, he nodded and replied in a raspy voice. "Resistance is futile and escape impossible. They're all doomed unless help arrives soon. Her Majesty's relief company, the Eighty-fourth Regiment, did us little good. They were so immediately bombarded by gun and cannon, they were all forced into the entrenchment with the civilians who were already dying of thirst and starvation." He reached for the water and drank again, choking and spewing most of it back up, tinged heavily with blood. "He's herding them like cattle, women and children through the hot sun, shoeless, naked. If they fall they're stabbed and minced by bayonets or shot."

"Who?" Jason demanded. "Who's doing this?"

"Nana Sahib. He's taken control and reestablished himself as peshwa. He's rallied his armies by spreading the rumor that the British have resolved to send seven thousand troops up the country from Calcutta to murder fifty thousand Hindus and convert all Hindustan to Christianity. To reinforce this army another thirty-five thousand British troops were sent from England, but the pasha of Egypt sank the entire British fleet at Alexandria and entirely wiped out the British force. They've grown drunk with power and murder. They believe they cannot be taken down."

A spasm ran through him and he clutched at Jason's hand. "If you value your life, sir, go no farther. It is death yonder. God has deserted them, and the devil feasts on their souls."

Men, if still we dare to argue that we're just as good
    as they,
We can seek the God of Battle on our knees, and
    humbly pray
That the work we leave behind us, when our earthly
    race is run,
May be half as well completed as our Father's work
    was done.

—CAPT. RONALD HOPWOOD,
"The Laws of the Navy"

For three days Destiny was forced to wait in camp two
miles outside the perimeter of Cawnpore while Trevor's
men assessed the increasingly bleak situation. She remained hidden in the long river grass during the day, sunk
partially in mud when the temperature soared to one hundred twenty degrees. Hour upon hour she listened to the
distant melee, smelled the acrid scent of burning thatch
brought to her by the hot winds, cringed at the booming
cannons and chattering musket fire that ricocheted over
the drumhead plains.

Dunleavy chose to remain in the shade of a tree,
perched on his canvas stool, drinking fine brandy from a
flask, and wearing his best English tweed as if flaunting
his citizenship and authority.

The city's situation was worse than dire: it was hopeless
without a mammoth number of European troops to back

up the dwindling, starving infantries holed up within their weakening barricades. Black smoke boiled continually into the air as the natives set fire to homes and shops and barracks, driving citizens and soldiers alike out into the open to be shot and left to die in the streets.

Each time Trevor or his men ventured into the melee Destiny waited in fear that they would return to inform her that her father was already dead—or worse, that he was indeed in league with the peshwa Nana Sahib. She feared, too, that they would not return at all, that the rally of gunfire that occasionally erupted would have cut them down, and then where would she be—stuck tottering on the edge of perdition with Harold Dunleavy, whose experience in combat had never extended further than paperwork and howling speeches to Parliament. The man didn't have the first clue how to load a gun. Then again, she thought, why should he, when he could so easily order men like Jason and Connie and Zelie, and even Trevor, into the fray to die.

On the third evening her fear came to fruition; Trevor and the dozen men who had accompanied him on their scouting expedition did not return at their anticipated time. Hours dragged on, and still they did not come.

Destiny, having changed into breeches and boots and a big linen shirt one of the men had given her, approached Dunleavy where he reclined, sweating, on a hammock. "I'm leaving," she declared. "I fear something's happened to Trevor and his men. I don't intend to bake here in this dreadful place forever, waiting to be found by a lot of bloodthirsty sepoys."

He blotted sweat from his brow and waved her away as if she were a pesky insect. "Fine. Get yourself shot. You and your father—a lot of damned trouble. These deaths are on his shoulders."

"What will you do if Trevor doesn't come back?"

He stared up through the leaves of the trees. Finally, he said, "Cobra fighters are the finest fighters in the world. I handpicked them myself. They'll be back. Something has detained them is all."

"Your arrogance astounds me," she replied. "You expect and demand too much of a lot of mortals. Perhaps that's why they all hate you so. In your quest to develop the perfect soldier you've forgotten that they're human first."

He snorted. "All humans are expendable for the attainment of the ideal, young woman."

"It seems that you and Nana Sahib aren't so very different after all. Your esteem for the human soul is less than that for a cur."

His eyes shifted toward her briefly, but he did not reply.

Destiny took up a rifle and filled her pockets with cartridges and chupatties, and she confiscated a canteen of water from the supplies Trevor had left behind. Lastly she took a *tulwar,* a sword that one of Trevor's men had taken from a sowar he had killed the previous day.

She did not speak to Dunleavy again as, keeping to the deep shadows of the trees, she struck out through the dark for the city, following the meandering shoal of the Ganges where pelicans and cranes nested so thickly they resembled embankments of snow in the moonlight.

Unlike most of the northern stations that were dull and sunbaked, Cawnpore had become an agreeable residence through the years. Gardens abounded and fine bungalows were painted in vibrant colors; there was a horseshoe-shaped theater with massive Doric columns and luxurious seating. As a child, Destiny and her parents had spent many enjoyable evenings there with friends, watching plays and listening to music. There was a Masonic temple, to which her father belonged, a library, where her mother had taught her to read, and a vast rich park where they picnicked on Sundays and where young men gambled extravagantly on the Arabian horses running in the Cheroot Races.

What greeted Destiny now, however, were blackened shells of buildings and shattered windows, roofs torn away by round shot and cannonballs, and walls chewed away by disintegrating shells.

She found a bloodstained *deputtah* on the ground and used it to wrap her head and face, leaving only her eyes uncovered. Were she discovered by a native perhaps he would believe her to be a sowar and allow her to pass. She was fortunate, however, to slip past the scattered groups of mutineers and finally, upon climbing the mortar walls surrounding the compound, she found herself on the broad boulevard known as the Course, where the wealthier and more influential Europeans resided within the city. Here the government officials, wives and children of the British officers, and well-to-do merchants lived. She had spent half of her life wandering this street lined with shade trees, playing marbles in the sand with the native children.

Now, however, the Course resembled a cemetery of lopsided tombstones, the laughter of the past echoing in her mind like ghost whispers.

A burst of conversation startled her. She ducked behind a rubble wall surrounding bullock sheds as a threesome of sepoys moved near, all carrying their rifles and *tulwars*. In voices vibrating with fervor they spoke of annihilating the infidels and reclaiming their religious destinies. At last they faded into the dark, leaving Destiny with her heart pounding wildly in her ears.

She continued cautiously down the avenue, bypassing the camel sheds and rum godown; then she ran through the shadows to the soldiers' cemetery, where she stayed long enough to allow her breathing to return to normal. Around her the small white crosses were aligned in perfect rows, and she could not help but think of how many more would be erected here when this terrible disaster finally concluded. Her own mother was interred not far from here. Thank God, the dear woman had not lived long enough to face such a horrible nightmare as the many men, women, and children who had been slaughtered the last days.

At long last she found her father's bungalow. How

small and simple it seemed to her now that she was grown. Its thick mud-brick walls were heavily blanketed by bignonia creepers her mother had planted not long after their arrival in Cawnpore. Over the years the vines had spread over the bamboo trellises surrounding the verandas as well as the small windows, so even the shutters could not be opened.

Sinking against the wall, she closed her eyes and did her best to breathe evenly. What would she do if she found her father dead, butchered in his bed or his little library that he loved so well? What if she had come all this way to find that he had died only yesterday?

Dear God, the heat, even at midnight. Had she actually once relished this insufferable temperature? Had she teased her poor parents who, in the beginning years, slumped like wilted flowers in the heat of the day and questioned their sanity for coming to India in the first place?

Dragging the *deputtah* from her head, she poured water from the canteen over her face and down her neck, allowed it to trickle like a cool damp tongue between her breasts.

She thought of Jason and prayed that he was still in Cape Town with Connie and Diana and Fritz, Franz, and Zelie. If God would grant her any wish, it would be that they would not find their way to this dreadful, doomed place.

He wasn't, of course, still in Cape Town. He was out there somewhere, in the dark and heat. She could feel it.

Destiny inched along the bungalow wall, to a tiny window that overlooked the parlor. A thin stream of light filtered through the bignonia leaves. She did her best to peer through the slats of the shutter and could just make out the figures of several natives hunkered about a collection of brass pots as they ate.

"Do not move," came the native voice from the dark, and the muzzle of a rifle was pressed against the side of her head. The man grabbed the rifle and *tulwar* from her hands then clutched the back of her shirt and dragged her around the house and in through the back door, shoving her to the clay floor on her hands and knees. The women eating jumped to their feet and babbled excitedly. Destiny looked up—into the familiar face of her old *ayah*.

The nurse's eyes widened first in confusion, then recognition. She flapped her hands at the others and began to shout: "Away, away, it is Fontaine Sahib's girl!"

With a little cry of relief, Destiny scrambled to her knees and flung her arms around the old nurse's thin shoulders. They hugged fiercely as memories flooded Destiny with images and sensations she had long forgotten: the texture of the *ayah*'s worn clothing, the pungent scent of her skin, and the smell of aniseed on her breath. The *ayah* had seemed ancient even when Destiny was a child. Her wrinkled, leathery skin looked no older than it had those years before when Destiny, with tears in her eyes, had bid her cherished *ayah* good-bye.

"Bring water and rice," the *ayah* ordered, and the others scrambled, delivering within a matter of seconds a cup of warm, sweetened rice water, which Destiny gulped thirstily. At last, she wiped her mouth and glanced around.

"*Ayah*, where is my father?"

The woman frowned and replied, "You must rest first. We will speak of it in the morning."

"No. I must know now. Is he alive?"

"Morning," she declared and firmly helped Destiny to her feet. The old woman then led her through the mostly empty rooms that had once bustled with activity, where the walls had been decorated with her mother's own watercolor paintings, and every corner of the rooms had sported Indian-made chairs and sofas with chintz and cretonne from England. Then the windows had been covered with bright, colorful material her parents had bought at bazaars and the floors covered in carpets soaked in corrosive sublimate to kill the white ants that feasted on everything edible. Now, however, there was little left but broken, scattered pieces of pottery, an old table with antelope horn legs, and rugs tossed about where the *ayah* and her family had been sleeping.

"But I don't want to sleep," she argued, knowing she wouldn't win the argument with her *ayah*. She never had.

Tugged along by the old woman, who carried a lamp in her free hand, Destiny was led into her parents' room. The bed she had so often climbed into with her mother and father remained, draped in yards of transparent netting. As she sat on the bed the *ayah* removed her boots, clucking in disapproval.

Sinking back into the pillow, Destiny grabbed the old woman's arm. "Please tell me. I have to know. Is my father still alive?"

Her dark brow wrinkled as she frowned, then nodded. "Fontaine Sahib alive. Yes, yes, now sleep. Go to sleep." She blew out the lamp and shuffled from the room, pausing at the door to look back at her briefly before dissolving into the darkness.

Destiny sat up and stared through the shadows as if she were blind again, allowing her senses to expand.

She could hear the *ayah* and her family arguing, but could not make out their words. Wearily, she fell back on the bed, too bone weary to care in that moment if the entire sepoy and sowar armies piled in on her. They wouldn't, of course. Once her *ayah* would have given her life to protect Destiny. If there was ever a guardian angel to watch over her, her *ayah* would be the one.

As dawn's light crept over the sunbaked plain, Connie wiped the blade of his Bowie knife on his shirtsleeve, then gently pressed the cold steel tip of the knife against the roll of fat under Dunleavy's chin. "Let me," he whispered to Jason. "The flippin' pig won't ever know what happened."

A rifle in one hand, Destiny's tattered and filthy wedding gown in the other, Jason listened to Dunleavy snore. He was tempted to allow Connie to cut the son of a bitch—damn tempted. He glanced at Zelie, then to Fritz, who had searched all the way to the riverbank for any sign of Destiny or Trevor and his men. Stepping back into the clearing, they shook their heads and lowered their guns. Then he glanced at Diana.

Her blue eyes glazed, her skin sunburned, she stared at the muddy lace material of the wedding gown as if Destiny were still in it. She would not scream, however. She had no voice left to manage it even if she could work up the energy.

Jason positioned the barrel of his gun between Dunleavy's eyes. "Rise and shine, Harold."

Harold's eyelids fluttered; he grumbled and snorted. His eyes snapped open as Jason cocked the trigger and pressed the muzzle hard into the flesh of Harold's forehead.

"Fancy meeting you here," Jason said through his teeth.

Harold's attempt to sit up was thwarted as Jason shoved the muzzle hard into his brow and forced him back down.

"What have you done with Destiny?" Jason said as calmly as his escalating fear and anger would allow.

Harold shook his head.

"What have you done with Destiny?" Jason repeated, pressing the muzzle so hard into Harold's flesh that the surrounding skin began to turn white for lack of blood. "Destiny," Jason sneered, jabbing Harold again with the gun muzzle. "Is she with my brother? Answer me, damn you. Have you killed her? Perhaps you'd like to experience for yourself exactly what Cobra does to torture the truth out of the enemy. Remember the code? Attain the truth and nothing but the truth by any means possible. As I recall, you encourage the use of torture. You've even gone so far as to suggest a few methods that have worked splendidly for us through the years."

Harold shook his head. "Christ, where is Trevor?" He tried to sit up. Connie shoved him back down.

Jason flipped open the buttons of Harold's trousers. Fritz and Zelie moved up beside him. Connie removed the sweat-drenched bandanna from his own forehead and, wadding it up, shoved it into Harold's mouth; then Fritz and Zelie yanked Harold's pants down to his knees. Harold bucked wildly as Jason grabbed hold of his flaccid penis and pressed a knife blade against it.

"Careful." Jason grinned. "You've got little enough as it is. One more wrong quiver and it's whoops to willie."

His body vibrating with fear and anger, and dripping with sweat, Harold nodded and grunted his acknowledgment.

Connie removed the bandanna from Harold's mouth. Harold gasped and gagged. His face looked as white as the sandbars in the middle of the Ganges. "Monsters," he croaked and gagged again. "I'll have your bloody heads for this."

Jason pressed the knife blade into the thin skin of Harold's organ, causing Harold to howl.

"Monsters?" Jason growled. "You're damn right we're monsters, Harold. As you always preached: there's no room in Cobra for conscience, compassion, regret. The objective is obtained by any means possible. Now tell me what I want to know or I swear to Almighty God that I'm going to stuff this cock down your throat and laugh as you choke to death. Is Destiny with Trevor?"

Harold shook his head. "Trevor and his men are gone— didn't come back at appointed time. The woman left last night—for the love of God take that knife away before you—"

"If I find out you're lying to me—"

"I'm not. I swear it. I told her good-bye and good riddance. A lot of good she's going to do me now, what with all hell broken loose already."

Pressing the blade deeper, until a thin stream of blood began to dribble over his fingers, Jason said through his clenched teeth, "If she's dead there won't be a rock in this world where you can hide that I won't find you. What I do to you then would make my lopping off this pitifully small appendage pale in comparison."

Jason backed away and gave the hammock a kick that

spilled Harold onto the ground, his bare butt in the air. Scrambling, Harold yanked up his pants and ran to the edge of the clearing, frantically buttoning his breeches and moaning as the crotch fast blotted with blood.

Wearily, Jason sat next to the tree and rested his rifle across his lap. Little by little daylight intruded on the meager camp nestled among the high river reeds. Trevor had chosen his hiding place well. The river would make for an easy escape should any mutineers happen by, which was unlikely this far from Cawnpore.

Zelie squatted beside Jason and offered him a canteen of water. "Trevor's in trouble, obviously. Or he would have returned by now."

"Maybe. I'm not worried about Trevor. He can take care of himself."

"You think Destiny's gone looking for her father."

Diana sank to the ground beside him and covered her blistered face with her hands. Connie squatted beside her, his expression concerned.

Jason drank from his canteen and wiped his mouth. He handed the canteen to Diana, who took it and gulped the water greedily, her eyes rolling back in her head in relief. He cut his gaze to Harold, who was trying desperately to stem the flow of blood by stuffing his pants with remnants of Destiny's wedding gown. "Come here, Harold," he shouted.

His legs slightly spread, Harold hurried toward him like an obedient pup.

"You're familiar with Fontaine's residence."

Harold nodded and winced. His eyes were beginning to tear.

"Good. Then you're going with us into Cawnpore."

Harold stared at Jason as if he had transformed into Lucifer himself.

Fritz let go a soft whistle and shook his head. "That's asking to be shot, Jay. Look at him. We might as well sashay down the middle of Grand Trunk Road wearin' a bleeding bull's-eye."

Harold nodded in agreement and checked out his crotch again.

"He came here to negotiate with Nana Sahib and Compton Fontaine. So . . . now he's going to negotiate."

"There will be no negotiating with madmen. They're killing us on sight," Harold argued. "For the love of God, you're all a lot of lunatics. How can you think to march a man into this bloodbath? Have you no loyalty, no care for human life?"

Jason looked at each of his men. They all burst into laughter. Finally they replied in unison, "Hell no."

Harold blanched.

Franz, who had walked to the edge of the river grass, turned swiftly on his heels and motioned. Jason grabbed Diana, slamming his hand over her mouth as he and the others dissolved into the reeds so swiftly Harold was left with his mouth agape, eyes fixed on the men who suddenly appeared at the edge of the clearing.

Stepping from behind a thatch of undergrowth, Jason pointed the gun at Trevor's temple and whispered, "Bang, you're dead."

Harold went limp with relief and sat on the ground.

Trevor slowly turned to face Jason, a smile curling one side of his mouth.

Jason shook his head but did not lower the gun. "Tsk, tsk, Trev. You're getting sloppy in your old age."

"Not nearly so sloppy as you." He pointed to the trees on the opposite riverbank. Within the highest branches perched Trevor's soldiers, with rifles all aimed at Jason and his men.

"I could still put a bullet in your head if I wanted," Jason said. "And I might yet if you don't tell me where Destiny is."

Trevor shrugged. "She was gone when we got back."

"And you haven't gone after her?"

"She's not my fiancée, now is she?"

"Why the hell didn't you leave a man here to stand guard?"

"If this camp were discovered by sepoys and sowars, the chance of their taking prisoners alive is greater if they don't associate them with infantry. Besides, she was safe enough had she stayed in one place like she was told." Trevor shoved the gun away and walked over to Harold, who had begun to bleed again and curse. Trevor laughed and shook his head, turned away, and dropped onto the hammock. He stretched out his long legs and closed his eyes.

"The entrenchment is completely surrounded, cut off from the roads and river by Nunne Nawab's garrison. The only water available is from a solitary well in full view of Nawab's men. In short, the men, women, and children in the entrenchment will either die by a bullet or die of thirst.

"Nana Sahib is in residence at Savada House. There's still concern among a great many of his men that he's taken no open stance regarding his alliance with Britain. In short, he's playing both sides of the fence, I suspect. Until he's certain that we're not about to march into Cawnpore with fifty thousand soldiers intent on wiping out his race, he's going to make no overt moves to declare himself totally hostile. He's getting pressure from his brother Bala Rao, however, to make his stand one way or the other. I suspect Nana Sahib will be forced to make an example of his leadership soon."

Trevor looked at Jason. "Compton Fontaine is alive and residing at Savada House with Nana Sahib. The babble among Sahib's men is that Fontaine is, in some way, influencing Sahib not to totally burn his bridges where the British are concerned. There are whispers that Bala Rao and Teeka Singh, risaldar of the Second Native Cavalry, are intent on getting shut of Fontaine in order to assure Sahib's loyalty."

"Is it possible that Destiny could have made it to her father's house undetected?"

"Yes. It's possible." Rolling from the hammock, Trevor reached for a stick and began drawing in the sand the eastern perimeters of the city, the Ganges River on the north, the canals and esplanades to the west, Nana's camp on the south, and the lines of the native infantries situated along the east and throughout.

Dragging the stick southeast of the canals, he pointed out the course. "There is an area beyond the soldiers' cemetery that is relatively clear of the enemy. If she were going to get through successfully, it would have to be there."

Trevor stood and faced Jason. "Chances are she's already captured. Even if there were to be someone in that residence who at one time held close relations to the Fontaines, there's no way in hell they would risk their lives to help her. To do so would mean instant death if they were discovered. Of course, they may spare her if she admits to being Fontaine's daughter, or they may kill her instantly. Her only hope is to get to Savada House. *Your* only hope of helping her is to get *into* Savada House."

"We stand as much chance of that," Connie said, "as our stealin' the Crown jewels."

Trevor added, "The only hope of getting in there without a sowar cutting you in two immediately is to somehow convince the garrisons between here and Savada House to take you directly to Nana Sahib. Let's face it, they take one look at us and there won't be enough left of us to feed those damn vultures."

Trevor pointed to the dozens of circling birds hovering over the river.

Jason turned his gaze on Harold. "This calls for an ambassador of sorts."

"Agreed."

Harold's eyes widened. "Forget it. If you think I'm walking into that fray then you're crazier than I thought. It would be suicide, I tell you. Get away from me, Batson." He jumped to his feet and backed toward the river. "I'll have you court-martialed for this. You'll spend the rest of your life buried so far under London Prison—better yet, I'll send you to New South Wales—you'll never walk this earth as a free man again."

"Come, come, Harold. As you so frequently like to remind us: all humans are expendable for the attainment of the ideal."

"Shoot him, Trevor! That's an order. I command you to shoot this bastard or I'll . . . I'll . . . bloody hell."

✄ 23 ✄

What men will fight for seems to be worth looking into.

—H. L. MENCHKEN

Destiny knew the ayah's wail of grief—it had shaken the rafters upon Destiny's mother's death, absorbed into every fragment of Destiny's body to the point of splintering pain. For months the memory of the dreadful sound had jolted her from her dreams as she had relived that terrible instant of her mother's death again and again. So she knew, before the sepoys fell upon her and dragged her from the bed, that, at this moment, she was in dire trouble.

The soldiers' hands tore at her clothes and hair as they wrestled her to the floor, slamming her head against the mud tiles so hard consciousness flickered like a flame in the wind. Voices shouted in anger and amid it all her *ayah* cried repeatedly: "Fontaine Sahib! Fontaine Sahib!"

Her instinct was to fight back; instead, she lay as docilely as possible, giving over to their barked demands as they shoved her to her knees. Surrounded by a half dozen black-skinned natives, their heads wrapped in *puggaris* and all with bloody curved swords, Destiny kept her eyes averted and her trembling hands folded before her in submission. She remembered some, though not all of their language. Her *ayah*'s husband had feared the retribution of the sepoys and so gave her up to the enemy. The sepoys were divided over what to do with her. Half wanted to kill her on the spot. The others feared Nana Sahib's retribution should he continue to be influenced by Fontaine Sahib. If they killed Fontaine Sahib's daughter, would Nana not exact his revenge on them?

Finally, one of the men dragged Destiny to her feet and shoved her toward the door, prodding her out into the street with the point of his bayonet. The sun cooked the ground and burned the bottoms of Destiny's feet as she stumbled into the street, where she was confronted by a group of rebels escorting a train of bullock carts filled with white men, women, and children, their wrists and ankles bound. A man grabbed her from behind, wrenched her arms behind her, and bound her wrists so tightly she was forced to bite her lip to keep from crying out. Then he tied her ankles, picked her up, and flung her into a cart.

The other prisoners, looking hungry and filthy, stared at her with vacant expressions. "Where are they taking us?" Destiny asked in a hoarse voice.

A woman with a very young child in her lap shrugged wearily and peered down at Destiny through limp strands of blond hair. "To Nana Sahib's headquarters. We surrendered, so they felt that their commander should decide what to do with us."

"For whatever good that will do us," another declared with a sharp laugh. "These fiends are taking no prisoners. From Meerut to Delhi to here, women are being stripped and raped in the streets, children tortured, men hacked to pieces and fed to dogs."

A man with a face so swollen by beatings he could hardly open his eyes turned on the woman and said furiously, "For the love of God Almighty, I won't hear you speak like that in front of the children. Nana Sahib has been a friend to the British. Even if he has become a rebel, why would he kill us for no reason? No doubt he simply intends to hold us all captive to make certain we carry no intelligence to British garrisons in Allahabad."

"There are no British garrisons in Allahabad," the woman spat. "If there were they would be here by now.

They're all dead, I tell you. These animals have murdered us all."

The carts creaked along the road at a snail's pace as the sun climbed higher and burned hotter into their skin. Destiny stared up at the yellow-tinged sky and did her best not to think about her father or Jason or Diana, all of whom she might never see again. She tried not to think of the child inside her who might never know life.

Rebels gathered by the roadside as the carts passed, shouting insults, taunting, and threatening, waving their weapons in the air and shouting at the top of their lungs, *"Maro! Maro!"* Kill! Kill! Amid the jeers the erratic clatter of the garrisons' musket fire added to the nightmarish melee.

Finally the carts arrived at Savada House. The sepoys dragged the prisoners from the carts and herded them like yoked oxen into the large central room of the building. At long last out of the blistering sun, the coolness of the floor and walls and ceiling was a tremendous respite to the parched, starved, and exhausted families who collapsed to the floor.

Turning on one of her captors, Destiny declared in their language, "I demand to see Nana Sahib this moment. I'm Fontaine Sahib's daughter—"

He struck her across the face.

She stumbled back, then repeated, "I'm Compton Fontaine's daughter, a friend of Nana Sahib. Take me to see him now."

He hit her again.

Her mouth filling with blood and her head ringing, Destiny drew back her shoulders and said, "If you kill me Nana Sahib will have your head and your mother's head and your childrens' because I am as family to him."

"Sahib has no British friend or family any longer. Sahib spits on the infidels." He spat on her bare feet and leered. "But perhaps you can persuade me, memsahib."

"I would rather rut with a swine," she declared with a smug smile.

His eyes widened and he grabbed a knife from his belt.

A door suddenly opened and men poured into the room, shouting orders and pointing to the prisoners. Someone took hold of Destiny and propelled her out into the sunlight, followed by the other captives who huddled together and moved as a unit, prodded on by *tulwars* and bayonets in their backs.

Odd how little sound there was—no weeping or pleading or praying. It was as if the group had long since accepted the worst.

The group moved over the dry ground toward a vast ditch surrounded by platforms and armed sepoys. The soldiers dragged the captives into the ditch one by one, and seated them in two lines: the men in the back, the women and children in the front. On her knees, trying to breathe evenly despite the dust and fear closing off her throat, Destiny searched frantically among the men surrounding the ditch for any familiar face.

Nana Sahib emerged through the flurry of dust.

He had changed little since she saw him last. Distinguished in his robes, his dark eyes sharp and surprisingly compassionate as they looked over the swarm of exhausted captives, he did not appear the sort who would commit such horrendous crimes.

One of the male prisoners jumped to his feet and cried, "Your believing you can exterminate all of the Europeans in this country is ridiculous. Why not imprison us instead? What good can come of murdering women and children? If you kill us more will come and they'll wipe you out."

Nana Sahib ignored him and turned his gaze toward Destiny.

"Sahib!" she cried. "I'm Destiny Fontaine. Compton's daughter. Fontaine memsahib!"

He turned away with no sign of recognition or acknowledgment that he had heard her. A sepoy walked over to him, glanced at Destiny, and spoke softly to the commander, gesturing toward her as he did so. Nana Sahib did not look back, but joined several others, who looked on with

impatience. Quietly he announced that he was disposed to
spare the captives. What good would killing them do?
They might prove more valuable to use as hostages.

"Absurd!" an officer declared angrily. "We must make
an example of what will happen to these Europeans who
come into our land and destroy us. If you spare them they
will live to rise up against us one day."

The argument continued until Sahib walked away.

Still, the captives waited under the broiling sun, the children so weak from thirst and hunger they could barely cry
as they clutched at their mothers' skirts and begged for
water.

Sinking to the ground, Destiny stared through the clouds
of dust at Sahib's back. What little hope had sustained her
the last hours, days, weeks evaporated like mist in the un-
relenting sun.

She closed her eyes.

The flutter began, low in her belly. For a moment she did
not breathe, did not hear the cries and pleas of the frightened, miserable humans beside her. "My darling Jason,"
she whispered. "I'm so very sorry."

The crowd of sepoys gathered around the ditch began to
chant "Death, death to the infidels!" and hurled stones
upon them, their voices rising as the men and women cried
for mercy. Several sepoys elbowed their way through the
jeering men and jumped into the ditch, dragging the few
*ayah*s who had faithfully remained with their children out
of the ditch as the officer who had argued with Nana Sahib
climbed upon a platform overlooking the scene and announced, "By Nana's orders the Europeans shall all be
massacred and their corpses strewn for the dogs, vultures,
and crows!"

It seemed in that moment that reality ground to a stop.
Voices came to her as if from a tunnel, drawn out and distorted as she watched the soldiers raise their muskets and
prepare to fire. Someone moved into her line of vision—a
dark angry face with yellow teeth and flashing black eyes,
shouting something at her as he reached for her arm, haul-

ing her out of the ditch as the hail of gunfire erupted amid screams and shouts of *"Maro! Maro!"*

She could not walk. The man flung her across his shoulder and ran toward Savada House; he ducked through a door and into the dim, cool interior, his feet padding softly upon the stone floor. At last he came to a door, kicked it open, and tossed Destiny onto the carpet. With a knife he severed the ropes binding her wrists and ankles, then as quickly he stepped from the room, slamming the door closed behind him.

The guns were silent.

Staring at the ceiling, shaking, Destiny dared not close her eyes for fear of seeing again the horrified faces of the women as they looked up into death's eyes.

A groan.

She thought at first that it was herself moaning. But no. Turning her head, she focused on the bed in the distance and the man behind the netting.

"Papa?" She crawled on her hands and knees to the bed. At last managing to stand, she threw aside the netting and stared down at her father's emaciated face. "Papa," she whispered, taking his face between her bloody hands and giving him a watery smile as he opened his eyes; they were sunken and dim.

"He has been very ill for a long time," came a voice from behind her.

Nana Sahib stood in the doorway, his hands clasped behind his back. "He has his good days and bad days. Occasionally he rouses enough to play me a good game of chess."

"What's wrong with him?"

"I do not know."

"Has he been seen by a physician?"

"My own." Nana Sahib moved to the bed. Destiny backed to the wall. Nana looked down on Compton's face with a sad smile. "We have known one another for many years, and though our ultimate objectives in life now differ, he is still my friend and I will keep him as comfortable as possible until the end." Lifting his sad eyes to Destiny's, he added, "For your own peace of mind, memsahib, he knows nothing of what has transpired here, which is for the best, yes?"

"What's become of you?" she asked in a voice trembling in anger. "The Nana Sahib I knew would never have murdered innocent families."

"Perhaps you did not know me as well as you thought."

"Obviously."

He gave her a thin smile. "Mayhap you will enlighten me as to how you came here, and who brought you."

Raising her chin and rewarding him with a smile as cold as his, she replied, "No doubt you believe that I came with vast armies who are waiting for dark to attack you."

The smile slid from his face, and his eyes narrowed as he regarded her expression. "I see you have grown into a woman much like your mother, full of fire and rebellion and much beauty." He shrugged. "I'm not afraid of your armies, memsahib. You, on the other hand, should be very afraid of mine."

Jason allowed Dunleavy to drink deeply of the brandy before taking the empty flask from Harold's shaking hands and tossing it to the ground. He handed Harold the white flag and tucked the loaded pistol into the top of Harold's boot.

"The gun is loaded, Harold. I suggest that you use it should they show signs of aggression. Aim here." He tapped at Harold's temple. "You'll be dead before you hit the ground."

"You're insane," Harold sneered.

Trevor slapped Harold on the back. "You'll be begging for a bullet should they decide to dismember you piece by piece with their *tulwars*."

Harold clutched at Jason. "You cannot send me in there. They're lunatics. They'll murder me."

Jason peeled Harold's fingers from his shirt. "You have a choice, Dunleavy. You can march into that compound with a white flag and ask nicely to see Nana and discuss settling this fray like gentlemen, or you can stay here and deal with me. What that lot of sepoys will do to you pales in comparison to what you'll endure at my hands. If you're very lucky you'll live long enough to see Nana Sahib. If you're luckier you'll convince him that you're an emissary of goodwill and that if you don't return to camp by nightfall ten thousand British troops are waiting beyond the river to attack."

Harold groaned.

Taking hold of Harold's shoulders, Jason shoved him out into the open road. Harold stumbled, dropped the flag into the dirt, then scrambled to pick it up. He looked from Jason to Trevor to the others, finding no sympathy or escape from his predicament.

Pulling his pistol and aiming it at Harold, Jason said, "Walk. If you attempt to run away you'll be dead within seconds."

Flag clutched in both hands, Dunleavy walked down Grand Trunk Road, looking neither right nor left nor back.

Trevor sank down beside Jason and both watched Harold stumble down the road toward the city. "Makes you feel a bit sorry for the little bastard, doesn't it?" Trevor said.

"No." Jason shook his head. "It doesn't."

"He'll never come out of there alive."

Jason glanced at Trevor. "Just saves me the effort of killing him myself."

Trevor looked back at his men. "We don't stand a chance, you know. At least not until more troops arrive."

"Then we wait. As long as Compton Fontaine is alive, there's no reason to think Sahib won't spare Destiny."

"Never thought I'd live to see the day you would risk life and limb for a woman."

"Neither did I."

"Not that I blame you. If there ever was a woman who could stand up to your bouts of mood and temper, she would be the one."

"She's having my baby."

"I know. Somehow I'm having a hard time imagining you with a lot of rug rats hanging off your legs."

"Stay alive long enough and maybe even you'll grow up enough to want a wife and children."

"Sure. Right." Trevor laughed and shook his head. "What are we going to do about Diana?"

Jason watched Diana as she sat beneath a tree, swatting at flies. "I'll take care of her if we're captured. I won't let her suffer."

There came a howl of voices in the distance and a cloud of dust rose in the air. Zelie, watching from the branches high in the tree, called down, "They've got him."

❧ 24 ❧

Give heed to thy words and thine actions,
Lest others be wearied thereby.
It is ill for the winners to worry,
Take thy fate as it comes with a smile.

—CAPT. RONALD HOPWOOD

To Destiny's despair, Compton Fontaine was a shadow of the man he once had been, hardly the robust, energetic, and youthful man of forty-five years she had expected to find. His hair had turned snow white and he was little more than skin and bones, his flesh thin and yellow with disease. His lungs wheezed as he breathed, and every few minutes he was racked by coughing that produced bloody spittle on his lips. For the time being, however, his fever had broken. As he opened his eyes and focused on Destiny, she touched his cheek.

"Hello, Papa."

His lips parted as he reached out disbelievingly with his frail hand. "Daughter?" He laughed weakly. "I'm not dead, surely, because I certainly wouldn't be meeting *you* in hell."

She blinked back her tears of relief and grief, and did her best to appear strong. "I see you haven't lost your wit."

"My sanity, perhaps, but not my wit. Dear merciful God, Des. What are you doing here?"

"I came to take you home, of course."

"Bad timing on your part, I'm afraid." He coughed and clutched at his sides, groaning in pain.

Destiny pressed a cup of cool water to his lips. He drank heartily before falling back on his pillow. He regarded her with a weak smile that further deepened the lines of pain in his face.

"You look just like your mother. Even more beautiful, if that's possible. Where is your husband?"

"My husband?"

"Lord Chesterfield. He is with you, isn't he?"

"Obviously you never received my letters." She squeezed his hand and wondered just how much of the truth she should tell him. To learn of the tragic circumstances of her brief marriage would distress him. On the other hand, she wanted desperately to share with him the news about his coming grandchild. What harm could come of lying to him if it meant his being happy? "I . . . never married Lord Chesterfield, Papa."

"Never married Chesterfield?" He frowned, confused.

"I met someone else. Someone I've grown to love very much. I'm . . . going to have a baby, Papa. Isn't that wonderful? You're going to have a grandchild soon."

A look of pleasure crossed his features and his eyes filled with tears. "A grandchild. But who is your husband, Des? Does he come from a good family?"

Destiny managed a trembling smile. "The child's father is Jason Batson."

"Batson!" His eyes brightened and he wheezed pitifully in laughter. "By God, the rascal took me up on it, after all. Looked you up, did he? I knew you could hook him, and you did. Imagine my little girl married to Batson. But why didn't Diana write and tell me?"

"I asked her not to. I wanted to tell you myself."

"And here you are." He coughed then gasped for air. Falling back on the bed, he waited until the spasms passed before attempting to speak. "Where is Nana? He'll be thrilled to see you again. We'll host a soiree and invite all the families—they loved your mother devotedly and will be most pleased to see what a lovely woman you've become."

Frowning, Destiny again took her father's hand in hers. "Papa, how long have you been ill? How long have you spent in this room?"

I . . . don't know." He sighed heavily and frowned. "Days. Weeks, perhaps. One loses track of time, I suppose. I've mentioned to Nana repeatedly that I must get well enough to return to Cawnpore. There's so much business to do, letters to write. . . ."

Bending near, Destiny smiled into her father's eyes and asked, "Where, exactly, do you think you are?"

"Bithur, of course. Nana's home."

"Oh, my God," she whispered, trying her best to keep the shock and concern from her features. "Papa, have you no idea of what's happening around you? Do you not realize that you're in Cawnpore?"

For a moment he appeared to float in and out of reality. Agitation flushed his cheeks, as if he were trying desperately to clear his mind of its confusion. He appeared to rally, then as quickly sank again into his stupor and drifted to sleep. Destiny dropped wearily into a chair by his bed and covered her face with her hands.

For the last few months Nana Sahib had sheltered her father away from the melee. Her father had no clue that all hell had broken out around him, that his countrymen were being slaughtered like helpless animals.

The door opened and servants appeared. They carried trays of food and drink. They ministered her father by bathing him in scented waters and removing and replacing his soiled clothes. They roused him enough to spoon broth and rice water through his lips.

Earlier they had delivered to Destiny a tub of hot, jasmine-scented water to bathe in and a bourka to wear. While the one-piece, head-to-heels cloak offered respite from the filthy rags she had worn for days, she had refused to cover her head with the material. The insufferable heat was hard enough to bear. Besides, she had no intention of showing respect for her enemies' customs.

"I demand to speak to Nana Sahib," she declared to the servants. But, just as they had before, they ignored her.

She ran for the door.

The servants shouted an alarm and instantly there were sepoys swarming around her with their muskets and swords, snatching at her hair and bourka, driving her to her knees with their hands.

"Enough!" someone cried. A young man Destiny had come to know as Chimnaji shoved through the soldiers and dragged Destiny to her feet. "You were told that she was not to be injured. I could have the lot of you shot. Now get about your business."

Turning to Destiny, he bowed slightly and offered her a sympathetic smile. "I beg your pardon, memsahib. Too often the men are caught up in their fervor, I'm afraid. But I must remind you that you are not to leave your quarters without escort."

"I wish to speak with Nana about my father."

A look of compassion crossed his face. "I remember how very close you were to your parents. Fontaine Sahib's heart was broken when he was forced to send you away." Chimnaji laughed. "You don't remember me, I think. Once we played marbles together in the sand. Your mother fed me steak and kidney pie and Yorkshire pudding. It was my first taste of British food. I thought you very beautiful then. . . ."

"If you were our friend how can you now be involved in this slaughter?"

"Some of us have little choice," he admitted sadly, his voice resigned and weary.

"Such as my father, Chimnaji?"

He frowned and glanced around, then lowered his voice and said, "I think that I do not understand your meaning, memsahib."

"The rumors that my father is in alliance with Nana against the Crown, are they true?" She held her breath as she awaited Chimnaji's reply. Her eyes held his as he considered his response, obviously unnerved by her question. "Please," she finally pleaded. "I have to know, for my own peace of mind. Did he in any way instigate this rebellion with Nana Sahib?"

"Let me say this," he responded carefully. "When a man is not of his right mind, he may be led like a blind man down false paths."

"Are you referring to his illness?"

"Memsahib." He smiled nervously and looked again toward the group of men converged in the distance, their conversation muted but quick and sharp as they watched him and Destiny. "You ask too many questions, I fear. I will simply say this: your father was worth more to Nana alive than dead. His signature scrawled upon a letter proved to be a blade of contention to the Crown . . . even if he wasn't fully aware of the letter's content, or intent."

"My father was tricked. Is that what you're saying, Chimnaji?"

"I'm saying nothing more, memsahib. Now come. I'll take you to Nana. There is someone with him that you will want to see, I think."

She walked with him from the house and to the colorful *shamianah* a short distance away. They worked their way through the crowd huddled about the entrance of the tent. Before entering, Chimnaji whispered into her ear, "Be cautious. He is not in good humor today. He lost two dozen men during the night not to mention one of his finest cannons."

Hesitating in her step, Destiny looked into Chimnaji's eyes, which were as strangely telling as his silence. For the first time in days her heart squeezed with excitement and hope that there might still be sympathetic friends among the natives.

"Go." He nudged her on.

A moment passed before her eyes adjusted to the *shamianah*'s dim interior. Nana stopped his pacing when he saw her.

"I was about to send for you." He looked to the man sitting in a chair before him. "It seems a friend of yours has joined us."

Harold Dunleavy stared up at her, his sweating face white as Destiny's bourka. She felt the blood drain from her head. Dear God, had the others been captured, or worse?

Harold stood, his hands clenched as he announced in a monotone: "I've come as an ambassador of goodwill. See the white flag? We would be pleased to negotiate. If not there are troops even now surrounding this city who will attack if I don't return to them by nightfall."

"Tell me," Nana smiled coldly at Destiny, "does he speak the truth?"

"How am I to know, when I've been held a prisoner for these last days?"

"Is this man a friend of yours?"

"He's no friend of mine," she declared with a narrowing of her eyes. "He came here to destroy my father. But then you've already done that, haven't you, Sahib?"

Nana sat on plush pillows and crossed his legs. "I don't know what you mean, memsahib. Your father is my dear friend. Have I not nursed him in his illness? He would be dead now if it wasn't for me."

"You're not his friend. You've taken advantage of his illness and delirium." She turned to Dunleavy. "It all makes sense now, the letters, the articles, his turning his back on his own countrymen and moving to Bithur with Nana Sahib. Perhaps he never wrote those letters at all. Perhaps when he signed them he had no idea what he was doing. Perhaps that's the only reason he's been kept alive this long."

Sahib smiled. "If that were entirely true, why would I not have killed him already? Now that the rebellion has begun I obviously have no further use for him."

"Because he's a diplomat. And because should there be troops preparing to strike against you this very moment you will at least have him to use as a hostage."

"Not true. Now I have Mr. Dunleavy, haven't I?"

Destiny shook her head. "If anyone cared about Harold's welfare they would not have sent him here, would they?"

"Then my shooting him would not matter."

"No."

Dunleavy jumped up. "Good God, woman, are you trying to get me killed?"

"On the other hand," she added, "he's obviously of some influence or he wouldn't have had the authority to supplicate himself to you in such a brazen manner. What good would his coming here do if his word was worth less than elephant dung? Allow him to leave and if there are troops prepared to strike they might look upon Nana Sahib's charity in a favorable light—should you be taken as prisoner."

Chimnaji entered the tent and bowed to Nana Sahib. "Your pardon, your majesty. I thought you should know. We have just learned of another twelve deaths during the night. They were decapitated and their bodies hanged from the eaves of the barracks in which they slept."

Outrage flooded Sahib's features, then as quickly it passed. He turned to Harold. "You are free to leave. But you may tell your associates that there will be no negotiations unless they are willing to surrender our land to us completely and leave this country for good." He shouted to the watching sepoys and ordered them to escort Harold to the edge of the city.

"The woman is to return with me," Harold said eagerly, pointing to Destiny.

"I think not," Sahib replied.

"I demand it!" Harold declared with his usual pompousness.

His eyebrows lifting, Nana sneered, "You are a disgusting little man who stinks of cowardice. Now get out of my sight before I decide to kill you after all."

Harold stumbled back, into the sepoys' grasp. They dragged him from the tent, shoving and kicking and cajoling him as they went.

"You're going to kill him, aren't you?" Destiny said,

surprised to acknowledge the dread she felt in her stomach for Dunleavy's well-being.

"What do you think?" Nana replied.

For four hours Dunleavy stood in the hot sun precisely where Jason had told him to remain should Harold survive his visit to Sahib's compound. He lifted his blistered face occasionally to look around him, back toward the vacant road down which the bullying sepoys had escorted him, prodding him with their bayonets when he stumbled. His back bled profusely from their cuts.

Jason lay on his stomach, his body mostly hidden by rotting straw he had dragged from the river's edge. He did not take his gaze from Harold even as Diana crawled up beside him.

"You cannot allow him to continue standing there like that," she said. "This sun is killing him."

"They're using him as bait, Diana. If he returns to our camp, they'll follow. If one of us were stupid enough to help him by showing ourself we'd be shot and so would he. I suspect that as soon as it's dark, they'll kill him. They won't risk the chance of being trapped out here should he be telling the truth about our troops."

"And you're going to allow them to kill him? You can't. Not until we know what's happened to Destiny and Compton."

He finally looked into Diana's thin face. "I don't need any reminders about my responsibilities regarding Destiny. Nor do I need a woman telling me how to do my job. If you care to skip out there and offer him a drink, be my guest." He shoved a canteen of water into her hands. "I'll be sure to put a bullet in your head before they dismember you."

Diana sank onto the ground, her face half buried in the sand. She did not so much as flinch as a large beetle crawled across her cheek and into her matted hair. Jason knocked it away, then turned his attention back to Harold.

"Tell me about Ceylonia Plantation," she said. "I like to

imagine your taking Destiny there. How peaceful and serene it must be. Is it very beautiful?"

"Very."

"Do you have a grand house?"

He shifted his gaze to a distant rise, where an eddy of sand suddenly spiraled into the air. There was, perhaps, another half hour before nightfall. The sepoys hidden beyond the distant rocks and trees would be growing impatient to return to Cawnpore before dark.

"Yes," he finally replied, closing his hands more firmly around his rifle.

"And servants?"

"Many."

"You grow tea."

"Tea is good. It's made me very wealthy."

"I don't doubt it, when we're forced to pay twenty guineas a pound for it in England."

"Expect to pay twice that now that the East India Company is dissolved." He grinned. "Lucky thing I got into shipping when I did."

Suddenly a black cloud of crows rose in the air, their wings popping in the silence. Jason glanced back at the line of trees across the river and scanned the shoals, which were oddly empty of birds.

Diana lifted her head and stared at him. "How can you lie there so calmly and so apparently unconcerned about what's happening here, and what may be happening to Destiny this very moment?"

"Is that what you think, Diana? That I'm calm and unconcerned?" He swallowed, reluctantly acknowledging the tightness of his throat and the slight tremble in his hands, which had always been so dead solid when he faced life-and-death situations. "Christ. I've never been more frightened in my life," he admitted quietly.

"Because you might die before this is over?"

"No. Because Destiny might."

Diana touched his arm. "You're blaming yourself for her predicament, aren't you? Don't. She would have found her way here regardless. In case you haven't noticed, she's dreadfully stubborn."

He grinned, thinking of Destiny's obstinate little chin. "I've noticed."

Turning to Diana again, he put his hand on her head, forcing her cheek hard to the ground. In a firm voice, he said, "Whatever happens in the next few minutes, don't move. Remain where you are until one of us comes for you."

Her blue eyes widened in panic, but when she started to speak, he stopped her, shaking his head.

"Good girl," he whispered and gave her a wink.

As the first dulled rays of sunset crawled over the west horizon, Jason took a deep breath, praying the effort would calm the trembling in his hands. If he intended to get Harold safely off that road, he would have to act now. He just hoped to hell that Trevor and his men had had time to sight the enemy and position themselves for a counterattack.

In one lithe move, he jumped to his feet, raised his rifle, and aimed it at Dunleavy, who, in that same instant, turned his head and stared directly at Jason, his jaw dropping in alarm.

"Don't move, you stupid son of a bitch," Jason growled and pulled the trigger.

Harold buckled and hit the ground.

A rainstorm of bullets began flying as Jason ducked and ran for the road. Harold writhed in the sand, blood pumping from the bullet wound in his leg.

From the opposite side of the road, Franz appeared, rifle in hand, leaping over boulders and brush as he, too, ran for Harold. Both reached him at once, grabbed Harold by the arms, and dragged him into undergrowth as he howled in pain. Reaching a dense copse of trees, they dropped him. Franz quickly tied Harold's leg with a tourniquet, easing the flow of blood while Jason scanned the horizon for any pursuers. Judging by the rapid volley of shots, Trevor and his men were taking care of the sepoys nicely.

Clutching at his thigh, Harold glared up at Jason. "Maniac! I'm bleeding to death."

"Calm down, Harold, and thank your lucky stars I didn't aim three inches higher." Dropping to one knee, Jason raised Harold's head enough so he could drink from the canteen. "Look at it this way. I could shoot you in the leg and get your flabby ass off that road now or I could have left you another fifteen minutes and every sepoy who followed you out of Cawnpore would have shot you."

Harold's eyes rolled back in his head.

Jason shook him. "Talk to me, Dunleavy."

"Go away. I'm dying, for Christ's sake."

"You die when I say you can die." He splashed Harold's face with water.

Harold gulped and gasped like a man drowning.

"Is Destiny alive?" Jason asked.

Harold nodded and closed his eyes. "With her father. Fontaine very ill. Don't know for how much longer, though. Killing everyone. Women, children, entire families. It's hell in there. Entrenchment hasn't yet fallen." Raising his head and staring at Jason, he said, "Did you decapitate those men and hang their heads from the barracks?"

Jason shrugged. "Why, Harold, would Cobra do something like that?"

Man's evil manners live in brass:
Their virtues we write in water.

—SHAKESPEARE, *Henry VIII*

Destiny spent her monotonous hot days ministering her father, whose health varied hour by hour. For a time he would appear to grow stronger, fueling her hopes for his recovery. Then as quickly he would plummet into his old delirium and coughing fits that seemed to wrench his body in two. Occasionally, Nana Sahib himself visited to check on her father's condition. Each time he boasted to Destiny that the entrenchment of wounded, starving British troops were on the verge of surrender. Help from any outside sources was impossible, as his sepoys had managed to cut Cawnpore off completely from the outside world.

Soon other prisoners were brought into Savada House. Old Rose Greenway, whose husband had owned vast properties and businesses in Cawnpore, and a widow Jocobi and her three children. However, much to Destiny's mounting desperation, she was not allowed to speak to them, and was kept locked in the suite of rooms she shared with her father.

Very late one night, she was tossing and turning on her cushions, unable to sleep due to the intense heat and mugginess and the sporadic gunfire in the distance, when the door opened slightly and a figure slipped into the room. She sat up, her heart racing.

"Who's there?" she demanded.

"Chimnaji, memsahib." He crossed the room on tiptoes, then dropped to his knees beside her. "Hush and listen. If I were to be discovered here I would be immediately killed. Nana grows very suspicious of spies among his ranks. Too many of us grow weary of this fight and wish to return to our families. This war does not go well for Sahib, despite what he might say to you. He expected his taking of the entrenchment to take a few days and it is now weeks. The British soldiers continue to pick us off one by one. Each morning we are forced to drive the bullock carts up and down the streets collecting our dead. Nana is not a superstitious man, but he wonders if the ghosts of the dead Brits are not returning to exact their revenge on the sepoys who killed them."

Chimnaji sank onto the cushions beside Destiny. "The sepoys grow restless and unhappy because Nana's promises of payment have run dry, as has his ability to continue funding this rebellion for much longer. He grows desperate for money."

"Why are you telling me this?" Destiny whispered.

"Because I am your friend, memsahib, and I feel you should know that soon change will come. You should not give up hope." He smiled. "I don't blame you for distrusting me. But perhaps you will trust me better if I give you this."

Picking up her hand, he placed something in it. Destiny touched it with her fingertips. "A ring?" She shook her head. "I don't understand. What does it mean?"

"A wedding ring, memsahib."

She frowned in confusion.

"He says that he hopes it fits you properly, as he was not able to size it to your finger before purchasing it in Cape Town."

A weakness suffused her. Wrapping her trembling fingers around the ring, she closed her eyes. "My God, he's still alive."

"And very eager to see you again." Chimnaji stood. "I must go now."

She caught his hand. "Why are you doing this, Chimnaji? If you're discovered the consequences would be terrible for you."

"I'm no fool. This mutiny will eventually end and those who stood against the British will suffer. Besides, your father and mother were very kind to me and my family. I have honor and would not turn my hand against a friend."

He left the room as silently as he had entered it.

Sinking onto the cushions, Destiny tried to breathe evenly as she gripped the ring in her hand.

Dear God, Jason was alive, she thought as her heart hammered in her chest. She almost laughed aloud. Not so very long ago she had cursed Jason's cunning and blood thirst—had even hated him for it. Now it was that very cunning and blood thirst that would hopefully save her and her father.

She slid the ring onto her finger, smiling as she whispered: "It fits perfectly, my love."

She awoke the next morning to a great ruckus taking place outside. Glancing out her window, she saw Nana Sahib riding toward Savada House on his gray Arab, flanked by others. She hurried to the door and, finding it unlocked, threw it open and ran into the main room, where a group of agitated sepoys were shouting and gesturing with their weapons. Chimnaji stood among them, sheltering a man on his knees, his hands clasped behind his head. His arms were bloody and partially shielding his face.

"Stand away," Chimnaji ordered the soldiers. "I know this man. He is a friend of the Nana's and has surrendered his weapons."

They argued heatedly as Destiny cautiously moved to better see the captive's face, though some niggling realization had begun to flutter in her breast. Heat rushed through her as she focused first on his long dark hair and the width of his shoulders within his tattered, filthy shirt. And then he turned his head, and his eyes met hers. Her knees gave and she sank back against the wall.

Nana entered the house and quickly walked to the crowd. They parted for him, one reaching down and grasping a handful of Jason's hair and yanking back his head to reveal his beaten face.

Destiny bit her lip to keep from crying out.

Chimnaji bowed to Nana and quickly explained, "You remember your old friend, Sahib. Lord Batson. His father is Earl Falkland. As I recall you have entertained Falkland many times through the years and he was much grieved over the Dalhousie ruling."

"I remember," Nana said thoughtfully as he regarded Jason. "I have spent many pleasurable hours with the earl." Frowning, he stooped closer to Jason and said, "So what are you doing here in this dreadful situation, Batson Sahib?"

Jason winced as the sepoy pulled harder on his hair. "I was in Fatehgarh on business for my father. I thought to make my way back to Calcutta when the uprising ensued. My horse fell lame. I was caught with little water and food. I've been hiding out near the river, but grew desperate with hunger. I thought it better to ask compassion from a friend than risk starving to death."

The officer Destiny had come to know as Bala, Sahib's brother, entered the room then, his hand resting on the hilt of a *tulwar* hanging from his belt. "Kill him now," he declared furiously, then drew the blade and raised it.

A scream worked up Destiny's throat.

Nana Sahib quickly stepped between Jason and Bala. "It is my decision who lives or dies, my brother. This man's father showed much consideration to Azimullah Khan during his journey to London. Falkland is a very important man."

"Why should you care?" Bala sneered. "We are done with the English once and for all."

"I have money," Jason said.

Nana turned to him.

"With my saddle there are twenty thousand rupees. There is much more in Calcutta."

"Are you attempting to buy back your life, Batson Sahib?" Nana asked.

"It seems I have little choice."

After a long moment of contemplation, Nana barked orders to the sepoys and they backed away. Chimnaji stepped forward. "Perhaps you will allow the memsahib to minister to Batson's injuries."

Nana glanced at Destiny and shrugged. "Do what you want with him."

Chimnaji helped Jason to stand and, draping Jason's arm around his shoulder, walked him to Destiny's quarters, where he eased Jason down on the cushions. Then, turning on Destiny, he said, "They will be watching him closely. I hope for his sake he was telling the truth about the rupees. Bala Rao would like nothing more than to display an important and well-respected aristocrat's head on the end of his *tulwar*."

As Chimnaji left the room, Destiny fell beside Jason and took his battered face between her hands. She began to cry, not only with relief, but over the severity of his wounds.

"What in God's name are you doing here?" she asked, carefully touching the open injury on his brow.

"I felt I could better help you here than out there."

"But they might have killed you."

"I've walked through the devil's door enough times to know the risks." He buried one hand in her hair and pulled her close, his eyes narrowing dangerously. "Has he hurt you? Because if he has, I swear to God—"

"No." She shook her head and smiled to reassure him.

"And my baby?"

"Thriving." She slid his hand into the folds of her bourka and placed it upon her rounding belly. The baby kicked in that moment, as if greeting its father, and Jason's expression melted into a softness that made her throat close with emotion.

"You look like hell, sir." Destiny carefully caressed his

unshaven cheek, which had grown nearly as dark as the natives' the last days. He had dropped weight as well, so the swellings on his face exaggerated the dark hollows of his eyes and the gauntness of cheeks.

"You don't." He grinned and pulled her close again. "You're as beautiful as ever."

"Diana. . . ?" she asked with a catch in her voice.

"Alive and hysterical."

"And the others?"

"All alive."

"Dunleavy?"

"Blustering, of course. I've been tempted to kill him just to shut him up."

Her father groaned. Destiny hurried to him. His fever was up. She bathed his forehead as Jason moved up behind her.

"Is he capable of being moved?" Jason asked.

"He's very weak and lapses in and out of consciousness." Destiny looked up. "Why?"

"There are negotiations going on between Nana Sahib and Major-General Wheeler in the entrenchment. Nana has offered safe passage to Allahabad for all those who were in no way connected with the acts of Lord Dalhousie and who are willing to surrender the garrison's money, guns, and ammunition."

"Can we trust him?" she asked, trying her best to keep her excitement in check.

Jason shook his head. "No way in hell do I trust him."

"Then what do you intend to do?"

"There's nothing we can do, Des. Trevor is powerless to help us until an opportunity presents itself."

Destiny turned away. "You were a fool to have turned yourself over to Nana like you did. Whatever were you thinking?"

Jason caught her arm and his voice became rough with emotion. "That I was a fool to have allowed you to ride away from me that day in the glade, but I wasn't accustomed to dealing with your kind of innocence. Hell, I wasn't accustomed to being seduced by virgins. Never wanted one, personally, unless, of course, she was the woman I intended to marry. Then there were those weeks on the *Pretender,* sleepless nights of tossing and turning in my bunk, thinking of you sleeping so close by, wanting you again like hell, wanting to reveal myself to you. But each time I came close you were still so damn angry."

His eyes watched her with an intensity that made her heart ache. She smiled and showed him the ring she wore on her left hand. "In case you haven't noticed, I've forgiven you."

He slid his arms around her, pulled her close, held her fiercely as he whispered, "And in case you haven't noticed, I love you."

He kissed her, passionately, tunneling his fingers through her hair, moving his mouth on hers with a hunger that made her body weightless and hot and mindless.

Gripping him fiercely, she looked into his gray eyes and did her best to steady her voice. "What will happen to us now?"

"We wait and hope that Nana Sahib's offer to boat the survivors in the entrenchment to Allahabad is honorable. One way or the other, I'm confident that you and your father are safe for the time being. The fact that your father so adamantly and publicly decried the Dalhousie ruling has made him well respected among these people." He pressed his lips to her forehead and closed his eyes. "Des . . . if something happens to me—"

"It won't. Trevor and Connie won't allow it." She gave him a watery smile and raised her chin with a touch of her old pugnacity. "I'm determined to marry you, sir. The child inside me will have it no other way."

There came a noise from the corridor and Jason shoved Destiny away. The door opened and several sepoys entered, Bala Rao among them. Taller and younger than Nana Sahib, he displayed an air of arrogance and anger that radiated like storms in his eyes. He walked to Destiny's father and stared down at him before turning back to Jason.

"You will come with me, Batson."

Destiny stepped forward. "Where are you taking him and why?"

"This is none of your affair. Stand back and be quiet."

"He's Nana's friend. "

"Nana has too many British friends as far as I'm concerned." He sneered at her, then at her father.

"Nana is peshwa here, not you."

He struck her hard, knocking her to the floor.

Jason lunged for him. The sepoys grabbed him and hauled him back on his heels; one of them thrust the point of a dagger against his throat so firmly blood trickled onto the blade.

Bala smirked and motioned to the sepoys. As they shoved Jason from the room, Destiny followed Bala into the main hall, her fear and desperation mounting as she searched for Nana and realized he wasn't present.

The sepoys ushered Jason into the courtyard and stripped him of his shirt. They forced him to his knees in the boiling sun. Bala removed his *tulwar* from his belt and stood over Jason, glancing around at his soldiers.

"Nana Sahib negotiates now with the British. Should they refuse to surrender we will renew the fighting immediately and will crush them by nightfall. We will take no survivors." Laying the blade of his sword against the back of Jason's neck, he declared, "This one will be the first to die. I will send his head in a box to Queen Victoria as proof that we will no longer suffer the injustices and humiliations of the Angrezi Sahibs."

The crowding sepoys shouted and raised their weapons in the air. They shook and rattled them at Jason, who stared straight ahead, not so much as blinking as they spat on him and prodded at him with their bayonets.

Still, he did not whimper or flinch. He fixed his gaze upon some distant object and, as if his mind no longer occupied his abused body, remained as still as a statue as the sun beat down on his shoulders.

Crouched within the shade of the veranda, her body shaking uncontrollably, Destiny wept first with fear, then with anger. She shook with the desire to fling herself across Jason and beg Bala for mercy but afraid her actions would only spur the sepoys into a greater frenzy. They were drunk with power and a need to kill. She realized also that Bala would not stop with murdering Jason. His threat had been directed toward her and her father as well.

The minutes crawled and the sun grew hotter; the heat and his injuries beginning to tell on Jason and his body swayed, his head dropping forward as his consciousness waned. Destiny feared that if Bala didn't kill him, the heat and his injuries would. Unable to tolerate the abuse any longer, she took a cup of water and bowed before Bala.

"I ask mercy of Bala Rao. Allow me to quench Batson's thirst or he'll surely die."

"Why should I?" he replied with a lift of his eyebrows. "This man means nothing to me."

"Because Bala is a great leader and a just man. He is not a cruel man."

He snorted in derision. "Do not mistake me for a fool, memsahib. You think me a murderer and a savage. You would like to kill me. Your respect for me is as minuscule as your respect for that scavenging crow yonder. True?"

Raising her eyes to his, she gave him a flat smile. "True."

He howled in laughter and slapped his knee. Then he nodded. "Go then. Give him water and tell him to drink deeply of it. It may well be his last."

Destiny fell on her knees before Jason. Carefully, she took his chin in her trembling hand and lifted his head. He stared at her blankly, his eyes dull.

She tipped the cup to his split, parched lips. "Drink. Drink, damn you. Listen to me. Please, you mustn't give up. You mustn't let them beat you. Nana will not allow

Bala to kill us. I know it." Closer, she whispered, "I love you. Do you hear me? I love you."

He blinked and his eyes focused on her face. There was life still, in their gray depths. When she tipped the cup to his lips again, he drank.

A group of riders approached, jumping from their horses before the animals stopped completely. The men ran into the house. A suddenly swelling silence fell upon the crowd of sepoys as Bala hurried inside. In moments he returned, his face smug with satisfaction. Still on her knees beside Jason, Destiny closed her eyes and held her breath.

"They surrender!" Bala shouted, and Jason sank to the ground.

❦ 26 ❦

I would like to go through life side by side with you, telling you more and more until we grew to be one being together until the hour should come for us to die.

—JAMES JOYCE

"Thank God it's all over." Destiny did her best to smile encouragingly as she tenderly applied salve to the dozens of cuts on Jason's back. "Isn't it wonderful? The garrisons have agreed to lay down their arms, to turn over all weapons and ammunition, money, and anything of value to Nana Sahib. In exchange, tomorrow morning Nana will transport us all to Sati Chowra, where he'll have boats supplied with enough food and water to see us to Allahabad."

Jason pushed himself up on his elbows, gritting his teeth against the pain. "I don't trust him, Des."

"But he eagerly signed the treaty," she explained. "He expressed his deep regret that the garrison has suffered so horribly and swore by the gods and upon the Gunga to protect us and have us safely taken to Allahabad. He's providing us with a palanquin to transport Papa to a boat. Even now he's sent men into the entrenchment to help the survivors collect up their belongings. I've offered to ride to the entrenchment to help them. Nana feels that if they see me, another white woman who has gone unharmed under his care, they'll trust his word."

"You're not going anywhere without me," he said and struggled to his feet.

"But your back—"

"My back will be the least of our problems if Nana gets into that entrenchment and still has an eye for murder."

Horses were provided to Jason and Destiny for the half mile ride to the entrenchment. Sepoys lined the road as did carts they were using to load up what little ammunition and guns remained with the garrison. As Destiny dismounted her Arab mare, women and children emerged from their hiding places to stare at her, to touch her clean hair and skin, their own caked with three weeks' worth of filth and blood. Others wandered the grounds, their eyes deep hollows, their teeth yellowed from a diet of nothing but lentils.

Jason and Destiny lifted the small ones in their arms and carried them to the well, where the adults lined up to fill their jugs with the first water they had had in days.

Jason searched the hundreds of sepoys flooding the entrenchment for any clue that they meant to harm their captives. His shirt cut into his lacerated back like teeth, but he suspected the pain he was experiencing in that moment was nothing compared to the torture these men, women, and children had survived the last weeks. They were little more than walking cadavers, wounded and starving and desperate to believe Nana Sahib intended to make good on his promise to transport them out of Cawnpore safely.

A company of sowars arrived and announced they would take several volunteers to Sati Chowra to inspect the boats Nana was providing for the trip to Allahabad. Jason stepped forward, along with several haggard and weakened officers.

"What are you doing?" Destiny demanded, her voice tight with fear as she grabbed his arm.

"It might be my only opportunity to let Trevor know we're still alive," he said. "Besides, I'll be a better judge of the situation at Sati Chowra than they." He pointed to

the dazed officers. "Poor bastards are desperate enough to
believe Nana Sahib is God if he told them he was."

"You're in no condition to go either," she pointed out.

He kissed her and held her close. "Let's pray the worst
is over."

"But you're still not convinced."

"I'll let you know when I get back."

He turned her away and gave her a nudge. He watched
as she walked to a group of women who were stacking the
last of their valuables into a bullock cart for the sepoys to
transfer to Savada House. Reluctantly, she looked back, rewarding him with that smile that, since the first time he
had laid eyes on her, made his stomach feel unsteady.

It was an effort to turn his back on her and join the
sowars, who had provided a pair of elephants to take the
delegation of inspectors to the river.

They rode the lumbering animals down the road and
through the crowds that gathered close, curious, silent,
many of them oddly sad, just as many still angry and
thirsty for blood. He searched their faces, looking and hoping to recognize his own men among them, knowing even
as he did that they would be as skeptical as Jason about this
unhealthy truce. They had fought in enough wars to trust
their feelings of uncertainty.

At long last, they reached the boatmen's village of Sati
Chowra, sitting low along the bank of shallow river. Once
this had been one of the most beautiful sights in Cawnpore,
a haven for the officers and their wives who wished to ride
in the morning and evenings. Its banks were lined with
palm trees and neem trees, ritual statuaries, and the lovely
Shivaite temple that had been built partially over the river.

Now, however, it was little more than mud strewn with
the flotsam and jetsam of the Ganges flow: garlands, floating lamps, shattered remains of huts and walls torn asunder by cannon fire. Here and there plovers and monkeys
ran along the waterline filching whatever food they could
find.

Captain Turner, who had commanded sentries by the

main guard throughout the ordeal, dismounted his elephant first and proceeded to inspect the line of twenty-four boats moored along the ravine's mouth. As Turner argued with Nana's *kotwal* regarding the pitiful shape of the boats, Jason moved cautiously along the shoal, his gaze constantly scanning the deserted buildings for any sign of trouble, and any sign of his brother.

Then a movement caught his eye near the upper level of the Shivaite temple. A dark-skinned man wearing a *puggari* stood there briefly, bowed to Jason, then turned as quickly and disappeared. Jason noted there were several sowars watching him, so he remained where he was until Captain Turner's complaints so aggravated the *kotwal* that an argument broke out between him and his underlings regarding the condition of the boats. Jason swiftly mounted the steps and on the uppermost terrace found a gun. He slid it into the top of his boot.

Captain Turner stood before the pitiful lot of men, women, and children in the entrenchment and spoke in a hoarse, weary voice. "The boats average thirty feet long and ten feet wide. They're decked over, throughout their whole length, with bamboo. There are oars, long bamboos with circular boards at the end, a longer one of the same sort to steer with, and a long enough bamboo for a mast. They're clumsy and dangerous, but if we keep our heads about us and practice caution they'll suffice to get us to Allahabad without drowning."

As the sun set on the yard and a slight breeze stirred the dust, the survivors listened raptly to the captain, who refused to acknowledge the occasional man or woman who spoke up to ask reassurance that this affair was no ploy of Sahib's to trick them. They then turned their attention on Nana's coolies who were loading up the remainder of the garrison's belongings and money.

Jason found Destiny helping several women bind up the remainders of their tattered clothing. Taking her hand, he tugged her out of the crumbling barracks, refusing to answer her when she demanded to know where they were going. He led her along a path through what was left of the soldiers' garden, to a gazebo that had somehow managed to survive the onslaught of gun and cannon fire. A man stood there in the shadows, and not until Destiny reached the steps did she realize he was a minister.

Holding Destiny's hand, Jason said, "This is my fiancée, Reverend Moncrieff."

The man regarded Destiny with a sad smile. "Lovely. After all that we've suffered and lost, this occasion gives me hope of new beginnings."

Jason took Destiny in his arms. She regarded him curiously. "I'm about to marry you," he told her, his voice soft and melancholy.

"Marry me?" She searched his haggard, bruised face.

"I assume you'll still have me." He grinned.

Her face brightened and her lips curved. "This is rather sudden, isn't it?"

"Not sudden enough for me." He slid the ring from her finger and turned to Reverend Moncrieff. "Get on with it."

Destiny laughed and stroked the tense line of his jaw, her love for him overwhelming her. "You act like the sky is about to fall on us again."

"If it does we'll be married, at least," he replied seriously, and added with an intensity that made her heart quiver, "I'm not taking any chances this time."

The Reverend Moncrieff married them in the little gazebo with the sun fast disappearing behind a thin finger of clouds on the horizon—the first hint that the insufferable dry heat would soon give way to monsoon rains. The emotions turning over in Destiny's chest were too much. Her eyes teared. Her hand trembled as Jason kissed it first then slid the pretty gold band onto her finger, solemnly repeating his vows while looking down into her eyes.

"I pronounce you husband and wife," the minister declared, then added, "May God protect and keep you."

They barely noticed as the minister walked away. Destiny sat on the gazebo bench and looked into her husband's troubled eyes. She struggled to breathe. She didn't want to think beyond the feeling of happiness that made her head fuzzy and her heart race madly. Jason's expression, however, was hardly that of a man delirious with pleasure.

"Somehow I sense this isn't so much a cause for celebration as it is an act of necessity," she said, pressing a kiss to his unshaven cheek. She desperately wanted to ignore her rising sense of fear. But it was there, nevertheless, clawing at her insides as her husband averted his eyes and released an unsteady breath.

"I told you"—he smiled—"I'm not taking any chances. I intended to make an honest woman out of you if it was the last thing I ever did."

"You saw something at the river that disturbed you."

"This entire situation disturbs me." He took her face between his hands. "Listen to me. Whatever happens tonight or tomorrow, I won't let them have you again. I fear that the slaughter they've perpetrated here will pale in comparison to what they'll do next should they turn on us again."

"Kiss me, husband," she whispered urgently, attempting to smile. "We may never get another chance. I love you," she said.

"I love you." He sighed, a part of him ripping open inside as her beautiful face turned up to his, her mouth parting and her eyes swimming with the intensity of her feelings. God, how he loved her. He would do anything, sacrifice anything to save her and the child inside her from what he suspected was going to happen the moment they boarded the barges for Allahabad.

Easing down to his knees before her, he brushed her lips with his and whispered, "We'll pretend this is a rainy forest glade and I'm half out of my mind with wanting you. Christ, how I wanted you that day, and every day since. I want to spend the last minute of my life inside you, Des."

Her eyes drifted closed.

He kissed her deeply and slipped his hand beneath the bourka, trailed his fingertips along the curve of her leg to her thigh. As night's shadows deepened, muffling the distant sounds of misery and hope, Jason embraced his wife. Her soft body opened to him, enfolded him, washed him in warmth and wetness that raged through him in a sort of sweet, damning ecstasy that made his blood roar and his injured body ache with a kind of pain that was as glorious as it was unbearably tormenting.

She kissed him back with a wild violence as she lifted her legs and wrapped them around his hips, drawing him in, crushing her body into his as if attempting to absorb him. Her hair flowed around them, slid like silk between them as they moved together, clutching gently then impatiently, unable to get enough of one another. As the close, velvet caress of her body stroked him like fire, his desperation for her built within him like the tempest that had once threatened to destroy them. He groaned. He gasped. He buried his hands in her hair so he could kiss her more deeply, bury his body more deeply until her fingers twisted into his shirt and her body bowed into his like a willow whip. She made a sound in her throat and her eyes flew open wide as she whispered, "Oh, my God."

Afterward they returned to Savada House and throughout the night they lay naked amid the piles of plush cushions, their intimacies shielded from her father by a *purdah*. Occasionally Destiny napped as Jason, with a *chuddah* wrapped around his hips, paced from window to window, unable to dismiss his concern that Nana Sahib was up to no good.

Destiny would lure him back to her with a smile or a sigh and an opening of her arms as she urged, "Come to me again, my love." Each time he loved her was as passionate and as tender as the time before, and afterward he lay with his head on her stomach, waiting for the instant his child fluttered inside her.

Just before dawn Destiny fell deeply asleep. When she awoke the sun was shining brightly through the windows and Jason was standing over her. He tossed her a pair of loose trousers and a shirt and said, "Put them on. It's time to go."

Hurriedly, she dragged them on as sepoys delivered the promised *dhooli,* a palanquin with doors that could be closed to completely shut the passengers inside. Destiny did her best to dampen her excitement as the lighthearted conversations outside drifted to her. It was as if the horrible cloud of hate that had gripped the natives the last long weeks had miraculously lifted.

Fortunately, her father's stupor had lifted enough so when she gently shook him, he roused and opened his eyes. Still, he frowned and called out "Marilyn? Is that you, darling?"

"No, Papa. It's Destiny. You have to wake up now and let me help you."

"What are we doing?" he asked.

"We're going home."

"To Cawnpore?"

"To England."

He shook his head. "I won't go back there, Des. This is my home. These are my friends. Your mother is buried here. I won't leave your mother."

Jason gently moved Destiny aside and picked Compton up in his arms so easily Destiny gasped in despair. What little protest Compton attempted failed as Jason carried him out to the palanquin surrounded by watchful servants who bowed slightly in Compton's presence and took turns kissing his hand. As carefully as possible, Jason laid Compton upon the cushions and motioned for Destiny to join her father.

"I'll walk with you," she said, shaking her head.

He grabbed her arm roughly. "Get the hell in the litter, Des, and don't argue."

His tone stunned her, yet she checked her normal combative response and climbed into the palanquin with her father. She did not close the curtains, however, just settled down on the pillows and took her father's hand as he stared up at her with a look of concern. Although his brow appeared moist with fever, his eyes looked cognizant and apprehensive.

The servants heaved the *dhooli* onto their shoulders.

Jason mounted a horse and positioned himself at Destiny's right while several sepoys, all armed with *tulwars* and rifles with bayonets, surrounded them on horseback. As Destiny looked out at Savada House, she saw Nana Sahib at the window, his face void of emotion. For an instant his dark eyes met hers, then he turned away.

A sense of cold trepidation turned over in her chest, and for the first time since word had come of Nana's treaty with the garrisons she felt swamped by the suspicion that had eaten at her husband all night.

By the time they reached the entrenchment, the progression to Sati Chowra had commenced. Headed by sixteen commissariat elephants and some eighty palanquins that carried the wounded, the caravan was fast surrounded by thousands of native soldiers and sentries who shouted their good-byes and good riddance and occasionally hurled stones that bounced off the sides of the *dhoolis*.

As their laborious journey took them slowly along, Compton stared out at the rubble of the bungalows, the shattered walls, the barefoot women staggering down the road. "My God," he managed in a thin voice. "What sort of hell has gone on here?"

"The natives have mutinied, Papa," Destiny said. "They're driving the English out of India."

Fear brightened his eyes and he clutched at her hand. "Who instigated such an act?"

"Nana Sahib mostly."

He stared up at her with his hollow eyes and his breath wheezing in and out of his dry lips. "Have I caused this, Des?" he finally asked in a thin voice.

"No." She stroked his wet forehead and smiled. "Dalhousie's greed caused this, Papa. Just like you always warned them."

"I never meant harm to come to anyone—"

"Hush." She placed her finger upon his lips. "Soon we'll

be away from this dreadful place and you'll grow well and strong again. My husband will take us all to Ceylona Plantation and we'll put this nightmare from our minds. You'll hold your grandchild in your arms and we'll recall the pleasant times we spent here with Mama."

Jason rode away. Long minutes passed and Destiny's concern grew. At last, he returned and positioned his horse close to the palanquin as his gray eyes moved constantly to assess their surroundings. "I don't like it," he said as quietly as possible. "Since yesterday the boats have been dragged high upon the sand. Shoving them into the river will be difficult if not impossible if they're loaded with passengers. They're crowding the women and children onto the boats as swiftly as possible and I don't care for the sepoys lined up along the riverbanks. They're all armed heavily. Why the hell should they be armed to oversee a lot of starving, wounded prisoners?"

"Stop!" a voice shouted behind them.

Jason looked around as Chimnaji and several riders approached. The riders fanned out on either side of them as Chimnaji ordered the palanquin to be put down and the carriers to continue on without them. Several sepoys broke from their ranks and ran toward them, but Chimnaji shouted, "Nana Sahib has ordered me to return these Angrezi to Savada House. They are not to be included in the journey to Allahabad."

The outriders, all but their eyes hidden behind their *deputtahs,* leapt from their horses and hurried to the palanquin. Hefting the conveyance up on their shoulders, they turned south again as Chimnaji convinced the suspicious sepoys that he acted on orders of the Nana.

Her panic rising, Destiny jumped from the *dhooli* just as Chimnaji raced through the dust clouds toward them, whipping his lathered horse. "Quickly," he called to Jason and pointed toward a footpath that led through trees to the river away from the landing at Sati Chowra. "It is a trick. The prisoners are to be killed!"

In that moment the chilling sound of a bugle rose in the

air and almost immediately gunfire broke out. The servants carrying the *dhooli* laid it down and dragged the scarves from their heads, tossing them to the ground as they withdrew guns from their belts. Destiny found herself staring into Fritz's face, smeared with lampblack and ashes.

On the opposite side, Zelie flung open the *dhooli* and hefted her father up in his arms.

Jason grabbed Destiny and slung her up behind him on the horse. He followed Chimnaji down the steep path, ducking beneath low branches that raked their shoulders and the tops of their heads. By the time they reached the concealed conveyance, smoke from the burning boats at Sati Chowra was boiling into the sky. Several of Trevor's men waited there and ran to help Zelie carry her father to the river.

Up and down the waterway, hidden behind the crumbling walls and trees, the sepoys fired on the dazed and confused crowd now running for their lives or doing their best to shove their stranded boats into the low water of the Ganges. Women scrambled desperately through shin-high water to reach the few boats that had slid off the sandbars. Others searched the bloody waters for their children who had fallen into the opaque shallows.

Because their boat was much farther down the shoal, away from the murderous barrage, Jason and Zelie managed to heft Compton onto the boat with little trouble. Jason handed Destiny off to Franz, who shoved her into the shallow hold and ordered her to stay there.

A dozen sepoys broke through the trees and fired on them as Jason and Fritz shoved the boat into the slow current. The bullets kicked up the water inches from them and pinged off the boat with bits of shrapnel. Chimnaji stared up at the sepoys with a look of panic as he realized that he had been discovered.

"Get in!" Jason shouted above the firing. "You can't go back now. They'll kill you!"

Chimnaji jumped into the river and waded to the boat. Zelie fired at the Sultanpore sepoys of the Seventeenth

Native Infantry who ran along the river's edge, shooting wildly, their grape whizzing by the frail bamboo structure as thick as hail. Laying her body over her father's, Destiny closed her eyes and covered her head. The sounds of guns and screaming tore at her ears and the stench of burning bamboo made her queasy.

A hot wind rushed unobstructed down the Ganges course, carrying with it the dense cloud of smoke above and the waves of blood below.

Destiny lifted her head in time to see Reverend Moncrieff standing behind one of the shattered boats, clutching his sodden Bible in his hands as he was approached by a leering sowar who struck him across the neck with his weapon. The reverend slowly slipped facedown into the water, his Bible floating on the surface momentarily before sinking.

Jason scrambled for one of the rifles Zelie had stored in the hold while the others did their best to pole the boat further into the pitifully slow and shallow current. One by one Jason picked off the snipers, his aim steady and sure until the remaining sepoys fell back and turned on the surviving refugees.

At last the boat, caught by a tenuous thread of current and propelled by Chimnaji and Fritz's poling, slid down the river and away from the melee. Jason sank to the floor beside Destiny, who cried with relief and thanked God that her father had lost consciousness again so he would be spared the horrible display of mayhem.

Franz had taken a bullet in his leg. He stemmed the flow of blood by tying his *deputtah* above it.

Chimnaji sat with his head in his hand and tears in his eyes. "I did not want to believe it," he said. "I did not want to think that Nana could so order the massacre of these people. Then I heard the sepoys talking among themselves. . . ." He wept harder and covered his face in shame.

"Where are Trevor and Connie?" Jason asked Zelie.

"Out there somewhere." Zelie nodded toward the tall

grass and trees lining the river. "I suspect we'll see them sooner or later."

"I'm hoping it will be sooner than later," Fritz cracked as he reloaded his rifle. "I'm feeling a bit like a sitting duck here."

They all looked up at the hazy sky and the hint of clouds scattered over the hot sun. The wind had begun to rise and coursed hard down the center of the river, forcing them to pole the boat closer to the steep banks that allowed coverage for any sepoy who might have ridden downriver searching for escapees.

Silent, their rifles prepared for the attack that would surely come; they clustered together as the men took turns navigating the boat along the currents, taking as much care as possible to avoid the sandbars and tree stumps.

Night was forever coming, it seemed, and not until building clouds crawled over the moon to blanket the river in total darkness did they relax. Destiny brought out the little food she found in the hold; chupatties and cold cooked lentils. She managed to rouse her father and coax him into eating, but, alas, his spasms of coughing became so intense he soon lapsed back into unconsciousness. For a long while Destiny sat with his head in her lap, mopping his brow with cool river water and doing her best not to think about what awaited them when the sun came up.

She dozed, awaking when Jason sat down beside her. He took her in his arms and held her close, kissed the top of her head and her closed eyelids.

"How is my baby?" he whispered in her ear.

"Which one?"

"Both."

She put his hand on her rounding stomach, and in a moment their child moved against his palm. "I'm certain he's wondering what all this commotion is about," she said sleepily.

"One day we'll have one hell of a story to tell him."

She looked up into his eyes. "Do you think so?"

He sighed wearily. "Of course."

"I've occupied my thoughts the last hours on our sailing to Ceylonia Plantation together. Of you carrying me across the threshold of your home."

He looked away.

She cradled his cheek in her hand and forced him to look at her again. "I've consoled myself with the fact that you've grown very weary of war, and that your fondest desire is to settle down and bounce babies on your knee. That *is* what you want, isn't it?"

"Yes," he said softly. "More than anything."

"And you want to make up for all the years you lost with Jenette."

He nodded.

She clutched his shirt in her hand and her voice trembled with emotion. "Then cease looking out there and look at me. Stop thinking that you should be out there, and not with me. You've seen what the sepoys have done. There's nothing one more soldier can do to stop them."

He pulled her into his lap and held her close, whispering only, "I love you."

At just before dawn the boat caught on a sandbar and despite the men's best efforts they could not budge it back into the current. Shin-deep in water, they braced their backs into it and pushed and heaved to the point of exhaustion.

His leg beginning to fester, Franz, with rifle ready, watched the banks for any sign of the enemy. "I don't have a good feeling about this, Cap. Trevor and Connie should have joined us by now with the horses."

"Could be they were caught," Fritz said.

Zelie grinned. "I'd hate to be the bastards who caught them. They'd be thinking by now that they got hold of the white man's devil."

Thunder rumbled and the monsoon clouds crawled over the sun. Wind whipped at the trees and stirred up dust, which made a hissing sound as it was driven through the tall river grass.

At first the sudden and unexpected pop sounded more like the crack of a dry tree branch. Then, from the corner of his eye Jason saw Zelie sink to his knees, his rifle sliding from his hands and bouncing on the boat deck. A bloom of dark red blood appeared on his chest before he toppled forward with a death groan.

Destiny screamed and clawed her way over Zelie's body to the hold, where her father struggled to sit up.

"Bastards!" Fritz yelled and began firing at the line of sepoys emerging from behind the trees from both sides of the river.

Jason tossed Chimnaji a rifle. Franz scrambled the best he could to take cover and begin firing on the wall of rebels wading into the river.

The rain began, driving like spears into the river and into their faces as the sepoys' bullets struck the boat's hull.

"Our only chance is to get this boat off this sandbar," Chimnaji shouted through the force of rain and bullets whizzing by his head. Tossing aside his rifle, he jumped into the water, and as Jason and the others continued to fire at the sepoys, he heaved as hard as he could against the hull, hoping the wind and rain would help to dislodge it from its mooring.

Still it did not budge.

Fritz jumped in beside him. A bullet struck him in the back, and as he spun to aim his pistol at the sepoy a second bullet hit him in the forehead. He sank into the muddy water. As Jason scrambled across the slippery deck to help Chimnaji back onto the boat, the man's eyes flew open wide, and Jason knew even before Chimnaji slowly floated back into the water that he, too, had been struck and killed.

Sinking to his knees, the rain stinging his face as he stared out at the sepoys who were splashing through the river toward the boat, Jason pulled the gun from his boot and turned to Destiny, who continued to huddle protectively over her father, her eyes frightened yet resigned, her chin set in courageous determination.

"We're done for," he announced as calmly as possible.

She nodded in understanding and held her father tighter.

"I won't let them have you," he said, angered by the emotion that was rising up inside him. "I love you."

"And I you," she replied softly and squared her little shoulders. "Do it quickly, husband, they're almost here."

He pointed the muzzle to her head, cocked the trigger.

His hand shook. His vision blurred. The sob inside him swelled through his chest and throat and raged like fire through his brain. As she stared up at him with her wide green eyes, he let go a low, heart-wrenched groan and dropped the gun.

"I can't," he whispered, sinking to his knees before her. "God help us both, Des, I can't hurt you."

Destiny took him in her arms and he buried his face into her breasts. "I'm sorry," he wept. "I'm so goddamn sorry."

A sudden volley of gunfire came as sharp and constant as the monsoon thunder overhead.

Gripping her shaking husband fiercely in her arms, her hands buried in his wet hair, Destiny raised her eyes to the line of sepoys no more than fifty feet from their boat. One by one they fell into the river or frantically stumbled toward the shore.

From the east, British soldiers poured down the embankments, firing their weapons at the outnumbered sepoys who were scattering for cover amid the river grass and tree stumps lining the shore. From the west, Trevor, Connie, and Trevor's men drove their horses into the river and toward the boat, shooting the horrified sepoys as they went.

As Diana ministered to Destiny's father under a nearby canopy, Trevor sat on a canvas cot and watched as Jason, Destiny, and Franz drank hot coffee and ate a mixture of rice and lentils. Harold lay on a nearby cot, drinking whiskey straight from a bottle. He glanced their way occasionally, his look wary, as if he anticipated one of them shooting him point-blank at any moment.

"We were cut off from the river just south of Aherwa,"

Trevor explained. "They had the river almost entirely covered, anticipating there might be a few Brits who slipped through their guns at Sati Chowra. You were lucky to have gotten as far as you did. We were forced to take the road south and double back. That's when we ran into this garrison on their way to Cawnpore."

"What about survivors?" Destiny asked.

Trevor shook his head. "I've heard they massacred all men, including the male children. The surviving women and children were taken back to Savada House. God only knows what will happen to them now. We can only hope that more troops get here soon. These few soldiers won't stand a chance against Nana's armies."

Destiny thought of the desperate families whom she had visited with the night before the massacre. Excusing herself, she went to her tent, curled up in the blankets, and tried to focus on the positive. She and Jason were alive. Her father was alive, and Diana. The child inside her would live to know and love his parents in a place of beauty and security.

In her exhaustion she slept fitfully, and when she awoke the rain had begun again and dark had descended. Jason lay beside her as he had for the last hours, watching her sleep. He had bathed and shaved. His clean hair fell in soft, rich waves over his forehead.

He did not speak as he reached out and took her in his arms, pulling her body to his. Opening her legs she allowed him in. His taking of her was gentle and yet furious, like a man grasping at his last breath of life. She clenched her teeth to quiet the groan of pleasure that sluiced through her, centering between her legs that became a hot apex and made her strain her hips against his, driving him to thrust almost savagely deep inside her.

The end came too swiftly. Spent, they lay tangled in each other's arms and legs, their bodies wet and flushed, their hearts beating as one. Desperately, she clung to him as the rain drove harder and night wore on, afraid to sleep, afraid when she awakened again he would be gone.

At last, she forced herself to look into his eyes. "You're not returning to Ceylonia Plantation with us, are you?"

"I can't," he said and kissed her lips. "I can't turn my back on those people—those desperate women and children, Des. I still hear them crying for mercy and finding none. Please understand."

She wept silently, knowing that if she pleaded with him he would turn his back on the war and return to Ceylonia with her. But she knew, too, that he would forever be haunted by his decision. It wasn't in Jason's character to walk away from women and children in trouble. Like Julia and Maggie and Mary and Carla, she must accept that these men were special, driven by some need to risk all for the cause. Julia had been right; she had fallen in love with Jason's air of danger; he was chivalrous, courageous. Forbidden. Unattainable. Unpredictable. The very attributes about him that she had come to love and respect the last many turbulent weeks were the very ones now that would ultimately break her heart.

Finally, despite her valiant attempts to remain awake, sleep dragged her down. And when she suddenly came awake at dawn she reached for him, knowing he would not be there, and swallowed back a sob.

A thick mist clung to the ground as Jason joined the others. Trevor tossed him a rifle. Connie shifted the pack on his back and said quietly, "You ain't got to do this, y' know. Dunleavy's willin' to look the other way if y' wanna turn yer back on all this and take a walk."

"Would you," he asked Connie directly, "take a walk?"

Connie shook his head. "I ain't got a new wife and a couple of kids."

"There's always Diana." Jason half grinned and slung the rifle strap over his shoulder.

"She's got somethin' for Fontaine. Too bad. The woman sorta grew on me after a while."

"She's there," Trevor said in a voice uncustomarily gentle.

His first instinct was to turn, to allow his eyes to imprint Destiny's image on his mind one last time. But he knew that if he turned he would stay; they would sail away to paradise and grow rich on love and tea profits . . . while the haunting memory of desperate women and children forever ate at his conscience. He was going to make damn certain that the next time he held his wife in his arms there would be no ghosts between them.

"Rule number five," he said aloud, focusing on the trail before him. "Never look back."

Standing outside the tent, tears stinging her eyes and her heart trembling in pain, Destiny watched her husband disappear into the mist.

∾ *Epilogue* ∾

Love in her sunny eyes does basking play;
Love walks the pleasant mazes of her hair;
Love does on both her lips forever stray;
And sows and reaps a thousand kisses there.

—ABRAHAM COWLEY

Spring 1859

Jason stood on the clipper's prow, the letter in his hand fluttering in the wind and his gaze fixed on the distant island plantation rising out of the sea like an emerald gem.

Would Destiny be there, still? Had she grown too weary of the wait and returned to England? Perhaps she had not received the hundreds of letters he had sent her since that morning he had joined the British troops on their way to Cawnpore.

Their worst fears had been realized. The women and children Nana Sahib took into Savada House as refugees were ultimately slaughtered. Nana Sahib fled Cawnpore just before the city was overtaken by British troops. For the last year and a half, Jason, Trevor, Connie, and numerous troops had chased Nana Sahib around the country in an effort to bring him to justice for the murder of over a hundred innocent women and children, to no avail. Despite the bounty of ten thousand rupees put on Sahib's head, his countrymen continued to protect him. Eventually he had lost himself in Nepal, much to Dunleavy's despair.

Harold had taken up residency in Bombay, where he could ride out the wave of rebellion in relative safety, certain that eventually the British would rally in their attempts to take back control of the country. Stories had reached Jason that Dunleavy had ordered the massacre of all natives, guilty or not of murdering Brits, whom the troops could capture. The atrocities that followed were scandalous, innocents by the hundreds slaughtered by vengeful British troops. In December of '58 a band of *bheels*, tribesmen with a reputation for banditry, accosted Dunleavy on a dark road outside Bombay and cut off his head. The authorities found it the next day spiked atop a *tulwar* at the entrance of the city. Upon hearing the news, Jason and Trevor had celebrated with a bottle of Connie's infamous rum.

Jason looked again at the only letter he had received from Destiny, delivered to him by a soldier in April of '58. Over the last year it had become tattered and soiled from his reading it every morning and every night.

December, 1857
My Darling Husband,
I have given you a son with dark hair and eyes that will certainly break women's hearts. He is beautiful and healthy, and I am feeling gloriously happy. When Diana is not buzzing about my father, who grows stronger every day, and Jenette, who grows more lovely every day, she is fluttering about me and the baby, certain without her attentions we are certain to expire. I have named our son Jason Compton Batson, by the way. I hope you approve.

I miss you. I love you. Each day I stand on the balcony of our home and stare for hours out to sea, praying that I will soon see your ship on the horizon, that you will return to me and we will live happily forever in this wonderful paradise. The bell on the dock awaits you, and I have informed Franz to announce your homecoming by ringing it three times.

*Until that day please remember, I need your love as
a touchstone of my existence. It is the sun which
breathes life into me. I await you with a heart filled
with love.*

> *Your devoted wife,*
> *Destiny*

Standing at the helm of the clipper *My Destiny,* Connie
shouted, "Shall I run up the flag, Cap'n?"

"Aye," Jason replied, nodding.

As Connie saw to the raising of the Union Jack, Trevor
joined Jason at the rail. Trevor had taken a bullet in the hip
during a skirmish in Oudh with Bala Rao a few months
earlier. The injury still bothered him, which was why he
had agreed to Jason's invitation to stay awhile at Ceylonia.
Eventually Jason intended to offer his brother a partnership
in the business, but not yet. He wanted Trevor to get a good
taste of paradise before he bothered, certain that once
Trevor experienced heaven on earth for himself, he would
want to stay.

"Think she'll still be there?" Trevor asked.

"She'll be there." Jason nodded.

"You're pretty damn certain of yourself."

"I know Destiny. She'll be there." Jason lifted the glass
to his eye and prayed to himself that he was right. Through
the last long months he had not allowed himself to consider what he would do if he arrived in Ceylonia and found
her and his children gone. The thought of them had kept
him from taking risks that at another time in his life he
would have taken and thought nothing of. But he hadn't
had a whole hell of a lot to live for then. He did now.

In the distance, men scurried along the docks, preparing
for the docking. Franz stared back at him, his mouth curving in a smile. He waved, then limped over to the big brass
bell and began to ring it.

From the top of the hill, Destiny came running, her hair
flying behind her, a baby balanced on one hip, his dark
curls bouncing, rosy cheeks smiling. Even from this dis-

tance Jason could imagine that he saw the flash of Destiny's green eyes; her smile radiated like the sun. The first thing he intended to do was to carry her off to their bedroom and spend the next week making love to her, making babies, making promises that would carry them into forever. Christ, he'd missed her. God, *he loved her more than life.*

Behind her trailed a slender Jenette with hair black as night, a half dozen puppies yapping at her heels as she sprinted for the dock. Farther back came Diana, skirt hiked to her shins, and behind her hurried Compton, laughing and shouting to Diana, who waved him on impatiently.

"Lucky man," Trevor said and slapped Jason on the back.

Lowering the glass and smiling, Jason whispered, "The luckiest."

Dawn. They lay tangled in sheets and arms and legs and Destiny's hair that coiled in loose sprays of dark tendrils around their shoulders. The wind through the open window chilled their damp, cooling bodies. They both shivered at once, but instead of reaching for cover they drew their bodies together again, warmth against warmth, heart against heart.

"I missed you," she whispered into Jason's sleepy eyes.

He grinned and kissed her, rolled his body over hers, his hands caressing, torturing by gentleness. "Thank you for my son. And for loving Jenette. And for loving me. Thank you mostly for that, Des. For loving me. What did I ever do to deserve you?"

"How can I help but love you?" She slid her leg up his, then down again, hooking her foot around his ankle and drawing her toe up the back of his calf. "Any man who will read a woman Shakespeare in the rain deserves to be loved."

His voice grew husky as he buried his face in the crook of her neck, breathed softly against her pulse. "Those months on the *Pretender*—I thought I had lost you. I felt desperate. And mad. I loved you more than life. I always will."

Smiling, Destiny turned her mouth up to his, breathless, yearning, loving him more than she could ever convey in words. "Promise me," she whispered, pulling his mouth down to hers in a kiss that possessed her and made her liquid with pleasure. "Promise you'll never leave us again."

"I promise," he vowed, and meant it.